SEA SHAKEN

J.M. Simpson

Authors Note

I have taken a degree of literary licence when depicting the wonderful work and crew members of the Royal National Lifeboat Institution (RNLI). I have embellished various aspects and fictionalised others to get the story right. So all mischaracterisations are fictional, and any procedural errors are entirely mine.

I have also taken a degree of literary licence regarding the practices of the military with respect to hospitalisation and recovery, following serious trauma and injury, for a serving soldier. For the purposes of the story I have embellished various aspects and fictionalised others to fit the storyline, so all mischaracterisations are fictional, and any procedural errors are entirely mine.

Protecting and healing the mental health of our serving soldiers and veterans is of paramount importance and there are now many organisations that exist solely for this purpose. These organisations do incredible work and are often a much-needed lifeline for those in need, providing guidance, support and a listening ear. Signposting those in need of these services could save a life and let them know they are not alone. Just a few of these amazing organisation are: Veterans Gateway; SSAFA; PTSD Resolution; The Veterans Mental Health and Wellbeing Service; Help for Heroes and Rock to Recovery.

Also by J.M. Simpson

<u>The Castleby Series</u>

Sea State

Sea Change

Twitter @JMSimpsonauthor

Instagram JMSimpsonauthor

For my sister Sal. 'Love your work'

When a good man is hurt, all who would be called good must suffer with him.

Euripides

PROLOGUE

He lay, barely conscious, on the hard earth-packed floor. The heat in the dark room was oppressive; hot, heavy, stifling. Vaguely, he heard flies buzzing. He felt them dance lightly on his skin and face, feasting on his open wounds. He felt small rodents nip at his fingers. He had no strength to brush them away. They could have their fill.

Death beckoned seductively; she had been teasing him gently for days, drifting around his semi-conscious state, plucking at his senses. He would give in to her soon; he was resigned to it.

He had gone to a dark place in his mind. To escape. To be free of it. Nothing could get to him there. It had been the only way to cope. To get through the pain, the agonising, relentless, brutal torture.

Three of the eight had died; unable to cope with the extreme abuse to body and mind. He knew he would be next. His body was shutting down; unable to sustain. His mind – shutting down; unable to process the extreme horror.

He thought she had come, wearing the thick cloak of disguise. Tricking him. The welcome seductive arms of death playing one last trick. Through the slits of his swollen eyes, he saw bright flashes. Heard gunfire, voices shouting, familiar accents from home. He tried to speak, but no voice came from his dry throat and cracked lips.

He felt himself being lifted, carried into bright sunlight over rocky terrain. The pain of the brightness and movement was indescribable. He felt broken bones grinding; extreme agony as he was hefted about. He tried to call out for them to leave him alone; leave him in the dark. He felt safe there. He heard the whumping sounds of a helicopter, felt the intense hot wind on his face.

Death hovered closer, her tendrils beckoning. She wanted him and planned to have him. Cleverly, she showed him the things he wanted to see. The bright comforting light; his family. She showed him the beguiling respite from the intense pain and the horror. He reached out a shaking hand to touch his wife's beautiful face and ruffle his son's hair. He dragged himself up and walked towards them.

Death drifted gently towards him, the consummate seductress. She showed him his family, stood with open arms, beckoning to him gently, smiling lovingly.

'Come on,' she whispered, reaching out her hand and gesturing to his family.

With a deep sigh of relief, he let go and stepped into their arms.

CHAPTER 1

Dr Kate Cooper wiped a shaking hand across her wet eyes and threw the last suitcase into the boot of her old Volvo XC60. She surveyed the contents of the boot and fresh tears came. So this was what five years of marriage amounted to when it was over. A boot full of half possessions that no one really wanted but felt obliged to take.

'I'll make sure your half of the house money gets transferred when it's complete,' Matt said, leaning casually against the front door jamb. It was the same position he'd been in for the last half an hour as he watched her carry heavy boxes and suitcases to her car.

'Solicitor will do that,' she said shortly.

He shrugged. 'Whatever. That it?'

She closed the boot. 'Uh huh.'

He walked towards her and stood close. She tensed, not knowing what to expect. He held out his hand.

'Key, please,' he said quietly.

Her eyes opened wide. 'Seriously?'

He waggled his fingers. 'Yup.'

She snapped the key off her fob and threw it at him as she marched towards the driver's side of the car and wrenched the door open.

'See you then,' he said pleasantly. 'Enjoy your new life in the arse end of nowhere.'

She slammed the door and started the car.

'Fucking prick,' she muttered, feeling better instantly. 'Stupid. Mean. Fucking. Selfish. Prick.'

She drove out of the road where they had lived for the past five years and refused to look back. That was it. Over. Five years ended in a single night, in a conversation that had lasted half an hour. She replayed it in her head, still shocked.

'Matt, look we need to talk. Dad's called again, he's really struggling since Jack left and just can't find a permanent GP. He needs me and I think it's time. I want to go and run the practice with him. You know it was always our plan.'

'Yes, but it's not *my* plan, is it? I've told you before, I don't *want* to do it.'

'This is why we need to have a proper discussion about it. I need to understand why.'

'Kate. How many times? I am not moving to some dead-end town by the sea so you can become queen GP and be treated like royalty by everyone.'

'What are you talking about?'

'Last time we went down – it's like your dad is the local fucking messiah or something. Oh hello, Dr Lawrence, let me find you a table, Dr Lawrence, anything for you, Dr Lawrence. Oh isn't Dr Lawrence amazing, you must be so proud.'

'It wasn't like that.'

'It was! I'm not going to do it. I don't want to do it. People will treat me like I'm some fucking groupie to the great Dr Kate Cooper.'

'Matt, you can work anywhere. Does it really matter?'

'Of course it matters. I don't want to leave here. I like it here.'

'What about what I want? Perhaps a fresh start might be good for us.'

She remembered him sneering and topping up his wine glass for the fifth time that evening.

'Do we want a fresh start? Really? Let's be brutal, Kate. You still haven't got over losing the baby, and it's been what? Nearly nine months? I mean Jesus… get over it. You're simply not the same person now and I'm not sure I want to be with you anymore.'

She remembered the crashing sense of disbelief that he could be so dismissive of something so huge and utterly devastating.

'The baby… *our* baby had a name, you know. Or did you choose to forget?'

'I didn't forget. How could I forget with you weeping everywhere and not being able to get out of bed for an eternity? I mean Jesus. Move on. Get over it. I moved on. No one bothered about how I felt or how it had affected me. No one even asked me.'

'How can you be so…'

'So what? So practical? Yes. You lost the baby at, what was it, thirty-two weeks? Yes, it was awful. But do you know what? Better that happened than have to deal with one that wasn't perfect, and he wasn't, was he? That's what the post-mortem said. He was far from perfect. So nature did us a favour. It all worked out.'

'But Daniel was *our* son.'

She remembered sobbing, unable to understand how he could be so callous.

'I think it's all for the best anyway. He would have been even more of a burden than we thought. I wouldn't have wanted that.'

'How can you say that? You wanted a child…'

'I wanted a *perfect* child, Kate, which you clearly are unable to give me.'

'What? Are you saying Daniel was my fault?'

She remembered him shrugging and slurping his wine.

'If the cap fits,' he had said.

Kate remembered looking at this man who was her husband. She remembered seeing him clearly for the selfish, cruel, lazy man he was.

'I'm going then. Without you.' She had decided almost instantly. Anything to be away from him.

He had shrugged. 'Whatever.'

'We'll put the house on the market.'

'No need. I'll buy you out.'

'Is it that simple to you?'

'Yes. And just so you know, Anna will probably move in pretty soon.'

Kate recalled a moment of wondering whether she was in a parallel universe.

'My friend Anna? You're telling me you're having an affair with her?'

'For ages now,' he had said irritably. 'You're close to useless on the sex front since Daniel died and I have needs, you know. Anna's always liked me.'

Kate remembered looking at him incredulously and realising that she had no idea who this man was. She remembered anger taking over.

'Well, Anna's welcome to you then. Perhaps *she'll* provide you with a perfect child,' she had shouted and stomped upstairs to start packing.

'Here's hoping!' he had called after her.

Kate had lived in the spare room for three months, working out her notice, packing her things and largely ignoring Matt. Her plans were to stay with her parents in Castleby until she found a house to rent or buy, but the prospect of being under the same roof with her nitpicking mother had almost made her change her mind. Kate assured herself, however, it wouldn't be for long and she could work long hours to avoid her.

They had a difficult, fractious relationship and the crux of it was that for some reason, Kate felt she had been a constant disappointment to her mother. She did, however, have a wonderful relationship with her father. When she thought about it, that was probably the root of many of the issues with her mother.

She tightened her fingers on the steering wheel. This was it. A new start. She felt a moment of pure freedom, turned up the radio, and floored the accelerator.

Six hours later, Kate pulled into the driveway of her parents' house in Castleby. It was a large red-brick Edwardian detached house, built deep into the slope of the hillside and had far reaching views over the golf course and Long Beach. She loved the house – always had. As a small child she had chosen her bedroom carefully so that she could sit on the broad window seat and watch the weather roll across the bay.

The ornate front door swung open spilling light onto the driveway. Her father's black Labrador, Otis, ran out barking and wagging his tail.

'Darling, you made it,' her father said with delight as he approached her with open arms.

'Hey, Dad,' Kate said, hugging him tightly. 'Good to see you.'

'Darling, I can't believe you're back for good to work in the practice. It's a dream come true.' He pushed her away from him so he could look at her face. 'You look tired, love. I'm sorry things went pear-shaped with Matt.'

'Let's just say I finally saw the light,' Kate said grimly. 'Hello, Mother.'

Kate's mother emerged from the house and proffered a powdered cheek for Kate to kiss. Hugging her was like hugging an ironing board, and Kate had learnt at a very early age, physical affection was not in her mother's repertoire.

'Hello, Kate dear. Oh it is so sad about lovely Matt. I did so utterly adore him, you know. Didn't you, Graham? Perhaps he'll still visit anyway.' She waved a hand vaguely. 'You know, when you aren't around, dear.'

'Hopefully not,' Kate said cheerfully, opening the boot and dragging out a bag. Her father offered to help but she waved him away. 'I'll get the rest tomorrow.'

She linked arms with her father as they walked into the house.

'Supper's nearly ready,' her mother said, drifting in the house towards the kitchen.

'Of course, I told your father, when Jack left the practice that he needed to get some help, but he would insist on using these dreadful locums all the time.' Kate's mother was in full swing at the dinner table, giving her opinion on everything with the assistance of a chilled Chardonnay.

'Did you? I don't recall that, Vanessa.' Kate's father winked cheerfully at her.

'How is Jack these days?' asked Kate innocently.

Graham sighed. 'Bless him. He's not good at all. Some days it's like there's nothing wrong at all, but other days the dementia presents as quite severe—'

'You know Sophie has come back to help out?' interrupted Vanessa. She pursed her lips. 'Not before time either in my opinion. The poor man was found in town in his pyjamas on more than one occasion.'

'Yes. She told me. It's been really difficult for her.' Kate and Sophie had been firm friends since school.

'Umm. Well not before time,' Kate's mother said waspishly, downing a glass of wine almost in one. 'Though quite how she can care for her father with that unruly boy and a missing husband I don't know.'

'I know Sam's still missing. That's what she said last time I spoke to her.' Kate looked at her father.

'It's been two years now, I think,' he said sadly. 'No sign of him at all. The MOD have told her he's presumed dead, but she won't have it.'

'It's so awful for her. I'll see her as soon as I can.'

'Of course he's dead. There's no way he could still be alive after all this time,' Vanessa piped up, topping up her glass and ignoring everyone else's.

'You don't know that, Vanny,' chided Graham, pushing himself up from the table.

'Of course I do,' Vanessa retorted irritably.

He ignored Vanessa and disappeared for a moment.

'I have a gift for you, my love.'

When he returned, he held a square wrapped in red tissue paper with a large bow. Vanessa clapped her hands and then her face fell when she realised the present wasn't for her.

'What's this about?' Kate said, taking the gift and looking lovingly at her dad.

'Just a little something,' he said, grinning.

'I never get any gifts,' Vanessa sniped.

Kate unwrapped it carefully. It was a new brass plaque that read *Dr Kate Cooper* and listed her qualifications.

'Dad,' she said, touched. 'Thanks so much.'

'I'm putting it up tomorrow,' he said, smiling and squeezing her hand. 'I'm so very happy to have you back. A practice with my daughter. I couldn't be any prouder. We should have a toast!'

'But I've run out of wine, Graham,' complained Vanessa plaintively, ruining the moment. 'Be a dear and fetch another bottle?'

Later Kate stood at her open bedroom window and felt the sea breeze on her face. She reflected on the evening, smiling at her father's delight in her return and finding a level of amusement in her mother's intermittent waspishness throughout the evening when the spotlight wasn't on her. She would start looking for somewhere to rent or buy tomorrow. She genuinely couldn't do any serious time in the house with her mother. They'd end up killing each other.

CHAPTER 2

Doug Brodie, full-time skipper of the Castleby lifeboat stood easily on the outside deck of the fast-moving lifeboat as it surged powerfully through the dark sea. Years of being on the water meant he was used to the roll of the ocean and the movement of the boat, whatever the conditions.

He was exhausted and almost asleep standing up. The crew had spent hours trying to find two missing kayakers in very rough conditions. The alarm had gone off early the previous evening and Doug and the team had searched all night. They had finally found the two men trapped in a rocky inlet, with one kayak lost and the other damaged. The search in the dark on rough seas, along with the tricky rescue, had left him and his crew shattered.

He narrowed his eyes against the wind and spray and saw the welcoming lights of Castleby harbour approaching in the gloomy dawn. He wanted to get home, see the kids, eat and sleep. In that order.

Finally, the station came into view. As the lifeboat turned and was slowly winched back up the ramp, Billy, a retired crew member who had suffered a stroke during a bad rescue, leaving him semi-paralysed, wheeled himself along the upper gantry and shouted urgently.

'DOUG! DOUG! Felix has been calling!'

Instantly panicked, Doug almost fell off the side of the boat in his heavy all-weather gear, as he tried to hear Billy properly over the sound of the heavy-duty winch.

'WHAT?'

Billy shouted louder. 'Felix said to get to the hospital as soon as possible. You need to hurry, Doug. I'll stow the gear and lock up. Just go.'

Doug leapt off the moving boat and ran to the locker room, stripping off his gear and leaving it in a heap on the floor. He dressed quickly, pulling on his jeans and polo shirt. He grabbed his phone and keys and sprinted towards the front door.

Billy grasped his arm tightly. 'I'll close up. You get to Jesse,' he said quietly, his face a mask of worry. 'You call me now, soon as you know, my boy. I need to know.'

'Aye. Will do,' Doug said grimly as he raced out of the station and around the harbour towards his truck.

'CLEAR,' shouted Dr Felix Carucci as he applied the pads to the patient's chest. He pressed the button and watched the screen for heart activity over his shoulder.

'Jesus. Nothing. COME ON. Charge again,' he shouted.

The team waited for the machine to charge and stood back.

'CLEAR,' he called again and pressed the button.

The team waited.

Felix watched the screen intently. 'Don't do this,' he muttered to the unresponsive patient. 'Don't fucking do this.'

'Still nothing,' a nurse said, fingers pressed to the patient's neck.

'Charge again.' Felix breathed deeply. 'CLEAR.' He shocked the patient again and closed his eyes. Waiting. Praying.

'Come on,' he said through gritted teeth.

'Sinus rhythm,' announced a nurse. 'Pressure's on its way back up.'

'Jesus Christ.' Felix slumped with relief. He peeled off the pads, put them back on the crash trolly and turned to talk to the unresponsive patient. 'Don't do that again. Doug would have killed me once and for all if I'd lost you.'

He checked the patient's vitals again and picked up a hand, squeezing it gently. 'Doug's on his way, don't go anywhere.' He leant forwards and whispered in her ear, 'By the way, Jesse. Pull that stunt again and I'll damn well kill you myself.'

Doug dragged a shaking hand through his hair. He leant against the wall with a sigh and tried to control the tears of frustration that threatened to fall.

Felix laid a comforting hand on his arm. 'I can't give you an explanation as to why it happened. It could be any number of things,' he said earnestly.

'Like *what*?' Doug asked, frustration bubbling up. 'Jesus, Felix. Like fucking *what*? Her fucking heart stopped. It stopped! Does this mean her body can't take it anymore? Or that she was trying to come round? Jesus, Felix, give me something, it's been nearly a month.'

'I don't think it was because she was dying. Far from it, in fact. I wonder if it wasn't…'

Doug stared at him. 'Wasn't *what*? Come on. Wasn't what?'

'I just got a feeling…'

'About?'

'That maybe she was fighting to come out of it.'

11

'A feeling?'

Felix took a breath. 'I had the same sensation when she was on the table. It was a touch and go moment and I sensed that she was putting everything into pulling through. It was just a moment, just a feeling.'

Doug exhaled heavily. 'I'll take that.' He looked across ICU to her bed.

'It was just a feeling, Doug,' Felix cautioned.

'I'll take anything at this point.'

'She's stable for now. It's up to her.'

'Can I stay with her a wee while?' Doug asked softly, his Scottish accent always more pronounced when he was emotional.

'Yes. Talk to her. She might well be able to hear and be fighting to come round.'

Doug gazed at the floor, unseeingly. He felt wrung out, emotional. Tears lurked dangerously close. 'Look. I just want to say—'

'You don't have to—'

'I do. Seriously. Thanks. For getting her back and… you know… Jesse and everything with Claire…' he struggled to finish.

Felix enveloped him into a half bloke-hug. 'Who knew, eh?' He pulled back and grabbed Doug by the shoulders. 'You look shattered. You should sleep. Look, you can't even dress yourself properly.' He pointed to Doug's T-shirt, which was inside out. 'I don't want *you* ending up on my operating table.'

Doug rolled his eyes. 'Ach, nagging like an old woman,' he grumbled.

Felix motioned to Jesse with his head. 'Go and see her.' He slapped Doug on the shoulder and headed off towards the nurses' station.

Doug sat down in a chair next to Jesse. He rested his forearms on the bed taking Jesse's hand and kissing it.

'Enough now,' he said. 'You've slept long enough. I need you here, Jesse. I can't do this without you, I don't want to do this without you. I need you to wake up.'

He dropped his forehead down to rest on her cool, unresponsive hand.

'Brock misses you. He's not done the stick on the back of the leg thing for ages. We miss you. Come on, Jesse. Even Bob's worried. Billy sends his love.'

Doug lifted his head and searched her face for signs that she could hear him. He tried again. 'When you're back, we're going to take some time. Some real time. You and me. We're going to go away. Just the two of us… OK, three of us. Brock will want to come. We're going to walk on beaches in the sunshine, drink wine at lunchtime, snooze in the afternoon and get tipsy in the evenings. Together. But you have to wake up. You have to come back to me, Jesse. You have to wake up.'

Doug closed his eyes and tried to will her to come back to him. Within seconds he had fallen asleep next to the bed, his head on his forearms, and holding Jesse's hand.

Jesse was the full-time mechanic to the lifeboat in Castleby. She was also the woman who Doug wanted to spend the rest of his life with. For nearly a month she had been in a coma following a brutal attack by her previous partner Christopher Cherry, who had escaped from prison on a mission to find her.

He had kidnapped her, beaten her and pulled her off a high cliff onto the rocks below when he himself had fallen. Two years before that, he had savagely beaten and raped her and left her for dead.

Jesse had recovered the first time. She had fought to stay alive. He had been arrested and she had rebuilt her life and started again in Castleby. She had met Doug who was struggling to get over a rescue that had killed two of his friends, and almost killed him too. He had been battling survivor's guilt as well as dealing with his wife suddenly leaving him and the kids for another man.

Over time, Jesse had completely fallen for Doug and his quiet manner and strength without realising it. She loved him completely with a force and intensity that surprised her. Much the same had happened to Doug and the depth of how he felt about Jesse still surprised him. He loved Jesse much more deeply than he thought he was capable, following his wife's betrayal.

When Jesse had been taken by her ex-partner, Doug had felt his head and his heart would explode. He had been frantic. And when he had seen her so broken and damaged and so near death, it had almost killed him.

Dr Felix Carucci was the man who Doug's wife, Claire, had left him for. Doug had then rescued Felix when he had been knocked unconscious and dragged along for miles while kite surfing. Neither man had been happy to see each other when Doug pulled him out of the water, but Felix had been lucky to survive.

For a time, Doug and Felix's relationship had been highly fractious, but Felix had stepped up. Despite Claire leaving Felix because he had been unfaithful, when Claire had caught a life-threatening infection following surgery for cancer, he had overseen her treatment and helped her through it. Although Claire was still improving and recuperating at Doug's house, Felix loved her deeply and wanted her back. He had promised to change his ways, but Claire was still largely unconvinced that he could remain faithful.

During Claire's' treatment, Felix and Doug had formed a reluctant friendship. This had been firmly cemented over the past month. It had been Felix who had operated on Jesse. He had also calmed down a frantic Doug who was convinced Jesse wouldn't make it through this time. But Felix saved her life. It had been an incredibly difficult surgery. Jesse had been in dreadful shape, but Felix had done everything he could and had felt her fighting to stay alive on his table, a sensation he rarely experienced from a patient.

Following the surgery, he had stayed in ICU for the first 24 hours to monitor Jesse. In Doug's eyes, his commitment to Jesse had elevated him from the rank of annoyingly good-looking lothario to salt of the earth. They were now firm friends.

Jesse was in a dark place. It was a vast cave of dark black rock. She smelt the sea but couldn't see it. She figured if she found the water, she could swim her way out. But she was tired. So tired. Her chest hurt to breathe. She tried short shallow breaths and that felt better. She was on the edge of panic, but she knew if she allowed it in, it would consume her, and she would lose it. She couldn't allow that to happen.

She walked around the cave, stumbling over rocks and tried to see a way out. She rested for a while, exhausted, and then tried again. She knew this wasn't normal. She couldn't place why though. Was it a dream?

She carried on walking, searching for any sign that she might be able to leave this dark place. Then she heard it. A low murmur. She stopped and strained to hear. Where was it coming from? She walked towards the sound, hearing it get louder. She saw a sliver of light in the rocks. She scrabbled at the hole where the light was, trying to make it bigger to squeeze through it; hearing the murmuring grow louder, but she couldn't make out the words and she couldn't get through.

The pain in her chest was unbearable. She breathed shallowly and forced rocks aside, pushing herself through the gap. She gasped as she felt pain sear through her chest. She fell to her knees, the pain coursing through her. She knew she had to move, but the pain was too bad. She closed her eyes and the pain struck again. She rolled on the floor, the rock felt cold, damp and gritty against her face. She closed her eyes. She needed to rest.

She felt it then, the cold tendrils of water swirling around her. She lifted a hand and the black water dripped through her fingers, like melted tar.

Then she heard it. A voice. Clear – like it was stood next to her.

The voice was telling her to stop sleeping and come back. The voice was beautiful, lilting, soft, male, with an accent. She pushed herself up, the water coursing in relentlessly, soaking her. She waded to the edge of the rocks and started to climb, to get away from the cold water. Her breath short and choppy. Her chest agony. The voice was louder. Urgent. Telling her to come back. She climbed blindly her fingers and feet scrabbling for traction. She reached the top of the cave and rested on a ledge in the rocks. She couldn't see a way out. The water was rising, and with panic she saw glistening reptilian bodies swimming. She curled herself up away from them. She could hear the murmuring now, louder. She panicked as the water lapped over her.

'I can't get out. I can't find a way out!' she screamed. 'Somebody help me!'

Doug felt the sensation of someone stroking his hair. In the delicious moment between sleep and consciousness, he assumed Jesse had awoken during the night.

'Doug,' Claire said softly. 'Wake up.'

Doug awoke, surprised to see Claire sat next to him by Jesse's bed.

'What?' he said, looking around. 'Jesse?'

'No change. She's OK,' said Claire, squeezing his shoulder. 'Jesus, Doug. Look at you, come home and get some sleep. Come back later.'

'How did you get here?' he asked. He knew Claire was still on sick leave from the hospital and too weak to have driven in.

'Your dad dropped me in on his way back to Scotland, he said he'll call you later. Felix wanted to come and get me though. He really is trying very hard,' she whispered, grinning.

'Why did you come?' Doug said, trying to work out why Claire was taking an interest.

'Because I care about you, Doug, and I know how you feel about her,' she said tightly, looking over at Jesse. 'Poor girl's been through enough. Nearly dying by the hands of a psychopath once is bad enough, having to do it twice is sheer misfortune. I want her to come through this. I wanted to see if I could help.'

'Can you?'

'I don't know yet. I want to see a brain scan and her obs. Felix is loading it all up in his office now.' She stood, holding the back of the chair for support. 'I'll try, Doug, I promise. Without wanting to sound arrogant, if I can't help her, nobody can.'

In his office, Felix folded his arms and watched Claire inspect Jesse's file.

'It's nice to see you back here,' he said softly.

'I feel better,' Claire said, not taking her eyes off the scans in front of her. 'Have you scanned her since she arrested yesterday?'

'No. I wanted her stable for a while.'

'Hmm.'

'What do you mean, hmm?'

'What does your gut tell you, Felix?'

Felix sat heavily in his chair. He scrubbed his face with his hands and then scratched his head.

'OK. Sounds ridiculous, I know, but I got a sense yesterday that…' he trailed off.

'That what? That she was going to die?'

17

'No… that she was fighting to get back… that there was a real struggle going on.'

'You sure? I've sensed when a patient gives up in surgery, that they want to go. That it's time. Sure it wasn't that?'

'No, because when I get that, I know when I can't fight it… But this… yesterday I felt this sensation. This sensation that she was there but fighting to make the leap back.'

Claire studied the chart. 'I can't see anything here to explain her current state. Everything suggests to me that she should be awake by now. Up and about. It must be psychological,' she said thoughtfully.

'Could be, I suppose. From what I hear, this is the second time this man has tried to kill her.'

'I think there's something blocking her from coming back.'

'You don't really believe that's the main reason, do you?'

'It has to be. I've read about patients like this.' She pursed her lips thoughtfully trying to recall what she'd read. 'Bring the dog in,' she said suddenly. 'Brock.'

'What?'

'I'm serious. The dog has the most profound, deep and loving bond with her. She's his world and vice versa. He's utterly miserable without her and pining. Bring him in. Let them sense each other. Take some time. If he can't get her out of this, no one can. I'll back you if the bigwigs don't like it.'

Doug held Brock's lead tightly. In typical Border collie style, Brock was very excited to be somewhere new and was straining to get ahead and sniffing absolutely everything. He had caught Jesse's scent and was desperate to find her. Doug stopped at the door of the single patient room she had been moved to since she became more stable and told Brock to sit.

'Listen,' he said to Brock who was sat expectantly, head on one side, ears alert. 'She's in bad shape and we need her to come out of it. To come back. Do what you can.'

Brock licked his hand and Doug realised the stupidity of the situation. He must be losing it to issue health instructions to a dog. He pushed open the door to the room and unclipped Brock's lead. Doug picked up a chair and placed it in the corner, sitting, careful not to interfere.

He watched Brock sniff around the room and then sniff the bed. He whined gently and gave a small yip, all the time sitting patiently by the bed. He sat with his head on one side and then circled the bed again. He made a small noise in his throat and then jumped up. He straddled Jesse's prone form and leant forward, sniffing her and the various tubes and machines she was attached to. He sniffed her hand and pushed his head underneath it, her hand flopping away. He carefully inspected her, then gently pushed a tube out of the way with his nose, wriggling length ways alongside her. He laid his head on her chest, his body pressed against the length of her, all the time making small noises at the back of his throat. He closed his eyes and appeared to sleep. Doug sat quietly and texted Felix to tell him Brock was here.

Jesse could feel warmth, although the cold water was nearly at her neck; it came from somewhere. She moved her head and felt an imperceptible breeze on the side of her face. Was that a way out? She scrabbled sideways and found another ledge that she could move to out of the water. The higher she went, the warmer it was away from the black water.

The breeze was stronger, and the cold black rock was feeling warmer to the touch. She found where the breeze was coming in and tried desperately to make it bigger, ripping her hands and nails as she tried to make the hole larger.

'Hello?' she yelled. 'Can anyone hear me?'

She made the hole bigger and saw it was night-time. A million stars were out; the night sky looked like it was close enough to touch. A large piece of rock came away in her desperate hands and she managed to pull herself half out of the hole.

'Hello?' she shouted. 'Anyone there?'

She pulled herself out of the hole, slipped and rolled down a steep incline, crashing into rocks and debris. She came to an abrupt stop and lay on the ground, her head throbbing and her chest feeling like it was in a vice, her heart pounding from the terror. She slowly got to her feet, knowing she had to move, but not sure why.

She glanced behind her and saw the black water rising up out of the hole and heading towards her, suspended in the air. She gasped, her eyes searching for an escape away from the water. She saw a small white cottage in the distance and staggered towards it. She kept falling over rocks and debris and it felt like she had lead boots on. Everything was such an effort, she could barely move her legs to run.

She kept hearing an old rock tune in her head, 'Summer in the City'; the first verse on some sort of repeat, going round and round in her head relentlessly. It played over and over again, until she found herself singing it as she staggered breathlessly over rocks. Every time she looked up, the cottage seemed to be the same distance away and the water was still following her like a giant snake.

Finally, she reached the door and the music in her head stopped abruptly, like someone had scraped a needle across a vinyl record. She saw an old painted and cracked door knob, and turned it, pushing the door open.

The brightness blinded her. She raised a hand to shield her eyes and staggered backwards. She had stepped into a hospital room. She couldn't understand where she was or how she had got there.

She looked around the room, in one corner she saw a man sitting quietly on a chair looking at his phone and on the bed she saw a black and white dog laid out along the side of a woman with dark hair. She frowned, wondering who the woman was.

She stepped forwards to get a closer look at the woman. She gasped and raised a shaking hand to her face, touching the scar she saw mirrored before her. *Was this her?*

The light was getting brighter and hurting her eyes. She turned and saw the open doorway filling up with a wall of dark water, the reptilian shapes hovering behind it, evil eyes glinting. She ran to the door and tried to close it, but the water was bulging out. She had to shut it. Why wasn't the man helping her? She screamed at him to help her, but he didn't hear.

With a final effort she threw herself against the door, just managing to close it. The light was getting too bright. She closed her eyes and slid down the door onto the floor, exhausted from her efforts. Her hands were still shielding her eyes from the harsh light, that only seemed to shine brighter. She felt a flash of immense white-hot pressure in her head and cried out from the pain.

Then felt nothing.

The bright light was back, flashing intermittently into her eyes.

'Pupils are equal and reactive,' she heard a man's voice murmur. 'She remains stable for now. Just unresponsive.'

'It's only been a couple of hours, give it a chance.' She heard a soft male voice with traces of a Scottish accent. It was the voice she'd heard in the cave.

Everything about her hurt. She knew she was lying down in bed. There was a warm sensation down one side of her body, which felt comforting, like a warm heavy duvet on a stormy, cold night. She moved slightly and the warm comforting thing moved too. She was so tired, but she knew she had to open her eyes.

'She moved.' There was the soft Scottish voice again. 'Jesse?'

Someone took her hand and squeezed it.

'Jesse.' A different voice. She liked the other voice better. 'Jesse, if you can hear me squeeze my hand.'

She squeezed, although it took nearly all her strength.

'Jesus Christ. She's back.' Felix glanced over at Doug.

Doug laid a hand on her forehead. 'Jesse. Sweetheart, open your eyes.'

Jesse's eyelids fluttered open. She frowned as she focused on things around the room. She looked with surprise at the dog on the bed who was sleeping soundly.

The man with the soft, nice voice was holding her hand, looking at her intently.

'Jesse, you've been out a wee while. How do you feel?'

'I'm so tired,' she mumbled. 'Whose dog is this?' She focused on the man's face who was holding her hand so tightly and looking at her so intently.

'Who are you?' she mumbled before she could fall asleep again. 'You have such a lovely voice. You were talking to me in my dream. I heard you.'

* * *

Former police officer, now escaped prisoner at large, Christopher Cherry lay on the narrow bunk in the old stone cottage. He was miles from the nearest human habitation. He heard birds squawking, the roar of the sea, the wind howling, driving rain but that was all. He was freezing and had been since he arrived there.

Nearly a month ago, he had been hauled out of the Irish Sea, very close to death by two old fishermen brothers, in an equally ancient trawler. They had roughly dragged him onto the boat and given him a bed, some food, but little else. They had forced him to stay and help them on the trawler over the winter if he lived that long. In his pain and desperation, he had agreed. That was the deal in return for them sharing their small cottage and meagre food rations.

They were an odd pair, who rarely spoke. Chris felt they weren't quite the full ticket. They had no car, just a small trawler, which they had spent years making a makeshift jetty for on this unforgiving wild piece of coast. To buy provisions, they stopped at their nearest harbour, sold the fish from their catch and went to the shops there.

They had helped him set his broken arm and leg, and he had managed to sew up his own torn skin. He was in intense pain every day but knew that he was improving slowly. The white-hot rage he felt kept him warm and his plans for revenge got him through the sleepless, pain-filled nights.

He knew it was a long road to recovery, until he was back to his normal level of fitness, but he could wait. He had all the time in the world. He would get better, walk again and then get fit. In his pain and desperation, he felt he'd had no choice but to agree to help the brothers.

They told him he was in Ireland, but there were no towns nearby; they lived alone – remotely. There was no way of getting back to Wales, except by boat. He had no money. The brothers seemed to have no money. So his only option had been to learn how to drive the boat and then get rid of the two old fuckers when he was strong enough.

He had no idea if Jesse had made it out alive when he had pulled her off the cliff with him, but he needed to find out. If she wasn't dead then he'd make her pay once and for all. Oh, how she would suffer and how he would enjoy every delicious second.

CHAPTER 3

Sixty-two-year-old Mrs Edwina Pomeroy carefully wrapped her parcel and placed it gently in her wicker shopping basket. She glanced at the clock, she had to hurry. She walked through the small house she shared with her husband, Fred, a fisherman, and tutted seeing him sprawled out dozing on the sofa, still in his fishing gear, the stench of fish hanging heavy in the air.

'Fred,' she snapped. 'Get that gear off and go to bed.'

Fred opened an eye and ignored her. Cursing him, she slammed the front door loudly and hurried down the road in the cold morning air. The autumn wind buffeted her up the path of the vicarage where she used her key to open the door. She stripped off her coat, hung it neatly, and bustled into the kitchen. Turning on the radio, she set about cooking breakfast.

As was her habit, she walked into the vicar's study, picked up the large appointment book and carried it through to the kitchen.

This was her empire – the vicar's appointments – all organised by her. Nobody else was allowed; she was most particular.

She also picked up a pile of unopened post from the vicar's desk and took it into the kitchen noting the time. She flicked on the kettle and set about steaming open the vicar's post. Not just parish business, but his personal mail too. She knew what he had in his bank account, his savings. She knew he had begun to get slightly warmer and more amorous letters from his late wife's sister recently – although she had withheld a couple of those she deemed inappropriate. She knew that the new curate had a troubled past and she also knew that the vicar had recently subscribed to Netflix. Nothing escaped Mrs Pomeroy.

She read the post, resealed the envelopes with her trusty glue stick and then replaced the stack of mail on his desk. As she was returning to the kitchen the vicar arrived, rosy faced from his shower.

'Good morning, Mrs P,' he said jovially. 'Wonderful autumn morning, I see.'

'Cold wind out there,' she said shortly, passing him a cup of tea.

The telephone rang shrilly in the kitchen just as Mrs Pomeroy had placed a plate of scrambled eggs and bacon in front of the vicar. She tutted and went to answer it.

'Castleby vicarage,' she said in the plummy voice she reserved for phone conversations in the vicar's presence. She listened and then sighed heavily. 'Vicar is *very* busy,' she said imperiously. 'I'll see what we have.'

She pulled the appointment book over towards her and flicked through it.

'He's there today from about three o'clock anyway. I'll ask him to call in and see her then. But he is very busy, you know.' She listened again. 'You are most welcome. Shall I send some broth in with him? Oh, it's absolutely *my* pleasure. Goodbye.'

She took her time carefully writing in the appointment and shut the book with a snap.

'Really, Mrs P, you are too kind. Quite wonderful,' said the vicar chomping away. 'Your broth and cakes are a godsend for the folk that are ill. Now, who am I seeing today?'

Peter, the new curate accompanied the vicar as they left to start a day of visits around the parish. He was learning the life of a vicar and he liked the peace of it and helping people. He liked the vicar very much but didn't, however, care much for Mrs Pomeroy. He thought she was a two-faced battleaxe, but he didn't mention it to the vicar. There was something about the older woman with the disapproving mouth that he disliked intensely. If he got to be vicar in that parish, she would be the first change he would make.

Mrs Pomeroy cleared up the breakfast dishes and set about her daily routine. She cleaned the kitchen and prepared some vegetables for the vicar and Peter's dinner that evening. She also unpacked her basket and set about making her special healing broth in the slow cooker. Satisfied it was bubbling away, she took a duster into the vicar's study.

After some desultory flicking around, she sat herself at his desk and proceeded to go through it to check there wasn't anything she had missed. She saw that he had made some notes following a few visits, so she read those in detail and also noted a letter from a parishioner asking him to call in and see her. She tutted at herself that she had missed this letter when it came in the post. She read it and pursed her lips. She knew this woman, this parishioner. She was up to no good. Mrs Pomeroy decided that the vicar couldn't be bothered by women like that, so she tore up the letter and threw it in the bin. Then she wrote herself a cheque from the parish account, carefully forging the vicar's signature, and left the study to go up to Peter's room.

It was immaculate with his bed neatly made. She flicked the duster around and then opened the drawers in his dresser and rifled through them looking for anything of interest. Nothing. She moved around the room looking in cupboards and lifting cushions. Nothing of consequence at all. She moved into the vicar's bedroom and performed the same routine, finding only a Stephenie Meyer *Twilight* novel, which she raised an eyebrow to.

She returned to the kitchen, her daily routine complete apart from the hoovering and cooking. Content she knew everything there was to know about both men for the time being, she helped herself to the petty cash and headed off to the supermarket.

* * *

Kate waved goodbye to the care workers, firmly shut the door to the care home and hurried down towards the high street, her doctor's bag swinging heavily from her shoulder. She checked her watch and increased her speed to a faster trot, rummaging in her pocket for her ringing phone.

'Hello?' she said breathlessly. 'Dr Coop... Whaaa—!' Her voice was cut off as she slipped on a patch of wet pavement and went crashing sideways into a café's table and chairs. She lay for a moment, awkwardly, wondering what had happened, until an arm reached down and firmly gripped her elbow.

'Madam, you can't lie down here, this is café. They don't allow loitering. Let me help you up,' a voice said, with some amusement.

Kate blinked and allowed herself to be hauled upright and politely dusted down.

'Anything hurt?' the voice asked.

Kate looked into the face of the person who had helped her up. He was a nice-looking blond-haired man with sparkly blue eyes. She guessed to be in his late thirties and he was dressed in jeans and a T-shirt. He was smiling at her. There was a large coffee stain up one side of his T-shirt and splatters on his jeans.

'I'm OK,' she stammered. 'I slipped. Did I fall on you?'

'You fell on my coffee. Are you OK though?' he said with concern.

Kate glanced down at herself and adjusted her clothes. She spotted her bag lying on its side and was looking for her phone when one of the waitresses handed it to her.

'I think it's OK, just the screen cracked,' she said semi-apologetically.

Kate took the phone. 'Thanks so much.' She gestured to the waitress. 'Wait. Please can I pay for this man's coffee and get him a new one?'

'No need,' he said, waving the waitress away good-naturedly. 'I have to go anyway.' He inspected Kate, frowning. 'Look I need to go, but are you OK really? Not seeing double or anything?'

She gave an embarrassed smile. 'I'm fine. Feel like total idiot and I feel even worse about the state of your clothes too.'

He glanced down at himself. 'What do you mean? I look like this all the time,' he said as a phone rang from somewhere on his person. 'Right. I've really got to go. Now, no more flying into people's breakfasts!' He turned and jogged lightly up the high street pulling his phone out of his back pocket as he went.

Kate watched him go, wondering who he was. She picked up her bag and continued at a slower pace to her destination.

'Hey, Maggie,' Kate said breathlessly as she walked into Maggie's Beach Café.

Maggie screeched with delight and came around the counter to envelop Kate in a huge cuddle.

'My favourite doctor!' Maggie beamed. 'So good to have you back, my darling. Are you OK? Glad you dumped that shit of a husband. Could never stand him. He was a right prick.'

'Christ, Mags, why don't you try saying exactly what you think every once in a while and not hold back?' Kate said dryly.

'Hey, lovely lady.'

Kate turned at the voice and saw her friend, Sophie, standing behind her. Immediately Kate dropped her bag and gave her a tight hug.

Dr Sophie Jones was a very busy marine biologist who wore a raft of different hats for different clients. She had moved back to the area with her son, Marcus, to care for her father, who had been Kate's father's partner at the GP practice until his retirement. Sophie's husband, Sam, a captain in military intelligence had been missing presumed dead in Afghanistan for nearly two years.

'Soph! So good to see you. I missed you.'

'Ditto. Oh, and Maggie's comment about your husband? Yeah… what she said.' She pointed at Maggie, her eyes sparkling.

'Sorry I'm late, I fell over in the high street.'

'Nothing changes! What happened?'

'I don't know, I was answering my phone and then next thing I know I'm lying on a table and chairs, and I've covered some poor bloke in coffee.'

'Who was the poor bloke?'

'No idea. He had to go. Wouldn't even let me pay for his drink.'

'Ooh intriguing,' said Sophie.

'Right, what'll it be, ladies?' Maggie clapped her hands together. 'It's on me. Go and enjoy the sunshine while you can, there's a table outside.'

'Mmm, that's good,' Sophie said, sipping her large coffee. 'I needed that. So, what's it been now? Three weeks since you got here? How are you finding it?'

'Busy! But hey, I'm so sorry this is the first chance we've had to catch up. I've been helping out at the hospital to avoid Mother. Tell me about you. Come on. Everything.' Kate leant forward and looked at Sophie intently. 'Your dad, Marcus and Sam. Whichever order you want.'

'Blimey, how long have you got?' Sophie said wryly.

'Long as you need.'

'OK. Dad. Dementia is progressing but is manageable most days, although it's becoming more of a problem lately. Dad has Carol who comes in and helps out. His latest obsession is how much he has to pay to use the toilet and whether he has enough underwear to last him the week.' She pulled a face. 'Carol got him into respite care a few weeks back and he really enjoyed it there; so that's an answer every now and again, I think.' She stopped for a moment. 'I'm not ready to send him permanently if that's what you're thinking.'

'OK. Do you want me to give him a once over and check his meds are current?'

Sophie touched her hand. 'I'd love that. Thanks, Kate.'

'Marcus? How's he doing?'

Sophie rolled her eyes. 'Did I tell you about the thing with Jude and Marcus getting lost in the Brecon's and falling down the old shaft?'

'Yeah, you told me last time we spoke. Jude did well to keep him safe and get him out.'

'That boy is a chip off the old block as Dad used to say. So like his dad, you remember Doug, don't you?'

Kate frowned. 'I think so. Is he the Scottish lifeboat guy? Tall, handsome... lovely way about him.'

'Who's tall and handsome with a lovely way about them?' interrupted Maggie, delivering their food.

'Doug from the lifeboat.'

'God yes. Gorgeous man. I can tell you, that man can rescue me any day,' Maggie said.

Sophie giggled. 'Rob and Rudi were amazing helping me find the boys.'

'Rob and Rudi?'

'Course, you wouldn't have met them, would you? Rob runs the climbing centre now and Rudi is a tree surgeon, but he's always around somewhere. They were in the forces together – they're really close.'

Maggie was clearing the next table and butted in again. 'Oh, those two,' she said wistfully. 'You know how I love a soldier and those two certainly hit the mark. I've got a soft spot for Foxy. Their friend Mack too. Lovely boys. I tell you when I see them all together it's like I've won a totty lottery.' She tittered. 'If only I was ten years younger,' she said, disappearing inside.

'Foxy?' asked Kate confused. 'I'm struggling to keep up here.'

'Foxy is Rob's nickname. Everyone calls him Foxy. He owns "ENDURE" over there.'

'I saw the signs had been changed. So, come on. Onto the super important stuff. Sam.'

Sophie's eyes filled with tears. Kate instinctively reached over and took her hand.

'Soph, I'm so sorry, I didn't want to upset you.'

Sophie shook her head and wiped her eyes.

'He's still missing then?' Kate said softly.

Sophie sniffed. 'That's the thing, Kate. They've found him, but he's in really bad shape.'

'What?' Kate was shocked.

Sophie lowered her voice. 'It's all very hush hush. A few weeks back, I get a knock at the door and it's someone from the MOD, some Casualty Informing Officer or something, and they tell me that they think they've found Sam and what's left of his unit. That he's in really bad shape… like… really bad shape, and that they don't even know if they'll get him out safely without him dying. Well, they did get him out, and he made it, but, from what I hear, he arrested a few times on the extraction. But they got him back. So, that's it in a nutshell really.' She blew her nose and wiped her eyes. 'They've said…' She struggled to compose herself.

'Said what, hun?' Kate prompted softly.

'Said that he's unlikely to be the same man,' she choked out. 'The things he's endured, had done to him… he's not likely to be himself.'

'Jesus, Soph. So where is he now? What's happening?' Kate grasped her hand.

'The last update was that he was still in one of the bases in Afghanistan and they were waiting until he was stable enough to move him to Portsmouth. I get news every couple of days.'

'Jesus. Can I do anything medically?'

Sophie shook her head sadly. 'It's just a waiting game.'

'OK. But next time you get news, insist on the doctor's name and get a contact number. I'll call and see what I can find out.'

'OK. Thanks, I appreciate it. It's just not knowing, you know, how bad it is.' She wiped her red eyes and blew her nose.

A tall, well-built man with a handsome, weathered face and enormous arms stopped next to their table. He placed a hand lightly on Sophie's shoulder looking concerned, his eyes flicking over Kate.

'Soph? Everything OK?'

'Hey you!' she said warmly. 'Talk of the devil. Kate, this is Rob, who I was telling you about.'

He gave Kate a quick nod and extended his hand. 'Hi there. Good to meet you.' He turned back to Sophie. 'Soph, has something happened?'

Sophie flapped her hands and wiped her eyes. 'I'm fine. I was just telling Kate about Sam. Kate's an old friend. She's the new GP, our dads were partners when the practice was first set up.'

'Uh-huh. So, nothing new today?' he enquired.

Sophie shook her head. 'Kate's going to try and talk to one of the doctors once he's back in the UK, so that'll be helpful.'

'Good idea,' he said thoughtfully and turned to Kate. 'He's clearly not stable enough to be moved otherwise they would have got him here by now. They don't mess about.'

Kate tilted her head, remembering that he was ex-forces. 'Voice of experience?' she asked lightly.

He looked grim for a moment. 'Of sorts. Look I've got to get back. I'm on my own, the boys are out on a shout. Good to meet you, Kate, see you around. Look after yourself,' he said to Sophie and headed back inside the centre.

'He's very protective.' Kate observed watching him enter the climbing centre and stop to stroke the Alsatian sitting in the doorway.

Sophie glanced over fondly. 'That's Solo. He's lovely, Rob found him injured in the middle of a war zone, rescued him and brought him home.'

'I didn't mean the dog,' Kate remarked. 'I meant him.'

'Oh yeah. He was with me when the MOD turned up. Asked all the right questions, he's been fantastic. Between you and me, he was captured and tortured on a tour, and I think he nearly didn't make it. I guess he has more insight on this than the rest of us put together.' She turned to Kate. 'He's been a good friend. He's been through a lot too.'

Kate raised an eyebrow. 'Like what?'

'His daughter died, his wife blamed him, divorced him, he's making a new start, trying to deal with stuff.'

'Are you two…?'

'No! Course not,' Sophie said indignantly. 'He is lovely though.'

'Didn't you say he stopped the guy who killed your mum from attacking you?'

'Yup, he's like a guardian angel of sorts.' She smiled. 'He's a good friend.'

'Does he see it that way?'

* * *

Inspector Steve Miller (known to most of the locals as Steve the copper) bleeped himself through the security door at the local nick. He raised a hand in greeting to a harried PCSO who was manning the reception desk and trying to explain to a confused pensioner that they weren't the local taxi office.

He jogged up the worn vinyl stairs and shouldered through the doors to CID, approaching a group of men gathered around a large table.

'Christ, what the hell happened to you?' Detective Chief Inspector Jerry Reed pointed at the large coffee stain across Steve's T-shirt and jeans.

'Man's entitled to a day off and some coffee throwing once in a while.'

Jerry laughed. 'Sorry to call you in. I needed your take on the hunt for the elusive Jake Jones.'

'Ah! The mysteries of missing pond life,' Steve said, leaning against a filing cabinet.

The police had been looking for Jake Jones, or JJ, a well-known criminal, who was a frequent flyer locally, for over a month. Rumours were that he had crossed the local mafia and had paid with his life, as his friend Huey had, in particularly unpleasant circumstances.

'We've had something through from the boys in Oxford.'

'Oxford?' Steve snorted. 'He wouldn't be there, far too upmarket for the likes of JJ.'

'I agree. They've sent a few CCTV pics, bit grainy, but I don't reckon it's him, and I'm buggered if I'm forking out on a facial recognition ID until I get your take.'

He threw some photographs across the desk at Steve. 'Your thoughts, please?'

Steve flicked through the pictures studying them carefully. 'I'm 99.9 per cent sure it's not JJ,' he said finally.

'Why?' demanded Jerry with his usual intensity.

'OK.' Steve pointed. 'Hair's a little too long compared to the last time I saw him and no one's hair grows that fast. He wouldn't be wearing a wig, he's not the sort. He's not got a tattoo on that arm either, plus one of that size I reckon would be a couple of hundred quid and he wouldn't want to fork out that much for something like that. Plus, those things take ages if there's loads of colours.' He narrowed his eyes. 'What else? OK, see him at that till there? Counting out coins with his left hand? JJ is right-handed. And this one of the guy leaving, look at the position of his feet, his right foot is turned outwards as he walks. I'm no expert in gait analysis, but I do know JJ's foot placement is actually turned inwards, he's really pigeon-toed. I've chased him down the street enough times to know it. So, in my humble opinion, this isn't JJ.'

Jerry beamed. 'Excellent. I thought it wasn't, but you've confirmed it. The search continues.'

'Unlike JJ to have laid low this long,' mused Steve. 'Perhaps the rumours are true.'

'That he got the same treatment as Huey?' asked Jerry, slurping his coffee.

'You have to wonder,' Steve mused. 'Although they do like to make their killings public, as a warning.'

'Little scrote will turn up somewhere, you mark my words. Now, bugger off. Get on with your laundry, or whatever it is you do on a day off,' he said, pointing at the stain.

'Your wish is my command,' Steve said. 'See you later.'

He took the stairs two at a time and headed out into the sunshine. He ought to really head home and change but couldn't help wondering who the blonde-haired woman was who dropped into his lap earlier.

I see them all. I see them. Into their souls. Their rotten souls. They are all lost and searching for something. Greedy for everything. Nothing satisfies them. Never are they sated. What is it they are searching for? Do they know?

This life of having everything and valuing nothing. They consume the world, with no regard to how it affects others. They seek blessing from their wasted lives. They seek atonement from the higher powers. They have no regard for the future of others. Do they know what they are doing? The damage they cause? The cost to society? Perhaps they need educating. Perhaps they need to be told. Perhaps someone needs to tell them.

CHAPTER 4

Jesse couldn't keep her eyes open. She was so exhausted she could barely have a conversation for five minutes before falling asleep again. This made it difficult, and frustrating, for her doctors and Doug to get any sense out of her.

Felix was standing at the foot of her bed.

'Jesse. I need you to focus. I need you to tell me the last thing you remember.'

Jesse struggled to remain awake. The effort of thinking was too much. 'The white house… I was trying to get across the rocks to it.' Her eyelids fluttered shut. 'Then I opened the door into here.'

'What do you remember before that?' Felix asked. 'Your life before that? Do you recall what you do for a living, where you live? Those things?'

Jesse thought hard. It was so exhausting. Her eyelids felt so heavy.

'I just remember the cave and the cottage. Oh…' she said as she drifted off. 'And that man's voice. That beautiful voice. It was calling me.'

Felix watched her. He wasn't particularly worried, coma patients often experienced post-traumatic amnesia, but he had sought a second opinion from various colleagues and their thoughts had been interesting; they had suggested that Jesse's psyche could be blocking the reality of her memories because the horror of her second encounter with Chris was so traumatic that her brain was refusing to process it. Whatever the reason for Jesse's amnesia, Felix was certain that she had a significant journey to recovery ahead of her.

* * *

Steve was driving when his phone rang.

'Miller,' he answered on the hands free.

'Guv. It's Jonesey. Don't know how you're gonna feel about this.'

'Oh Christ, what is it?'

'Er, we've got a head. In a lobster pot.'

'Say again, Jonesey?'

'We've got a head. In a lobster pot. The Davy Jones Salvage boys brought it up, they called us. SOCO have had a look and sent it to the morgue to see if we can ID it.'

'Whoever said police work was dull?' Steve said dryly. 'Who is it?'

'Dunno. Wanna go and look?'

'Yup. I'll do it now. I'm halfway there anyway. See you later.'

Steve ended the call, turned the car around and headed towards the morgue.

Suitably gowned, Steve waited patiently for the pathology technician to slide open the large drawer to the chilled cabinet.

'We've left it in the pot for now. Dr Murphy isn't ready yet, so it stays as is for photographs etc.'

'OK.'

The item was covered in a sterile cloth which the technician lifted carefully. He turned the pot around so that Steve could get a good look at the face.

'Well, well, well,' Steve murmured, bending down to get a closer look. 'I wondered where the hell you'd got to.' He turned to the technician. 'OK to take a few snaps?'

The technician nodded solemnly.

Steve smiled. 'Stuff like this makes my Instagram and Facebook page way more interesting.'

The technician looked horrified before realising Steve was joking.

'Not really very appropriate to joke about these things, I think,' he said stiffly.

Steve chuckled. 'If you knew who this was you'd realise it's wholly appropriate.' He put his phone away. 'Thanks very much. If you could let me know when the investigations take place that would be helpful.'

The technician gave a nod and glided away. Steve stripped off the disposable gown and shuddered, desperate to get out into the open air away from the cloying smell that frequented the morgue. Standing outside he yanked out his phone and dialled.

'Jonesey,' he said. 'Just left the morgue.'

'Who is it, Guv? Anyone we know?'

'It's your friend and mine, Mr Jake Jones.'

'No way!'

'Yes way. And I have an idea about someone that might know a little bit about it.'

'You on your way back?'

'Yup. Couple more calls to make, then I'll be in. Keep it on the down low for a bit, eh?'

'OK. See you later.'

Steve dialled another number and left a message on DCI Jerry Reed's answerphone.

'Jerry. JJ has turned up. Well, his head has anyway. Call me back.' His phone rang again, and he answered it. 'Miller.'

'Guv. Me again. Chief Superintendent's been on the phone. Can you come and see him pronto? I think that means, like, right now.'

Steve shut the door to the Chief Superintendent's office and swore quietly but colourfully under his breath. All he fucking needed. A pet project for the Chief Super to breathe down his fucking neck over and make his life a misery. He thumped grumpily down the stairs, marched along the corridor, into his office and kicked the door shut. All the time, fuming quietly at the politics of the higher echelons of the police force and the impact the funny handshake brigade had on some investigations.

Loitering outside and slightly wary of going in directly, Jonesey knocked lightly and stuck a hand around Steve's office door that held a steaming coffee cup.

'Come on in, Jonesey,' called Steve.

Jonesey put down Steve's coffee.

'What did the Chief Super want?' He plonked himself down in a chair, unwrapped a Penguin biscuit and stuffed it in whole.

Steve rolled his eyes. 'Jesus, at least break it in half.' He sighed. 'New case, bit hush hush.'

'What is it?' Jonesey said, chewing noisily.

'There's been some unexplained deaths at a couple of the local care homes for the elderly in the last few months, nothing significant to explain it, I think, but the press have been sniffing about.'

Jonesey frowned. 'Isn't it like, you know, fairly normal?'

'Fairly normal?'

'Well, you know, for old people to die in a care home?'

'Well, yes. But I think these deaths were… unexpected, shall we say. Plus, it just so happens that the Chief Super has a very good friend…' he mimicked speech marks, 'and I suspect this very good friend is also a member of the funny handshake brigade. But also happens to own at least two of the care homes where these deaths occurred.'

'Ah.'

'Exactly, ah,' said Steve grimly. 'And you are the lucky fellow who gets to assist me.'

'Lucky me.'

'My thoughts exactly. So, your mission if you choose to accept it, which you will, is to get me the list of victims and the results of their PMs please. Soon as you like, while keeping this on the down low. Capiche?'

'Capiche,' Jonesey said, rising. 'Your wish is my command, oh great one.'

'Just as I thought,' said Steve, grinning and slurping his coffee. 'I'm popping out in a mo, gotta see a man about a head.'

* * *

Local fisherman and part-time criminal Jimmy Ryan was crapping himself. So much so, he was considering doing a runner. Early that morning, he'd been chatting to one of the fishermen on the quay who had told him that the Davy Jones Salvage boys had found a head in a lobster pot and the police had it. Jimmy had almost wet himself in panic but had tried to appear nonchalant.

Well over a month ago, Jimmy had been a reluctant fence for fellow criminal, Jake Jones. JJ had stolen a stack of ordnance from the MOD camp, before the local mafia had got to it. Unfortunately, the local mafia had considered it theirs for the stealing and JJ's sidekick in crime, Huey, had been found and murdered horribly to make the point that no one fucked with the Camorra. JJ was greedy and had refused to give up the stash, instead he approached Jimmy and asked him to broker a deal with a Russian contact that Jimmy had run a few drugs for previously. Reluctantly, Jimmy had brokered and done the deal with his contact Alexy.

The payment, however, hadn't been what Jimmy negotiated and had, instead, been a large bag of cash for him, which unfortunately also contained JJ's head. Jimmy not being the sharpest knife in the drawer, had not known what to do with it. Eventually he'd had the bright idea of taking it out to sea in an old lobster pot and chucking it over the side. He'd thought that was the end of it.

Until now.

Jimmy had visions of forensic testing throwing up his fingerprints on JJ's head and the lobster pot and the very thought of being done for it was making his knees weak. He was already on a suspended sentence for giving up the gang that he had been bringing drugs in for.

He tried to think logically, which was hard for him. Would they come to him? Why would they? Plenty of other blokes with lobster pots they could bother. He gave himself a talking to. The fuzz couldn't prove a bloody thing. Didn't stop him worrying about it though. It later occurred to him that he also had no idea where the rest of JJ was.

Steve drove through the town and headed down towards the harbour. He was on the lookout for someone specific. He parked next to the RNLI parking bays and strolled down to the quayside to see who was there. He checked his watch. Some of the fisherman would be rolling in about now. He looked out to sea and saw a line of boats heading in. Steve grabbed himself a takeaway coffee and settled on a bench to wait.

After a while he got lucky. Exactly who he wanted. He watched the boat arrive and have the catch unloaded on the quayside. Rising, he tossed the empty cup in a bin and wandered over.

'Afternoon, Jimmy,' he said softly, leaning against one of the iron ladders that ran along the edge.

Jimmy had his back to the quayside and almost shat himself when he heard Steve's voice. He closed his eyes and breathed in deeply. Turning to face the policeman he did his best to appear casual.

'What d'you want?' he said grumpily.

'I'm very well thanks for asking, Jimmy. How have you been?'

Jimmy shrugged. 'Y'know.'

'Just wondered whether you'd heard the jungle drums?'

'About?'

'I think you know, Jimmy.'

'About what?'

'OK, we'll do it this way then. The rumours about JJ and his trip in a lobster pot. Any clues about where the rest of him went?'

'I haven't seen JJ for ages.'

'I feel sure you have.'

'What you gettin' at?'

'Jimmy, I realise playing dumb comes fairly naturally to you, but this really isn't an Oscar-worthy performance.'

'Bit harsh. All I've heard is a rumour that the Davy Jones boys had found a head in a lobster pot. You sayin' it's JJ?'

'Bingo. Know anything about it?'

'Like what?'

'Like, who put it there, how did it get there and where is the rest of him?'

'How would I know anything about it?' Jimmy tried to look affronted.

'You have a boat, lobster pots and did deals with JJ. It's not rocket science to join the dots here, Jimmy.'

'You can fuck right off with your dot to dot. I don't know nothing about it.'

'OK,' said Steve brightly. 'Just wondered. Forensics will get to it in a day or so and then we'll know more. I might even come and have a chat with you then. Have a good evening. Oh, and Jimmy? Don't leave town.'

* * *

It was bright and early, and Steve had elected to call into one of the care homes on his way into the station. He knew it would be breakfast time, but he figured the hustle and bustle might elicit a few more answers. He buzzed the door entry, the receptionist let him in and asked him to sign the visitors' book. As he walked into reception he saw the local vicar, a jolly, rotund figure in his early sixties with a balding head. He was accompanied by a younger, tall, thin man with dark hair and a pale complexion.

'Morning, Vicar,' Steve said good-naturedly. 'How are things in your heavenly kingdom?'

The vicar chuckled. 'Ah, Steve. Good to see you, how have you been? May I introduce you to Peter, my new curate.'

Steve shook Peter's hand. 'Peter, nice to meet you. Been here long?'

'About a month now,' the young man mumbled shyly.

'Peter, this is Steve Miller, the local police inspector.'

'For my sins.' Steve gave a small mock bow. He gestured to the dining room. 'Working breakfast, Vicar?'

The vicar chortled. 'I wish, it looks quite delicious, but Mrs P did breakfast this morning. We're just popping in to pray with Mary and Olive, twin sisters. Their older sister Mabel has suddenly become quite ill. Quite the surprise isn't it, Peter? She was fine when you held prayers with them earlier in the week.'

Peter nodded.

'Is she very ill?' asked Steve.

'She is poor thing. Dr Cooper saw her last night when she took a turn for the worst and she's not hopeful of a recovery.'

'May I ask what she is ill with?' Steve's interest was piqued.

The vicar shrugged. 'I think it's a bad flu. Dr Cooper is coming in again later.'

'I won't keep you from your good work then, Vicar. Good to see you both,' Steve said, moving aside so they could pass him.

The vicar moved off down the corridor talking earnestly to Peter as they went. Steve approached the reception desk.

'Hi there,' he said, flashing his warrant card and giving the receptionist what he hoped was a winning smile. 'Is the manager about?'

Thirty minutes later, after much smoothing of ruffled feathers with a slightly irate care home manager, Steve left holding photocopies of the visitor logs for the past two months. He climbed into his car and flicked through the logs. He noted the name of the victims and who had been in to see them. He noted that various doctors called in, and that the vicar and Peter visited regularly. There was also a lot of locals popping in and out for various reasons.

He sat thinking for a while, planning ways to collate the logs across care homes to look for any patterns that might emerge.

'So… It's mainly blimmin' do-gooders and God botherers,' Jonesey said, chewing noisily on a toffee while scrutinising the photocopies. 'You know the sort. I'll help, but is there anything in it for me?'

'You are a very jaded man,' remarked Steve, pinching a toffee.

'I call it realistic,' Jonesey said, snatching the bag away and stuffing it in his desk drawer.

'So, collate it all, please – chuck it on a spreadsheet, let's look for patterns,' Steve said. 'I'm off to the next one on the list.'

CHAPTER 5

'For fuck's sake, Carla, it's not like that at all,' Foxy snapped into his phone angrily. 'I really don't know what your problem is here.'

He scowled as he listened to the tirade on the other end of the line.

'Carla, for the last time. We're just friends. You know that. You met her when you were here. She needs support right now. Her husband's in a bad way. Do you not remember what that was like?'

He listened for a moment and closed his eyes.

'Carla, I'm not going to do this. You live there and don't want to move here. You have a life there, which I know very little about. You literally cannot say to me that you aren't happy about my friendship with Sophie. I'm not having it. I will not be told who I can be friends with.'

Foxy rubbed his face, frustrated at yet another tedious conversation with his ex-wife about his friendship with Sophie. A few weeks ago, Carla had arrived out of the blue at Foxy's to stay for a couple of weeks and it had seemed like an olive branch. He was hopeful that perhaps she had finally forgiven him; she had blamed him for their daughter's death and ended their marriage because of it. Things had been good for a while; they had rekindled their romance. Until Carla had met Sophie.

Carla simply couldn't understand that they were just friends and not involved. She refused to believe it, leaving Foxy in a difficult spot. He still had feelings for Carla, but he was a loyal friend to Sophie, and he would not abandon a friend. There was silence on the other end of the phone.

'Carla,' Foxy tried again. 'Be reasonable.'

He was rewarded with more silence. He stared at the phone in disbelief. She had hung up on him. She knew that was his pet hate. Nothing irritated him more than someone hanging up on him during an argument.

He shook his head, swore under his breath, and stuffed the phone back into his pocket.

He walked back into the climbing centre, which was busy with the after-school crowd.

'Everything alright?' Sophie ventured.

'Carla is being ridiculous,' he said, his eyes narrowing. He watched Sophie's son, Marcus, navigate a difficult corner and pull himself up with sheer strength.

'Good turn, Marcus,' he called out. 'Well done.'

'Ridiculous about what?' Sophie asked, nudging him.

He glanced down at Sophie. She looked shattered. Dark smudges under her eyes.

'You sleeping?' he asked.

'I said, what is Carla being ridiculous about?'

'And I asked if you were sleeping.'

'Bad night last night. By the time I got home, sorted dinner, helped Marcus with his homework and finished a paper that I was late submitting, it was really late. Dad has started wandering in his sleep and trying to get out. He gets quite belligerent at 3 a.m. in the morning when he wants to check on the hens we don't actually have.'

Foxy looked sympathetic. 'Soph, you need to think about getting some help at night.'

'I know, I know. It's just what with Sam and everything. I just don't know whether he'll need any help too. Everything's up in the air.'

'It must be. Look, tonight, you go home now. Get your work done. I'll close up and bring Marcus home with pizza for us all, Jack too. I'm staying at yours. You're coming back here to sleep. You need to sleep, Sophie. You're absolutely wrung out.'

'I couldn't do that.'

'Look, I've changed the sheets and everything today. I've even put the winter duvet on. It's like a tart's boudoir up there. Tempted yet?'

'Are you calling me, or you a tart?' she said, grinning, and thought for a moment. 'Winter duvet? I'm in. The prospect of a good night's sleep sounds wonderful. Thanks. You're such an amazing friend.'

'Try telling my ex-wife that,' he muttered. 'Go on. Bugger off. I'll see you in a couple of hours.'

* * *

When Foxy arrived later with Marcus he found Sophie trying to coax her father back in from the garden.

'This happen a lot?' Foxy asked as they stood in the kitchen and watched the pair.

'Most days at some point,' said Marcus. 'Come on, pizza's getting cold.'

Foxy opened the back patio doors and walked into the garden. Sophie was pulling her dad's arm trying to get him inside. He was firmly refusing and very red in the face.

'Hello, Jack,' said Foxy pleasantly. 'Can I borrow you for a minute I need some help in the kitchen?'

Jack, instantly distracted by Foxy and a new request, acquiesced immediately.

'Of course, my boy! I'll come now. Sophie, find the chickens and get them back in, please.'

Sophie glanced at Foxy, smiling as he winked at her and steered Jack in the kitchen.

'Ooh, pizza,' Jack said, sitting down at the table immediately and helping himself to a slice. 'Sophie, love,' he called. 'Will I need my wellingtons for dinner or am I OK in my slippers here?'

'Slippers are fine, Dad,' said Sophie, closing the patio doors.

'Great. Sit down then. Sophie what on earth were you doing outside in the garden?'

'Trying to get you inside, Dad.'

'Rubbish. Oh, hang on. I'm not sure I have enough money to pay for dinner and be able to use the loo later.'

'Dad, it's fine. You don't have to pay for anything.'

'Wonderful,' he beamed. 'Dig in everyone.'

Foxy sat at the kitchen table on his laptop. Sophie had just left for his place after putting Jack to bed, which Foxy hoped might mean she managed a good night's sleep. Foxy was catching up with some mates via e-mail and paying some bills. Marcus appeared in the kitchen for a glass of water.

'Hey,' he said, shuffling into the kitchen.

'Hey.'

'So,' Marcus said, sitting at the table with his water.

'So,' echoed Foxy, shutting the lid of his laptop, knowing this was the way kids communicated these days.

'About Dad.'

'OK. What about Dad?'

Marcus picked at the corner of the table. 'Do you think he'll be like… disfigured or something?'

'I genuinely don't know, mate,' Foxy said quietly. 'We don't know what sort of state he's in. I think he's pretty banged up, not just physically, but up here a bit too.' He tapped his forehead.

'What, like mental problems?'

'Bit like that. As a soldier it's hard to be captured and tortured. It does damage to you. Not just physically, but mentally too. You have to go to battle with them in your mind as well as your body.'

'Were you captured? Tortured?' Marcus was wide-eyed.

'I was.'

'You're OK though.'

'I wasn't. I'm better now, but it took a while. I was in a bad way physically and mentally. But I got help.'

'You're the strongest person I know.'

'No way, mate. Your mum is.'

Marcus pulled a face.

'See, it's not about strength here.' Foxy pointed to his bicep. 'It's about strength up here.' He tapped his forehead again. 'This is where you need to be strongest. Your dad has a long road to recovery in front of him and it's going to be hard on everyone. You, your mum particularly, since she's coping with your grandad too.'

Marcus thought for a second. 'I need to help out more.'

'She'd probably like that.'

'Are you going to stick around when Dad's back?'

'I'll try and help out if I can. Why do you ask?'

Marcus shrugged. 'Dunno. Got used to you being around. I quite like it.'

'Me too. You can come and find me anytime, mate.'

Marcus grinned. 'OK. Night, Foxy.'

'Night.'

Foxy watched him go and went back to his laptop. The phone in the kitchen rang shrilly in the quiet and Foxy moved to answer it before the sound disturbed Jack.

'Hello?'

'Is Mrs Jones there, please?'

'Who's calling?' Foxy frowned, recognising the voice from somewhere.

'This is Mark Jericho, the CNO for the MOD. Who is this, please?'

'Hi, Mark. This is Rob Fox, we met when you first visited Sophie. Look, Mark, I'll be straight with you. Soph's shattered, she's out for the count. Is this anything you can share with me. Is Sam OK?'

There was a hesitation from the other end of the line.

'OK. I was just calling to say Sam has left Afghanistan and is en route to the UK. He's responded well to the last round of treatment and the doctors felt it was better to move him when he was the best he'd been for a while.'

'What's his ETA?'

'Early hours of the morning, straight into the hospital. He'll be assessed first thing and a plan of action prepared. I'll ask the doctor to call Sophie tomorrow afternoon for an update.'

'OK. Her friend is the GP here, she'll want her in on the call or to at least speak to the doctor. Can you let the doctor know?'

'Fine. If you wouldn't mind letting Sophie know for me, please, Rob?'

'No problem. Thanks, Mark.'

'Oh, and Rob? Sophie's going to need a lot of support, as is Sam. It's an incredibly steep and rocky mountain for them both to climb.'

'Mountains I can do, Mark.'

'Good to hear. Night, Rob.'

'Night.'

Foxy ended the call and sat thinking. Sam was improving and on his way to the UK. He was torn about calling Sophie and telling her or waiting until the morning. He figured it was better to let her sleep; he was sure if she knew Sam was being moved she would fret all night. He switched off the lights in the kitchen and removed the keys from the outside doors placing them up high, as instructed, where Jack wouldn't find them. He checked on Jack and Marcus and settled himself down for the night on the sofa.

* * *

Kate had been on call all night. She'd had to go out to a clueless woman with a tiny baby in the early hours. Seeing the tiny baby boy, holding him and dealing with the clueless mother had broken Kate's heart wide open again. She hadn't been able to stop herself from crying when she had eventually returned to the car.

She had sobbed herself dry with grief for her baby son and she wondered whether her heart had actually been broken in two. She drove home to change and have some breakfast before setting out again, bleary-eyed, to some early appointments before surgery. She was shattered and emotional, not a good recipe for a long day ahead.

She pulled into the care home and grabbed her bag. She wondered about a worrying trend she was seeing; perfectly healthy older people were suddenly dying with no obvious diagnosis apart from food poisoning-like symptoms that came on suddenly. She made a mental note to ask her father if he had seen the results of the post-mortems performed on patients in similar situations who had died suddenly.

As an afterthought she grabbed a pack of sterile swabs for testing as she left the car. She saw two patients who were receiving palliative care before sitting with a cup of tea in the common room with a few of the other residents there. She wanted to get to know some of her new community.

One elderly lady with bright, beady eyes and a very proper grey bun sat herself next to Kate with her tea and produced a handful of biscuits from her pocket, laying them on the table.

'Hello,' she said, gesturing to the biscuits and saying in a matter-of-fact voice, 'if you don't grab a handful early on, Marvin over there takes a bite out of each one and then puts the ones he doesn't like back. Quite disgusting really. You must be Dr Lawrence's daughter. You have his look around the eyes.'

'That's a relief,' Kate said. 'If you'd said I looked like him around the mouth I would have had to go and check I hadn't grown a beard overnight.'

The old lady gave a rumble of laughter and held out a hand. 'Mollie,' she said.

'Kate.'

'Lawrence?'

'Cooper.'

'Married then?'

'Was.'

'Sad about it?'

'Not especially.'

'Then it wasn't meant to be.' Mollie handed her a biscuit. 'Trust me. I'm not a doctor, but I know these things.'

'How long have you been here for then, Mollie?'

'Too long, my dear. Too long. It's not too bad here. I couldn't be at home because I just keep falling over all the time. I miss it though.'

'What do you miss most about home?'

'Oh, you know, dear. Things like spending all day listening to the cricket or the tennis on the radio and having three Mars bars for tea and no one tutting about it or telling me off.'

'Mars bars for tea? You rebel, Mollie. Were you married?'

'I was, dear. To a man older than me. Gorgeous fellow but died far too soon for us to have a quality retirement together.'

'I'm sorry, Mollie.'

'That's life, my dear,' she said, picking another biscuit. 'The perils of falling for the older man.'

'Not tempted to try and meet anyone new?'

Mollie chortled. 'In here? Well, George Clooney did pop in last week for a visit, but I was busy washing my hair. Perhaps he'll come again soon.'

'I'll keep a look out for you, you never know.'

Mollie leant forward conspiratorially. 'Don't judge me but whenever there's a spate of deaths here, I always quite look forward to the new arrivals.' She rubbed her hands. 'Fresh meat! I keep suggesting speed dating, but the staff won't have it and most of the residents can't remember to move to the next person or what their name is half the time.'

'There's always Tinder.'

'I've done that.' She twinkled. 'Anyway, have you come back to help your dad out?'

'I have.'

'How long have you been here?'

'About a month now. Feels like forever.'

'Busy work does that for you. Now, I'm going to take my leave from you. I've just seen the bloody vicar and that idiot curate arrive and I simply won't be preached at, which is what will happen if I stay sat here.'

'Atheist?'

'Of the very highest form, dear. I figure if God wasn't around to stop things like the Holocaust, then he's certainly not rocking up for anyone or anything now.'

Kate smiled. 'You've shared these thoughts with the vicar then?'

Mollie chuckled deeply. 'Yes. I fear he's on a mission to convert me, dear. Him, the curate and the dreadful Mrs Pomeroy and her cakes and soup. But I'm not having it! I'm off. Let's have tea again soon. You were a bright light in an otherwise dull morning, dear.'

'Bye, Mollie. We'll definitely do another tea together soon,' Kate said firmly. 'How about I bring the biscuits next time?'

Mollie's eyes danced merrily. 'Excellent plan. I shall look forward to it.'

Amused, she watched Mollie shuffle off, deftly avoiding the vicar and the curate. She finished her tea, spoke briefly to the care home manager, and headed off for morning surgery.

Kate sat in the chair reserved for patients next to her father's desk.

'Dad, did you see the post-mortem results from the recent deaths in the care homes?'

'Which deaths?'

'The ones where the patient wasn't having palliative care.'

'Oh… yes, it's been a few hasn't it? I thought they were flu related, but I'm not too sure. If it was flu, then I would expect others to have caught it, but it's not that widespread. That does remind me, I should chase those up.'

'Can we ask for them, Dad? I don't understand why a few of them suddenly died and I'd like to know.'

'I'll ask Carol to chase it up.'

'Thanks, Dad. I met a lovely lady today in the Hollies.'

'Who was that?'

'Mollie. Grey bun. Very direct.'

'Ahh. Mollie. Lovely lady. Bright as a button. Just a little unsteady on her feet. Fit as a fiddle though.'

'We had a cup of tea together.'

'And a pocket full of biscuits knowing Mollie.'

Kate grinned as she stood. 'That's the one. OK. So, you'll chase Carol?'

'Yes. I'll do it now.'

There was a knock, and the receptionist stuck her head around the door. 'Good, you're both in here. I have a policeman in reception who wants a word.'

'About what?' Kate said with surprise.

'Don't know, he didn't say.'

Kate looked at her dad. 'OK, we'll chat to him together.'

The receptionist turned. 'I'll send him down.'

She disappeared and Kate grabbed another chair from the corner of the room. The door was knocked lightly and pushed open to reveal a face Kate recognised.

'Hello!' she said. 'It's you!'

'Ah,' Steve said, smiling. 'So you are genuinely a flying doctor.'

Kate laughed. 'Dad, I fell over in the high street the other day into this man's coffee, it went all over him. He was a real gentleman. Picked me up and dusted me off.'

'Guilty as charged,' Steve said, extending his hand to Kate's father. 'How are you, Dr Lawrence? I think we've only met once or twice before, but I'm here officially. Inspector Steve Miller.'

'Good to see you.' Kate's father shook his hand.

Steve turned to Kate. 'Intensive police training and outstanding deductive powers lead me to deduce that you are Dr Kate Cooper.'

'Guilty as charged,' Kate said, shaking his outstretched hand, appraising him quietly.

'What can we do for you, Inspector?' asked Graham.

'I need a bit of an off-the-record chat, please.'

'Oh?' Kate was intrigued.

'I've been asked to look into some unexplained deaths in some of the local care homes. I've looked at the logs and see you've both been in and out of them and wondered if you had any thoughts?'

Kate looked at him in surprise. 'Dad and I were just talking about that.'

'What? Deaths in the local care homes?'

Kate nodded. 'Yeah. I've asked Dad to source the post-mortem reports on the deaths of those that weren't being treated with palliative care, those that were pretty healthy.'

'So you have your suspicions?'

'I don't know if suspicion is the word. I have *concerns*, nothing concrete or finger pointy though,' Kate ventured.

'Finger pointy?' Steve seemed amused.

'As in no firm conclusions about anything just yet,' Kate said, smiling.

'OK. Could we have a chat when you've seen those reports, please? You can interpret them to a dumb copper.'

'Of course. But you know sometimes, older people do just die, without any particular warnings. Brain bleeds, heart attacks, etc., so it's not totally implausible that these elderly people have died in normal ways. We're in flu season too and that has a much higher mortality rate. There are some possible explanations as to why.'

Steve nodded thoughtfully. 'Yes. But despite all that, you are concerned enough to question what they died of.'

Kate gave a half smile. 'Perhaps I'm just thorough.'

Steve chuckled. 'A highly admirable quality if I may say so. Now, I'm aware you have morning surgery. I was told in no uncertain terms by the receptionist not to be too long and my own personal mantra is to never cross a doctor's receptionist.'

'Excellent mantra to have.' Kate liked this man's sense of humour and warmed to him. 'Look, if I can help with anything just call me. Take my mobile number and call me on this rather than go through the system.' She scribbled the number down and handed it over.

'Thank you. I appreciate that,' he said, taking it. 'Right. I won't keep you. Pleasure to meet you both. I'll be in touch to talk about those PMs. Bye then.'

'Nice to see you,' chipped in Graham as Steve left. 'He's a nice chap,' Graham remarked as Kate put the chair back.

'Umm. He was very sweet when I fell on him the other day. Right, I need to crack on, I've got Mrs Bevan first. I swear the woman is here every single week with something or other.'

'She's lonely. This is half the issue with some of these elderly people. Signpost her to the church group that meets a few times a week. Tell her there are people there who are lonely and would benefit from someone as lovely as her to chat to. Get her to call Mrs Pomeroy, although she's a battleaxe, she'll point her in the right direction.'

'We are talking about the same Mrs Bevan, aren't we? Would we say lovely?'

Graham chortled. 'Play the long game, Kate dear. Tell her she's wonderful and it would help others. It makes her feel wonderful and incredibly self-important. Chances are she'll join the church group and hey presto… your visits will reduce.' He winked. 'Trust me, I'm a doctor.'

I have been chosen. I have his blessing. I experienced the revelation. He's left it for me to decide. To select. To cull. He's put me in charge of their future. I look at all of them… Needy. Wanting. Expecting. Hands grabbing. Always taking. So helpless. So annoying. So feeble. They are nothing but a drain on society and people's time. This stops now. Now he has told me. I bask in his glory. I will be the one to decide. I will be his servant and I will not fail you or forsake him.

CHAPTER 6

Military Intelligence Officer Captain Sam Jones was on the cusp of consciousness. His brain was processing unfamiliar noises, smells and memories. He was lying on a long-forgotten softness, not on a hard-packed mud floor. His confused brain told him this wasn't where he had been. This wasn't the hot, fetid room, with the hard ground; with the rodents that ate his fingers and the flies that buzzed constantly. This was different.

He struggled to come to the surface of consciousness. Tried to drag himself upwards in his mind to the surface. To the light, to the clean air. He was somewhere new. He opened his eyes into tiny slits, blinking at the brightness, and closed them again as the bright light sent a sharp pain into his head, which was already throbbing.

He was thirsty. So thirsty his tongue felt three times the size and his throat was so raw any liquid would be painful to drink, no matter how welcome. He tried to move his arms, but they were heavy; too heavy to move. He didn't want to open his eyes again. The pain was too much. The light too bright. He tried to speak and call out, but no voice came from his dry throat. He tried to move again, and waves of intense pain shot through him. His brain promptly decided that this was more than enough activity and he slipped into unconsciousness again.

Sam had been dreaming. Mixed wild dreams. He had seen a row of graves in a hot, dry and dusty place, with nothing for miles. He had seen his dog tags hanging from one of the crosses and the silver seahorse that Sophie had given him as a wedding gift, which he always wore with his tags. He had been with a child. He didn't know whose child it was, but he took it everywhere, the small hand in his, wherever he went.

He saw words suspended in the air. Different languages. Phrases in cursive script floating freely. They made no sense. He saw a busy market bazaar somewhere, completely foreign to him. Coloured fabric in oranges and yellows with flashes of bright pink. Then he saw her. Saw her blonde hair.

She was searching, looking for something. She was shouting and calling. In her hand she had his dog tags and the seahorse. Where did they come from? He couldn't reach her, and the floating words were getting bigger, obscuring his view. He tried to push them out of the way, but more kept appearing. Then he realised he'd lost the child. He looked down and his hands were covered with rats and flies and dripping blood. He screamed, trying to get them off. Shaking his hands and brushing them off.

'Sam. SAM. Leave your hands alone. They're fine,' said a soft, soothing voice.

Sam struggled to wake. He opened his eyes slowly and saw soft, dimmed light. A figure stood by his bed.

'You're safe now,' the voice said firmly. 'You're safe and being cared for in the UK. We've got you, Sam. You're getting better. You're home now.'

Sam absorbed the sparse information. With superhuman effort he raised his head off the pillow and peered down at himself. His hands were in enormous bandages and there was something like a tent over his legs. Did he still have legs? He couldn't feel them. Couldn't see them.

He experienced a sensation he had all but forgotten. Relief. It washed over him, consuming him, engulfing him like a powerful wave. He was free? Free from the brutality, the absolute and unending horror, the extreme pain. He felt a wave of emotion build at the back of his throat and surge forward. He couldn't stop himself. Tears ran down his face and huge gut-wrenching sobs came uninhibited. Two years of pent-up grief, anger, loss and pain were released, unchecked. The sobs turned into roars of anger and frustration until Sam slipped back into unconsciousness again.

* * *

Sophie ended the call and sat at the kitchen table, her head in her hands. Sam's doctor had called again and told her that Sam had regained consciousness. He had used words like, 'extreme exhaustion, highly emotional state, significant forthcoming surgery.' The words buzzed around her head. The doctor had suggested that Sophie come and see Sam. He had stressed that she should come alone this time. The doctor had tried to be subtle. When Sophie had instructed him not to pull any punches, he said in typical clipped British Army tones to, 'Expect the worst and hope for the best. He's in extremely bad shape.'

Sophie glanced at the kitchen clock and called out loudly. 'Carol? Are you OK with Dad for a couple of hours? I need to pop out.'

'OK! See you later. Could you grab a pint of milk, please?'

'No worries!' Sophie called, grabbing her keys.

Sophie drove through town and headed for the climbing centre. Her friendship with Foxy meant he was her 'go-to guy' with respect to all things British Army. As ex-special forces, he had good insight, which she found invaluable, plus she knew now she could talk to him about anything. They had shared their fears and talked about their demons with each other, and this had cemented the close friendship they had.

She parked next to his Defender and hopped out. He was on the beach, throwing the ball for Solo. She placed her fingers in her mouth and let out a piercing whistle. Foxy turned and Solo forgot the ball, hurtling towards Sophie.

As she bent to make a fuss of the battle-scarred Alsatian, Foxy jogged up, his cheeks rosy from the chilly wind.

'You OK?' he asked, frowning.

Sophie bit her lip, the tears threatened. Foxy missed nothing.

'Come on,' he said, propelling her up the outside stairs to his flat. 'Coffee.'

He opened the door and flicked the kettle on, pointing her to one of the big comfy chairs by the picture window. She sat and, as always, was enchanted by the view over the bay and the beach. She could sit there all day and watch the world go by.

'Right. Spill,' he said, handing her a large mug and settling into the chair opposite. 'Is it Sam?'

She nodded, not trusting herself to speak.

'Have they said you can go and see him?' he asked quietly.

'Yes,' she whispered, the tears spilling over.

'Soph, come on. You knew it was coming. Let me guess, you're frightened of what you might see and how he might be, aren't you?'

She sniffed and Foxy took one of her hands.

'I bet you're a right mess inside, aren't you?' he said softly. 'Now the waiting is over, and the reality is here. You sort of want it, but you don't because the reality is way scarier than the idea of it.'

Sophie sobbed out loud. 'How do you always know what I'm thinking?' she wailed. 'Doesn't that make me a bad person to think that way?' She wiped her eyes. 'There's a part of me just wants to go back to hoping, rather than this. Not knowing.'

'Soph, you're tired, running on empty. This is just your brain not wanting to cope with another challenge. Not wanting to process it. It just wants to go back to something comfortable that it can handle. Tell me what they've said.'

Sophie relayed the news, adding, 'Kate is talking to the doctor later and she's calling in on her way home to tell me all about it.'

'OK. So we'll hear it from all angles,' Foxy said. 'Do you mind if I come and sit in on your chat with Kate?'

'I'd like you to. Kate said she'll be in around seven.'

'OK. I'll close up here and then come over,' he said. 'Soph, I know you're under no illusions, but this is the start of an epic recovery for him. Look, does he have any family who could help? Be a support?'

Sophie shook her head. 'He was an only child and his parents died about five years ago. Car accident in France.'

Foxy frowned. 'It's going to be really fucking hard and I'm not pulling any punches here. Do you want me to come with you to see him? I won't come in, but I'll drive you and be there for you.'

Sophie looked at him gratefully. 'Thanks, Rob. I don't know when I'll go. I need to look at my work diary first and see what I can shunt about. Everything feels up in the air suddenly,' she said, wiping her eyes and blowing her nose.

* * *

Foxy sat in the warm kitchen at Sophie's nursing a glass of red wine. Kate had just appeared, but had ducked upstairs to see Jack before coming to talk to Sophie. Sophie was bustling about making a pasta bake.

'Calm down. You're a nervous wreck,' observed Foxy with amusement.

'I can't help it,' Sophie said. 'I just want to know.'

'Okey dokey,' said Kate, coming into the kitchen and dumping her bag. 'Hello again. It's Rob, isn't it?'

Foxy nodded. 'Most people call me Foxy though. She's the only one who calls me Rob,' he said, gesturing towards Sophie.

Kate tilted her head. 'You actually look much more like a Foxy than a Rob I have to say. Any of that going?' She gestured to the wine.

'Here you go,' said Sophie, passing her a glass.

Kate took a huge slug and smacked her lips. 'Christ, I needed that. What a fucking day. Right. Let's crack on.'

Foxy smiled at Kate's use of one of his favourite phrases. He was beginning to quite like her no-nonsense approach.

'Come on then. What did Sam's quack say?' Sophie pestered.

'Sophie, not everyone is a quack,' scolded Kate. 'Anyway. Very helpful man. Not the most forthcoming on the detail. It was a bit like pulling teeth. It's only when I told him I would be Sam's GP when he's eventually home, did he thaw out a little.'

'And?'

'OK. In the here and now. He's in and out of consciousness, but that's improving. Classic state for recovering from what he's been through. Best thing he can do is sleep, to be honest. He woke fully yesterday and then had quite an emotional episode. Bit of a meltdown, but the docs think it was because he had finally realised he was home. So, they think they saw some sort of emotional release at being rescued, if you like. He is aware that he's not in captivity anymore and his mind is likely busy processing that.' She took another slug of wine. 'Right. Physically. His hands are very damaged. There's a lot of rodent damage.'

'What?' Sophie's hand flew to cover her mouth in horror.

'I said rodent damage on his hands and feet and some residual frostbite.'

'Frostbite?'

'It gets incredibly cold at night in the desert,' Foxy murmured.

Kate continued. 'He has a plethora of infected wounds and some very bad skin infections. Lice, scabies – you name it, he has it. He's a walking antibiotic at the moment. They're throwing everything at it, trying to get on top of it.'

'God,' Sophie whispered.

'There's something else, Soph. You need to brace yourself. It gets much worse.'

'Worse?' echoed Sophie.

'His legs were so badly broken… they were…' She searched for the right word.

'Smashed,' Foxy finished quietly.

'You know then,' she said after a pause.

'Smashed?' Sophie asked faintly.

'They smash the legs of prisoners in captivity, basically to stop them trying to run away,' said Foxy softly.

'Absolutely and utterly fucking barbaric. These people are beyond redemption. Anyway, Sophie. Focus, darling.' Kate nudged Sophie. 'They've tried to operate on them to save them, but in simple terms, they are too smashed to repair or rebuild, plus there is necrosis of the surrounding tissue. They've tried to restore blood flow and fight the infection, but they do think the reality is they may have to amputate in the next day or so.' She stopped and took Sophie's hand. 'I'm so sorry, Sophie.'

Tears were rolling down Sophie's face. 'My God,' she said. 'I didn't think…'

'Soph, loads of ex-military operate full and active lives without legs. Sam could too, with time and the right support,' Foxy said quietly.

'That's it though. Ex-military… His army career is over if that happens.'

'Not necessarily,' said Foxy. 'He's a Captain in the Intelligence Corp. They won't want to lose him or his insight.'

'He won't want to stay if he can't be active.'

'You don't know that, Soph. Not now. Not after what he's been through. You can't make that judgement.'

Kate waved her hands, halting the conversation. 'Too early to say any of this, guys. The other thing is that he will have some significant issues with PTSD and that sometimes takes longer than flesh and bones to heal.'

'Amen to that,' said Foxy under his breath.

'You have experience of PTSD?' Kate asked.

'Not my finest hour, but I got through it,' Foxy said grimly.

'I've treated a few patients with it but I do want to learn more about it from people in the forces. Would you have a chat with me when you have time, only if you'd feel comfortable. It might just help me to help Sam get better.'

Foxy thought for a moment. The idea of revisiting his darkest hours was not in the slightest bit appealing. But then he saw Kate and Sophie's expectant faces.

'Anything to help,' he said quietly.

'I appreciate that, Rob,' Sophie said, touching his hand. 'I know it'll be tough.'

'Doctor has suggested that you might want to come in a few days, Sophie. The decision on his leg will be made and done by then and it might be perfect timing,' Kate said gently.

'OK,' sighed Sophie. 'I'll talk to Carol about Dad maybe going into respite for a few days, and perhaps Doug will have Marcus for a couple of nights.'

'Good plan. If none of that works out, I'll come and crash here,' Kate said.

'You'll do anything to get away from your mother. But thanks. I might take you up on that.'

'I assume you'll drive Sophie down there?' Kate turned to Foxy.

'I will. I'll amuse myself and catch up with a few people. I can make myself scarce.'

Kate regarded them both. 'That's that sorted then. It's just a waiting game now. I have to say this whole thing is an absolute bastard. It's going to be really tough for everyone involved. So, I think we should drink to Sam's good health and to him coming through this.' She raised her glass.

* * *

Jesse sat waiting in the uncomfortable chair and had the strongest sense of déjà vu. She was experiencing that a lot lately. Part of the healing, they'd told her. She knew that she'd been here before. In therapy. She remembered flashes of conversations in a certain room, a vase of flowers, and then saw snippets of scenes from her kitchen. She knew the woman who had been her therapist had then tried to kill her.

Jesse thought harder and shuddered. She was too afraid to think about it further; to try and remember. Shivering at the half memory, she concluded that therapy in general was not a happy place for her. Since waking, she had recovered well physically, but her memory was still blocked.

'Jesse?' Dr Jonathan Lewis came in the door quietly and sat down in the chair opposite her. He was a tall trim man in his early forties with dark hair and a beard, and very warm brown eyes.

'Hello, Dr Lewis.'

'I saw you had a memory a moment ago. It made you shudder. A physical reaction to something. Can you tell me about it?'

Jesse shook her head as if trying to clear it. 'I just remember snippets from the last time I was in therapy.'

'So you remember?'

Jesse closed her eyes. 'Pieces. Flashes. Like scenes from a film. I remember her. Emma. In my house. I remember being in her office. Telling her things.'

'Anything else?'

'Her in my house… I remember being scared. Terrified.'

'OK. Anything else?'

'Is there something else?' Jesse frowned.

'There is.'

'What is it?'

'I was hoping you'd tell me.'

Jesse exhaled deeply. 'I think there's something else… I can feel it.'

'Relax and think for a moment.'

Jesse closed her eyes and relaxed, trying some of the techniques they had been working on since she had woken. She breathed deeply and let her mind wander.

'Fire. There was a fire.' Her eyes flew open.

'There was... What else?'

Jesse tried again but couldn't get anything else.

'I can't,' she said. 'You know though.'

'I do.'

'So you tell me.'

'That's not how it works.'

'Telling me will help me remember,' she insisted.

'It's not always the case, Jesse. I am hoping your memory will kick in and flesh out the detail.' He paused. 'You had gone to Doug's house for dinner.'

'Were we?' She gestured vaguely.

'Intimate? Together?' he asked. 'You were in the beginnings of a relationship. You both felt strongly, but you hadn't been intimate yet. According to Doug there has been a series of constant interruptions and he was set on "wooing" you. Those are the words he used. Wooing. He said he wanted to make it special.'

Jesse had a sudden flash of him stood in her kitchen, holding pastries.

'Pecan slice,' she murmured. 'He told me he had things to say. He told me he loved me.' She blushed at the memory. 'I can't believe I remembered that.'

'This is good, Jesse,' said Jonathan warmly. 'Excellent.'

'Carry on. So, I went to Doug's for dinner.'

'You had dinner and then started to get intimate. You moved upstairs, and very simply, there was a fire. Doug's neighbour called the fire brigade and they got you and Doug out of the bedroom window.'

'What happened then?'

'The person who started the fire, died in it.'

'And that was Emma? My ex-partner's sister.'

'Yes. Then by all accounts, Doug's wife arrived and told him of his mother's illness.'

'And then he went to Scotland,' Jesse echoed. 'She died.'

'You remember.'

'I remember feeling that he had been gone for so long.'

'OK. This is very healthy. You're doing well today. I want to move things along a little.'

'OK.'

'I want to explore how you feel about Doug. What you remember. The same with Brock. You've spent some time with them both now. Tell me, Jesse, how do you feel?'

'Brock. I think I remember his *presence*, more than him. Does that make sense?'

'From what I hear he went almost everywhere with you,' Jonathan replied.

'I feel a sense of… what is it?' She searched for the word. 'When I walk about, and I look down and expect to see something there and there's nothing… then I get a sense of loss. Almost like grief, I think.'

Jonathan nodded. Jesse carried on.

'I don't remember physical things with Brock, like walking anywhere or doing anything specific, I just remember a presence. Like when I sleep at night, it's like there is something missing, and I suspect it's Brock.'

'So you know, he's important to you,' Jonathan said.

'Yes.'

Jonathan regarded Jesse for a moment and said quietly, 'I've spoken at length with Doug.'

Jesse stared at Jonathan for a moment, not sure whether to share. 'There's a…' She stopped and waved the words away. 'Nothing… me being silly…'

74

'Come on,' Jonathan urged. 'Nothing is silly here. Everything is relevant.'

'But I don't know if it's a dream, or a memory.'

Jonathan leant forwards. 'Doesn't matter.'

'I don't know if it's real, but I dream, or remember, I'm falling. Completely weightless.'

'And?'

'And it's like I know I'm going to die. I'm absolutely certain of it. Completely.'

'What else?'

'As I'm falling, knowing I'm going to die, I see Doug's face. I see his incredible eyes, I see him smile and I hear him whisper my name and then I feel Brock's head under my hand and I know it's OK. Even though I am going to die, it's OK.'

Jonathan blinked and glanced away, clearing his throat.

'What?' Jesse asked.

'Nothing. That's incredibly moving,' he said. 'But then I cry at the drop of a hat. I literally well up at all sorts of things. I even found myself crying at an old re-run of ER the other day.'

Jesse gave a half laugh. 'Well, if it's the one where they found the letter from Mark Green on the noticeboard after he died. I can sympathise. That slayed me. I was a wreck. So – memory or dream?'

'I would suggest it's similar to a sensory memory. But it tells me a lot about your feelings for Doug.'

Jesse's eyes filled with tears. 'But I don't remember them!' she blurted out. 'Why can't I remember them? It's awkward when we're together. I don't know how to be. And he looks at me. There's something I remember, something I feel, but it's like it's out of reach. I just can't get to it,' she said desperately. 'I so want to reach it.'

Jonathan sat back in his seat, folding his arms. 'Right. Radical treatment time. You, young lady, are going on a field trip for the day. You will go to the lifeboat station and see your crew. Go to your home, go to Doug's home and take Brock for a walk. Then you will return here. And the next day. We'll do some hypnosis to try and bring those memories to the forefront.'

'Hypnosis?'

'Hypnosis. Your words about your feelings for Doug – "I so want to reach it" – we can reach it. I'll be here. You'll be safe.'

'Can I think about it?'

'Absolutely not. I'm calling Doug in a minute. Your field trip is tomorrow. He'll pick you up at 8.30 a.m. and return you after dinner. No arguments, Jesse. We need a little radical action. Now. Off you go. You've got physio and no one wants to be late for Fatima. Trust me.'

CHAPTER 7

Doug pulled into the hospital grounds and parked around by A&E. He told Brock firmly that he would be back in a minute with a surprise and then locked the car. He jogged lightly across the car park to the entrance of the hospital, waving at paramedics Phil and Liz as they pulled out in their ambulance.

Phil put down the window and yelled. 'How's she doing, Doug?'

'Aye. Not too bad. I'm taking her out for the day to the station. Bit of sea air.'

Phil gave a thumbs up. 'Give her our love.'

'Will do.' Doug waved as they disappeared.

He walked across reception and headed up towards Jesse's room. At her door he stopped, suddenly nervous about the day ahead with a woman he knew and loved, but who didn't seem to know him.

He knocked lightly and pushed the door open.

'Good morning,' he said seeing Jesse sat in her chair by the window with her eyes shut. He walked in and stood looking down at her. He watched her sleep for a while dropped down to his haunches, so he wasn't looming over her.

'Hey, sleepyhead,' he said lightly, touching her arm.

Jesse shifted slightly in her sleep. Doug touched her arm again.

'Jesse.'

Jesse awoke slowly, stretching luxuriously like a cat. She opened her eyes and, seeing Doug next to her, blushed.

'Sorry,' she mumbled.

'It's OK. It's not the first time I've watched you snore.'

'I don't snore.'

'Do so,' he murmured. 'You look good. How do you feel?'

'After too long being in here, I feel ready to go out for the day.'

'And yet, here you are napping at eight in the morning.'

She laughed. 'I had early morning physio with Fatima, the woman's a bloody machine.'

The door opened and a nurse walked in pushing a wheelchair.

'No way,' Jesse said, pointing at it.

'Yes way,' said the nurse. 'Dr Carucci said, and this is a direct quote. "No chair. No trip out." He said if you were walking you wouldn't even make it to the front entrance.'

Jesse stood slowly, grabbed her bag and plonked herself in the chair.

'Tell Dr Carucci he's a bloody killjoy,' she said angrily.

'You're not the first to mention it,' the nurse said, grinning and holding the door open for Doug to push Jesse through. 'He's used to it.'

Doug pushed her along the corridor and out into the chilly morning sunshine. He noticed Brock through the truck windscreen running around in excited circles as soon as he saw Jesse.

'Brace yourself. He's beside himself.'

Doug stopped the wheelchair by the passenger door and Jesse stood slowly. He opened the door and Brock flung himself out of the car and circled Jesse, brushing against her legs, giving yips of happiness. She patted his head and climbed into the passenger seat and Brock immediately jumped up and sat on her lap, licking her face and making noises in his throat.

Doug put the wheelchair in the back bed of the truck and climbed in the driver's seat.

'Brock, on the floor,' he ordered. Brock obediently sat on the floor with his head on Jesse's leg, looking up adoringly at her.

'He's missed you,' Doug remarked quietly as he started the truck and pulled away. 'We all have.'

Jesse closed her eyes and enjoyed the sensation of Brock's head on her knee. He was the presence she was missing. She felt content with his warmth against her leg and his head under her hand.

'I had a good memory yesterday,' she said, stroking Brock's head gently.

'Tell me more,' said Doug, giving her a sideways glance. He was encouraged by her peaceful face as she stroked the dog.

'I feel a bit awkward saying it.'

'Just say it.'

'I was in a session with Jonathan, and I asked him if you and me had… you know, been intimate.'

'Right.'

'You've spoken to him a lot, haven't you?'

'I thought it would help you.'

'I think it has.'

'So what was the memory?'

'My kitchen. Pecan slice and you telling me how you felt about me.'

'Ahh, when I came back from Scotland. That was a good day from what I remember.'

'You told me you were "all in".'

Doug took his hand off the wheel and reached over to hold Jesse's hand.

'I've not changed. I still feel that way,' he said. 'No pressure though. Any other memories of that day?'

'You talked about wooing me. We were kissing and you stopped it. Because you wanted to woo me.'

'That's not changed either.' Doug stopped at some traffic lights. 'I want things to be special when we get together. I want you to feel special. But I'm not making a move until you do – Jonathan's orders.'

'OK,' Jesse said, looking down at her hands. 'It's just a bit confusing. It's like I know we were together, but I just don't really remember it. I remember you now, but not necessarily *you*, now we're together. Do you understand?'

'Must be really difficult.'

'We're doing hypnosis tomorrow. Trying to work out what's stopping the memories.'

'You feel OK about that?'

Jesse shrugged. 'I feel at a point where I know I have to do something. Unlock it somehow. I trust Jonathan. He thinks it's the only way.'

'Let me know if I can help... or be there... or not be there... up to you.'

They rode in silence for a while, entering the outskirts of the town. Jesse gestured to the signage that had gone up along one of the fences.

'Oh it's the carnival of the sea in a month or so, isn't it?'

Doug glanced at her. 'You remember that?'

'Yeah. It's weird. I can remember lots of things, but the thing that I can't seem to reach is the few weeks or so before the accident.' She gazed out of the window. 'So I remember the festival and stuff like that, I remember Emma in my kitchen and stuff, and then after that the memories are really spotty.'

'Well, don't even think you'll be on duty for that, but shall we see if we can get you out of hospital by then?'

Jesse nodded happily. 'That would be good.'

'OK. Where to first? Your house? My house? The station?'

Jesse thought for a moment. 'My house.'

Doug nodded. 'Your wish, my lady…'

Jesse stood in her kitchen and ran a finger down a photo of herself and another woman.

'This is Angela,' she murmured to herself. 'I remember that.'

She moved stiffly across the kitchen and sat at the table, looking out of the window down the garden, suddenly exhausted by the day so far. Doug wandered over, flicked the kettle on and leant against the worktop with his arms folded.

Jesse turned around and watched him. 'I remember you standing there. Saying how you felt.'

'What else do you remember?'

Jesse looked around the kitchen. 'I remember Emma in here. Cooking for me, long before that. I thought it was you.' She inhaled sharply. 'I remember so wanting it to be you.' She touched her hand to the scar that Emma had left on her face. 'I remember she died. In the fire.'

'She did.'

'I remember you and me in here. I remember you kissing me.' Her cheeks flushed at the memory of it.

'I remember it too.'

'This must be difficult for you.'

Doug made them a coffee and came and sat down next to Jesse at the table. 'Sorry, no milk. Do you remember the boat? Gavin's boat?'

Jesse thought for a moment. 'I do remember, I think... You bought Gav's boat and did it up.'

'Uh-huh.'

'Yes! I remember it! You had strung lights outside along the boon and oh it was so pretty! We had dinner on the boat... then... I can't remember. What happened?'

'Claire collapsed and I had to go, she was at home with the kids, they were frantic.'

'She was having the cancer treatment, wasn't she?'

'She's been in a bad way, but she's out of the woods now. Felix is driving himself crazy trying to win her back.'

'You two have become friends,' Jesse observed. 'Who'd have thought it?'

'He's alright,' Doug conceded. 'He saved you, so basically if you give me grief I can say it's all his fault.'

Doug leant forward and took her hand. 'Jesse, I want to try and understand what you remember about us. Anything? A snapshot in time?'

Jesse met Doug's wolf-like light-blue eyes. Her stomach lurched and she felt a rush of something, but she couldn't place what it was. She felt slightly breathless. She reached out and touched his face gently.

'It's all so muddled,' she said softly. 'I feel things I don't understand when I'm with you. I have these feelings and I don't know what they are. I had a memory... a... a sensation sort of thing. I told Jonathan and he got quite emotional – funny really.'

'What was it?'

She took a breath. 'I'm on this high cliff and then I'm falling. Completely weightless, like I'm flying, but falling, slowly, like slow motion. And it's like I know I'm going to die. As I'm falling, I know with total and utter certainty that I'm going to die. I don't know how I know it; I just do. Then I see your face, Doug. I see your beautiful eyes, your smile and I hear you whisper my name with your lovely voice, and then I feel Brock's head under my hand, and I know it's going to be OK if I die.'

Doug stared at her. 'Jesus,' he said hoarsely.

'I know. I don't remember anything else. What does that mean?' she said, feeling embarrassed.

'I know what I want it to mean,' said Doug. 'What else do you remember?'

'I remember staying at a house, but there were other people there and I don't know who they were. It was like we were waiting for something. We were on edge, but I can't remember why or what we were waiting for.'

'OK. We can't force it... but what you said... just now? Gives me hope. Right. Station next?'

Jesse stood slowly. 'Bring it on,' she said, smiling.

'Oh my goodness!' Jesse exclaimed as Doug wheeled her into the station.

Most of the crew were there and they had created a banner that read, 'Get well soon, Jesse' and had strung it across the back of the boat.

'You guys,' she said, smiling and not wanting to admit to Doug that she didn't remember all of them. An older man in a wheelchair bumped against her chair and she looked into familiar blue eyes which were filled with tears.

'Billy,' she said softly, touching his weathered face. 'So good to see you. I've missed you.'

Tears ran down Billy's face and he clutched her hand. 'Jesse,' he said. 'My special girl. I've been so worried. You mean the world to me.'

'Billy.' Jesse held his hand.

Another man with very short white hair and a grumpy expression, touched her arm.

'Jesse, he's been a nightmare. Crying everywhere. Only happy when he's been looking after the dog.' His expression softened and he took her hand. 'Missed you,' he said gruffly. 'Hurry up and get better.'

'Who are you and what have you done with Bob?' Jesse laughed. 'I've missed you too, Bob. Everyone's so cheerful in hospital. I've craved your grumpy company.' She looked around. 'So who did the banner?'

'Er, that would be us,' said Mike and Tom, two of the younger crew. 'We're going to come in and see you soon, plenty of fit nurses from what I hear.'

Jesse spent a few hours at the station, time in her precious workshop, talking to Billy. It occurred to her that she hadn't forgotten anything about her work or the boats. It was more like she was facing a black blank wall when it came to what happened to her before she thought she was going to die.

Doug appeared in the workshop and put his hands on her shoulders.

'Come on. Back to mine for a bit, then back to hospital.'

'Yes, boss.'

Jesse said a tearful goodbye to the crew and then Doug drove her to his place. The motion of the truck sent her off to sleep almost immediately, she was exhausted.

When they arrived back at Doug's, he lifted her gently into the house and laid her on the sofa, covering her with a blanket.

Claire, who was still recovering and staying with Doug, appeared in the lounge and watched with a critical eye.

'Felix says she's improving every day,' she said quietly.

'Seems so.' He tutted at Brock who had jumped up on the sofa to lie next to Jesse. 'It was a good idea of yours to get Brock in. Do you reckon that's what brought her round?'

'I don't know. I'd like to think so.' She tilted her head to watch Jesse sleep. 'She's doing well. Her face is better, her jaw has healed. That cast will come off soon. Felix said the internal injuries were repaired. This girl wants to live, I think.'

Jesse stirred in her sleep and Brock snuggled closer. Jesse moved so that the heavy cast on her arm now lay across Brock's body.

Doug watched her sleep for a moment. 'I can't believe she had to fight that madman off twice. She must have experienced the sort of terror that we can't even imagine.'

'I suspect that's the key thing behind the memory loss,' Claire said quietly. 'Did they ever find his body?'

'Not that I know of. We searched for days, but nothing. I'll check with Steve now I remember.'

'Do we actually know he's dead, Doug? Could he come back?' Claire whispered.

'The fall must have been near fatal. It was so high. Plus, Jesse fell on him, so there was the impact from that. I can't imagine any normal person surviving that.'

'He's not a normal person though, is he? He's a psychopath. It constantly surprises me what the human body can recover from.'

'I know. Steve released a bogus press report that said a woman was killed in a fall from a cliff on Kirby Island, so we have to hope that if he did make it, he'll see that and assume it was Jesse.'

Claire glanced at Doug. 'You believe that?'

'Until a body shows up, I'm not convinced of anything, Claire.'

'Very wise,' she said briskly. 'Anyway, I'll leave you be. I'm going for my walk.'

Claire left and Doug sat on the edge of the sofa pondering the conversation. He pulled his phone from his pocket and texted Steve to ask whether any bodies in the shape of Chris had shown up.

Doug was in the kitchen heating up some soup, when he heard Jesse call out.

'Doug?'

'Here,' he said, walking back into the lounge.

Jesse was sat up, her arms around Brock.

'Sorry. I didn't know where I was. This is the place we were staying, waiting for something.'

'This is my place.'

Jesse was silent for a while. 'I can't remember it here. Why were we here?'

'Come and have some soup and I'll tell you.' Doug held out his hand.

He placed the soup in front of Jesse along with a basket of bread.

'Sure you want to know?' he said quietly.

'Yup.'

The soup sat untouched.

'OK. Chris had escaped from prison. I think the easiest way to describe it is, he was hunting you.'

Jesse closed her eyes. 'Jesus. And you thought I'd be safe here?'

'Absolutely. Steve agreed. We had coppers here too and at the station.'

'So how did he get me?' Jesse whispered, her eyes filling with tears.

'He tricked us. Said the inshore boat was being broken into, you and one of the policemen went around there and that's where he got you and knocked the copper out. Another old guy too, stole his RIB.'

Jesse swallowed hard. 'Where were you?' she whispered.

'I was at the hospital. Claire was in a really bad way. Bob called me. Then I came back, and I had to go on a shout while the police went to the island to find you.'

'What was the shout?' Jesse asked quietly.

Doug dropped his head into his hands. 'Never ever in all my years of doing this have I not wanted to go on a shout – I felt so conflicted.' He raised his head and looked at her. 'I had to go, but I wanted to go to you. To find you.'

'It's OK. What was it?'

'Two young girls on an inflatable unicorn, caught in a rip tide blown into the channel.'

'Did you get to them?'

'We got to them and there was only one on the float. I had to dive down for the other. We got them both, but one died in ICU about a week later, they just couldn't bring her around.'

'God. You must have been in pieces.'

Doug gave a wry smile. 'Slight understatement, I think.' He leant forward. 'It was so hard to have to go and rescue the girls and not come for you. I felt like I'd failed you even on the most basic level. I promised to keep you safe, Jesse, and I couldn't.'

Jesse watched him across the table. She felt the odd sensation again and couldn't place it.

'Don't think that.' Her eyes filled with tears. 'Look, I need to remember, Doug. It's so frustrating, it's like this black wall blocking everything. I want to know what happened.'

'I'm worried for you. You're blocking it out for a reason. I worry about you remembering. How you'll feel. What you'll remember.'

'I have to trust Jonathan. We're going to try tomorrow. I've got to look at it like this, in a way.' She gestured to the cast on her arm. 'Part of my mind is broken, so I need to do something to fix it.' She smiled at Doug. 'Look on the bright side. Tomorrow I might remember.'

'That's what I'm afraid of,' Doug replied.

* * *

Foxy put Sophie's overnight bag in the back of the Defender and held the door open for her to climb in as she precariously balanced two takeaway coffees.

'Ta.'

Foxy climbed in and started the engine. 'Good to go?'

'Good to go,' she said firmly.

As they left the town, Sophie sipped her coffee and tried to organise her thoughts about what she was approaching.

'Do you have the building number?' asked Foxy.

She scrabbled around in her bag.

'I don't need it now, just when we get near.'

'OK,' she said, fiddling with her bag, twisting the handle.

'Soph, calm down,' Foxy said quietly.

'I can't,' she said, tears suddenly rolling down her face. 'I'm so frightened of what I'm walking into. How awful is that? Nothing's happened to me. It's all happened to Sam and I'm blubbing like a bloody idiot.'

'Soph, cut yourself some slack here. It's OK to feel bad, to feel nervous. What's happened to Sam has happened to you too. You just can't see it.'

Sophie sniffed and stared out of the window. She watched the countryside flashing by and wondered how she would feel when she was watching the same countryside on the way home. Would she feel different?

'They took his legs. Yesterday. They called me this morning,' she said softly and closed her eyes.

'Christ. You have to remember though, they did it because it saved his life.'

'I know. He won't see it like that though.'

Foxy was silent. He recalled friends who had lost limbs. He recalled their funerals when some had taken their own lives; unable to cope. Thinking they were half a person.

'You have to get him through this and out the other side.'

'He has to want to, Rob. I can't do it if he doesn't want to.'

'True,' Foxy agreed.

'I'm so frightened that the wonderful, gorgeous, funny Sam has gone. He was such a joker. I'm frightened that the Sam I love has gone, lost forever in a desert somewhere and this is a person I just don't know. A shell of someone that just looks like my husband… or some of my husband.'

'Too many unknowns at the moment to even think that,' Foxy said softly, wanting her to be wrong, but knowing she was probably right.

Sophie turned to the window, the tears rolling freely down her face, not wanting Foxy to see them. She was a wreck. She felt like she was hanging on to sanity by her fingertips. She was so frightened of seeing Sam she trembled whenever she thought about it. In her mind it had always been a happy, ecstatic reunion when she finally saw him. Not like this. She raised a trembling hand to wipe her eyes with a damp tissue.

'Soph, it'll be OK. If I can make it OK, I will. I'll be here for you,' Foxy said softly, gripping her hand.

CHAPTER 8

'NO! I don't want her in here. Get her OUT of here. OUT of here. GET HER OUT!'

Sophie sat in the chair outside Sam's room and wept into her handful of already soggy tissues. She kept hearing the words in her mind, over and over in a constant loop. His angry, contorted face as he said it. This wasn't Sam, with his wonderful big smile and huge dimples. This was an angry, emaciated stranger.

Two years missing, presumed dead and that's what he said when he saw her. She focused on her trembling hands and for once in her life, was at a total loss about what to do. She tried to think.

She watched the nurse through the window calming Sam down and adjusting his pillows. Then she left, giving Sophie a sympathetic look as she passed. Sophie sat and cried some more. She wasn't sure how much time had passed. She didn't remember thinking about anything in particular or forming a plan. She just stood. Wiped her eyes. Blew her nose and took a deep breath. She realised that anger was driving her. There was no way she was going to put up with this and fall at the first hurdle.

'No,' she muttered. 'Fuck this,' she swore uncharacteristically, took a deep breath and marched into Sam's room. She dumped her handbag on the table, his eyes flew open. She pointed at Sam with a trembling finger as he went to open his mouth to shout at her.

'No. You don't get to do that. Not to me. Not now. Not after everything. I'm going to have my say. Then if you still want me to go, I will.'

The nurse came hurrying in and started to say, 'Mrs Jones, I really think—'

'No!' said Sophie firmly, holding up a hand. 'I'm saying something to my husband, and I would like a minute, please.' The nurse didn't move, just eyed her. 'And then I'll go,' Sophie said quietly.

The nurse retreated and stood by the door outside the room, watching through the window.

Sophie steeled herself and said in a low, shaking voice, 'Two years, Sam. I've had two years of being told you were dead. But I didn't believe it. Not once. Two years of hoping, wanting… longing. Missing you. Trying to keep the hope alive.'

She pointed a shaking finger at him as the tears ran down her face.

'I never gave up hope. I didn't believe them. I knew my Sam wouldn't leave me. And then one day there's a miracle. My beloved husband! Alive! Just as I have always known and felt in here.' She banged her chest and the tears continued unchecked. 'And finally, he's here! In the UK! So I listen to the doctors, and I come to see my beloved husband when I'm allowed to. My husband. My beautiful Sam, who I have ached for all this time. And when you see me your first words are to tell me to go away? No, Sam. It's me. You don't get to do this. This has happened to both of us.' She paused and watched him for any sign of a response. 'Come on,' she said desperately. 'We're the A-team, remember?'

She stood trembling, watching him. He looked different. His face was gaunt. His cheekbones stood out sharply, with deep hollows beneath. He watched her with dead eyes. She saw no emotion or depth behind them. She didn't see the mischief that used to live there. She saw a shell. He looked at the nurse who had just entered the room.

'Get her out of here. I don't want to see her again.'

Sophie stared at him in disbelief. 'Sam? Come on,' she said desperately. 'We can get through this together. Marcus will help us. We can be a family again, Sam?'

'Nurse, I said GET HER OUT and make sure she doesn't bother me again.'

'I'm sorry, Mrs Jones, but I am going to have to ask you to leave.' The nurse took Sophie's arm.

Sophie shook her off and talked to Sam directly. 'So that's it? I don't want to see my wife again? My son? That simple? That's OK, is it?'

'Get her OUT!'

'Mrs Jones, I will have to call security…'

'OK, I'm going. But I will be back tomorrow, and we will have a discussion about this, Sam, and you won't be hiding behind this bloody nurse.' She turned to the nurse. 'Sorry, I didn't mean that.'

'It's fine, Mrs Jones,' the nurse said desperately, managing to propel Sophie out of the room and close the door behind her. 'Look, Mrs Jones, this isn't unusual. This reaction to family. It's a huge mix of emotions for them. I think you would benefit from sitting down with a couple of the doctors here. I'll arrange it for you tomorrow. Would that be OK?'

Sophie nodded, mopping up her tears, embarrassed that she couldn't seem to stop crying. 'Thank you… and sorry about the bloody nurse thing… no disrespect and all that.'

The nurse winked. 'Actually, between you and me I thought you were pretty cool if the truth be known. It's what some of these guys need. They become embarrassed – ashamed of their injuries. Silly really, they don't realise their family love them no matter what. So look, you'd better go. I'll sort out the doctors and see you tomorrow, shall we say around 10? Yes?'

'Yes, OK, and it's Sophie. Please. Look… is he likely to be like this tomorrow?'

The nurse pursed her lips. 'I would say there's a good chance of it yes, so prepare yourself. But keep trying. Talk to the doctors. But expect him to be the same. I need to go. See you in the morning. I'm Lottie by the way.'

Lottie went back into the room with Sam and Sophie stood watching for a moment. Sam caught her eye and then turned his face the other way. His face completely devoid of any emotion.

Never before had she ever felt so hurt, so lonely, so helpless. So utterly devoid of any idea of what to do.

* * *

Foxy had dropped Sophie off and driven into the city. He had parked at the main hospital and taken a gamble, surprising his ex-wife, Carla, at work. When he walked onto the ward, Carla had greeted him coolly with a raised eyebrow, and he knew from years of experience that she was still angry with him.

94

Carla managed to wangle a long lunch break as a result of approving glances and winks from her colleagues, and the two had found a quiet place in the hospital coffee shop.

'So, what are you doing here?' she asked, sipping her coffee.

'Surprising you,' Foxy answered levelly.

'Bullshit,' she said, eyeing him. 'What are you really doing here?'

'Busted. Sophie's husband is back in the UK. He's on the base in the hospital there. I took her to see him, he's been missing for two years. She's in a right state.'

'Jesus. What's the matter with him?'

'Cast your mind back to me after I was captured. He's ten times worse. They had him for two years, for me it was three months. Plus, she found out yesterday that they've just taken both legs too.'

Carla watched him over the rim of her cup. 'That's awful. It was tough with you and physically you were intact.'

'Just not mentally, eh?'

She shrugged. 'You were in terrible shape, whichever way you looked at it. What's the prognosis with him?'

'Early days. If the truth be known they actually didn't expect him to make it back over here. I think a couple of the guys died in the rescue and it was touch and go for a while with Sam just getting him out.'

'Sounds bad.'

'It is.'

'Will she cope?'

'It's rough for her. Dad with dementia, teenage son. She's pretty strong though.'

'And obviously she has you to lean on,' Carla said sarcastically.

'She has lots of friends that'll help, that she can lean on, and yes that includes me.'

'What are we doing, Rob?' Carla put her cup down.

'What do you mean?'

'Don't play dumb.'

Foxy leant back in his chair and regarded her coolly.

'Carla, see this from my point of view. You come and spend a wonderful couple of weeks with me in Castleby. We reconnected, laid ghosts to rest. It was like it used to be… with Charlie… before Charlie. And now, it's like you're dead set on busting my balls because I have a good friend who needs help?'

'I don't think you are friends though. There's something more there.'

'There isn't. I don't think about Sophie like that.'

Carla snorted. 'You're a man. You have a pulse. She's smart, gorgeous, funny. Of course you look at her like that. Christ, I'd bang her if I was that way inclined.'

'Carla.'

'Look,' she said firmly. 'Cards on the table. It was a wonderful couple of weeks. Like old times. I'll never forget it. But I have a life here. I love my work, my friends, my house. I'm happy here. I don't want to leave. You're there, with your friends and your new business. And you don't want to leave and I'm not asking you to.'

'So what… that's it for us?' Foxy said testily.

'I think deep down you agree with me.'

'I don't agree with you at all.'

'I'm sorry about that. I don't see this working longer term. Look we had a great time recently; it was great to reconnect and spend time together. I love it where you are. But I have no desire to be there permanently. I'm happy to come and visit and have a repeat performance, but I don't see why we have to keep tabs on each other and pretend this is a long-distance relationship.'

'So just occasional fuck buddies then?' he said sarcastically.

'Well, that's one label to put on it,' she said, amused.

'So basically, you were using me for sex and a free holiday.'

'And I'm happy to again. Don't look so affronted. You're a big boy. You'll get over it. As I recall you didn't suffer too much in the equation.'

'How many other occasional fuck buddies do you have, Carla?' Foxy narrowed his eyes.

'I don't have to tell you about my private life.'

'I kind of thought we were involved enough for me to give a shit.'

'I completely absolve you of responsibility on that front. I see who I like, you can see who you like.'

'If that's the case, why the hell do you have such an issue with Soph then?'

Carla sat back in her chair and folded her arms. Her eyes narrowed.

'Ah… the million-dollar question. From what I see, there's no way she's in occasional-fuck-buddy territory. Not in your eyes anyway. She means way more to you than that. You just haven't realised it yet.'

Foxy dragged his hand through his hair. 'Fuck's sake, Carla…I thought we—'

'Rob, I can't be involved with you exclusively. Not when I see what I see when you're with Sophie. It's self-protection.'

'But I don't think of her that way,' Foxy said, exasperated.

'You can keep telling yourself that, but your face, your eyes. All say something different.'

'You're talking shite.'

'I'm not. Deep down you know it, you just don't want to admit it. You will. One day.'

Foxy folded his huge arms grumpily and scanned the room. He noticed a man in blue scrubs and a white coat heading over with a takeaway coffee and frowned at his approach.

'Carla?' said the man. 'Thought it was you. Just wanted to say hi. I've been away for a bit, I've been meaning to come by and catch up.'

'Hi, Jamie, you were teaching in Toronto for a month, weren't you? How did it go?' Carla beamed at him.

'Fantastic!' he said enthusiastically and then turned to Foxy who was scowling at him. 'Look, Carla, sorry to interrupt with your friend here.'

'No problem. This is Rob, my ex-husband. He's got a friend at the military hospital down the road and popped in to say hi. Rob, this is Jamie Hunter, one of the orthopaedic surgeons here.'

Jamie shook Foxy's hand. 'Good to meet you,' said Jamie pleasantly. 'How's your friend doing? Nothing too serious I hope?'

'About as serious as it gets unfortunately.' Foxy pulled a rueful face.

'Can I be bold and ask?'

'He's been in captivity for two years, tortured, etc. The works. Just lost both legs too.'

'Drylands? They smashed his legs huh?' Jamie looked sympathetic.

'They certainly did. You served? Sounds like you've been there.'

'Barbaric fuckers,' muttered Jamie. 'Sorry. Look, if I can help with anything, don't hesitate. This is kind of my field. I served a while back. Treated lots of these sorts of injuries and the problems that are left while I was out there. Jesus, man, it's true when they say you can never unsee some things. Carla said you were out there.' He glanced at his watch. 'Look, I've gotta go. Good to meet you. Meant what I said. If I can help, just shout. Any friend of Carla's. She'll give you my details, although I'm off training the army surgeons out in the Sudan for a while.'

Foxy inspected the man he had taken an instant dislike to a moment ago. 'Appreciate that,' he said warily. 'Might take you up on it. Be safe out in the Sudan, it can get brutal.'

Jamie kissed Carla on the cheek and then jogged off across the café.

'Hmm,' observed Foxy. 'One of your fuck buddies?'

'Nope,' Carla said, taking out her phone and tapping into it. 'He's just a great surgeon. I'm sending you his number. If he can help, he will.'

'Isn't it too late now? The legs are gone.'

'Everything else is left though. Thighs, hips, maybe knees? People have terrible issues with those after amputation.'

'OK. Thanks.'

Carla stood up. 'Go and find Sophie. She'll be a wreck and will need a stiff drink. I can tell you that for nothing. Text me how her husband's doing.'

'So that's it? Where does that leave us?'

'It leaves us where we should both be. You're free, I'm free. Text me if it looks like you'll be free at Christmas. Maybe I'll come to the seaside again then.'

'For sex and another free holiday?' Foxy snapped.

'If that's on offer. If not, I'll be happy with a turkey dinner, a walk on that beach and a cuddle with Solo.'

She bent and kissed him lightly on the cheek. 'Look after yourself. You know I still love you, right?'

'Doesn't feel like it.'

'Stop being childish. Go and find Sophie. She'll need you. See you later.'

She picked up her coffee, ran a quick hand across his back and left with a cheerful wave, leaving Foxy sat in the café slightly put out at being friend zoned.

Foxy started the Defender and drove out of the car park, thinking about Carla's words. It was early afternoon, but the skies had turned dark, and it had started to rain heavily. As he drove back across the city towards the military base, he thought about Carla's words and what she had said about his feelings for Sophie. It troubled him. Sophie was his friend and he cared about her hugely. He'd not thought about her in any way other than as a friend. Besides she was a married woman. He dismissed Carla's words and changed lanes to head into the right area of town.

The sky had become so dark Foxy had to put his headlights on. The rain was approaching biblical and the Defender's windscreen wipers were only just coping. Traffic had slowed and all Foxy could see was a wet blur of red tail lights. Foxy spent almost an hour crawling through the traffic heading for the base.

Finally, he turned into one of the back roads that ran along a harbour wall and his headlights lights flashed over a lonely figure sat on a bench in the pouring rain. Foxy frowned and quickly pulled over. The figure looked like Sophie. But she wouldn't be here. She'd be at the hospital, with Sam. He buzzed down the window and peered out.

'Jesus!' he shouted, climbing out of the car. 'Sophie?'

Sophie barely registered Foxy calling her name. She had been sat for hours, oblivious to the weather. Playing the conversation over and over. Seeing Sam's contorted, angry face. Who was he? The huge veins in his neck as he yelled. She had no clear idea of where she was or what she was doing.

'Sophie,' her name was said sharply, and she looked up to see Foxy standing in front of her soaking wet.

'Jesus. What are you doing out here, Soph?'

She opened her mouth to respond, and no words came out. Instead, a strangled cry emerged, and her face crumpled as she thought about having to tell Foxy what Sam had said. She sobbed. She was barely aware when Foxy sat down next to her in the pouring rain and pulled her into a hug.

Foxy sat on the bench silently, hugging Sophie, his heart breaking as he listened to her gut-wrenching sobs. He held her tightly, gently stroking her back. He had a fair idea of what had happened, and he had been half expecting it. He had been torn as to whether to tell her to expect it or not. The rain continued to pour down and they were both soaked to the skin. When her crying eased slightly, Foxy nudged her gently.

'Soph, come on. We need to get you dry and warm.' He led her to the Defender like a small child, tugging her along by the hand. She was in some sort of shock he guessed. She wasn't really aware of her surroundings or what was happening. He gently helped her into the passenger seat, then climbed in the driver's side and gunned the engine, heading off to the hotel he knew she had booked for the night nearby.

'Sophie, drink this,' he instructed, handing her a brandy that he had got from the mini bar. She obediently drank it, coughing as the liquid burnt down her throat. He took the tumbler from her and propelled her to the bathroom where the shower was running on hot, and the room was already warm and steamy.

'Get in there and get under the shower and only come out when you're warm,' he ordered, pushing her in the door and shutting it. 'I'll be back in a while.'

Foxy headed back down to the Defender, for the small bag he had brought with him. He had planned to crash at Carla's that night so had brought a change of clothes. He grabbed the bag and went back to reception.

'Do you have any single rooms free tonight, near room 421, please?'

The clerk checked the computer.

'Yes, sir, I can do you the room next door for a single rate as it's late. With breakfast for one night?'

'Yes please.'

Relieved, Foxy paid and grabbed the key card, heading back up. He dumped his bag and put his head around Sophie's door and listened. He could hear her in the shower, so he closed the door and went back to his room to shower and change into dry clothes. Fifteen minutes later he knocked on Sophie's door and she opened it, dressed, but red-eyed.

'Hi,' she said. 'Wondered where you went. I was just going to call you. How come you're dry?'

'Got a room.'

'Aren't you seeing Carla?'

'Let's not get into that now,' he said grumpily.

'Okaaay.' Sophie frowned.

'How're you doing? You look warmer… better.'

'I feel human again. Thank you for sorting me out. Bit of a meltdown,' she said guiltily. 'Look, I'm starving. Haven't eaten all day. There's a Thai place just over the way. Want to eat?'

'Always. Do you want me to get a takeaway?'

'No, I need to be out. Among normality. If I hide in the room, I'll feel worse.'

'Let's go then.'

They walked across the courtyard of the new-build development complex that housed their hotel, some restaurants and offices, stopping at the trendy looking Thai place.

'Doesn't look too busy,' said Sophie, eyeing up the long benches and smattering of people.

They were led to the end of a table and Foxy was relieved they were the only people on it. The waitress rattled off a load of information, took their drink orders and then disappeared, briefly re-appearing with their drinks.

'Christ, I need this,' Sophie said as she drank deeply from her glass of wine.

Thoughtfully she put the glass down and twirled the stem, unable to meet Foxy's eyes.

'Sorry again. About earlier. I think I must have been in shock or something. Thanks for looking out for me. You seem to always come to my rescue.'

'No problem. That's what mates are for.'

'Tough day,' she said, finally looking at him.

'Was always going to be.'

'I didn't think…' Her eyes filled with tears again. 'Shit.' She fumbled for a tissue in her bag. 'I'm sorry…'

The waitress was approaching again with another couple and looked as if she was going to sit them near Foxy. He caught her eye and shook his head, inclining his head towards Sophie who was wiping her eyes with a tissue. The waitress veered off and sat the couple at a bench further down. Foxy rewarded her with a wink.

Sophie blew her nose. 'Sorry.'

'It's OK… So, you didn't think?'

She blew out a big breath. 'I didn't think seeing Sam would be how it went today.'

'Tell me.' Foxy picked up his beer.

Sophie drained her glass, caught the eye of the waitress and gestured for another round of drinks.

'I had to wait ages outside the room and then when I finally got in…' Her eyes filled with tears again, but Foxy saw her set her jaw and she continued. 'Basically, he shouted that he didn't want to see me. Told the nurses to get me out.'

'Soph…'

'He shouted at me to get out.'

She murmured thanks to the waitress who put another round of drinks down.

'So I sat outside his room and I thought… I thought… Fuck this.'

'You never swear,' Foxy said, amused.

'Well, I marched in and told him what I thought.'

'Oh? What did you say?'

'I was honest. I told him that I never once believed he was gone. Never believed he had died. That we wanted him back.' She sniffed, her eyes filling again. 'I told him that it was me. His wife. That we were the A-team.'

'And what did he say?'

'He shouted again. Told the nurse to get me out. Said he didn't want to see me again.'

Foxy took a swig of beer and watched as Sophie suddenly shivered.

'You cold?'

'No. I'm just remembering what he looked like.'

'Bad?'

'No, not in that way. How he was when he was saying it. He had these…' She searched for the words. 'These dead eyes. He didn't look like Sam. He was gaunt. Pale. Emaciated. He had these huge veins throbbing in his neck when he shouted at me. He didn't look like my Sam at all. He looked like a scary ghost of Sam. With Sam there was always mischief behind his eyes, and they were always warm. He had such a beautiful smile and huge dimples. He didn't look like anyone I knew today.'

'He's been gone a long time, been through a lot,' Foxy said. 'Are you going back tomorrow?'

'Yes. The nurse thinks I need to talk to the doctors there.' She rolled her eyes.

'It'll be useful.'

'I'm dreading what they'll say, that it'll be all doom and gloom.'

'Soph, one day at a time. It's not going to be good news from the doctors, is it? It'll be practical and honest. It's just about getting through it and getting him better.'

She glanced away, her eyes filling again. 'I just thought…'

'What did you think?'

'That he might be pleased to see me, that's all,' she said quietly, another tear escaping.

'Soph, look this is hard to say, but you have to trust me here. You can't think like this. He's not thinking straight. As far as he's concerned, he's come back half a man. Broken. No good to anyone. I suspect he's pushing you away because deep down he thinks you can do better. He'll probably be thinking that he's a burden and you'd be better off without him, which is why he's pushing you away.'

'Why would he think that?' Sophie asked tearfully, wiping her eyes.

'Because he's a bloke. A soldier. A proud man.'

'But that's ridiculous. We're his family. We love him, no matter what.'

'That may be, but I almost guarantee this is how he'll be feeling.'

105

'Was that how you felt?' she asked quietly. 'When you came back after being captured.'

Foxy felt guilty as he closed his eyes, remembering.

'Yeah. I was awful to Carla and Charlie. Pushed them away. Physically I wasn't too damaged. But I felt too broken to be of any use to them.'

Their food arrived and Foxy thanked the waitress. Sophie was sitting staring into her wine glass.

'Dig in,' Foxy said, his mouth full.

'How long did you think that?' Sophie asked quietly. 'That you were too broken. No use.'

'Er, I don't know… few weeks.'

'Jesus,' said Sophie. 'Poor Carla.'

'Oh yeah,' said Foxy ruefully.

'I thought you were seeing her today. What happened?'

'Don't ask,' replied Foxy, picking up his beer and looking over Sophie's shoulder, avoiding her enquiring gaze. 'Don't fucking ask.'

I feel like time is running out. There's so much to do. So many to help. That's what I'm calling it. Help. I wonder if I'll have enough time to help them all. I see this as a service. A gift, or a blessing if you like, from above. The authority to be able to do this for the greater good.

My only sadness is that people won't know it was me who helped them. Does that make me selfish? Self-centred? To want some acknowledgement for all of my hard work? Perhaps the fact that God knows is good enough. He knows. He must know. I feel his hand guiding me.

CHAPTER 9

Steve was sitting in his office with his feet up in a desk drawer. He was unusually stumped and despite his best efforts at internet research, he was at a dead end. He had been through the post-mortems for the care home deaths, and they seemed fairly inconclusive. Sighing, he picked up his phone and made a call which went straight to answerphone.

'Hi there,' he said, leaving a message. 'It's Inspector Steve Miller, your personal crash mat. We need to have a chat about all things post-mortem. How about a chat over a beer or a coffee as long as you promise not to fall into the beverage of my choice. Happy to fit around you, but I do need to catch up if that's OK. Or...' he added as a cheeky afterthought, 'happy to spring for some food as long as you don't end up lying in that too. Call me back or text, whatever's easier, I know you're busy. Speak soon. Bye.'

'Are you trying to get a date with the new doc?' Jonesey asked, peering around the door, scoffing a tube of smarties.

'Don't you ever stop eating?' asked Steve. 'Give me an orange one.'

'I don't think they taste like the orange ones anymore though.' Jonesy shook some out and gave Steve a few. 'Haven't they taken all the E numbers out? So… talk me through your date with the doc then,' he said, plonking himself down in the chair. 'Word on the street says she's single and ready to mingle.'

'Jesus Christ. Which word, which street?'

'Town grapevine of course,' said Jonesy, chucking a handful of smarties in his mouth and looking at Steve as if he was a moron. 'People have couple-goaled you two already. Both professionals, single, some people think you're not too shabby looking. I don't see it mysel—'

'Couple-goaled? What's couple-goaled?'

'You know… want you to get together. They think you're a match.'

'Who does?'

'Duh, are you not listening? The town.'

'Do you have town meetings or something to decide this crap?'

'No, it's just, you know, word on the street.'

Steve stared at Jonesey in amazement. 'Bugger off. Go and do something.'

Steve's phone rang and Jonesy craned his neck to look at who it was.

'It's the doc,' he said, grinning and waggling his eyebrows. 'Better get that.'

'Bugger off,' said Steve, answering the phone. 'Steve Miller.'

'It must be love. Love…' sang Jonesey loudly.

'Bugger off!' shouted Steve. 'Sorry,' he said into the phone. 'Annoying staff member who is about to be sacked.'

'You love me really,' called Jonesey as he walked down the corridor.

* * *

Kate had been up for a bite to eat in the pub. She had joked that she would do anything to avoid going home to her mother, so an evening in the pub sounded heavenly. They had arranged to meet at the Hope and Anchor and Steve had got there a few minutes early. He greeted Genevieve who worked at the pub to supplement her lifeguard job on Castle Beach in the summer months.

'Hey, Gen,' he said, pleased to see her. 'How's it going?'

'Good thanks,' she grinned. 'What can I get you?'

Steve selected a beer and asked after Genevieve's boyfriend, Mack, who was one of Foxy's soldier friends. He was currently in Germany recovering after being shot while he was on an operation overseas.

'He should be back in the next couple of weeks,' she said happily. 'They kept him for longer because there was some tendon damage, I think. But he's all good. I went over last weekend to see him.'

'Good to hear, give him my regards,' said Steve as he headed towards a free table.

'Are you eating tonight?' she called.

'Yeah. I'm just waiting for someone,' he called back.

'It's the doc, isn't it?' She grinned when he turned around and raised an eyebrow. 'Town grapevine,' she added.

Steve rolled his eyes and turned to see Kate in the doorway.

'Hi,' he said warmly. 'Drink?'

'God yes,' Kate said, plonking herself down at the table. 'Red wine, please. A bucket of it and perhaps even a crack chaser. Jesus, what a day.'

Genevieve heard the order and motioned that she'd bring it over. Steve sat down at the table.

'Good to see you – upright,' he joked.

She laughed and then looked mortified. 'That was so embarrassing. I'm so sorry. Did the stain come out of your jeans and T-shirt?'

'Jeans yes. T-shirt went to the big T-shirt graveyard in the sky.'

'Oh Christ. Let me replace it. Please.'

'Absolutely not. Thanks, Gen,' he said as she brought over Kate's wine. 'Have you met? This is Kate Cooper. Kate this is Genevieve. She's either here or saving people's lives on Castle Beach.'

'Hi. Genevieve is such a beautiful name,' said Kate.

'Most people around here can't spell it, so Gen it is,' she said good-naturedly. 'Nice to meet you. I'll be back in a minute to get your food order.'

'Good to see you, Kate. Cheers.' Steve raised his glass.

'Cheers,' echoed Kate.

'Right,' Steve said. 'Put me out of my misery. I've read all the PMs and am coming up with nothing.'

Kate sipped her wine. 'Me neither. It's nothing plainly obvious. A few ultimately died of kidney failure, while for others it was things like a heart attack or stroke, for example.'

'So, what do we deduce from this?'

'God that's good,' she said, sipping again and thinking for a moment. 'The thing to think about is that PMs just really look at cause of death and not necessarily anything surrounding that, or what led to it.'

Steve nodded. 'For us, in the context of a suspicious death, we use a PM to confirm cause of death, which might tell us how they died, which sometimes helps, sometimes doesn't. Our problem is having the budget to run the myriad other tests that sometimes have to be done.'

'So, we have the results for a pretty basic set of PMs,' Kate mused. 'Not any real extra analysis, or additional tox screening. But we are still waiting for the basic tox screens to come back. There's an issue at the local lab. They're seriously backed up. And it's worth considering that with older people, it's awful to say, but usually it's a foregone conclusion that they died of something pretty simple.'

'So, what you're saying in an extremely politically correct way, is that the pathologist is essentially ticking boxes with older person deaths that aren't in any way suspicious?' Steve probed.

'It was very politically correct, wasn't it? But sometimes, yes.'

'So where does that leave us?' Steve asked.

'I was thinking—'

'What'll it be for food, guys?' Gen interrupted.

They ordered and resumed their chat.

'You were saying, that you were thinking…' Steve prompted.

'I want to pull their records from our systems and the care home systems to look at what was recorded about their health beforehand.'

'What might that show?'

'Might shows a trend in symptoms, or medication for example. It might even be a bad batch of meds – it's not unheard of.'

'Jesus, I didn't think of that.'

'We'll see what their records show. Did you say you were looking at visitor logs?'

'Uh-huh. Lots to wade through and collate,' he said, amused. 'Hark at us. Holmes and Watson.'

'Dempsey and Makepeace,' she said. 'Much cooler. So, anything in the visitor logs so far?'

'Nothing finger pointy,' Steve said dryly. 'Early days though, I want to dig a little deeper.'

'We should do that when I've gone through the records too and then perhaps reconvene to discuss,' Kate said, smiling. 'Any discussions involving wine I am totally up for.'

'Good to know. I like that idea,' Steve said. 'Even though I know you're only out because you can't stand your mother.'

'Busted.' Kate laughed. 'If you'd met her you'd be running for the hills. I don't know how Dad does it.'

'OK. So we'll both dig deeper and then compare notes.'

'Sounds like a plan.' She raised her glass.

'If you don't mind me asking, what brought you back here?' he said gently.

Kate thought for a moment and then decided she liked this man enough to be honest. She was a strong believer that people should be straight and honest at all times.

'Total heartbreak, then the discovery that my husband was an unfaithful prick, plus Dad was desperate for help. The locums weren't up to much.'

'Ah.' He sipped his drink thoughtfully. 'I'm sorry about your heartbreak,' he said softly.

She looked rueful. 'Apparently, life goes on, no matter how difficult that may be. It's a certainty. Me and Dad had always talked about sharing the practice. So, what about you? How long have you been here?'

'I was posted here after training, when I was young and stupid and wet behind the ears. I've been here on and off ever since, apart from a longish stint in CID in Cardiff.'

'You must like it here.'

'I do, very much. Most of the people are lovely, with the exception of the local pond life and I realised I hate to be away from the sea and this coastline.'

'I love the sea. I've always missed it when I've moved away. So, what about you? What's waiting for you at home? Any family?'

Steve thought about it for a while. 'Nothing's waiting for me at home,' he said. 'God that sounds bloody sad, doesn't it? A pile of ironing and a broken remote control.'

'I know a lady who might do your ironing for you. She's a tad on the lonely side. She might like the idea of it.'

'Bring it on,' he challenged.

'Have you never married?' Kate asked. 'Sorry if that's really nosey.'

Steve was quiet for a moment and gazed into his drink. 'I was engaged. It seems ages ago now.'

'What happened?'

He cleared his throat, remembering how heartbroken he had been when he discovered the betrayal.

'Erm… she completely omitted to tell me that she didn't believe in sleeping with just the one person while being engaged to someone else.'

'Ah… Perhaps she knew my husband.'

'Perhaps.'

'Were you heartbroken?' she probed quietly, looking into his blue eyes.

'I was. Completely. But it was more about the betrayal.'

'I'm sorry about your heartbreak,' she said softly.

'Thank you,' he said quietly. 'As you say, life goes on.'

'Right grub up. Plates are hot folks. I'll grab you some cutlery.' Gen appeared, interrupting the moment.

* * *

It was evening and Foxy and Sophie were driving home. There had been silence in the car for the last few miles, with Sophie staring out of the window as they rattled along.

'So,' Foxy said, interrupting the silence. He figured he'd given her long enough to process. 'What did the doctors say?'

Sophie had been lost in thought. Trying to understand what Sam's doctors *had* said and think about the kind of help they needed. She felt her head would explode with everything she needed to do and think about.

'As predicted. Doom and gloom,' she said, trying to lighten the mood.

'Be specific.'

'OK. They said he's improving. Day by day. Weight gain. Responding to drugs, etc. The wound, his legs, you know – all look good. Few issues with phantom pain, but they are managing that with meds. He starts on physio soon. The focus will be to help him get his strength back and his stamina back up. They suggested he come home for a long weekend in a few weeks, as long as we can make the house wheelchair accessible for him, get him used to being at home and in a different environment. Something to look forward to and all that.'

'How do you feel about that?' Foxy gave her a sideways glance.

Sophie snorted and glanced out of the window. 'I love the idea of him coming home for a weekend. It might mean he might actually fucking well speak to me.'

'You appear to be getting into the swing of swearing now.'

'Hmm.'

'Still wouldn't see you or talk to you?'

'Nope. I also spoke to one of their psychiatrists.'

'Useful?'

'Not particularly. They said what you said about him feeling I'd be better off without him, but no real help in how to address that with him.'

'Really?'

'Well, they banged on about time and giving him space and all that.'

'So that's their advice? Time and space.'

'Apparently so.'

'I think that's very wise advice. I think give it a couple of weeks and go back. Any medication that they'll have him on to help him cope will have kicked in by then and he might have a different outlook on things.'

'Hmm. We'll see.'

'This isn't a quick fix, Soph.'

Sophie bit her lip, then turned to look at Foxy.

'So… what happened with Carla? Why didn't you stay with her last night?'

Foxy hissed out a breath. 'We're not getting into that.'

'Yes we are. Come on. Spill.'

'In very simple terms she told me we weren't involved. We were both free to see who we wanted. She was there and I'm here and a long-distance thing wouldn't work. She's got issues with us being friends for some reason – got a bee in her bonnet about that. But very simply, next time she wants sex and a free holiday she's going to give me a ring and see if I'm free.'

Sophie laughed. 'Will you be on Tripadvisor soon offering sex and free holidays? Sounds pretty tempting to me.'

Foxy glanced at her grumpily. 'I just thought the time she spent with me meant something, you know, that maybe we were connecting again.'

'But you did. You reconnected. She forgave you for Charlie, not that there was anything to forgive in my book. You got close. It would have meant something. She certainly doesn't strike me as the heartless type. She doesn't want to live in Castleby and you don't want to go back there, so what's the problem?'

'I don't know. I just feel a bit, you know…'

'What?' She eyed him with amusement.

'Used.'

Sophie guffawed loudly. 'You had two weeks of female company and, what I assume was, great sex with no strings attached and you feel a bit used?'

'It's not funny.'

She patted his leg chuckling. 'It really is. You're a big boy. You'll get over it.'

'That's what she said.' He scowled.

* * *

Fisherman Jimmy Ryan was avoiding the police like the plague. When Steve the copper had appeared on the quay asking him about JJ's head in the lobster pot, he had almost done a runner then and there. He couldn't be done for it. He wasn't the one who killed him. He just lobbed the head over the side of the boat.

As he drove out to his lock-up, he fretted over what to do now. Would it be better to come clean and fess up to Steve? But then he'd have to explain the deal with the guns and ammunition, the money and the bag. He shuddered. Nope. Couldn't do that. He'd not even told his long-suffering partner, Marie, about the money and JJ's head. His view was, what she didn't know wouldn't hurt her. He arrived at his lock-up, parked across the doors and hopped out, frowning at the broken padlock lying on the ground.

'Oh for fuck's sake,' he said crossly, bending down to pick up the padlock. He heard footsteps behind him, felt something heavy crash down on his head and then blackness.

When Jimmy awoke he was tied to a chair. His head throbbed and he was desperate for a pee; there was some sort of sack over his head. He had no idea where he was or what he was doing here. Something that smelt horrible was stuffed into his mouth too. He wondered for a moment whether he might be sick. Abruptly, the bag was whipped off his head and a bright light shone in his face. Jimmy blinked and tried to avoid it, turning his head.

The smelly rag in his mouth was removed and someone threw cold water at his face.

'Where am I?' he mumbled to the dark figure behind the light. He saw the large table that had been put in front of him and felt panic swell in his chest as he saw the holes in the table and the blood.

Rumours had been that Huey's hands had been nailed to a table before the Camorra had killed him in the most horrible way. All to prove no one messed with Mickey Camorra. Jimmy's blood ran cold and he almost wet himself.

Shit, this was the Camorra's doing. It had to be.

He heard footsteps and the scrape of a chair but couldn't see anything past the bright light. He smelt perfume, heavy, rich. Heard high heels on concrete. He frowned and tried to peer through the darkness. He heard the rustle of fabric; the perfume stronger in his nostrils. He heard the flick of a lighter and smelt cigarette smoke.

'Sort the light out, Stanley,' a female voice commanded.

The light was adjusted, and Jimmy could suddenly see. In front of him sat a middle-aged woman, he guessed late-fifties, with a very attractive face and short, stylishly cut white blonde hair. She bore a striking resemblance to Helen Mirren. She wore all white. Trousers, shoes, top and trench coat. She inhaled her cigarette deeply and blew the smoke out lazily while she scrutinised Jimmy through the haze.

'Tea please, Stanley,' she demanded.

A huge, thick-set man appeared with a bald head and enormous hands. He placed a cup and saucer of delicate bone china on the table.

'Ashtray, Stanley,' she said sharply. 'Christ, it's not rocket science, is it? If I have a cigarette, I need an astray. Keep up. What's the matter with you today?'

Stanley provided an ashtray, and the woman carefully rested her cigarette on it as she picked up the delicate cup and took a sip. Replacing the cup and saucer, she picked up her cigarette again and took a deep drag.

'So, you're Jimmy,' she observed.

Jimmy nodded warily.

'Do you know who I am?'

Jimmy decided to play dumb and shook his head.

'I'm Pearl Camorra. Mickey's wife. You know who Mickey is, yes? I understand you've met?'

Jimmy swallowed and tried to control the fear and his pressing need to pee.

'Yes, I do. I'm very pleased to meet you, Pearl.'

She inclined her head and waved her hand vaguely as she spoke. 'Mickey is away. Up north, dealing with some… unfortunate… business.'

'Oh?' Jimmy managed.

'Yes. Now I had dinner with Alexy last night,' she said, picking up her cup and saucer again.

119

'How is Alexy?' Jimmy stammered, trying to pretend this was a casual exchange and not that he was tied to a chair being held hostage. Also suffering the indignity of being in increasing danger of wetting himself like a small child in front of one of the most powerful women in the region.

Pearl smiled indulgently. 'I like Alexy. He amuses me very much with his pidgin English. But he tries with the language. And I love a trier.' She leant forwards. 'Do you love a trier, Jimmy?'

'Er, yes. Yes, I do,' he said desperately.

'So, Jimmy. Alexy speaks very highly of you. Says you are solid and reliable,' she said. 'At least that's what I think he said, I can't understand him half the time.'

'OK,' said Jimmy warily.

'Says you're not a grass and can be relied on.'

'Yes,' said Jimmy, nodding stupidly.

'Well, I'd like you to talk me through this please, Jimmy.' Pearl snapped her fingers and nothing happened. She turned and shouted. 'Stanley! What's with you today? Pay attention.'

Stanley lumbered over and passed her an iPad. Pearl swiped through a few things until she got what she wanted.

'Talk me through this, please,' she said and turned the iPad to show him.

Jimmy focused on the picture and saw himself standing on his boat talking to Steve the copper, who was leaning against a metal ladder on the quayside.

Sweat broke out on Jimmy's forehead. 'He was asking me about JJ's head.'

'Ah… JJ's head. Talk me through what you did with it.'

'I weighed it down in an old lobster pot and chucked it out to sea.'

Pearl took another drag. 'Hindsight being the wonderful thing it is, do you think that was the best course of action, Jimmy?'

Jimmy squirmed in his seat, the need to pee was becoming tortuous.

'In my defence… Pearl,' he said carefully. 'I had never been handed a head before, I was a bit stumped as to what to do with it.'

Pearl gave a peal of laughter. 'I like you, Jimmy. But that aside. What did you tell the copper?'

'Nothing. I didn't say anything. I said I had no idea about it.' He tried to look affronted. 'I wouldn't say anything.'

Pearl watched him carefully. She picked up her cup and drained the last of her tea.

'Two things, Jimmy, and I need you to listen.' She leant forward. 'Can you listen, Jimmy? Because some people find it hard to listen properly, don't they, Stanley?' she shouted over her shoulder. 'So,' she said, extracting a cigarette from a packet in her pocket and placing it in her mouth. She waited for a moment and then turned and shouted, 'Stanley!'

Stanley ran over, producing a Zippo lighter and lit her cigarette. She regarded him with narrowed eyes, frowning. 'Why must I have to ask you for everything today, Stanley?

'Anyway. Two things.' She focused back on Jimmy, inhaled deeply and closed her eyes, waving Stanley away. 'First thing, Stanley has a little gift for you.' She turned and shouted over her shoulder. 'DON'T YOU, STANLEY?'

Stanley lumbered back wheeling a large black suitcase.

'What's that?' Jimmy eyed it suspiciously.

'That…' Pearl pointed, 'is the rest of JJ.' She took another drag of her cigarette and then blew smoke from her nostrils. 'Probably start to thaw out in a couple of hours so you might want to think about what you're going to do with him, well, the bits of him that are in there. We've got a couple for insurance purposes.'

'Why are you giving him to me?'

'To finish the job and to cement our friendship.'

'I'm assuming this isn't a choice for me.'

Pearl laughed delightedly. 'Jimmy, you are sweet. Of course not. I've asked you to do it for me as a new special friend and I'm hoping you'll agree happily.'

Jimmy decided to say nothing. He figured he'd live longer that way.

'Good. That's settled then,' she said brightly.

'What's the other thing?' Jimmy was fairly close to wetting himself and would have agreed to anything to be released just so he could pee.

'Ah yes. I've got a boat coming. Just a little yacht. None of us here are particularly good sailors and I know you are. I'd like you to drive it in for me, please, and park it in the harbour.'

'Park it?' Jimmy said with amusement.

'You know what I mean.' She waved a hand.

'What's in this boat?' Jimmy asked warily.

Pearl gave Jimmy a look. 'Now, Jimmy. Darling. Best you don't ask me things like that. It's a boat. A yacht. And it's for me. That's all you need to know.'

'Where do I pick it up from and when?'

'Alexy will let you know, you've got a while yet. You've also got more pressing matters to attend to, unless you've got a decent-sized freezer at home, then you can take as long as you like.' She stood and smoothed down her coat. 'I've enjoyed our chat, Jimmy. I think this is the start of a beautiful friendship.' She regarded him closely. 'You know what, Jimmy, you're quite good-looking in a surfer boy kind of way.'

'Thank you.' Jimmy was nervous about where this was going. 'It'll be such a shame to have to ruin that lovely face,' she said softly. 'Are we clear here, Jimmy?'

'Crystal,' he mumbled.

'Stanley,' she commanded. 'It's time.' She clicked her fingers.

Stanley walked over to Jimmy and hit him again, knocking him out. Stanley picked him up easily, put him in one of the trucks and issued an instruction for him to be dumped back at his lock-up.

CHAPTER 10

Peter the curate was out in the pouring rain, running errands for the vicar and Mrs Pomeroy. He was not happy. As he trudged through the streets with the heavy bags, he asked himself again why he didn't push to take the car. He had various care homes to call into with broth and cakes for the poorly and Mrs Pomeroy has also asked him to pick up a delivery from a woman called Sadie, who he disliked intensely as she always smelt of patchouli oil and stared at his crotch for too long.

She always made him feel a mixture of uncomfortable, yet semi-aroused at the same time. She had trapped him in a doorway once, pretending to stumble as she went past him. Her hand had gone straight to his crotch, and she had pressed her enormous breasts hard into his chest. That episode had made him most uncomfortable, but he had thought about it almost constantly for a week or so.

Peter made his deliveries and firmly refused to enter Sadie's house, waiting on the doorstep for the package before setting off back to the vicarage. He was going via a residential home to say some prayers with sisters Mary and Olive, their sister Mabel was not expected to last much longer. It saddened him greatly. She was a nice old lady and had been the life and soul of a quiz afternoon a few weeks ago. Her team had beaten everyone else's by a country mile, including the vicarage's team. The ever-competitive Mrs Pomeroy had been very put out to have lost.

Peter stayed for an hour or so, saying prayers and words of comfort and then left, vowing to return in the morning. He chatted to the receptionist on the way out and left some more broth that Mrs Pomeroy had made for Mabel. The carer had said it was about the only thing she was able to eat since she had become ill. Although Peter didn't particularly like Mrs Pomeroy, he commended her efforts in making her broth and cakes for the sick and infirm.

* * *

Mrs Pomeroy had an errand of her own. Once she had dispensed the vicar and Peter for the day, she had set about her daily routine of steaming open the vicar and Peter's post, reading and digesting the information and then re-sticking the envelopes. She noticed with annoyance that there was another letter from the irritating and pushy parishioner requesting desperately that the vicar pop in and see her to discuss important and highly confidential matters.

Later that afternoon, when her chores were all done, she re-read the letter again and made a decision.

'I'll give you important matters, lady,' said Mrs Pomeroy firmly as she rammed on her outside hat and popped into the kitchen for her tin of cakes to take to the lady. 'Vicar won't look twice at a harlot like you so don't be bothering him,' she said to herself. She had awarded herself the status of controlling every aspect of the vicar's personal life since the death of his wife. Armed with her umbrella and cake tin she marched off up the road in the wind and rain.

When pressed, Joy Brown's doorbell played a deafening version of 'Amazing Grace' in a tinny key that was sheer torture to anyone listening. Mrs Pomeroy waited impatiently and adjusted her coat and hat as she heard Joy approach the door. The door opened and Mrs Pomeroy became a different person.

'Oh hello, Joy. How are you?' she began in her plummy telephone voice. 'Vicar's asked me to pop in and see you. He's so busy, but he sends his warmest thoughts and apologies. He asked me if I could come and chat to you about what's bothering you.'

Joy looked crestfallen. 'How disappointing! Is there not even a chance he'll make it around soon?'

Mrs Pomeroy adopted her best sympathetic face. 'I'm so sorry, Joy. He's just so busy! He is so in need by the town. He did ask, though, that I make you something special and pop it in and have a chat.'

Joy viewed Mrs Pomeroy with a degree of caution. In her view the woman was an absolute Rottweiler where the vicar was concerned, which was why she had written to the vicar directly and marked it private and confidential. It raised an eyebrow as to why the vicar was sharing private letters with the housekeeper.

'Well the matter is rather confidential,' she said loftily, not wanting to chat to Mrs Pomeroy at all. 'I did note that specifically in my letter.'

Mrs Pomeroy leant forward, saying in a conspiratorial tone, 'Vicar likes to share with me. His burden is a heavy one. He felt perhaps I might be better suited to advising you in your confidential matter than him. Also it's a little more… now how did he put it? Yes… proper. Much more proper.'

Joy's hand flew to her mouth. 'Are you saying the vicar thinks I'm improper?' she whispered, appalled that he might think that of her.

'I'm not entirely sure,' said Mrs Pomeroy. 'Perhaps he is erring on the side of safety – you know how rumours start, Joy. Now shall we have a cup of tea?'

Three quarters of an hour later, Mrs Pomeroy left Joy's house and headed back to the vicarage feeling triumphant. She had left the cakes she had baked and taken the tin, so as not to provide Joy with an excuse to come calling. Mrs Pomeroy had done as much work as she could to try and persuade Joy that she shouldn't set her sights on the vicar in any way. Mrs Pomeroy felt she wouldn't have any trouble with her anymore. As a final point, she had told Joy that she had scheduled Peter the curate to come and talk to her the next day and perhaps share her confidential issues with him. Joy had agreed somewhat reluctantly.

Mrs Pomeroy let herself into the vicarage and heard the murmur of conversation, she closed the large front door quietly and inched towards the study where she could hear the vicar's jovial tones. She did her best to eavesdrop, quickly moving down the hall when she heard the vicar ending the call.

Appearing in the kitchen, the vicar said, 'Ah, Mrs P. Such excellent news. Marion, my sister-in-law, will be coming to stay in a few weeks. I've told her to come for the sea carnival as it's such a delightful weekend, isn't it? I say Mrs P? Did you hear me?'

'Yes, Vicar,' she said shortly. 'You can't really spare the time, can you? You're terribly busy.'

'I think we would need to try and keep the time she is here light on appointments so I can spend some time with her. If you could oblige that would be wonderful. She mentioned that she has written a few times, but I don't seem to have got those letters. Do you think our post is going astray, Mrs P? Perhaps I'll talk to Dylan next time I see him around.'

'Post is unreliable now anyway. How long will she be staying?' asked Mrs P through gritted teeth. 'Perhaps Peter can pick up the slack.'

The vicar beamed happily. 'Wonderful. Oh, I'm thrilled Marion would want to come and stay. I do so love Marion. We'll have a wonderful time and she can stay for as long as she likes. Right. Now,' he said, rubbing his hands, 'may I ask what's for supper tonight, Mrs P?'

Mrs Pomeroy looked at his beaming face and saw red. 'Fish and chips,' she said shortly. 'You can send Peter and get them yourselves. Goodnight, Vicar.'

She picked up her bag and basket and swept out angrily. She marched down the road fuming. What a thankless task it was looking after these idiot men. One swish of a skirt and or the promise of something and they were ridiculous. She vowed to make Marion's stay as difficult as possible. She had met her a few times previously when the vicar's wife had been alive, and she had taken an instant dislike to her and her overfamiliar ways.

She let herself in the front door of her small cottage and marched inside, still angry. Fred was sitting in the lounge watching television, still in his smelly fishing gear.

'Alright?' he said, not taking his eyes off the television. 'What's for tea?'

She stood for a moment looking at him and felt a rush of rage.

'I don't know. It depends what you are damn well cooking for yourself!' She turned around and left the house again, slamming the door. She stomped into the town and wondered for a moment what to do. She had no real friends. She couldn't call in to see anyone she knew. She felt very lonely most of the time. She had at various times over the years had some friendships with women the same age as her – they had gone out for meals, the cinema and some drinks – but these friendships had always ended badly.

Edwina had a habit of coming on too strong and being too possessive, too needy, too desperate. She also had a nasty habit of giving her opinion on things when it simply wasn't wanted. This was the main reason that she had no friends; no one could stand it after a while.

In life, Edwina was a troubled and discontented woman. She had been forced by her very elderly parents to marry at the age of 16. She had been seduced by a boy whom she had loved from afar, but he hadn't even been aware she had fallen pregnant. He was so drunk he hadn't even remembered that they had slept together. Edwina had then gone and trapped the first man who had been interested in her and she had told him the baby was his. He had stepped up and done the right thing. She had thought Fred had a good future; he had talked of joining the navy and that suited her fine, a husband she didn't love being away at sea for a long time.

Fred's father had suffered a heart attack shortly after their wedding and died as a result. This left Fred to take over his dad's small trawler, to keep the family business going to provide for his mother too. The navy became a pipe dream.

Fate then dealt Edwina and Fred another blow when their baby contracted tuberculosis at a few months old and died.

Edwina found herself stuck in a loveless marriage, with a man she loathed. In her mind, she had married well beneath her station, and she had always been destined for greater things.

Feeling unloved and unappreciated, she headed into one of the big hotels on the front for dinner. She deserved a treat, she thought. She asked for a table for one by the window and ordered herself a three-course meal and a small carafe of wine, justifying the expense of the dinner with the fact that she would write a cheque from the parish account to herself tomorrow to cover it. It was, after all, no more than she deserved.

Fred stood in the kitchen with his hands on his hips and tutted. Bloody woman, never here anyway, was it too much to ask to have a meal made for him when he was out fishing at all hours. She fawned after the bloody vicar more than she did her own husband.

He poked about in the unfamiliar domain of the kitchen and found a basket of mushrooms. He opened the fridge and found bacon and eggs. Job done, he thought, opening cupboards, looking for a frying pan. He could rustle dinner up for himself.

He grabbed the loaf from the bread bin and hacked a huge slice from it and slathered the butter on generously. Edwina was exceptionally stingy with butter, so he went all out in her absence.

Sitting at the kitchen table with his plate of mushrooms, bacon, fried eggs, and bread and butter he congratulated himself on being a highly capable man. He also thought to himself as he happily tucked in, how much he had enjoyed having the house to himself, being able to eat exactly what he wanted to eat, wearing the clothes of his choice.

* * *

Jesse was sitting comfortably in Jonathan's office with her eyes closed. She was warm and relaxed and listening to his voice. Her limbs were loose and she felt wonderfully calm.

Jonathan had been talking to her quietly for some time. He was using a technique whereby Jesse imagined she was watching or flying above her memories. They weren't her, and she was an observer of the proceedings. Like she was watching the events on television. Jesse had liked this idea. She wanted to be removed from it. She was clear that she didn't want to experience it or feel what she must have felt. She was certain she would never recover from the terror again.

Jonathan's clear voice was prepping her brain to access the memories, but to not be a part of them. Doug, at her request, was sitting quietly in the corner.

Following her day with Doug she had felt much closer to him. She still couldn't explain how she felt when he was around, but she knew she felt so much better when he *was* around, and it was the same for Brock.

She had asked Jonathan if Doug could sit in on the sessions and listen. She had explained to Jonathan it was as important for Doug to know what happened on the island as it was for her, since Doug felt guilty for choosing to do his duty over helping to rescue her.

They were nearly ready to go. Jonathan was instructing her to think back to the day when she was at the station, and they received the phone call that someone was tampering with the inshore lifeboat. Jesse had settled back and started to talk.

Doug watched Jesse nervously; deep down he was terrified for her. He knew this was an incredibly big deal for her. To try and remember. He knew that she was petrified of reliving it, but at the same time she was determined that she wasn't going to be held prisoner by an attack by Chris a second time. Doug's admiration for Jesse was off the scales.

He didn't think he knew of anyone quite so gutsy in facing their demons and their worst nightmares. He hoped that this would help her remember past the attack. Help her to remember their life together and their relationship.

Jesse had requested that the session be recorded so she could listen to it again. Jonathan had advised against it, but Jesse was adamant. Doug pressed record and closed his eyes as she started talking; describing walking around the harbour to the boat shed.

An hour later, Doug opened his eyes again. He was exhausted, wrung out. Tears had been flowing freely down his face unchecked for some time now and his shirt was covered with splotches of wet.

Jesse was sitting quietly.

Jonathan was still talking, bringing her into the room and the present day, reminding her gently that she was in hospital, she was safe, and that Doug was in the room. He told her that she could open her eyes and join the conversation.

He watched her open her eyes and blink a few times. She stretched and rolled her shoulders and glanced at Doug.

'You OK?' she asked, frowning. 'You look upset. Why is your shirt all wet?'

'I'm fine,' Doug croaked.

Jesse turned to Jonathan. 'Guess it didn't work, huh?'

Jonathan gave a sideways look to Doug.

'Do you feel it didn't work, Jesse?'

She glanced at Doug. 'I don't remember anything new. Sorry, Doug,' she said. 'What a waste of your time.'

'I wouldn't call it a waste of time at all, Jesse,' said Jonathan.

'How's that? I genuinely don't remember anything new.'

'The thing is, Jesse, you can remember. In that session, you remembered everything. Right up until where you went off the cliff. You shared it all,' Jonathan said quietly.

She blinked. 'That's nonsense,' she said disbelievingly. 'I'd remember it now surely?' She looked at Doug. 'Wait… is that why you look so—'

Jonathan cleared his throat. 'Jesse, I want to consult a colleague. Don't be disheartened. I think we're close. Really close. I think we should try again tomorrow to link the two. Past memories to present consciousness.'

Jesse ran her hands through her hair in desperation.

'So what? I've just gone through it all? Told you everything that happened?' She frowned. 'So you both know everything that happened, and I can't remember a bloody thing about it?' She focused on Jonathan. 'How is that even possible?'

Jonathan pulled a rueful face. 'Jesse, it's your conscious mind not wanting to face it and accept it. Your mind is happy to recall it when safe parameters are set. Like today for example, you were an impartial observer. Not emotionally connected. So it was easy to see what happened.'

'But I want to remember,' Jesse wailed tearfully. 'I just want – no – I *need* to move on.'

'Same time tomorrow, Jesse. We will make progress, I promise. Now the best thing you can do is go and sleep for a while. You need to. It's like pressing reset on the brain.'

'No. I want to… I need to go to the beach. Just to be on the beach with Brock for a while. I won't walk too far. Just to clear my head. Please, Jonathan? Just for a few hours?'

'I'm happy to go along with this,' Jonathan said. 'It suggests you're healing well. Doug, do you have the time to take Jesse?'

Doug nodded. Still not trusting himself to speak.

Jonathan pointed at Jesse and said sternly, 'Don't overdo it. A few hours, then back here for a rest.'

The two rode in silence towards Castleby to collect Brock. Doug felt emotionally exhausted and had no idea what to say to Jesse. Jesse had been looking out of the window, largely thinking the same thing. Doug drove down to the beach and pulled up next to a row of benches at the end of the car park.

'Hang on here. I'll pop home and get him.'

Jesse gave him a wan smile. She appreciated the gesture, meaning she wouldn't have to walk all the way down the steep path from Doug's house to the beach. She also suspected he knew she needed a minute or two by herself. She moved slowly to the edge of beach and sat on one of benches.

She sat and watched the sea, soothed by its relentless motion. She breathed deeply and felt herself relax. She breathed in the salty air and listened to the sounds of tide and the seagulls calling. This was her music. Sounds that soothed her.

She heard an excitable bark and opened her eyes to see Brock running flat out towards her. She knelt to greet him, and he covered her face with licks. She hugged him tightly and felt tears prickle behind her eyes. She sat for a moment on the sand, holding Brock's warm body tightly and closed her eyes.

'Better?' asked Doug, smiling down at her.

She nodded.

Doug held out a hand to help her to her feet and was careful to keep his distance.

She stood awkwardly, brushing sand from her trousers. 'Have you got time to walk with me?' she asked.

'Of course.'

She held out her hand for him to hold.

They walked for a while and Brock scampered off, his ears up and tail whirring around. He stopped and picked up a huge stick and proceeded to follow them along the beach clouting the backs of their legs as he ran past with it.

'He's happy, he's not done that for ages,' Doug said.

'It's his happy thing,' Jesse observed.

'It is. He's pleased to have you here. So am I.'

Jesse squeezed Doug's hand. 'So. Earlier... Bad, huh? What you heard?'

'I don't know what to call it.'

'Do you think about me differently?'

'Why would I think about you differently?'

'I don't know. You know what happened. I don't.'

'I don't think any differently about you, Jesse. I feel exactly the same as I always have.'

'Did I do something so bad that I'm blocking it out?'

'Not in my view.'

'Why do you think I can't remember?'

'Ach, I'm no shrink, but I do see sense in what Jonathan's saying. What his theory is... that the terror, the fright of it, is enough to keep it buried. It must have been off the scale terrifying to face him again.'

Jesse was quiet as she breathed in the salty air. 'I don't want to go back tonight, Doug.'

'Then call Felix and ask him for a night pass.'

'You reckon he'll allow it?'

'He's at home sucking up to Claire at the moment, I'm sure he'll agree to anything. But he won't let you be by yourself.'

'Can I stay at yours on the sofa?' Jesse asked.

'You know Claire's at home, right?'

135

Jesse snorted. 'She doesn't scare me, she's been quite good to me. I just need to be away from the hospital.'

Doug slung an arm loosely around her shoulders.

Jesse had a sudden memory of him doing that and then him kissing her in an alleyway. She blushed.

He eyed her. 'Sorry. Is this not OK?'

'It's fine. I just had a memory that's all.'

'What?'

'Your arm around my shoulders and you kissing me in an alleyway.'

'Ahh… I'm nothing if not resourceful.'

Jesse smiled. 'Let's go and ask Felix.'

Felix agreed readily. He would do anything to impress Claire at the moment. He was taking her out to dinner that evening, so Doug and Jesse had some time together as the kids were at a sleepover.

Jesse was exhausted from the day. She and Doug had eaten a takeaway and she had fallen asleep on the sofa. Doug had covered her with a blanket.

She woke with a start in the middle of the night and experienced a moment of disorientation. She got up and went through the quiet house to the kitchen to get a glass of water.

Sitting at the kitchen table, sipping the water, she noticed Doug's phone on the counter. She picked it up and scrolled through the apps until she found the one she was thinking about. She placed the phone down in front of her and stared at it for an eternity.

Then she pulled the phone towards her, and her finger shook slightly as it hesitated over the play button. She took a deep breath and pressed play.

CHAPTER 11

Chris Cherry lay on his makeshift bed in pain. He had healed, but badly. His fall off a high cliff onto rocks below had been exacerbated by another body landing directly on top of him. He cushioned the fall of the other person, but it had caused him significantly more injuries. His face was not as handsome as it had been and was a patchwork of scars. He now walked with a significant limp and suffered constant pain in most of his body. He hated himself. Once fit, healthy and trim, he was now thin, bony, scar-ridden and walked like a fucking cripple. But he was determined. Every day he forced himself to do more and more. Walk further. Run further. Lift heavier. Swim longer. He needed to build up his stamina and get back to full health.

On one of his longer runs he had come across a small town that housed a pay per use computer with internet access in a tiny café. He had gone back to the brothers' cottage and scrabbled about for some cash, returning the next day. He had sat and waited for what seemed like hours for the computer to connect and finally a Google search engine popped up. He searched for news about himself and the events on Kirby Island. He saw the usual news, the same thing re-written by different outlets.

Then he saw it. 'Woman Killed Following Attack and Cliff Fall'. He inhaled sharply. The woman wasn't named, but it had to be Jesse. He read the article again and again. It had to be her. She couldn't be dead. No way. He knew she was tougher than that.

There was something familiar about the article, but he couldn't place what it was. He printed it out at a further cost to himself, which took another ten minutes and then left.

As he ran back to the cottage his mind kept spinning. What was it about that article? Then he realised. It was the language. The phrasing. Classic police comms department. Suddenly it all fitted together. In the absence of finding him dead the police had issued a press release. Just in case he'd been looking. Just in case he wanted to come back and finish the job properly. He felt rage building in him like a white-hot sensation. Finish the job? He'd find her and fucking kill her properly once and for all, even if he died in the process. Now he knew she was alive, he felt reborn, full of energy and drive.

He'd get to her soon enough.

* * *

Doug woke in the early hours of the morning. He quietly crept to the kitchen for a drink and as he approached, he heard Jesse's voice and wondered who she was talking to.

He rounded the corner of the kitchen and saw her sitting at the table. She was listening to the recording. She was absolutely still, staring out of the window into the darkness as she listened to herself tell the story of what happened on the island. Doug quietly poured a glass of water and sat at the table. He reached across and held her hand.

They didn't speak at all in the time it took to listen. Sunrise was pushing aside dark cloud with autumnal oranges rising across the sky.

Jesse ended the recording with a shaking hand and pushed the phone away. She closed her eyes for a moment.

'Christ,' she whispered. She turned to Doug and her face crumpled. 'Doug, I—'

'Come here,' he said, pulling her to him. He stood and wrapped his arms around her while she sobbed into his chest.

'I don't know what to think about it,' she whispered. 'I'm so tired. I can hardly stay upright.'

'It's the shock,' Doug said. 'Come on, you need to sleep.'

'I just want to sleep for a week,' she mumbled.

Doug led her into the den where he had been sleeping since Claire had been back recovering in his bedroom. He pulled back the covers and pushed Jesse into bed gently. He went to pull the covers back over her and she held his hand.

'Stay? I want you close.'

Doug climbed in next to her, curling around her back with his arms around her.

She exhaled deeply. 'This I remember,' she said and fell asleep immediately.

Doug had awoken to hear Claire organising the children for school. He had thoroughly enjoyed the sensation of being wrapped around Jesse, having her near. He slowly extracted himself and closed the door carefully, letting her sleep.

Jesse had slept until lunchtime and Doug returned from the station to find her sitting at the kitchen table, with Nessie, Doug's elderly neighbour, tucking into pancakes.

'Looks like I made it back just in time,' he said as Nessie put a plate of pancakes down in front of him. 'Thanks, Nessie.'

'I knew Jesse was here and that she loves pancakes. Claire came and told me she was off for her walk and could I keep an eye on this one.'

Jesse nodded, mouth full. 'They are too good, Nessie. You are too good to me.'

'Who else is going to look after you two?' Nessie chided.

Doug reached out for Nessie's hand. 'Couldn't be without you, Nessie,' he said softly.

Nessie swiped him away with a tea towel, her eyes filling up. 'Oh don't be getting soppy with me, you know I cry at everything.'

'You and Billy both,' Jesse murmured.

Nessie glanced at the clock. 'I have to go,' she said, stacking the dishwasher. 'I'm picking the kids up tonight, so I might see you later.'

'Thanks, Nessie,' said Jesse.

Nessie approached Jesse and held her face in her hands. 'Good to see you here, my love. I've missed you.' She squeezed Doug's hand and disappeared off through the back door.

Doug watched her go and felt a surge of love for her. She had become even more of a mother to him since the loss of his own mother recently. He cleared his throat and looked at Jesse.

'You look good. Rested.'

'I did sleep well. Perhaps it was you,' she said quietly, meeting his eyes.

'Happy to help,' he said. 'OK. Million-dollar question. How do you feel?'

Jesse thought for a moment. 'Relieved.'

'Really?'

She scooped up the last of her pancake. 'Absolutely,' she said with her mouth full. 'I feel... like I've finished the book, if you know what I mean?'

Doug raised an eyebrow.

'Before, it was like this mystery up until a certain point and then nothing, but now I know what happened.'

'Do you feel OK about it?'

'Do I feel OK about it?' she echoed thoughtfully. 'I think I do. I know what happened, so that's a big relief.'

'But, Jesse, do you remember? Do you remember any of it?'

'I don't remember a bloody thing.'

* * *

For hours, Peter had sat quietly by Mabel's bedside. He had been there since 11 p.m. the night before when the sisters had called him for comfort. She had been on the brink of passing. He had seen it before, death. Been there in its presence.

He held Mabel's hand lightly and quietly recited the Lord's Prayer to her. Then he heard it. The last breath of life leaving a body. To him it always sounded very deep and very final, like the spirit was blowing out a large candle. He murmured another prayer and blessed her and sat for a moment feeling melancholy at her passing. He left the room, to inform the nurses.

Peter had arrived back at the vicarage after breakfast, he'd let himself in quietly and heard Mrs Pomeroy hoovering upstairs. He'd wandered into the kitchen and made himself some breakfast and sat for a while drinking a coffee.

Mrs Pomeroy had bustled in with a pained expression and started having a go at him.

'Where have you been? I'm telling you, young man, the vicar won't have you staying out all night getting up to all sorts.'

'Well I can always rely on you to tell him, can't I?' he said sarcastically.

'I beg your pardon?' Mrs Pomeroy placed her hands on her hips, looking affronted as he brushed past her.

'I'm going to grab a few hours' sleep,' Peter said over his shoulder.

'I think I'm entitled to know where you've been all night,' she said tartly.

Peter had stopped and met her eyes levelly. 'Judge not, that ye be not judged, Mrs P.'

'I beg your pardon?'

'Goodnight.'

Peter entered his bedroom and knew instantly that she had been going through his possessions. Suspecting this for some time, he had carefully arranged some things that if moved, he would know. If he guessed correctly, she had been through his drawers, bedside table and wardrobe. *Nothing if not thorough for a nosey old bag*, he thought and then chastised himself for being uncharitable. He would discuss it with the vicar when he got the chance. Some things had to remain sacred.

He lay down on his narrow bed and fell asleep almost instantly. He woke a few hours later to find Mrs Pomeroy standing over him scowling.

'What?' he said.

'You didn't tell us Mabel passed away last night.'

'Yes. It was very peaceful. I was with her. Why is it an issue?'

'Because Vicar will need to go and see the sisters now!' she exploded. 'And that mucks up the whole day!' She rolled her eyes and tutted. 'Lunch is ready,' she said, stomping down the stairs.

Peter entered the kitchen and found the vicar tucking in.

'Ahh, Peter, good job with the sisters and Mabel last night. Such a lovely lady.'

'She was. Life and soul of the party,' Peter said quietly.

Mrs Pomeroy snorted in the corner of the kitchen. 'I don't want to speak ill of the dead, but she was a dreadful cheat. We saw that at the quiz. We should have won fair and square.'

The vicar eyed Peter and pulled a face. 'I don't know about that. I liked her very much. She was always at church and did the most beautiful flowers.'

'Hmph, far too overfamiliar for me. Right, no rest for the wicked. I'm off to get some groceries.' She picked up her basket and shopping trolley on wheels and left.

'You must be shattered if you were with her most of the night, Peter,' the vicar said with concern.

'I've had a few hours' sleep this morning.'

'Right, dear boy, I must get on. You're down to see Joy Brown this afternoon, aren't you? Do give her my best, won't you? Mrs P has left her some soup, I think.'

Dusk was falling as Peter let himself out of Joy's door and headed back to the vicarage. She had been very unhappy at Mrs P's visit yesterday and felt that nothing was confidential anymore. Peter assured her that everything was confidential, but he wasn't sure if that had convinced her. She seemed to have quite the bee in her bonnet over Mrs P and had requested pointedly that the woman not come and bother her again. Peter had agreed and told her that she should just call and make an appointment with him. They had talked about her loneliness and a few family issues and Peter had asked her to come and help out at the next coffee morning which was two days away. Delighted at feeling useful she had agreed.

* * *

Mrs Pomeroy had trudged back to the vicarage with the groceries, muttering about a couple of parishioners she had run into. She stopped to collect a special delivery from the woman who made Peter feel uncomfortable, and then let herself back into the vicarage quietly.

She unpacked the shopping, careful to keep all the things she had purchased for herself using the money from the church tucked into her basket with a cloth over the top. Things that were 3 for 1, or 2 for 1, she would always take advantage of and feather her own nest with. After all, it was no more than she deserved.

She finished her chores, made dinner for the vicar and Peter, then made some more cakes and broth for the parishioners.

She arrived home after 9 p.m. that evening to find the house empty. She concluded Fred must be out on a long fishing trip. Sometimes they went a few days without seeing each other. She made herself one of her special teas and went upstairs to bed to catch up on a few soaps she had missed and to write in her diary.

Fred, Mrs Pomeroy's husband, was lying on the deck of his boat writhing in agony in the darkness. He had cut the engine much earlier and deep down he knew the boat was drifting aimlessly, but he couldn't get up to drop the anchor. His stomach felt like it was on fire and he had been retching for hours. He wanted to pull his insides out just for some relief from the pain.

He was on the boat on his own and had been for at least twelve hours now. He felt so bad he couldn't even make it up to the wheelhouse to call in a Mayday. Fred had a sixth sense that he wasn't going to make it back. He had started vomiting blood and he was losing it from his back passage too. The deck beneath him was slick with vomit, blood and excrement. He felt like his skin was burning and he screamed and thrashed about trying to make the pain stop. With superhuman effort he managed to raise himself to the edge of the boat. His brain was telling him that the water would put out the flames. He tipped himself over the edge of the boat and had a blissful thirty seconds as the cool water touched his skin.

Then the sea took him.

He hears me when I call to him. He has told me to bring forth justice to the nations. I will begin my work. This work is so important – no one else can perform it. These people, some are so desperate, so needy. So selfish. Do they not know that the life they lead will send them to Lucifer and not to the heavenly kingdom? How can they not know? Where is their faith? I have assured Him. I will help you cleanse. I will forsake those who choose not to come with me on my journey to enlightenment.

CHAPTER 12

After Jimmy had come round following his visit with Pearl, he had stashed the contents of the suitcase in a knackered chest freezer that he used for bait in his lock-up. He had tried not to look at JJ's limbs and torso, but noted that the Camorra had kept one of JJ's hands.

Jimmy was very unhappy on two counts. The first being that he now had to get rid of the rest of JJ and secondly, he was now on the Camorra's radar as one of their 'special friends'. Meaning he basically had to do whatever they wanted him to. This made him very uncomfortable. He knew the parameters they would stretch to, and he certainly didn't want to end up like Huey or even worse – JJ.

He was having sleepless nights wondering what to do with JJ's frozen body. Part of him felt the sensible thing to do was to take him out to sea and drop him over the side; but then if he was washed up, then they'd be able to match it to the head or worse, him.

He was struggling to think of options – didn't pigs eat people? Did he know anyone with a pig farm? He was sure he'd seen that in a Guy Ritchie film before.

He could dig a deep hole and bury it, but there was always the risk of someone finding it, usually a bloody dog walker. He could burn it he supposed, but then he'd have to defrost it. He just couldn't think what to do with it. He wondered to himself what the slippery JJ would do if it was him, and then the answer came to him. He would give it back to the Camorra.

He just needed to find out which places they used and put it back there without them knowing. By the looks of it, they were fairly well versed in cutting people up and freezing them. So that was his plan.

Thing was, Jimmy had no real idea where they operated from. It wasn't something he could google either, let alone ask around locally about, that would raise too many eyebrows. He'd have to somehow talk to Alexy and see what he knew.

Then he remembered. They had pictures of him talking to Steve. This must mean that they were either watching him, or Steve the copper. Jimmy vowed to be more aware of who was around him and if he could, he would follow them. Follow the follower. Very pleased with his deductive prowess, he decided to reward himself with a swift pint in the pub.

* * *

Steve had received the call about Mabel's passing from the care home manager that morning and had promised to call in and collect a copy of the visitor logs. Steve pondered her death as he drove, and his mind drifted to the evening he'd had with Kate in the pub discussing the issue. He liked her very much, she was funny, dry and smart and had a refreshingly no-nonsense approach to things. He

148

found it amusing that she used the same phrase as Foxy liked to use: 'crack on'.

The town was busy with the Saturday farmers' market and Steve edged his car through the crowd and down the high street. Halfway down the narrow street he saw Kate walking up the road towards him, dressed casually in jeans and a jumper. She had a windswept rosy glow about her. She was being pulled along the road relentlessly by a black Labrador. Steve stopped his car and buzzed the window down.

'Excuse me, madam, I think I'm going to have to take you in for questioning regarding your control of animals,' he called out of the window.

'Hello!' Kate said, laughing as the Labrador put both feet on the side of the car to see Steve.

'You off today?' he asked.

'I am. I've been on the beach, I'm desperate for a coffee now.'

'Fancy some company?' he asked hopefully.

The car behind blew the horn loudly and Steve glanced in his rear-view mirror.

'Hang on one minute.' He climbed out of the car and walked back towards the truck. He saw the queue of traffic behind it and pulled his warrant card from his pocket, holding it up to the queue of drivers to indicate he would be a few minutes.

He leant on the side of the truck. 'Hello, Jimmy,' he said pleasantly. 'How are you?'

'Fine thanks,' Jimmy said, looking directly ahead and not meeting Steve's eye.

'You in a hurry? Hooting at people would suggest there's some sort of emergency?' asked Steve mildly.

'Not particularly.'

'We'll need to have a chat soon about JJ.'

'What about JJ?'

'Well, a chat about where the rest of JJ might be and how his head appeared.'

'Whatever,' said Jimmy. 'I don't know. Are you going to be much longer chatting up that woman? I need to get on and you're holding up traffic.'

'That woman over there?' Steve pointed to Kate who was leaning against Steve's car. 'Do you know where she's from?'

'No.' Jimmy frowned.

'She's Scotland Yard's finest forensic pathologist.'

'What?' Jimmy almost wet himself.

'Oh yeah, I've called her in to look at JJ's head and the pot. She's quite confident that she'll be able to retrieve a raft of DNA and samples from them.'

'Surely it was in the water too long? From what I heard,' Jimmy said desperately.

'Not according to her. Anyway, better let you crack on then, Jimmy. No rest for the wicked and all that. Be seeing you.'

Jimmy didn't trust himself to speak. Steve wandered back to his car and got in, saying something to the woman. She walked back towards the harbour, chatting to him as he drove slowly down the high street. Jimmy stared at Kate as he pulled past Steve and accelerated away.

'Why was that guy staring at me? What did you say to him?' she asked as they walked up the road to a café overlooking the harbour.

'I told him that you were a top forensic pathologist for Scotland Yard, here to look at a head that was pulled out of the sea.' Steve laughed.

'Why would you tell him that?' she asked, incredulous.

'Because he's got something to do with it. That's why, and I want to put the wind up him.'

'Inspector Miller are you fabricating evidence?' she asked in mock shock.

'No. I am merely creating a narrative to prompt some activity. Latte? Cappuccino?' he asked, standing by the counter.

'Latte, please,' she said, then went to sit down on the outside balcony in the autumn sunshine.

'Who is he anyway?' she asked when Steve returned.

'Local fisherman and lightweight criminal. He's alright, just gets himself into trouble. He's a bit hapless. Had a couple of brushes with the law and helped us put away a drug smuggling ring. But he can't seem to keep his nose clean.'

'So a head was found? Who did it belong to?'

'A guy called JJ. Bit more of a serious criminal, a frequent flyer with us. His mate was killed horribly few months back. Local organised crime proving a point and I reckon JJ met the same fate. Jimmy is on the periphery of it somehow.'

'Organised crime? Here?' Kate was shocked.

'It's everywhere, Kate. The criminal underbelly doesn't differentiate by postcode.'

'Who's the organised crime here?' she leant forward whispering, eyes wide.

'Local gangsters, Mickey and Pearl Camorra. Ruthless, but like Teflon. Nothing sticks. We've got other smaller groups, drugs, trafficking, etc.'

'Christ.' Kate was surprised. 'Who knew?'

'Life is never quiet.'

'And yet you have time to have coffee with me.'

'Happy to take the time out,' he said, looking her directly in the eye. 'I really enjoyed the other night.'

'Me too,' Kate agreed.

'So. Any luck finding somewhere to live?'

'Yes!' she said, delighted. 'I found somewhere this morning! It's perfect. I'm going to rent with a view to buying. I've done the deal already.'

'Where is it?'

'It's the Watchman's Cottage near the castle. The owner mentioned to Dad that he was thinking about renting it and Dad told him I was after a place. I saw it this morning – it's perfect. Gorgeous views from every window!' She pulled a face. 'It's a total "chintz-a-thon" though. Needs a good coat of paint, a clear out and a bit of love, but it's perfect and pretty reasonable. They're happy to let me paint it.'

'Great! When do you get the keys?'

'Got them now! I'm off to buy paint and things in a while and then I'm going back to crack on and start painting.'

'Need a hand later?'

'Really? You any good with paint?'

'I like to think I can hold my own,' he said mildly.

'You're on. I'd love that. Thanks,' she said, grinning. 'Don't you have plans later? Saturday night and all that?'

'I now have plans with a paintbrush it appears,' Steve said, rising. 'Look I've got to go, but I'll see you up there when I've knocked off and got changed. OK?'

'Perfect. See you later.' She grinned at him. 'Look forward to it.'

Steve winked and jogged back to his car and headed off to the care home. He realised that he had forgotten to mention to Kate that there had been another death. But he would be insisting on a post-mortem for Mabel, so he made a mental note to tell Kate later.

* * *

Sam Jones lay in in his hospital bed. He had seen his beautiful Sophie this morning, seen her face full of hope, wanting to see him. To talk to him. But he couldn't do it. He couldn't look into her hopeful eyes and lose himself, being as broken as he was. The annoying nurse called Lottie had gone to talk to her and she had left.

He had concluded that he would like to die and would try to do so at the earliest opportunity. He wasn't the same man who Sophie had known. He was useless. No legs. No career. Can't provide. Probably couldn't even make love to her. Not a peep out of his old man. Not even the morning horn had appeared. Like she would even want to think about sex with him now. Like this.

Sam saw no future. He hated lying in bed with the cheerful nurse faffing about nattering on. He wanted to scream at her to shut the fuck up and go away forever. Give him drugs to make him die. Make him forget. That was what we wanted. He didn't want to rehash his experience. He didn't want to get better. He wanted to die. Part of him missed lying on the hard floor in the hot fetid room. When he was there he knew he was going to die. He'd accepted it. He knew he'd welcome it in the end. He had searched for news of his rescue, but nothing. No news of any kind of the torture and horror he and his fellow soldiers had endured. He had found other news though.

He had found news of his son being lost on the mountain with his friend who rescued him, and he watched the short footage of two soldiers who had helped with the rescue. He presumed Sophie must know them.

He read about the man who tried to strangle Sophie and had killed her mother all those years ago. The news had said a friend had saved her and intimated it had been a man. Sam wondered if he had been one of the soldiers. He had studied them on the short film, they were both good-looking chaps about her age. Sam wanted

Sophie to move on. Start a new life. He wanted to make her happy. He wanted to die so she could be free. That would make him happy and no doubt make Sophie happy in the long run. He just didn't want to live anymore.

Sophie was sitting in the canteen with Lottie, Sam's specialist nurse, having coffee and discussing Sam. He still resolutely refused to see Sophie, despite her best efforts.

'I don't know what to do about it,' Sophie mused unhappily. 'What's he said to you?'

'Nothing. He doesn't say anything to me apart from yes or no. This isn't unusual though, Sophie,' Lottie said reassuringly.

'I don't understand. Why wouldn't he want to see me, so we can work towards getting him better?'

'Honestly? At this stage, many patients who have experienced what Sam has, think it's over for them. That life isn't worth the effort.'

'Well that's rubbish. Of course it's not over,' Sophie said.

'In their view it is. Their livelihood is over, their career, their physical freedom. For some men, it's the end of an active sex life. That's pretty tough to accept if you're fairly young and healthy.'

'What can I do?' Sophie dropped her head into her hands.

Lottie laid a reassuring hand on Sophie's. 'Time. You need to give him time. Write to him too. He has an iPad he uses. He doesn't have to see you to read the emails.'

'He uses an iPad?'

'He's been watching the news, catching up with things.'

'OK. I'll email. Is he likely to reply?'

'Probably not, but it might be the difference between seeing you and not seeing you. It's happened with other patients. They wanted to see their spouse after a while.'

'What about coming home for a weekend in a few weeks?'

'I think we should plan for it. He'll want to hide out here. But we'll have to almost bully him into it. We can't let his world get too small.'

'Shall I write to him about the weekend?'

'Yes. Tell him what's going on and what to expect. He'll kick off about coming but it'll be good for him.'

'So it's no use going back upstairs and trying to talk to him?'

Lottie shook her head. 'Sorry, Sophie. He'll just get agitated again. Tell you what. Go home, write to him a little every day, about everyday life. Tell him you're not coming next weekend. But you will the weekend after and then after that he's coming home for a weekend. The regularity of contact might help.'

'Right. I'll go then,' Sophie said sadly. 'Thanks, Lottie. Appreciate it. The weekend when he comes home. Will I drive him? How do I get him home?'

Lottie waved a hand. 'Leave that to us. We want to get him to you, minimum of fuss and discomfort. Sometimes they dig out a chopper and take them if it's a way away.'

Sophie's eyes widened. 'Fly him home?'

'Maybe. Also, if transport is booked, many of these guys don't tend to want to mess anyone around by refusing it, so it's a win–win. I'll look into it. Which weekend is best?'

Sophie thought for a moment. 'We have the carnival of the sea in the last weekend in November. It's brilliant. Sam's always loved it. Even before I lived there permanently we would come for the weekend just to see it. The whole town comes alive, there's a big procession, then a huge beach bonfire and then in the morning there's a huge swim around the point with everyone dressed up like sea creatures or characters.'

155

'Sounds wonderful!' Lottie exclaimed. 'You know, sometimes, they ask a nurse to accompany. Would you mind if I came? It sounds perfect if he's always loved it.'

'I'd love it if you came with him. It would be such a weight off my mind, with all his needs.'

'Consider it done,' she said firmly. 'I'll book transport. If there's a helipad at the nearest hospital they'll land there, and we'll get to you that way.'

'There's an MOD base a few miles away.'

'Well, then that's blimmin' perfect!' She looked at her watch. 'I have to get back. Feel free to drop me a line if you want to,' she said, whipping out a pen and scribbling her email on a napkin. 'Be good to keep in touch.'

'Thanks, Lottie.' Sophie felt more reassured.

'Drive safely,' she said. 'See you.'

'Bye,' echoed Sophie.

Sophie stood feeling wrung out. A four-hour drive this morning and an hour at the hospital, only to face a four-hour return drive home, left her feeling exhausted. As she was climbing into her car the phone rang. It was Foxy.

'Hello you,' she greeted him.

'Hey yourself,' he said. 'Hang on a minute.' She heard him raise his voice. 'Jacob. I see that again and you're out. For good. Do you understand me? Marcus, keep an eye on him and report in. Comprendo? You there, Soph?'

'What's Jacob up to?'

'Being a little fucking shit,' Foxy muttered into the phone. 'Before you ask, Marcus is fine. I was just checking in with you. How's it going?'

Sophie felt a huge rush of affection for her friend.

'Still won't see me. Refused point blank. Got really agitated.'

'For fuck's sake.'

'I've just had a coffee and a really good chat with his nurse, Lottie, though. She's suggested a few things. She's going to bring him home for the carnival of the sea weekend.'

'Wow. Good news.'

'Hmmm.'

'What are you doing now?'

'Sat in the car just about to drive home.'

'You OK to drive? Not too tired? How about I cook you dinner?'

'Carol's got to leave by seven tonight, somethings come up for her.'

'OK. I'll close up later and bring his lordship home. He can help me cook at yours. OK? Give you a break. You'll be home by what? Six? Seven?'

'Sounds like heaven. Thanks. Rob. I really appreciate everything you do for me.'

'It's no problem. See you later. Drive safe.'

Foxy had resorted to spaghetti bolognaise as Marcus had moaned about everything when they had called into the supermarket for dinner. In desperation Foxy had sent Marcus off to get something for pudding while he had grabbed a couple of bottles of wine.

The sauce was simmering, and Marcus was sitting at the kitchen table doing his homework when Sophie walked in. Carol, Jack's carer, had just left and Foxy had put Jack in front of the news for a while. He could hear him arguing with the newsreader and was keeping a subtle ear on him. Sophie looked shattered.

'Hey,' she said, coming in and kissing Marcus on the head.

'Ugh, get off. Did you see Dad?' he said, shying away.

'No. Still won't let me. It smells amazing in here,' she said, going over and sniffing the sauce.

Foxy handed her a glass of wine. 'I'll stick the pasta on now. You OK?'

'Yes. Thanks. Where's Dad?'

'Watching the news, arguing with the newsreader.'

Sophie watched Marcus working diligently at the table.

'Who are you and what have you done with my son?' she teased Marcus. 'You never do homework in here.'

'I was helping Foxy. Wasn't I?' he challenged.

Foxy turned to the stove smiling. Marcus hadn't helped at all. He had just turned up in the kitchen and announced that he would work there in case Foxy didn't know where anything was. It amused Foxy, as the likelihood of Marcus knowing where anything was in the kitchen was quite slim. Foxy assumed he just wanted some company.

Sophie went into see Jack and Foxy set about finishing dinner.

'Why doesn't Dad want to see Mum?' asked Marcus in a small voice.

'Not really sure. But I can give it my best guess.' Foxy had been expecting questions.

'Go on then.'

Foxy leant against the worktop and folded his huge arms.

'So your dad's a soldier. Not just any soldier. A super bright one too. The guys in military intelligence have brains like planets. So his life, who he is – in here and here.' Foxy pointed to his chest and head. 'It's what defines him as a person. And suddenly that's gone. Taken away. Taken away in the most horrible circumstances too. That's gotta be hard. I suspect he doesn't feel like a man anymore, without his legs. Nor a soldier. He would have realised that his career in the field is over and that everything in life is going to be different and difficult and really hard. He probably feels like he'd be a huge burden to your mum and you, and doesn't want to see anyone because that's how he feels.'

'Savage,' Marcus whispered, his eyes huge.

'It is.'

'Do you think he won't want to see me?'

'That's tougher in a way, I think. Your son seeing you when you feel like that about yourself. I suspect in most dads' eyes they want their sons to see them as heroes and not broken.'

'I think he's a hero for making it through that.'

'Then you should tell him that.'

'I will.'

'Good. Pasta's ready. Pass those plates.'

Marcus called through the door that dinner was ready, and Jack appeared.

'Ahh hello, my boy,' he said to Foxy. 'Just wondering whether you know if I have to wear full school uniform for dinner, or am I OK in this?'

'No. Schools out today, Jack, no uniform needed.' Foxy guided him to a chair.

'Excellent,' said Jack happily. He glanced at Marcus. 'Hello. Who are you?'

'This is Marcus,' Foxy said, passing Jack a plate.

'Boy needs a haircut,' Jack said, pointing at Marcus's hair.

'I'm sure he's planning it.'

'Excellent,' said Jack, tucking in. 'Hello, dear,' he said as Sophie came in. He waved his fork at Foxy and Marcus. 'This young man has said he will cut this boy's hair before the school term starts, so you don't have to worry. Oh, and we don't need to wear school uniform today.'

'There's a relief.' Sophie glanced at Foxy.

After dinner Marcus reluctantly washed up and Sophie collapsed on the sofa after putting Jack to bed.

'Man, I am knackered,' she said, leaning back on the sofa and closing her eyes. 'Thanks so much for dinner. You are so good with Dad. I really appreciate it.'

'No problem. Now, tell me what the nurse said.'

Sophie recounted what Lottie had said, explaining about the emails and how they would get him home for a weekend. Foxy listened, nodding.

'Sounds very sensible. Let me know if you need some furniture moved about for that.'

Sophie closed her eyes. 'God, yes. So I was thinking I'd use Dad's study for Sam. It's on the flat, next to the loo and kitchen.'

'Seems sensible. Shout when you want that done. I would just say…' he stopped himself.

'What?' Sophie opened her eyes and glanced at him. 'What?'

'Just think about what you put in the email. Don't give him any cause for concern about anything.'

'Like what?'

'Like talk about who you're spending time with, etc. Just in case he reads it wrong.'

'Like Carla reading us wrong?'

Foxy looked rueful. 'Yeah, like Carla. So is that all Lottie said?'

'She asked if she could come too.'

'You OK with that?'

'Hell yeah. I need all the help I can get. She's given me her direct email so we can sort out the details.'

'Sounds like a plan then,' said Foxy. 'He just needs to go along with it.'

* * *

160

Dressed in an old paint-spattered Guns 'n' Roses T-shirt and equally paint-spattered faded jeans, Steve chucked his tool box in the back of his car along with a couple of dust sheets that he'd dug out and slammed the boot. He drove off looking forward to the evening ahead with Kate.

It had been a couple of years since he'd done any decorating. He just didn't seem to find the time with work, or more to the point, find the inclination, which he semi-justified with the fact that he had bought a brand-new home purposefully, so it didn't require anything doing to it.

He had surprised himself by offering to help, but he found he couldn't help himself. He liked Kate a lot and wanted to get to know her better. He parked up in the space next to the cottage and what he assumed was Kate's Volvo, and grabbed his gear. Kate greeted him at the door.

'That's a good look on you,' she said, raising an eyebrow as she appraised his outfit. 'Nice to see you out of a suit. Didn't Guns 'n' Roses do "Sweet Child O' Mine"?'

'Absolute bloody anthem,' he said seriously. 'How have you managed to get paint on your ear already?' he asked, squeezing past her with his gear.

'What's that for?' She pointed at his tool box.

'In case anything needs putting up, taking down or sorting out.'

'There's a rude joke in there somewhere.'

Steve chuckled. 'Right. What first?'

She pointed to the lounge. 'Painting in here and kitchen. Prepare yourself, it's a 1970s fest in there.'

He followed her through. 'Jesus, you're not wrong,' he said, looking around in wonder. 'It's like a time warp. What's the plan?'

'Everything white to start with and then I'll decide. I need to get a sense of what the light's like, so we'll get rid of the 70s paint and give ourselves a blank canvas. You OK with that?'

'You sound like you know what you're doing,' he said.

'OK. Let's crack on. There's an industrial size pot of white paint in the kitchen.' She handed him a tray and a roller.

After finishing the kitchen and the lounge, they moved upstairs to the bedroom. As Kate busied herself laying out dustsheets over the enormous bed and wardrobe, Steve started painting.

'Meant to tell you, there's been another death,' he said as he stretched up to reach the higher parts of the wall.

Kate wasn't really paying attention. She had been slightly sidetracked by Steve in those jeans and his old T-shirt all evening. The jeans were old and worn, but Christ alive they fitted him well. She stood for a moment checking out his backside as he bent and stretched with the roller.

'Kate?'

'God, sorry. What?' She blushed.

'You were miles away. I said there's been another death.'

'Oh no. Who was it?'

'Mabel. She was in The Grange.'

'So sad. Poor thing. I expect Dad's been informed. I've not seen him today at all. I'll make sure there's a PM done.'

'Can you do me a favour and look over her notes? And those from the care home? I've got the visitor logs. We're analysing them.'

Kate nodded thoughtfully. 'Someone mentioned Mabel the other day. Said her illness was sudden.'

'All the more reason to look into it.' Steve raised an eyebrow.

'Absolutely. Come on. We'll finish this wall and the bathroom, and I'll spring for a beer.'

'Promises, promises.'

'I'm good for it.'

'Best we crack on then. I'm getting thirsty.'

CHAPTER 13

Steve and Kate were sitting in Maggie's having breakfast, both nursing Sunday morning hangovers.

'When you said you'd spring for a beer, I didn't think it would be that many,' Steve moaned as he sipped his double espresso.

'Lightweight,' Kate chided, downing two paracetamols and a huge glass of water. 'Come on. Work through the pain.'

'You're ruthless. No heart. No soul,' Steve grumbled.

'Shut up and take two of these,' she said, putting two paracetamols in front of him.

Maggie appeared with food. 'Heart attack in a roll?' she asked, holding up a plate.

'That would be me,' Steve said, raising his hand. 'If this doesn't make me feel better, I'm going to be useless today.'

Kate regarded him with amusement. 'May I remind you that you were the one calling for shots when the lifeboat boys joined us.'

'God, was I?' he said guiltily. 'What else?'

'What happens in the pub, stays in the pub.' Kate pretended to zip her mouth shut.

'I remember getting a cab home.'

'Oh, the gossip of your car being outside my place all night.'

Steve tucked into his roll and closed his eyes. 'I genuinely think I have died and gone to heaven.'

'What's even in there?'

'Bacon, egg, sausage, portobello mushroom and a hash brown. It's the breakfast of champions.'

'Christ. You'll be on heart pills before long if you carry that on.'

'Are you offering me a free physical check-up?' he asked, looking innocent.

'Depends how you perform today,' she teased. 'A man's stamina is so very important. Eating stuff like that affects it.'

'Is stamina important now? Is that a proven medical fact?' He raised an eyebrow.

'It is,' she said, delicately eating her scrambled eggs. 'Crucially important. There's been some quite extensive research around the area too.'

'Has there now?' Steve was intrigued and enjoying the banter. 'Best you talk me through that.'

'Well, there's a great deal of intervening factors that affect a man's stamina...'

'Which are?'

'Age. Weight. Fitness. Diet. Alcohol consumption. Profession.'

'Thorough research...'

'There are areas where the research can be improved through, you know... through further research,' she said.

'Which areas would those be?' Steve asked mildly.

Maggie walked behind them. 'Oh for God's sake you two, get a room,' she said, rolling her eyes.

Feeling better after one of Maggie's breakfasts, the two headed back to Kate's to carry on painting. They were on a second coat in a lot of the rooms, and Steve had offered to take off the shower head in the bathroom so Kate could descale it. It was just a pathetic trickle and caked in limescale.

He was standing in the shower with a couple of adjustable wrenches carefully positioned when he felt the thread give. Or what he thought was the thread. Water suddenly gushed out of the shower head soaking him. He swore loudly and quickly tightened the pipe back up again until it was just a dribble.

'What are you swearing about? Oh, look at you!' Kate laughed, appearing at the door. 'Did it not want to come off?'

'It would appear not,' he said, shaking water out of his eyes 'I've turned the water off, so I don't know where it's coming from.'

'Your T-shirt's soaked!'

'I need some tape to sort that joint,' he said to her. 'Come and hold this.'

Kate giggled and stepped carefully into the bath. 'This and this?' she asked, carefully holding the wrenches.

'Yup. Don't move. I'll be back in two minutes. I've got some in the toolbox,' he said, climbing out of the bath and heading down the stairs.

A minute later he was back with the tape.

'Right,' he said. 'I'm going to get even wetter doing this, I think.' He glanced at her. 'Sorry,' he said stripping off his T-shirt and chucking it over a towel rail.

'It's… er… fine,' Kate said, aware she was standing very close to a half-naked man who was becoming more attractive to her by the minute.

Oblivious, Steve peered up at the shower.

'Bugger, there's a tiny anchor screw there. Hang on. Don't move,' he said, climbing out of the bath again. As he ran down the stairs to his toolbox the front door knocker sounded.

'I'll get it,' shouted Steve.

He grabbed the screwdriver and opened the door to a tall man with strawberry blond hair and a disdainful expression.

'Help you?' asked Steve, wondering who this man was.

'I'm looking for Kate. I'm her husband, Matthew,' the man said snippily. 'Her mother told me that I could find her here.'

'I see,' said Steve, suddenly aware that he was just in jeans.

'Who are you?' the man asked haughtily, looking him up and down. 'The plumber? A workman?'

Steve took an instant dislike to the man. He knew he had mucked Kate about and that made him dislike him even more. He couldn't help himself.

'I'm Steve,' he said. 'No, I'm not the plumber or a workman.' He gestured behind him vaguely. 'Kate's in the shower. All this decorating is hot and dirty work, you know.'

Behind him he heard Kate call. 'Hurry up! It's dripping everywhere!' And he knew Matthew had heard it too.

'Coming, gorgeous,' he called over his shoulder, winking at Matthew. 'I was taking her up a towel. I'll tell her you called. She won't be free for a while yet.' Steve slammed the door in his face and ran back up the stairs laughing.

'Why on earth are you calling me gorgeous? Who was that at the door?'

Steve stepped in the shower with the screwdriver in his mouth and took one of the wrenches. He unscrewed the small screw and carefully manoeuvred the shower head off. There was a gush of water that mainly went over him and then it stopped.

'One shower head for descaling,' he said, handing it to her.

'Thanks,' she said, peering at it. 'Ugh, look at the state of it. Who was that at the door?'

'OK. Two things. Don't be cross. No, three things. So that was Matthew at the door.'

'Matthew?'

'Your husband.'

'Why am I going to be cross?'

'Eh, I opened the door like this, he thought I was the plumber. He annoyed me. I thought I'd have some fun.'

'Fun?'

'I told him you were in the shower. That decorating was hot and dirty work…'

'I see.' Her mouth twitched.

'And then you shouted down, and I might have pretended that we were…'

'Pretended we were in the shower? Ah… hence calling me that.'

He looked guilty.

He grabbed a wrench off her. 'Besides,' he said, giving her a quick peck on the cheek and climbing out of the bath. 'You are totally gorgeous. A man can't help himself.'

Kate smiled to herself as she stepped out of the bath. She was perfectly happy that Steve had told Matthew that, and she was even more happy that he had kissed her cheek and told her she was gorgeous.

The door knocker went again, and Kate stood on the other side of the door, determined not to open it.

'Who is it?' she called.

'It's Matthew,' came the irritated voice. 'For goodness' sake. Let me in, Kate.'

Kate leant back against the closed door. 'Well, it's not very convenient at the moment, Matthew. I'm not really dressed and I'm a bit… busy.'

Steve had chosen that moment to walk into the hall and saw Kate leaning with her back against the closed door having a conversation over her shoulder.

'Perhaps you could come back in an hour or so, Matthew?'

Steve took a chance. He walked towards Kate and stood in front of her, so they were close. Bodies touching. He took her face in his hands and then kissed her gently.

For Kate it was totally unexpected and made her feel things she hadn't felt for years.

'Really, Kate. This is highly inconvenient,' Matthew whined through the door.

Kate broke off from kissing Steve for a moment. 'I'm sorry, Matthew,' she said breathlessly, wrapping her arms around Steve's neck and kissing him again. 'I'm just really busy here.'

Kate felt like a giddy teenager. She and Steve had got sidetracked and had been snogging like lovestruck adolescents for at least an hour. She didn't feel like a mature adult who was the local GP.

'This is the sort of decorating I like,' Steve said, coming up for air.

'We're going to run out of rooms to paint,' Kate said, sighing and nuzzling Steve's neck.

'There's always the woodwork,' Steve said, going in again for another deep kiss.

The front door knocker rapped out again, making them both jump.

'Kate.' Matthew's voice came through the door. 'Kate, I'm back. We need to talk.'

Kate reluctantly pulled herself away from Steve. 'I need to go and have this out. I've no idea what he's doing here,' she said, resting her forehead on Steve's chin.

Steve kissed her gently. 'Go on. Take him to Maggie's then he won't make a scene and she'll have your back.'

'OK.' Kate went to the door and called through it. 'Matthew, I'll see you in Maggie's Café in ten minutes. I've just got to finish something up here.'

She heard Matthew swear irritably and then stomp away.

'What are you finishing up here?' asked Steve. 'I'll finish the second coat on the bathroom.'

Kate grabbed him again. 'I'm not finishing up anything,' she said, pulling him close. 'Hopefully I'm starting something. I just wanted another ten minutes of this,' she said, kissing him again.

'I'll take whatever I can get.' Steve grinned.

Kate walked down the hill towards Maggie's and found Matthew who was sitting at a corner table looking out to sea with a grumpy expression.

Maggie caught her eye as she passed and winked.

'Coffee, love?' she asked as she passed her.

'Please, Mags,' Kate said gratefully and slid into the booth opposite Matthew.

'Hello, Matthew. You should have mentioned you were visiting the… what did you used to call it? Oh yeah… the arse end of nowhere,' she said quietly.

Matthew looked annoyed. Kate found herself scrutinising his face and saw deep lines of discontent and frown lines. Mentally she compared him to Steve. Steve had loads of laughter lines and wonderful sparkly eyes. She shook herself.

'I don't need an appointment to visit my wife,' he said irritably.

'Actually, most of the time you do,' Kate said dryly. 'Incidentally, it's soon to be ex-wife, isn't it? Solicitor has the paperwork. I'm sure Anna is keen for you to move this along. Is that why you're here? To bring me the papers to sign?'

Matthew regarded her critically. 'I've come to see you. I can come and see my wife, can't I?'

Kate rubbed her head and thought how much she'd like to be back up at her house decorating, in the broadest sense, with Steve. She sighed. 'Not wanting to appear pedantic, our marriage ended some time ago. I moved here. You had no desire to and if I recall correctly, you described it as the arse end of nowhere, plus Anna was moving in as soon as possible.'

Matthew said nothing. Kate's coffee arrived and she sipped it, watching Matthew over the rim.

'Why are you here, Matthew?'

'Who was that man at the house?'

'None of your business.'

'Of course it is, he looked like a bit of local rough. What is he? Some local builder you're having a bunk up with?'

'I repeat – it's none of your business. Why are you here, Matthew?'

'I've been doing some thinking,' he said theatrically.

'Oh?'

'Well, I don't want to, but I am prepared to.'

'Prepared to what?' Kate was confused.

He rolled his eyes. 'Prepared to move here. With you. As I said. I don't want to, but I'll do it for you.'

'Why do it then?' Kate said, aghast.

'What?'

'Why move here if you don't want to? Hardly a fresh start, is it?'

'As I said, I don't want to, but I'll do it for you.'

'Will Anna be coming?'

Matthew refused to meet her eyes. 'Of course not,' he snapped.

'Ah, that's a shame. I thought you were going to start a family together.'

'Well, it seems that Anna just wants to lie about all day watching television, spending what little money I have,' Matthew said tightly, his eyes sliding away from Kate's.

'So no work for Anna then?' Kate said, amused.

'No, she said because I worked, she wouldn't have to. She appeared quite content to bleed me dry.'

Kate choked back a snort of laughter. 'I'm sorry to hear that,' she said, trying to hide a smile.

Matthew continued, oblivious to Kate. 'So, I ended it and told her to pack her bags. I've put the house on the market and accepted an offer above the asking price.'

'Good for you. So, I can expect my half soon then.'

'Well, we'll use it to buy a house here together,' he said testily.

'Oh, is that your plan?'

'Of course,' he snapped. 'Jesus, keep up, Kate. Clearly your brain has gone to sleep living in a dead backwater like this.'

'Quite the opposite,' Kate said, not prepared to enter into it anymore. 'Matthew, I don't want you here. In fact, I don't want you anywhere. I want out. I can't wait to sign the papers to be free of you. And just so you know, I haven't cited your infidelity as a cause, but I will, and make it very public if you try to screw me over for my half of the house or any sort of maintenance. I will not support you playing *Assassins Creed* all day on the premise of being a consultant.'

Matthew stared at her in amazement.

'Kate, have you taken leave of your senses?' he snapped. 'I have said I will move here to be with you. It's what you wanted, and I've said I'll do it. That's surely enough.'

Kate stood up. 'Matthew, go home. I don't want you anywhere near me. You really are the most self-absorbed and insufferable man. It's taken me a break from you to realise it.'

'Sit down, Kate,' Matthew boomed in his authoritative voice.

'Goodbye, Matthew,' Kate said.

Matthew clamped a hand around her wrist and yanked her back towards him. He spoke quietly and viciously. 'It is quite obvious to me that you're not thinking clearly. Carrying on with some knuckle dragger who doesn't have two brain cells to rub together. I am prepared to forgive you for that minor indiscretion. But I have come all this way to tell you that I will move and make a fresh start with you. It's what you wanted after all.'

Kate snatched her arm away from his painful grip. She rubbed her wrist. 'Interesting that you're talking in past tense about what I wanted.'

'It is what you wanted.'

'Yes, but it's not what I want now, is it?' Kate hissed.

'Your mother seems to think it is.'

'What? My mother? I don't give a fuck about what my mother wants.' Kate was incredulous.

'Don't swear, Kate, it's unbecoming. You've clearly been mixing with the knuckle draggers to start using that sort of language.'

'Matthew, this is getting out of hand. I don't know how much clearer I can be. I don't want you here or in my life anymore. It's over between us. Whatever we had died with Daniel and your behaviour afterwards cemented it. I will be going ahead with the divorce.'

Matthew grabbed her hand again. His face was flushed and his mouth a thin line of anger. He yanked her close to him. 'I will decide when and if it's over for us,' he said through gritted teeth. 'My behaviour after Daniel? Jesus Christ, woman. I could ruin you. Tell everyone that their precious new GP is an absolute mental case. That she couldn't get out of bed for a month. Cried constantly, never slept, didn't eat and was a bloody wreck. I wouldn't want someone like that treating me. Some nutter who can't even sort her own bloody head out. Useless. You were and are bloody useless. I mean who the fuck do you think you are telling me it's over?'

'I think it's time for you to leave,' a voice said softly next to them.

Kate closed her eyes in relief.

'And who the hell do you think you are to make me do that?' Matthew sneered.

Steve produced his warrant card. 'Detective Inspector Steve Miller,' he said. 'I received a call from a member of the public who was concerned for this young lady's safety.'

'That would be me,' Maggie called out, giving Matthew a dirty but triumphant look.

Matthew looked at Steve's warrant card in disbelief. Steve stepped forward and removed Matthew's hand from Kate's wrist.

'Now,' he said in a low voice. 'We have two ways in which we can do this. One, we can do this knuckle dragger style and I can take you outside and we'll settle it out there, which incidentally after what I've just heard I am more than happy to do. Or, two, you will apologise to Kate, leave, and not return. Now which is it?'

'Are you threatening me?' Matthew asked loudly. 'He's threatening me. This policeman is threatening me. Who heard it?'

Maggie looked around her customers. 'I didn't hear anything,' she said. 'Any of you hear that?'

Everyone shook their heads.

Steve folded his arms. 'Which is it going to be?' he asked softly.

Matthew got up from the table. He pointed a finger at Kate. 'Happy to be rid of you. You're a useless bitch anyway, why do you think I went elsewhere? Useless and boring. I'm pleased to be rid of you. Can't even get a kid right.'

He brushed past Kate knocking her back against a table. Steve followed Matthew out into the street.

'Oh… oh are you following me now?' asked Mathew nervously in a loud voice. 'Is this police intimidation?'

A few passersby looked with interest at the exchange. Steve gave them a reassuring nod and a long-suffering expression.

'No, sir. Now move along, please. I've already asked you respectfully to leave. Unfortunately, if you carry on I will have to take you into custody.

'Don't even think about it,' Steve said quietly, years of experience giving him the sixth sense of knowing that Matthew was going to take a swing at him. 'Just go.'

'You're welcome to her.'

'Good to know. Bye now. You take care now.'

Steve stood in the road, his hands in his pockets, and watched Matthew walk up the street quickly.

Matthew was clearly fuming and kept looking back at Steve before eventually disappearing around the corner.

Kate was sitting on the rocks just past Maggie's Beach Café, cradling a mug of hot tea when Steve came back to find her. He'd stuck his head inside and Maggie had pointed to the beach, handing him a coffee.

'Just so you know. She's not upset over him going. She's upset about something he mentioned. She'll tell you.'

'Thanks, Mags,' he said gratefully. He walked over to her and sat beside her on the rocks. She had her eyes closed and her face tilted towards the weak autumn sunshine. He took her hand gently and sat there silently, their fingers linked, his thumb lightly stroking her hand.

'He's gone. Hope you didn't mind me stepping in.'

'On your white charger,' she said, smiling, eyes still closed. She sighed deeply. 'I think it was the nicest thing anyone has ever done for me.'

'I find that hard to believe,' he said.

She squeezed his hand. 'Seriously. It was pretty damn sexy too, warrant card, jeans and a wet shirt. My God. This is the stuff of some women's dreams.'

Steve burst out laughing. 'Well, we aim to please here in the local force.'

Kate turned to him. 'You have this ability to make me feel better. Make me laugh,' she said softly. 'Thank you. I'd forgotten what that was like.'

'Happy to be taken on for those duties on a trial run, leading to a perhaps a more permanent contract,' he said lightly.

'A trial run, eh? I'll give that some serious consideration, I think. Do I get to have any more free samples, just to be sure I can assess it properly?'

'Perhaps… if you play your cards right,' he said gently.

They sat silently for a while, Steve still holding her hand. She exhaled deeply.

'Aren't you going to ask me? About what he meant? Ask me who Daniel was?'

'I'm guessing you'll tell me when you want me to know.'

Kate turned to look at him and said with amusement, 'Who are you? And where have you been all my life?' She laughed. 'Seriously, I'm just not used to this.'

'Tell me, don't tell me. It's your choice.' Steve squeezed her hand.

Kate focused out to sea and started talking quietly. 'Daniel was my son. He died at 32 weeks. I think that was the most difficult thing I have ever had to do, give birth to a baby that I knew had died already. It broke me. I didn't think I would ever come back from it.' She inhaled deeply. 'There's part of me that knows it was for the best. The post-mortem threw up a raft of issues that we hadn't seen in the tests and would have meant…' She broke off and gulped. 'Basically, he would have needed lots of hospital care. But Matthew was right. It broke me. I couldn't get out of bed, couldn't eat. Couldn't sleep. I was useless.'

'This isn't something that you feel better about overnight, that's easy to deal with. It must be one of the hardest things to cope with,' Steve said quietly. 'Sounds like you suffered from some sort of post-natal depression. Did you get any help?'

'Eventually. Dad rocked up and got me back on the straight and narrow. Some counselling and medication.'

'Surely it should have been your husband's job to help with that?'

'Well, he was busy shagging my friend Anna because apparently I was useless on that front after the baby. Apparently he coped with it OK and I should have too. He made it sound like it was all my fault. That I had failed in creating Daniel with all his medical issues.'

'*Such* a nice guy,' Steve said dryly. 'Still struggling to work out why you left all that support and joy.'

Kate laughed and rested her head on his shoulder. 'So that's my sad story.'

Steve brought her hand up and kissed it gently. 'I'm sorry about Daniel,' he said. 'Really sorry. I don't know how you got through that on your own. I'm not sorry you left your husband though. As for you being useless and boring, he couldn't be more wrong. I wish I'd met you years ago.'

CHAPTER 14

Steve stood on the quayside, waiting for the lifeboat and the trawler it was towing to come back in. Jonesey was standing next to him, noisily chewing gum. Doug had made the call when they had found the fishing boat in a state and no sign of anyone aboard. As Mike brought the boats carefully alongside the quay, both Steve and Jonesey gazed down at the deck of the trawler.

'Jesus.' Steve frowned at the sight.

'Ugh. Looks like a scene from *Alien* or something,' Jonesey observed. 'They said it was Fred Pomeroy's?'

'Yup. Whatever it is, it doesn't look good,' Steve said. 'Call forensics, put them on standby. We need to see if we can find Fred first before we press the button on whether this is a crime scene or not. Let's get an address for him.'

Jonesey pressed the doorbell of Fred's house for the third time and turned to Steve. 'Nothing.'

The front door of the house next door opened and an elderly lady stepped out.

'If you're looking for Fred he went fishing the day before yesterday. Early. I saw him go. If you want *her*,' she said with contempt, 'she'll be at the vicar's. She's his housekeeper.'

Jonesey produced his notebook. 'What time exactly did you hear Fred go?' he said pleasantly, pen poised.

The old lady frowned, remembering. 'About 3.30 a.m. I saw him.'

'Are you often up at that time Mrs…?'

'Mrs Evans. And yes. I often wake and have a cup of tea around that time, then go back to bed.'

'Have you seen Fred come back at all?'

'No. He's often out for a few days at a time. Who can blame the poor man living with that?' She gestured with her head.

'So we can find Mrs Pomeroy at the vicarage?'

Mrs Evans shrugged. 'She'll either be there or lording it up at the vicar's coffee morning.'

Jonesey snapped shut his notebook. 'Thanks, Mrs Evans. If you should see Fred, give me a call?' He handed her his card.

She took it. 'Will do.'

Steve and Jonesey had no luck at the vicarage, so headed into the village hall and saw a sea of white hair – the pensioner coffee morning was in full swing. The vicar spotted them immediately and came rushing over.

'Steve my boy. Wonderful to see you,' he boomed, shaking Steve's hand furiously.

'Morning, Vicar. Not here for niceties today, we're a bit pressed for time. We need a word with your housekeeper, please? Is she here?'

'Whatever is the matter?' The vicar looked worried.

'If you could just tell me where she is, please?'

'Er, yes… She's in the kitchen. It's just through there.' He went as if to follow them.

Steve held up a hand. 'It's a private matter if you don't mind, Vicar.'

Steve and Jonesey walked into the kitchen and found Mrs Pomeroy stirring a pan on the stove.

'Something smells good,' Steve said, closing the door firmly.

Mrs Pomeroy turned with a frown. 'I don't like anybody in here while I'm cooking, there's coffee and cake in the other room,' she said rudely.

Steve held up his warrant card. 'Detective Inspector Steve Miller. Many thanks for the offer, but we'll pass won't we, Jonesey?'

'Well,' Jonesey said. 'I wouldn't rule out a piece of—'

'Mrs Pomeroy? Yes? Mrs Edwina Pomeroy? Wife to Mr Frederick Pomeroy?'

'Yes?' Mrs Pomeroy folded her arms.

'Mrs Pomeroy, I wonder if you could inform me of your husband's whereabouts, please?'

Mrs Pomeroy snorted. 'I've no idea. I expect he's on the boat earning a pittance.' She eyed the men critically. 'Why are you here?'

'Mrs Pomeroy, the lifeboat was called out to a fishing boat drifting aimlessly at sea around 4 a.m. this morning. They found the boat which was reported to be your husband's. Unfortunately, there was no sign of him. As a result, along with some other factors, we are considering his disappearance to be suspicious.'

'What?' she scowled. 'If he's not in the boat or at home, then where is he?'

'This is what we're asking you, Mrs Pomeroy.'

'I have no idea,' she said shortly and narrowed her eyes. 'What other factors?'

'The deck of the boat looks like there is a significant amount of blood on it and it looks like there may have been a struggle.'

'Well, he might have been gutting fish. That makes a hideous mess,' she snapped.

'There were no fish on the boat, Mrs Pomeroy. We need to ask you, when did you last see your husband?'

Mrs Joy Brown was excited about helping the vicar at the coffee morning, but she had awoken that morning feeling terrible. She had felt very ill the night before and had only managed another small bowl of broth. She was determined to help the vicar though, so had gone to bed early. She got herself up and dressed and tried to have some breakfast but didn't feel much better. She took a couple of paracetamols, did her face and hair and set off up the hill towards the village hall.

She entered the hall much to the delight of the vicar and Peter who both greeted her warmly. Mrs Pomeroy, however, raised an eyebrow and stalked off to the kitchen, informing Joy that the chairs needed putting out.

Joy had been putting out the tables and chairs with Peter helping her. A few early arrivals had drifted in and soon the place was busy with conversation. Joy was allocated the task of putting out cups and saucers, and plates for the cakes when she saw the two men come in.

She was feeling even worse and kept having to sit down as waves of dizziness and cold sweats swept over her. But amidst this, she knew they were police officers by the way they looked.

Her father had been a policeman and she could spot one a mile off. She saw to her delight that they were pointed towards the kitchen where Mrs Pomeroy was. Joy hoped to God the woman was in trouble about something. She stood, shakily, on the premise of going over to see if she could surreptitiously listen to see whether Mrs Pomeroy was going to get some sort of comeuppance.

As she stepped forwards, she felt a pain in her chest and suddenly saw the floor come rushing towards her. She felt a sharp pain in her head as it struck the corner of a wooden table.

Mrs Joy Brown died on the floor of the village hall, never having the satisfaction of knowing whether Mrs Pomeroy was in trouble or not.

Steve heard the commotion through the closed shutter of the serving hatch and frowned.

'One moment, please,' he said, leaving the kitchen and heading back into the hall.

He saw a group of people gathered around a woman on the floor. He called back over his shoulder.

'Jonesey – ambulance. ASAP.'

'Guv.'

Steve approached and saw Peter performing CPR on an elderly lady.

'She's not breathing and there's no pulse,' he said breathlessly.

'You OK? Need a hand?' asked Steve.

'No. I'm pretty well trained for this sort of thing. Occupational hazard,' he said quietly. 'She didn't look well today though.'

Steve cleared the crowd away and winced at the gossip already emanating from the group over tepid coffee and biscuits, while Peter carried on. The ambulance team arrived in the form of Phil and Liz. The two took control immediately but very soon, Phil turned to Steve and shook his head.

'Sorry, mate. She's gone.'

'I saw her head hit the corner of the table,' piped up an old lady sitting in a chair nearby.

'You saw what happened?' Steve asked.

'Yes. She was sitting down, saw you two come in and stood up, then she just fell forwards, hit her head on the corner of that table and then it hit the floor again.' She shuddered. 'Horrible noise.'

Peter walked over to stand next to Steve. 'Such a nice lady. I was only with her the day before yesterday. She was feeling lonely, wanted to speak to the vicar, but I went instead. She was lovely. Just lonely.'

Mrs Pomeroy had emerged from the kitchen to see the end of the commotion and Phil and Liz wheeling out a blanket-covered stretcher. The vicar came and stood next to Mrs Pomeroy.

'Such a terrible shame,' the vicar said, watching the stretcher go past. 'We'll say some prayers for her in church.'

'Well, that's certainly one less person to bother you, Vicar,' said Mrs Pomeroy, brushing past him to pick up coffee cups. 'She was getting to be quite the nuisance.'

The vicar was speechless for a moment. 'Really, Mrs Pomeroy,' he said. 'That's quite unnecessary. Very inappropriate under the circumstances.'

'Just saying how it is,' she said briskly, walking off.

Steve watched the exchange with interest. He found himself mildly fascinated by Mrs Pomeroy. For a woman who had just been informed that her husband was missing at sea, she was acting as if she wasn't in the slightest bit bothered. Her comment about the recently deceased had further piqued Steve's curiosity in the woman.

Steve nodded to the vicar and Peter. 'Mrs Pomeroy,' he called to her retreating back. 'We'll be in touch.'

'If you must,' she replied, heading into the kitchen.

Steve and Jonesey left the village hall and walked back towards the station.

'Something funny about that one,' Steve said as they walked along the road.

'What, like no apparent feelings?' supplied Jonesey.

'Well, we don't know what goes on behind closed doors.'

'She seemed like a right old battleaxe to me. Closed doors or no closed doors. What's that about? Slagging off a dead person when they're not even cold. Ignoring the fact that your husband's missing at sea, and I think we all know what that means?'

'We'll be digging a little deeper there, I think,' Steve said thoughtfully, stopping outside the station. 'Go on in, I'll be a minute,' he said, pulling his phone out.

Jonesey headed in and Steve dialled Kate's number. She answered breathlessly.

'Hello, Inspector.' He could hear the smile in her voice.

'Hello, Doctor.' He couldn't help smiling. 'How are you today?'

'Very well, thanks. I have fond recollections about my weekend. How about yourself?'

'Very similar position.'

'Good to know. Everything OK?'

'So… bit weird. I was just at the vicar's coffee morning—'

Kate guffawed loudly. 'You and your rock and roll lifestyle. Police chases, criminal underworlds and church coffee mornings… Netflix will be after you soon. *The Wire* has competition.'

He chuckled. 'Seriously, one of the parishioners keeled over and died. Right there. Hit her head, but had been feeling unwell. I consider that suspicious. I'll be asking for a PM.'

'OK. What can I do?'

'I need you to look at her records. I'll text over her name and date of birth, see if she's one of yours.'

'Steve, pretty much the whole town is one of ours. But yes, I'll look into it. Text me her name and address.'

'OK, thanks. So, I wondered whether you had any interest in dinner cooked by me tomorrow night.'

'Um. That sounds tempting. What's on the menu?'

'Me.'

'Umm. I wonder how nutritious you are though. What should I bring?'

'You.'

'When and where. Text me, I've gotta go. I'll look forward to tomorrow. Bye.'

Steve ended the call and turned to see Jonesey lounging in the doorway nodding knowingly at him and waggling his eyebrows.

'Couple goals. Told you so.'

* * *

Jesse was running. Full pelt. Flat out. Her legs screamed and her lungs felt they couldn't give her enough breath. She was being chased by something, but it was dark, and she couldn't see it. She knew it was evil though. She could hear it behind her. It was terrifying. She was so frightened she felt like her heart was going to burst out of her chest in fright. She knew she couldn't last much longer running like this.

She felt it over her shoulder, heard it closer and she pushed herself forwards again, running faster. Suddenly she tripped. She felt herself flying through the air and landing on rocky ground. She sat up, searching the blackness for the evil. Then she heard it. Throaty, growling. Inhuman. The sound of evil. She smelt the foul smell of death. She scrabbled away from it and tried to stand, but tripped again. She felt the evil tendrils snake out and grab her, holding her arms, pulling her into the blackness.

The panic almost overwhelmed her. She screamed and fought to pull away, her hands scrabbling at the evil tendrils. She managed to prize some loose and felt one close around her ankle. She screamed again. A profound sense of helplessness overcame her. She fought like her life depended on it and screamed again as its grip tightened.

'Jesse, wake up. Come back into the room. You're safe. You are in a safe place with people you trust.'

Jesse opened her eyes. She was in Jonathan's office. She was panting and sweaty. 'Jesus,' she said.

'Jesse, tell me you feel safe?'

'I feel safe.'

'Water?'

'Please.'

'I woke you because I sensed you were at the point of not coping with the situation anymore.'

Jesse drank a glass of water down in one and exhaled loudly.

'Jesus. I was fighting something I couldn't see. I was so tired. I couldn't run anymore. I fell over and it got me.'

'Are you OK to talk about this?'

'I think so. That was like a dream.'

'It was your subconscious creating the situation, while dealing with the issues we are working through. Tell me how you felt before I woke you up.'

Jesse breathed deeply and poured some more water.

'I was being chased in the darkness by this large, terrifying malevolent thing.'

'Could you see it?'

'No, but I had a sense of it. It was horrible. Black, growling, smelt like death, pure evil. I couldn't see it, but I felt it.'

'OK.'

'I was outrunning it, then I fell. And it had these tendrils that were wrapping around me, pulling me. I was trying to get them off, but they were coming too quickly. Then I felt…'

'Felt what?'

'Felt helpless. That I was losing the fight.'

'Interesting. What would have changed the situation?'

'What do you mean?' Jesse was confused.

'If your mind could have created something else to help for example.'

'If I had a weapon I could have used it against the tendrils.'

'OK, anything else?'

Jesse thought for a moment. 'Are you saying my mind could have created something to change that situation?'

'That's exactly what I'm saying.'

'So if we went again, you know I went under again, I could save myself?'

'You could.'

'I don't understand.'

'OK. This awful, terrifying event you endured at the hands of Chris. Not once, but twice, is so terrifying to you that you can't get past it. Your mind won't let you think about it, or remember it in the sense of "a live replay" because of the terror you felt and that you, by your own admission, felt certain you were going to die. So your mind has created this traumatic experience as a "thing" and I'm certain that this is the malevolent thing that you sense. In reality, it's the bulk of the bad memories that you don't want to face. It's chasing you because we're working on bringing them out for you to accept them and incorporate them into your memory bank without it being a traumatic experience.'

'Christ.'

'So it's chasing you and you feel terrified because we're getting closer. We could try and create an environment where you are in control of this "evil being" and I suspect that this is the key to the memories finally being incorporated into your present consciousness.'

'So let's go again.'

'No.' He shook his head firmly. 'Not today. You need to sleep to reset and heal the subconscious. We'll try again tomorrow. Set yourself the task of fighting the evil force.'

'Call upon my inner powers?' Jesse said dryly.

'Exactly that, Jesse.' Jonathan stood up. 'Go and rest. Tomorrow is a big day for trying to beat this thing.'

'I'm not sure I've got enough power in the inner tank,' Jesse said, walking towards the door.

'I think you'll be surprised,' he said. 'See you tomorrow.'

* * *

Doug drove home feeling frustrated. He had been out most of the day looking for Fred, firstly in the larger lifeboat and then in the smaller inshore boat with a smaller crew. They had even roped in the coastguard helicopter to help search, but they had found nothing. He had notified Steve that they had to call it a day today, but he would go out again in the morning.

Doug and Claire were sitting in the kitchen sharing a bottle of wine, with the remains of a pizza on the side. There was also a large envelope on the table in front of them.

'Last time we shared pizza and a bottle of wine, we ended up in bed,' Claire said quietly.

'That seems like a lifetime ago. Don't go getting any ideas,' Doug said dryly.

Claire laughed. 'Highly unlikely. I don't think you've ever looked at me the way you look at Jesse.' She sighed dramatically. 'A girl can only dream.'

'Stop talking pish,' Doug said, embarrassed.

'I think it's lovely,' Claire said. 'Genuinely. I'm happy for you. It's taken me a while to get to that place. I realised as soon as you knew about Felix, it was over for us. I know how you feel about trust. So, my fault, my mess. I've had to live with that and move on.'

'Things look like they're going well with Felix,' Doug said, sipping his wine.

Claire smiled indulgently. 'He's changed. I didn't think it was possible. I don't think he would muck me about again.'

'He's a good bloke.'

'He is.'

'I'm happy that you two are back on speaking terms.'

'Doug, Felix had a surprise for me today and I… well, we, wanted to get your blessing on it before we committed to it.'

'Sounds interesting.'

'The last couple of months, being here with the kids and getting on so well with you has been wonderful. Made me realise how much I miss it, but also made me think that we can still have all of it, even if we aren't together. Felix loves the kids and spending time with them too. So, he surprised me today by telling me that he's made an offer on number one, around the corner. So we could live there and be near the kids and be part of their lives. How do you feel about that?'

Doug sipped his wine. 'I think that it's a great idea. So close the kids can be in and out and still see the both of us easily. Go for it.'

'Owners want a quick sale. They've been posted overseas and have already gone. Felix is going to negotiate a rental agreement for a couple of months until the sale goes through, so we can move in straight away.'

'Why the hurry?'

'Partly because I feel better and want to start going into work maybe part-time, and I want to feel settled in a home for good. You know? And secondly, Jesse needs to be here. To heal. She can't be on her own. She loves you and needs you. That's difficult with me around. So it works out for everyone.'

Doug felt a lump in his throat. He'd not expected Claire to be so considerate about his relationship with Jesse.

'You're getting soppy on me,' she observed.

'Talking pish again,' he muttered, looking away.

'That's settled then,' she said, picking up the envelope. She took out some paperwork and signed it a few times and handed it to him with the pen. Doug picked up the pen, signed it and put the paper back in the envelope. He picked up his wine glass and clinked it with Claire's.

'Here's to the continuing good health and good fortune of the ex-Mrs Brodie.'

'Here's to the continuing health and good fortune of the wonderful Mr Brodie.'

They clinked glasses again.

'Will you keep the name or go back to your maiden name?' Doug asked.

'OK if I keep the name? I'm kind of attached to it now.'

'Call it my divorce gift to you. Better tell Felix it's a definite yes to the house.'

Claire stood and bent to kiss Doug on the cheek. 'I might just go and do that,' she said.

Doug pushed open the door to Jesse's hospital room. It was lit by a small corner lamp which cast a soft glow. He frowned when he saw the empty bed.

'What are you doing sneaking in here?' Jesse said, giggling as she walked in the door holding a large mug of something.

Doug was relieved. 'I wanted to see you. It's not right me being at home and you being here. Just wanted to be with you.'

'Ah bless.' Jesse sat on the bed cross-legged and patted the sheet beside her.

'Come on. Tell me about your day,' she said.

Doug stretched out on the bed and started to tell her about the discovery of Fred's boat. Jesse finished her drink and lay down beside him snuggling into the crook of his arm.

'Oh, and one more thing,' he said, smiling. 'Actually no, two more things.'

'Tell me.'

'One, I had a glass of wine and pizza with the soon to be ex-Mrs Brodie tonight. All very civilised and we signed on the dotted line quite happily. And two, Felix and her are buying number one around the corner so she can see more of the kids. So… what do you think about that?'

'I think that all sounds pretty bloody perfect,' said Jesse sleepily. 'I'm going to use my inner power tomorrow to fight the monster.'

'Fight the what?' Doug asked quietly.

'To fight the monster. Big day tomorrow,' she said, slipping into sleep.

He is my rock. In him will I trust; He is my shield, my salvation, my tower, and my refuge, my saviour; He saves me from violence. He trusts me to choose. I look upon these faces and they disgust me. They fawn over everything; they consume everything and give back nothing. They are not thankful. They are not blessed. They are greedy and undeserving. What right do they have to carry on living? They have no right. The kingdom would be better off without them. Their disagreeable ways, never considerate, always needing. Always wanting. Never thankful for any small act of kindness. They don't deserve to live. I must gather them together, and deliver us from these heathens, so we can glory in His praise.

CHAPTER 15

Christopher Cherry was as fit as he could get himself. With primitive living conditions, a poor diet and no medical assistance, he knew he would not get significantly better.

He was biding his time, trying to build up his strength and stamina. The old brothers had insisted he work with them on the boat, and he was now learning how to navigate and fish. He was not a natural sailor. He hated the sea. Every day he was seasick, but his rage pushed him through it. He didn't give a fuck about the fishing, but he needed to show willing. He needed to know how to get the fuck out of this shithole.

Day after day he worked long hours with the brothers, rarely being allowed to learn the navigational tools, but he stuck at it. Every day he got a little stronger. Revenge fuelling his tired bones. He felt that the time for action was fast approaching, as soon as he learnt how to navigate properly. He had no clear idea where he was.

He was also hoping that the brothers were building up a cash reserve that he could take when he eventually dumped them and left. So far, he couldn't work out where they kept the money they earnt from fishing. But he was wily. He'd find it.

* * *

Jimmy was way out of his depth. In his search for the Camorra lock-ups, he had done his best to follow who he thought was the follower. However, after a few false starts, and an unwelcome punch in the face from a boyfriend who thought Jimmy was stalking his girlfriend, it had struck him that whoever had taken the photographs was either very good or not taking them anymore.

He was at a loss. He had to get rid of JJ's body, but he couldn't think how. He tried to remember JJ and his various dodgy locations of lock-ups and drops. And then it came to him. He had met JJ at a barn once which he knew was the Camorra's. Jimmy tried to remember where that was. Then it came to him.

JJ had sent him a text with a pin drop in it. Bingo.

Jimmy drove slowly along the country lane. It was all coming back to him now. He remembered that JJ had left his car in a layby and gone on foot. He parked the truck and crept down the lane and over a gate into a field. Ten minutes later, after a traumatic encounter with a bull, Jimmy was breathing heavily and crouched at the back of the large barn, looking for any signs of activity. The place was deserted; the doors were securely padlocked, but frustratingly Jimmy had nothing that would help him pick the lock.

Ever resourceful from a life of crime, he climbed up the back of the barn and got in through the roof, dropping down onto a roof brace.

He climbed awkwardly down into the building. It was a large semi-industrial farm unit, which had a big open space in one area with a couple of cars under tarpaulins and a series of small rooms at the other end of the building. Jimmy found nothing of interest in the rooms apart from a few tables and chairs. He wandered back into the larger space and through into a single-storey outhouse area which housed two large chest freezers.

'Bingo,' Jimmy said quietly. He lifted the lid of the first freezer and looked in horror at the assortment of frozen arms and legs before him. He turned to the other freezer and found a series of torsos.

'Jesus fucking Christ,' he muttered. There was simply no room in either of the freezers. 'Fuck,' he said, shutting the lid. He turned to look at the rest of the room. Nothing in there, apart from the two cars under the tarpaulins.

With some difficulty he pulled himself back up again and out through the roof. He crouched down behind the building and waited for a while. Listening. A plan forming, he took a photo of both access doors and padlocks and went back to find his truck, carefully avoiding the over-friendly bull.

Jimmy sat in the pub. This is where he came to think. He had an idea that involved getting rid of JJ. It was highly risky and could probably result in both legs being nailed to a table, and Pearl and Stanley being extremely nasty to him.

He was sipping his beer when his mobile rang. It was Alexy. Alexy was an Eastern European gang leader who Jimmy had done some dodgy work for in the past, and he was also firmly ensconced in the embrace of the Camorra, with Pearl having a soft spot for him.

'Hello?' Jimmy answered.

'Ah, Jimmy the fisherman. It is your good friend Alexy.' Alexy's cheerful voice boomed out.

'How are you, Alexy?'

'I am very good, Jimmy. You have missing me, no?' he asked in his pidgin English.

'Missed you? Of course, Alexy. Every day,' said Jimmy sarcastically.

'I am thinking you are pulling my leg off?' Alexy chided him good-naturedly.

'Absolutely. What can I do for you, Alexy?'

'What? No chitty chatty with Alexy?' he teased. 'Straight to business?' He laughed. 'OK, Jimmy the fisherman. I have date for you.'

'To do what?' Jimmy asked, dreading the answer.

'To park boat in harbour and drive it around from… hanging on… I find piece of paper.' He scrabbled about and Jimmy heard rustling. 'Kilmore Quay… yes.'

'Where the fuck is Kilmore Quay?'

Alexy snorted with laughter. 'It is the Ireland. You do google.'

'Hang on.' He googled Kilmore Quay. 'Jesus, Alexy. It'll take me two days to sail back from there going flat out. How do I even get there?'

'The er… the big boat from Fishguard. You know… big boat… er, what *is* word?'

'Ferry?'

'Yes, Jimmy the fisherman. Catch ferry there and drive boat back.'

'It's too far.'

'Jimmy, you will do it. Yes?'

'I wasn't aware I was being given a choice.'

Alexy laughed heartily. 'Ha. You do have choice. You do it. All OK. All good. You don't do it. Hmm, remember Huey and JJ? Yes? Are we understanding me?'

'Yes.'

'OK. Last weekend in November. You go Thursday be back for weekend. Yes?'

'I don't have a choice, Alexy.'

'Exactly, my friend! I will send ticket for big boat. I have to go now.' The call ended abruptly, and Jimmy was left looking at his phone.

'Fuck,' he said quietly, a sense of dread creeping over him.

* * *

The long sands of Pendine Beach stretched into the early morning gloom. Steve stood on the beach looking down at a body. The young PCSO who had accompanied him stood looking wide-eyed with his hands tucked into his pockets.

'How do you reckon he died then?' he said, nodding towards the body.

Steve groaned inwardly. He tried to be supportive of training younger officers, but sometimes he wondered whether the basic entry qualifications for coming into the force were that you just had to have a pulse.

'Well, my deductive training says this to me. There's a body on a beach. It's wet. There's no boat around. The sand is still wet. This suggests to me that the body was washed up here by the tide. Hence I could consider the probability of drowning to be high.'

'Uh-huh,' said the PCSO, nodding. 'Cool.'

'Not for him,' said Steve, walking off the beach. He stopped a member of the SOCO team who was about to take pictures. 'When pictures are done. Check the pockets for ID, please, ASAP, I think this is someone we've been looking for.'

Steve walked off the beach and stopped to chat to the woman who had found the body. As he was finishing up the forensic officer came over with a wallet in an evidence bag. Steve manoeuvred the wallet around in the bag to open it and saw the name he had been expecting it to be.

He gazed out over the railing towards the beach. 'Hello, Fred,' he said quietly. He placed a call to Doug who answered on the second ring.

'What's up?'

'I've found Fred,' Steve announced.

'The fact that you've found him suggests to me that his end was not a happy one.'

'Looking at him I would be inclined to agree,' said Steve dryly.

'Come on, where was he?'

'Washed up on Pendine in a right old state. Forensics taking pics now and then we'll take him in.'

'OK. I'll inform the coastguard. We were due to go out again today looking.'

'Appreciate it.'

'No problem. Catch you later. Hope your day gets better, Steve.'

'Informing next of kin never makes a good day. See you, mate.'

Steve and Jonesey stood on the doorstep to the vicarage. Even through the door they could smell breakfast. Steve pressed the doorbell and Jonesey sniffed the air like a dog.

'I hate NOK calls. God, I'm starving,' he said. 'Reckon we'll get some nosh?'

'Nope,' said Steve. 'Stop calling them NOK too. It's disrespectful. It's next of kin.'

The door swung open and Peter the curate looked surprised.

'Hello, officers. What can we do for you? Do you want to come in?' He stood back and allowed the men to step inside.

'We need a word with Mrs Pomeroy, please,' Steve said.

'She's in the kitchen. Come through,' Peter said, heading down the corridor.

The kitchen was warm and smelt of bacon and coffee. The vicar was sitting at the table eating and Mrs Pomeroy was at the sink washing up.

'Ah, Steve!' the vicar said, waving a fork in greeting. 'Come in! Sit down! Coffee? Breakfast?'

'We're fine, thanks,' said Steve.

'I could always—' Jonesey started.

'There's no breakfast,' snapped Mrs Pomeroy, her back to the men as she washed up.

Steve eyed her with interest. In his view, she must have known what they were there about, but she didn't seem overly bothered.

'I need to have a private chat with Mrs Pomeroy, please,' said Steve quietly.

'Can do it here,' Mrs Pomeroy said, continuing to wash up. 'No secrets from the vicar.'

'Would you like to sit down for a moment?' Steve asked, trying to be sensitive to this abrasive woman.

'What for? You're going to tell me you've found Fred, aren't you? I don't need to be sitting down to hear that.' She heaved a large saucepan noisily onto the draining board.

'Mrs Pomeroy, I regret to inform you that we found the body of your husband this morning on Pendine Beach,' Steve said. 'I'm very sorry for your loss.'

'Hmmph,' said Mrs Pomeroy.

'Oh, Edwina. I'm so very sorry,' the vicar said, standing and laying a hand on Mrs Pomeroy's shoulder.

'Unfortunately, we will need you to come and identify the body as soon as you are able,' Steve said.

'Where is he? I'll come now,' she said, undoing her apron.

Steve held up a hand. 'Er, no. We're still processing Fred, Mrs Pomeroy. Can I suggest tomorrow, please?'

'Peter can drive you,' the vicar volunteered, missing Peter rolling his eyes at the prospect.

'Processing?' Mrs Pomeroy said haughtily. 'What does that mean?'

'Collecting evidence from him and the area concerned.'

'He fell overboard surely?'

'We are treating his death as suspicious, Mrs Pomeroy.'

'What's suspicious about being stupid enough to fall overboard?' she snapped.

Steve was struggling to be polite to this woman, she had such an unpleasant nature. 'As I mentioned previously. There was a lot of blood on the deck, signs of a struggle.'

'Probably drunk,' she said, snorting.

Steve decided it was time to go. 'Let's say tomorrow morning at 10 a.m.? At the mortuary. I will assign a family liaison officer to you, Mrs Pomeroy.'

'Don't need one.'

'It's standard practice.'

Mrs Pomeroy scowled at Steve. 'Is that it? You can go now.'

Steve took a moment to look at this woman. Over the years he had done a good share of NOK calls and had seen a range of responses, but never anything like this woman's reaction. It was almost pure ambivalence. Steve turned to the vicar and Peter.

'Vicar. Peter. Always a pleasure. We'll see ourselves out,' he said and propelled Jonesey down the corridor and out of the front door.

'I'm starving,' Jonesey complained as they got in the car. 'Can we at least swing by Maggie's to get a bacon sandwich?'

'What did you make of that?' he asked, ignoring his request.

'What? The woman with the emotional depth of a gnat?' Jonesey glanced back at the door.

'Yeah,' said Steve, thinking. 'I can't decide whether she's just not bothered about the fact that he's died or whether she wasn't bothered because she had something to do with it.'

'Can't call it,' said Jonesey. 'Pleeeease can we go and get food? Look I'm even doing the puppy eyes.'

Steve rolled his eyes and started the car. 'Stop doing the weird eye thing. I'm only stopping for takeaway though.'

Steve had decided to make Thai curry for dinner. Primarily because it took about 20 minutes and, in his mind, anything else was wasted time when he could be hopefully kissing Kate again.

Kate arrived with a box of files and a bottle of wine resting on the top. With difficulty she pressed the doorbell, trying not to drop the box and the wine. Steve swung open the door and grabbed the box from her, pulling her towards him for a quick kiss.

'Hello, Doctor. Have you come to give me the once over?' he said, smiling.

'Hello, Inspector, am I here for you to take down my particulars?' she asked, laughing.

'Come in,' he said, kicking the door shut with his foot and walking through to the kitchen. 'Drink?'

'Christ, yes.'

Kate wandered through the house. 'This is so lovely,' she said, liking the style, which was Scandi-type simplicity.

'Great view,' she said, looking out of the window. 'You can see the sea.'

'Why I bought it,' he said, passing her a glass. 'So, what's in the box?'

'Medical records of the deceased. I figure I'm not breaking any rules as you'd need to see them as part of the investigation anyway.'

Kate walked through into a large open-plan kitchen/dining room with another sea aspect at the back through the bifold doors.

'God, this is such a lovely house!' she said. 'I love that you can see the sea from almost every angle.'

'You hungry?' he said.

'In the words of my friend's husband, I could eat a scabby horse,' she said grinning.

'So,' Kate said, munching appreciatively, 'I've had a look through all of their notes and there's nothing that suggests they had any underlying health conditions which would account for suddenly becoming ill and dying shortly after.'

'What about Mabel?'

'She was fit as a fiddle that one. Couldn't see anything to explain it really. I've not seen a PM for her yet.'

'Hmm. What about the way in which they died? Their symptoms?'

'Nothing conclusive,' Kate said, frustrated. 'Mabel had become very sick with something like food poisoning, but not enough to kill her. I would hazard a guess that she died of liver failure.'

'How can you tell?'

'I won't bore you. But we'll see what the PM says.' Kate sipped her wine. 'So, Dad says you found old Fred Pomeroy on the beach?'

'Yup. Doug found his boat empty and floating – couple of things looked suspicious.'

'Like?'

'The state of the deck. It was awful, what looked like blood, shit, piss, sick. You name it.'

'Was he out with crew or on his own?' Kate asked, frowning.

'On his own we think. No sign of anyone else. He sometimes takes crew, but they're all accounted for.'

'What do you think happened?'

Steve shrugged.

'Do you think he just fell overboard?'

'I just don't know... I've been looking at the boat and wondering what happened.'

'What are your amazing deductive powers telling you?'

'Looking at the state of the boat I think we can safely rule out someone else being on there. We'd see different evidence. Instead, we see evidence which is a mix of bodily functions. That suggests to me that perhaps he was suddenly taken ill and maybe ended up falling overboard or something. So my question to you, lovely doctor, is... what would make him lose control of himself causing blood, sick, piss and shit to be all over the place in the space of, what, between twelve and twenty hours?'

Kate thought for a moment. 'The combination of all of those things suggests that he couldn't actually control what was happening to him. So I suspect he was incapacitated in some way on deck. Otherwise he would have been below deck using the loo, just because that's human nature. Yes?'

'Agreed.'

'So what happened to him must have been quite bad for him to be on deck losing control of his basic functions.'

'So what would do that?' Steve asked, pushing his plate away and grabbing a pad and pen from the drawer behind him.

'Some sort of fit. Er, maybe some sort of poisoning. Some poisoning is dreadful, the body expels pretty much everything. A fit wouldn't really account for a lot of blood at all, if there was a lot?'

'There was a lot.'

'I think perhaps it was something he ingested. Unless he had a fit or something and then cut himself badly. Any sign of a cut on the body?'

'Looked clean as a whistle.'

'See what the PM turns up. It sounds to me something like severe food poisoning of some description, or he ingested or came into contact with something that had that effect on him.'

'God.'

'Some types of gas or toxins have that effect on a person, but I can't think how he would come into contact with anything like that on a small fishing boat. I'd hazard a guess this is more of a domestic issue.'

'What like basic poisoning or something.'

'Maybe. See what the experts say.'

Steve thought as he stood and collected the plates and carried them out to the kitchen. Kate picked up the serving dishes and followed him.

'For what it's worth,' she said, musing, 'Mabel exhibited signs of some sort of food poisoning prior to organ failure. What about any of the others? Exactly how far back are we going?'

'I guess we need to pull PMs for, what? Last twelve months and then backtrack,' said Steve, loading the dishwasher. 'We need to look for patterns, people, places, etc., and start analysing.'

'Where do you even start?'

'Long hours and legwork.' He raised an eyebrow as he closed the dishwasher with his foot. 'This is why I have such impressive stamina levels.'

'Oh? Even if you say so yourself?' Kate was amused.

He yanked her towards him and pulled her close. 'I have to do my own PR here.'

Kate wound her arms around his neck, smiling. 'Yes, but what if you're just all mouth and no trousers on the stamina front?'

'Then after extensive research by a qualified medical practitioner, you will perhaps recommend an approach that will improve my stamina, but I'm pretty confident.'

'Don't forget modest… Sooo modest.'

'That too. Come here,' he said, kissing her.

* * *

Jesse felt strong. She was in Jonathan's office again and was relaxed. She felt good. Jonathan sat down.

'OK to start?' he asked. 'I will wake you again if I feel you're in a place where you're not coping.'

'OK,' she said.

'Close your eyes,' he began in his soft voice.

Jesse was standing in a field. The field and all the surroundings were in black and white, with a sepia tinge. The wind was strong, and the air had a scent that made her feel slightly nauseous. Like sulphur, or something rotting.

She looked down and saw that the field was muddy, and her feet were bare and dirty. She stood for a while looking around. She saw broken burnt-looking trees. The branches bent over like crippled old men. In the distance she saw the roof of something red.

She sensed that she needed to head that way, so she started walking towards it.

She reached the edge of the field and saw it. It was a house, but it had the lifeboat logo on the front of it. Why was there a lifeboat station with no water? She rounded the corner and almost fell down a steep drop. Hundreds of feet below her was a deep, rocky chasm with water gushing out from underneath the lifeboat house, straight down into it. The roar of the water was deafening and she felt the spray, cool on her face. How had she not heard that earlier? she wondered.

She stepped back and walked away from the edge. The lifeboat house had a large wrap-around porch, completely empty except for a bright red rocking chair. She stepped up on the porch and sat in the chair, rocking gently, and closed her eyes, enjoying the motion.

When she opened her eyes again, the maize was growing in the muddy fields. Before her eyes it grew, taller and taller. She heard it creaking and rustling as it got taller, taller than a person. Then she saw the maize move and leant forward. She stopped rocking and gripped the arms. She heard it then. The growl. The sound of evil.

She saw the movement of the maize as it came towards her, the plants withering and dying as the malevolence passed by it. She didn't feel scared. She felt safe. Safe in the house. Safe on the porch. Safe in the red chair.

She could smell the foul and rotting stench of death. It was at the edge of the maize. She could hear it grunting and growling.

'Come on then,' she muttered, standing. 'If you're coming.'

It was then she saw it. Properly. Fully. She gasped. This was the stuff of nightmares. A huge moving silhouette of dark mass. It moved like it was made up of dense black smoke. It had bright yellow eyes and long arms with long spikey fingers. It was the shape of a huge human. The noises it emitted were guttural – feral.

It moved towards her; the smell was unbearable. The noises – growling and snuffling.

Jesse watched it approach. She wasn't scared. The creature sensed this and roared at her. It held up an arm and she was immediately thrown backwards, hard against the side of the house. Jesse lay for a moment dazed and then pulled herself up. She was winded from the fall, but still felt no fear. She told herself repeatedly that she was in control.

The mass moved around, watching her, snarling. Stalking her. Again, it raised an arm and she was thrown back hard against the side of the house. Winded again, she lay for another moment and then rolled over and managed to stand. She was hurt and aching, but still she wasn't scared. The creature sensed this and howled at her in frustration.

Jesse decided then that enough was enough. She turned her back on the evil, hearing it grunt and snuffle after her. She ran around the side of the house, jumping off the porch and balanced precariously on the edge of the deep chasm. The huge torrent of water roared in her ears and the spray soaked into her clothes.

The evil roared, upset the game was over, unsure of her plan. It drifted towards her, so close that she could smell the cloying, rotting flesh. It seemed frightened of the water. She could see confusion in its yellow eyes. It swiped, trying to grab her, but instead Jesse closed her eyes, stretched her arms out and gracefully fell backwards down into the chasm. Straight into the mass of moving water.

As she fell, she heard the scream of frustration from the evil. She opened her eyes and watched it, hanging over the edge, screeching down at her, swiping at her with its long arms.

Silence. Quiet. Coolness.

Jesse opened her eyes. She was underwater, her lungs were hurting. She had to get to the surface, to breathe. Drowning was close. She struggled upwards, feeling weak. The surface was a long way up. She flailed for a moment and hung in the water, too tired to move.

Then she heard it. The voice, telling her to swim. To kick and float to get to the surface. Calmer, she closed her eyes. She felt a hand encircle her wrist and pull her at speed. She burst through the surface and lay floating for a moment on the water, gulping in huge breaths. She looked around her. No one there. *Who had grabbed her wrist?* Land was behind her. She struck out weakly towards it.

Finally, she lay on the sand, the tide breaking over her legs. She was exhausted, she had never felt so tired in her life. As she lay, she felt some strength returning. She felt different. She raised herself onto all fours and coughed, clearing her airways, choking up some water and then she finally got to a standing position.

She staggered through the tideline and up onto the beach. She saw a decked area in the distance and on the deck was another chair. She lurched towards it coughing, feeling bruised from being thrown against the side of the house. She reached the deck, climbed up and collapsed into it closing her eyes from exhaustion.

'Jesse, back in the room, please. Do you feel safe, Jesse?'

'I do.'

'What's the first thing you remember?'

'The red rocking chair.'

'Come awake for me now, Jesse. Slowly.'

Jesse blinked. 'Christ,' she said. 'I feel like I've gone ten rounds with someone.'

'You feel physical pain?'

'Yes. Very bruised. From being thrown against the house.'

'You told me that hurt.'

'I was talking?'

'Yes. You were telling me how you felt and what was happening the whole time.'

'I was? Wow. Heavy stuff.' Jesse shook her head in disbelief.

Jonathan leant forwards. 'I would like you to think, Jesse. Not about the struggle you've just had. But before. What do you remember?'

Jesse thought for a moment. She inhaled sharply and her eyes filled with tears. She looked at Jonathan in horror.

'Oh my God. I tried to kill him.'

Jonathan shifted in his chair. 'Calm down. Tell me what you remember.'

Jesse looked at him, eyes wide. 'I tried to kill Chris. I remember. Oh my God.' She covered her face with her hands. 'That makes me as bad as him.'

'How did you try to kill him, Jesse?'

'He was hanging on to a rock off the cliff with one hand and I was dragging myself along and I saw it. He yelled at me to pull him up and I found a rock. And I started hitting his hand with it.' She looked horrified again. 'That's when he grabbed me and pulled me over the cliff.' She covered her face with her hands. 'Oh God. I tried to kill him. I wanted to kill him. I remember the feeling of wanting him to die.'

I think we can safely say it was self-defence, Jesse.'

Jesse suddenly felt awful. She felt dizzy and sick and had the cloying smell of death in her nostrils. She stood unsteadily.

'I think I'm going to have to—' she said and promptly passed out.

CHAPTER 16

Sophie had religiously been emailing Sam every day, telling him news of everyday life. She talked of Marcus, his schoolwork, his friends, his love of climbing. She talked about her dad and told Sam some funny, but heart-breaking stories about his deepening dementia. She told him about the seal colonies and the babies and even sent some photos.

Nothing came back from Sam.

As suggested, she hadn't gone back to see him the previous weekend, but she was planning to this weekend: the weekend before he was due home. She wasn't expecting any significant progress, but felt a conversation would be good. She emailed him to say that she was coming and that he would be home the following weekend. She reminded him about the carnival, hoping to prompt some memories of the years they had gone together. She found it incredibly disheartening to not receive any type of response, but Lottie had told her to expect it and that Sam was doing well.

She closed the lid of the laptop after telling Sam she would see him in the morning. Unusually, she was alone in the house. Marcus was at Doug's for the weekend, the boys were off on a two-day Scout expedition. Sophie's dad was in respite care for a few weeks, arranged by Kate to give Sophie a break and make it slightly easier for Sam to come home. Jack was quite happy in there, he said he liked having a postbox in the reception to be able to pay in his cheques. He also told Sophie cheerfully that it was lovely that he didn't have to pay to use the toilet, or wear his school uniform there.

The sound of a loud engine jolted her back to reality and she peered out of the window to see Foxy's Defender pull up. She rose and went to open the door.

'Hello, you,' she said, pleased to see him. 'What brings you here?'

Foxy jumped out of the driver's seat, holding a white bag which he thrust at her and walked around the back of the Defender, opening the back door with a flourish.

'I have brought you a bed, and dinner.'

'Because?'

'The bed is for Sam, silly. It's an orthopaedic mattress. One of my regulars has lent it to us for Sam. Nice, eh?'

'What are they sleeping on?' Sophie ventured.

'They're all better. They were going to put it in storage, but I asked if we could borrow it.'

'Wow. Thanks. That's great. I was worried about what he'd sleep on.'

'Well,' Foxy said triumphantly, 'it's a done deal now, isn't it? Right, I need to eat before I unload this, or it'll get cold.'

'What's this?' she asked, holding up the bag.

'I figured, as you were on your own you wouldn't cook so I took the chance and brought you some too, but I'm happy to eat it if you've had dinner already.'

'Smells gorgeous.'

'Moussaka and Greek salad.'

'You are a god.'

'I do my best,' he said. 'Come on. I'm wasting away.'

Sophie followed him in. 'Do you ever stop eating?' she asked with amusement as she watched him unload the bag.

'Why would I? Come on. Dig in.'

Sophie hadn't realised how hungry she was. It occurred to her that she had missed lunch too. They ate in silence for a while until Foxy glanced at her.

'You worried about seeing him tomorrow?'

She shrugged as she chewed. Nothing escaped Foxy, so she was always honest with him.

'Little bit.'

'Any response to the emails?'

'No. I was told not to expect any response though.'

Foxy eyed her. 'Maybe he'll talk. Gotta give it a go.'

She pushed away her empty plate.

'Hope so, next weekend's going to be fucking awful if we can't even exchange pleasantries.'

'You're really getting into the swing of using bad language,' Foxy observed.

'I feel the current situation completely requires it.' Sophie raised her glass.

'You're not wrong,' he said. 'Right. OK to get this bed in?'

Together they manoeuvred the frame of the bed out of the Defender, in through the front door and into the study.

'I've cleared the decks a bit already. I thought we'd put it over there,' she gestured with her chin.

'OK, watch out and I'll swing it round.' Foxy effortlessly moved the bed round and pushed it into the corner.

'Right, mattress,' he said and disappeared.

Sophie followed, grabbed one of the handles and together they brought the unwieldy mattress into the study. Foxy picked it up to swing it round, not realising that Sophie was in the way and caught her full in the face with it.

'Oommph,' she said, staggering slightly, and burst out laughing.

Foxy turned in alarm and caught her again with the other edge, which made her laugh even more. He dumped the mattress down and she sat down on it, laughing.

'What?' he asked.

'You barged me twice with the mattress!'

The look on his face was enough to set her laughter off again. Once she started laughing she found she couldn't stop. Her laughter made Foxy laugh and together they sat on the bed laughing at each other. Finally, Sophie got the giggles under control and wiped her eyes. She bounced on the bed and then lay backwards, still chuckling.

'Hey, this is pretty comfy,' she said, wriggling. 'Try it.'

Foxy lay down next to her. 'It is pretty comfy. Bugger Sam, I might take it back tonight for me. The bed in my flat is dreadful.'

Sophie looked across the bed at him.

'But you won't because you're a good man,' she said softly. 'And you care about other people. You didn't have to do this. So, thank you. Mind you, I reckon once Sam's gone home you'll think bugger that and commandeer this for yourself!' She lay chuckling.

214

Foxy glanced across the bed at Sophie. Her face was flushed from her laughing fit and her hair was spread out around her head like a blonde halo. She was laughing gently to herself. Foxy felt his stomach flip. He had the most ridiculous urge to lean over and kiss her. To want to kiss her and not stop. Undress her. He felt a tidal rush of emotion and had to physically stop himself acting on it. He sat up suddenly confused and horrified with himself.

'I need to go,' he said, frowning and standing up. 'So, the bed's a hit? Yes? Right. Good luck tomorrow. Let me know how it goes.'

'Rob?' Sophie began.

'See you, Soph, take care on the drive tomorrow,' he called over his shoulder.

He walked out through the kitchen and grabbed his keys and phone and walked out of the front door as quickly as he could.

'Thanks for dinner and the bed,' Sophie called after him, frowning. What the hell was his sudden and uncharacteristic departure all about?

Foxy gunned the engine and drove off, taking out his anger on the Defender who was more than used to it. He decided he needed to clear his head, so he drove out to Pendine Beach and took the Defender down onto and along the huge stretch of deserted beach. He pulled to a stop facing the sea and sat thinking things he didn't want to be thinking. Shit.

Carla was right after all. She had seen that his feelings ran deep for Sophie. How could he not have realised? When he had seen her laying on the bed, her face flushed and happy all he wanted to do was to have her. There and then.

'Fuck!' he shouted out loud, hitting the steering wheel. 'Fuck, fuck, FUCK! You stupid FUCKING TWAT!'

He didn't want to ruin one of the best friendships he had ever had by wanting to shag his best friend. There was absolutely no future in that. He had single-handedly gone and ruined everything. Sophie knew him so well the likelihood was that she'd read it in his face in an instant and run a bloody mile.

* * *

Sam Jones lay in his hospital bed and read the latest email from his wife. He'd looked at the pictures of the baby seals and laughed at Sophie's descriptions of her dad. He felt proud of his son's climbing progress. He had done some research of his own and researched the climbing centre in Castleby, viewing the extensive gallery of pictures.

His son, Marcus, and his best friend Jude, were in many of them, up very high or dangling off dangerous corners and he couldn't believe the young man his son had become. He read the biography of Foxy with interest and saw he was an ex-special forces soldier. He had studied his picture carefully, making comparisons. Sam had also come across a picture of Foxy standing next to Sophie with another guy the other side. The three of them laughing and pointing up at something. They seemed comfortable with each other, relaxed and happy.

Sam had decided to see Sophie tomorrow. He didn't know what to say to her but felt he ought to. He supposed he should try to think of things to talk about, but he couldn't think of anything. It wasn't like he was going to say, 'Hey, did I tell you about my two years in captivity?'

He didn't want to go to Castleby for a long weekend. Well, part of him did, just to get out of the hospital. But he didn't want to go anywhere or do anything if the truth be known.

He just wanted to die. The sooner the better. He figured he'd talk to Sophie. Make her see he was a lost cause. Go to Castleby and then that was done and dusted. He could die and be free of this shit existence called a life.

* * *

Jesse woke in her hospital bed. She saw the clock and realised that she must have slept for around eighteen hours straight. She glanced down at the covers and it seemed like she hadn't moved at all during the night. She stretched and swung her legs over the side of the bed. She inhaled sharply as her brain awoke properly and flooded her consciousness with memories.

She sat on the side of the bed for a moment and breathed calmly, relaxing as Jonathan had taught her. She allowed herself to access the memories and tried to sort through them. She found herself breathing heavily and sweating and she lay down on the covers of the bed to use the relaxing techniques she had learnt to try to keep herself under control.

Four hours later she woke to find Jonathan sitting in the chair by the window, making notes in a stack of files.

'Ah,' he said. 'She wakes. How do you feel?'

'Pretty good,' Jesse said, thinking carefully. 'I woke up… I remembered… then I fell asleep again.'

Jonathan nodded. 'Excellent. In very simple terms, you know with a computer when you have updates? And then you have to restart to make all the updates work?'

'Yup.'

'Well, this is what happens with the brain. We've unlocked a huge, staggering amount of raw data, not just in the form of memories, but in the form of emotions, feelings, actions, etc., and the subconscious needs time to sort through these and allocate them correctly in your mind. Hence the need for sleep.'

'I remember waking up after I fell into the chasm… I remembered everything and then I passed out.'

'In computer terms, that was the computer crashing. Unable to cope with what it was being asked to do. It's no biggie. Very healthy, in fact. I'm so pleased with your progress I'm tempted to write a paper about your recovery if you'll allow me.'

'What happens now?'

'I still want to see you to check these memories are where they need to be and that there are no residual issues. But, Jesse, I want to see you as an outpatient.'

'I can go home?'

'That's up to Felix and the surgical team. But from my perspective, I have one condition. I don't want you living on your own. You're not well enough, I think, to live totally alone. But you are well enough to leave hospital. In fact, I have a surprise for you.'

'If it's my own personal wheelchair, I shall pick it up and throw it at you.'

Jonathan laughed, went to the door and stuck his head out into the corridor. A few seconds later, Doug came in, wheeling a small suitcase.

'Call me if you need me. I'll see you next week. Wednesday morning at 9 a.m., please.' Jonathan grabbed his files.

'Yes, boss.'

'Rest up. Look after her, Doug.'

Jonathan left and Doug leant his back against the door. 'You've got mad, crazy bed hair,' he observed.

'You don't like my new look?' Jesse asked, lightly feeling a rush of emotions as she stared at Doug.

'I love it,' he said softly. 'Right. I'm busting you out of here, as you said to me once. I need to go and sort out a couple of things with Felix, so I'll be ten minutes, OK?'

'Great. I need a shower.'

'Fresh clothes in there,' he said, pointing at the case. 'See you in a bit,' and he left the room.

Jesse went into the bathroom and frowned at her reflection.

'Oh for the love of God,' she said crossly, looking at the state of her mad hair, the dry line of dribble down the side of her face and the big clump of sleep in her eye.

She stripped off, feeling dizzy for a moment, but stood under the hot shower and slowly felt like a new woman. When Doug returned, she was dressed, with all of her possessions packed. He walked in the room and grabbed her suitcase.

'Better?' she asked.

'More like you. Ready to go?' he asked, his hand on the door handle.

'Ready,' she said, wondering why he hadn't touched her.

They walked slowly to the car together. She saw Brock through the window running in excited circles on the front seat.

'Are we going home?' Jesse asked, making a fuss of Brock as she did up her seat belt.

'Nope,' Doug said, starting the engine.

Jesse raised her eyebrows, smiling widely.

'Er… If I'm not mistaken, that means we're not discussing it.'

Doug inhaled sharply and stared at her.

'How much?' he swallowed, clearly emotional, his voice cracking. 'How much do you remember?'

Jesse reached over and touched his face lovingly. 'All of it,' she said softly. 'Every single thing.'

Three hours later, Jesse stood soaking in the sight of the beach and its gentle curve of bright white sand, with the lazy tide drifting in. She looked at the small cottage which stood directly above the beach, the front door of the cottage opening directly onto steps carved into the rock leading down to the sand. She turned her face to the sun and felt its warmth, despite the chilly autumnal nip to the air.

'So, this is our own beach? Our own private beach?' Jesse turned to Doug who was unloading the truck.

'Aye. Comes with the cottage.'

'So, technically, we can do anything we like on this beach.' She raised an eyebrow.

Doug stopped unloading the truck and turned to her. 'Aye. Did you have something in mind then?'

Jesse gave a teasing smile.

'Just checking. I'll give it some thought. Come on. Give me something to carry.'

Doug had thought of everything. He had packed food, drink, and stuff to make a fire on the beach with. They were sorted for the entire weekend. They'd unpacked hurriedly and gone to explore their surroundings. Evening was falling and they were walking along the sand together with Doug's arm resting loosely across her shoulders as had always been his habit; their fingers entwined. Brock had found a stick and was hitting them alternately on the back of the legs with it.

'It's getting dark,' Jesse observed

'Shall we have a fire on the beach?'

'Perfect,' she breathed. 'I could live here forever.'

'If only,' said Doug. He stopped at the bottom of the rocky steps. 'You hang on here and I'll go and get the gear. You must be exhausted after today. Find a spot, see if there's any driftwood.'

He jogged up the steps lightly and picked up a crate. He put in fire-lighters and some kindling, some wine and a couple of glasses, crisps and dips. He chucked a warm blanket over the top and headed back down the steps.

Jesse had settled herself against a large battered tree trunk and got together a pile of wood. The fire lit and crackling, Doug leant back next to her and passed her a glass of wine. The sun was in the stages of dropping slowly and the beach was bathed in a golden peachy light.

Doug sipped his wine. 'If this is what heaven is, I'm in.'

'Me too.' Jesse yawned. 'God, sorry. I can't understand why I'm tired, I think I must have slept for nearly a whole day.'

'You've been busy fighting monsters.'

'That'll teach them to mess with me,' she said.

Doug turned to face her. 'Can you tell me? What you can… or want to… I just want to understand.'

Jesse gazed into the fire. 'It's hard to explain. The only way I can describe it is that it's like a dream. Nothing makes sense, but you don't question it. Yesterday was no different except for the fact that I wasn't scared anymore.'

'What changed?'

'No idea. Jonathan told me I could change the course of what happened in these sessions whenever I wanted. I could be in charge, and it was like someone had flicked the switch. I thought, well, I'm in charge now. I'll call the shots.'

'What do you remember?'

'About fighting the monster?'

Doug nodded. Jesse sipped her wine and recounted the dream-like experience as she remembered it. When she'd finished Doug was silent for a while and she was shaking slightly.

'Jesus Christ. It sounds terrifying. Then what? You woke and remembered everything?' he asked quietly.

'I woke and then promptly passed out cold for eighteen hours.'

'But you remember now… things you've said today… mean you remember?'

'I do. It feels great to be able to. I just need to reconcile with myself that I tried to kill him.'

'I think you need to look at it differently. Would you do it again if you had to?' Doug asked.

She thought for a moment. 'In a heartbeat.'

'Nothing to reconcile, Jesse,' Doug said quietly. 'It was him or you.'

'It was.'

'Do you remember how you feel about me? About us?' he asked, his light wolf-like eyes searching her face.

Jesse felt the powerful rush of emotion she felt whenever Doug looked at her in a certain way. It filled her heart and twisted her gut in an intense way.

'I do remember,' she said softly. 'You know, all this time, when I was with you, when I saw you, I experienced this feeling… this rush… of something. It was like a physical reaction. But I didn't know what it was. I couldn't process it. But now I know. Now I remember… the feeling is how I *feel* about you. It's like coming home.'

'Are you sure?' Doug asked quietly.

Jesse scooted around to face him. She put her glass down.

'You said to me once that you were all in. You said you wanted me in your life, that you didn't want a life without me.'

'I remember.' He stroked her face. 'Thank God you remember.'

Jesse took his hand and interlaced their fingers. 'Doug, I came back to you. You saved me. I saw your face. I heard your voice. That's what brought me back. You. None of this matters if I'm not with you.' She stroked his face. 'I don't want to spend my days without you.' She paused. 'I'm all in.'

222

Doug stood. He reached down and pulled Jesse up. He gently took her face in his hands and kissed her. He took her hand and walked back towards the cottage, pulling her gently up the stone steps. As he stepped through the doorway, he kissed her again, taking the warm blanket from around her shoulders and dropping it on the floor. He kicked the door shut gently with his foot and pulled her towards the bedroom.

'Don't we usually get interrupted at this point?' she asked as Doug pulled her jumper over her head and started nibbling her neck.

Doug yanked his T-shirt over his head. 'You have my 100 per cent guarantee that I'm not stopping for anything. Not this time,' he said as he pushed her gently back onto the bed.

Jesse lay in bed with her head on Doug's chest. She could hear his heart thumping rhythmically and he was breathing deeply and evenly. His arms were around her and their legs were entwined. She had never felt so loved, so safe, so content in her life. She was on the brink of falling asleep and her last thought before she drifted off was that she wanted to be with this man until the end of her days.

Doug woke early and gently disengaged himself from Jesse. He ran a finger down her naked back, gently kissed her bare shoulder and quietly climbed out of bed. He grabbed a pair of jeans and stepped into them, half doing them up. He let Brock out and quietly made some coffee. Pouring a large mug, and, despite the chill, he opened the front door to enjoy the beach in the early morning light, leaning against the door jamb and sipping his coffee.

He smiled as he felt her arms slide around him from behind and felt her naked body press against his.

'That really is the most delicious sight in the morning,' she murmured, kissing his back. 'You in a pair of jeans and nothing else. Girl could get used to it.'

'Question is… would a girl want to get used to it?' Doug asked softly.

Jesse ran her hands across his chest, her hands creeping further down towards the open waistband of his jeans.

'Oh I think perhaps with a little more persuasion I could maybe get used to it.'

'Only a little more persuasion?'

'OK, a lot more persuasion might be required then.'

'I'd better get started then,' he said, kicking the door shut again.

CHAPTER 17

Sophie stood in front of the door to Sam's room and took a deep breath. She needed to focus on today, she'd been sidetracked. For the whole drive to the hospital she had been wondering about Foxy's sudden departure and change of mood the previous night. She had texted him early asking him if he was OK and she had yet to receive a response. Highly unusual for him not to reply immediately. Lottie interrupted her thoughts as she opened the door and stepped out.

'He's all good to go, Sophie,' she said. 'Little bit grumpy this morning so watch out.'

Sophie nodded and pushed open the door, wondering why she felt nervous.

'Hey, you,' she said, trying not to be too falsely cheerful, walking around to the side of the bed where the visitor's chair was.

'Hi,' he said.

'It's good to see you.' She scrutinised his face, trying to swallow the tears that threatened at his careless tone 'You look good. Lottie says you're doing well.'

Sam snorted and turned away from her gaze. 'She's far too fucking cheerful that one.'

Sophie sat in the chair and put her bag down. 'I've been sending you emails,' she said.

Sam remained silent.

'I don't know if you've read them,' she tried again.

Sam nodded.

'Dad's in respite care for a couple of weeks. To give me a break. Make it a bit easier for next weekend when you're home.'

Sam remained silent.

'Marcus is looking forward to seeing you,' she said brightly.

'I know,' he finally spoke.

'You've talked to him?' Sophie looked surprised.

'He emailed me.'

'Oh,' she said awkwardly. 'He's so tall now. I look at him somedays and I can't quite believe he's our son.'

Sam remained silent, so Sophie ploughed on cheerfully. 'We've got a proper orthopaedic bed for you that a friend has lent us. That came last night.'

'Right. Nice of them.'

Sophie searched for something else to say and then grasped at a subject.

'So it's a big secret in the town what people are doing for the carnival next week. Fishy John won last year. He basically encased the whole of his shack into the mouth of a great white shark. Just like the old *Jaws* posters. I have no idea how he did that, but it was amazing. The Hope and Anchor covered the whole place with these amazing floaty jellyfish.'

'Does Maggie still have the mermaid with the flashing boobs?' Sam asked suddenly and then grinned. For a moment Sophie was reminded of her old Sam, the gorgeous big smile, the dimples she had always loved.

Sophie laughed, delighted that he could remember. 'Yup. She never does anything else. There's a few new businesses, so we'll see what they do. Everyone's really looking forward to it.'

Silence stretched between them and Sophie searched desperately for something to say. She leant forward and tried to take his hand.

'Sam, how do you feel? Really feel?' she asked quietly. 'I feel like I'm visiting someone I work with, not my husband. Talk to me.'

'You don't want to talk to me,' he said tiredly, taking his hand away. 'I've got nothing of interest to say. I'm happy to listen to you though.'

'But, Sam… there's so much to—'

'I don't want to talk about it. Rehash it,' he snapped. 'You must realise that? It serves no purpose.'

'Come on, Sam… we've got to—'

'Talk about something else or go,' he said shortly.

They sat, silence like a gaping chasm. Sophie nervously twisted the handles of her bag.

'Why did you move from our home?' Sam asked suddenly.

Sophie was quiet for a second.

'I didn't have a choice really. All the signs pointed to Castleby. Dad was getting worse, needed help. Marcus was involved with a group of kids that had some gang ties. After a series of stabbings on young boys where that gang was involved, I figured I had to get him away.'

'A nice fresh start then?' Sam's mouth twisted.

Sophie frowned. 'I didn't believe for a moment that you had died. Even when they paid me out the death dues, I never touched that. It's in a separate account.'

'It would have been better for everyone if I had died,' Sam said bitterly.

'You don't think that.'

'Don't tell me what I think,' he snapped. 'You're not the one who is now a fucking useless cripple.'

'Sam, don't talk like that.'

'It's fucking true.'

'Look, plenty of ex-servicemen who have lost their legs go on to have a full and happy life.'

Sam stared her in disbelief. 'And how the *fuck* would you know that? Oh, let me guess. Your new soldier friend tell you that? Your new special friend? Who by the looks of it has both arms and BOTH FUCKING LEGS!' His face grew red from shouting, huge veins stood up on his neck and he was panting with the effort of yelling.

'Calm down, Sam.'

'I want you to go.'

'Sam, I don't want to leave when you're like this… we've not talked, nothing's been said. I feel like we're miles apart.'

'Well, feel free to blame me for all that.'

'I'm sorry for making a statement that I knew nothing about. I can't understand it. How it feels. But I want to, Sam. I'm trying to.'

Sam closed his eyes. 'Just go. You didn't sign up for this, Sophie.'

'I signed up for you. Sickness and in heath. Love and cherish. I meant it.' Sophie's voice shook.

'Sophie, I am no use to you. I have no career anymore. I'm useless. All I am is a burden. To you, to Marcus.' Sam scowled.

'Don't talk that way!' Sophie cried. 'You're not a burden. There is so much you can still do, you just can't see it yet.'

'Stop telling me how I feel,' he said through gritted teeth. 'I know how I feel. Look, I think you should go. I'm tired.' He closed his eyes.

'But—'

'GO!' He opened his eyes and glared at her. 'I'm just not in a good place right now, OK? I'll see you next weekend.'

'Can we talk then?'

'Maybe. Just don't keep pushing it. I don't want to talk about it. I don't want to endlessly relive it. I just want to forget it.'

'Whatever you want. I won't push it. I just want to understand how you feel, Sam. Help you live a normal life.'

A tear trickled out of Sam's eye and down his cheek.

'A normal life? What the *actual* fuck is that for me now? Eh? I think that ship has well and truly fucking sailed,' he said tiredly. 'Just go. See you next week.'

Sophie sat in her car in the hospital car park. She felt helpless. Her finger hovered over a number on her phone and she exhaled deeply and pressed. The phone rang a few times and was answered by a deep male voice, tinged with surprise.

'Sophie?'

'Hi, Connor. How are you?' she stammered. 'Sorry to call.'

A deep sigh came from the phone. 'What can I do for you, Sophie?'

Sophie took a breath. 'They found Sam.'

'I heard that.'

'Did you hear that he's in a bad way?'

'No. It's all highly classified apparently.'

'Well, take it from me. He's in a bad way. Lost both legs. He's pretty damaged on all fronts. Two years of relentless torture in captivity will do that to you.'

'Jesus. Will he make it?'

'Don't know. Look, I need to know. Give him something to hope for. Do you think he'll still be able to work as an intelligence officer even though he can't be operational now?'

'I've no idea. I think it depends on his disability, his state of mind. A raft of things. He would have a great career in the security services though with his mind, his background and his skill for languages.'

'Will the MOD encourage him to leave?'

'I think it's expected that he'd probably be pensioned out on a medical discharge at the very least. Maybe with a hefty whack of compensation.'

Sophie was silent for a moment and then asked, 'Who can I ask? Who'll give me a sensible answer? No company line bullshit. I need to be able to tell Sam he has hope.'

'Leave it with me. I'll talk to some people tomorrow. I promise. I'll let you know. I'd want to know.'

'Thanks, Connor, sorry to ask you.'

He was silent for a moment. 'I half hoped you wanted to talk about…' He trailed off.

'Connor, there isn't anything to talk about,' she said softly.

'I loved you,' he said fiercely. 'I still do.'

'Look,' Sophie said. 'I'm sorry you felt that way. We were friends. But I would never be unfaithful to Sam. You knew that. You always knew that.'

'I waited to tell you. Till he was…'

'Until you thought he was dead?' Sophie asked. 'I never believed that he was dead though.'

'But that kiss.'

'We remember it differently. You remember it meaning something and I remember it as something you tried, and I said no. Because I love my husband. I'm sorry, Con. I never wanted to hurt you. I always loved you as a friend.'

'But never how you loved Sam?'

'I'm sorry.'

'I'll be in touch. Call me if you need anything,' Connor said briskly, ending the call.

Sophie sat for a while, thinking and then checked her phone again, still nothing from Foxy. She rang him.

'Hey,' he said as he answered. 'Is everything OK?'

'Well, that depends on how you look at it,' she said playfully.

There was silence from the other end of the phone.

'Rob?'

'What?'

'What the hell is up? Why are you being weird? Have I done something?'

'Nothing's up. Look, Soph, I'm really busy, can we catch up later? Hang on…' His voice was muffled for a moment. 'No. You need to grab the other hold. The orange one. Do it precisely. More precision and less speed.' His voice was back, clearer now. 'Sorry, Soph. Can we catch up later? I'll call you, I need to go. OK? Bye.'

Sophie sat staring at the phone. Something was up. She knew it. What the hell was that all about? She'd call in on her way home and see him. She was worried that something had happened, and he wasn't telling her. They were friends for God's sake they were supposed to share stuff like this. Satisfied that she would have it out with him later, she started the long drive home.

Sophie had hit every traffic jam there was on the way back. The four-hour drive had turned into a six-hour drive. She almost wept with relief when she saw the outskirts of Castleby. She glanced at the clock on the dashboard and tried to calculate where Foxy might be. It was nearly eight. She supposed he was either in the pub or at home; she would try both and if she didn't find him, she'd head home.

She parked at the climbing centre and ran up the outside steps, peering through the glass window in the door. She knocked and waited, reassured when she heard Solo bark.

'Two seconds,' she heard Foxy's voice call. She watched him approach the door, he had clearly been in the shower and strode towards the door in jeans, barefoot, pulling a T-shirt on. He opened the door and frowned as he saw her.

'Hi,' he said. 'What are you doing here? I thought you were staying the night there.'

'Did I get you out of the shower?' she asked, looking at his wet hair sticking up in odd angles.

'Not really.'

'Your T-shirt's on inside out and back to front,' she said as she stepped past him. 'Something smells nice what'ya cooking?'

Foxy tutted and pulled off his T-shirt and shook it the right way and put it on again.

'What are you doing here, Soph?' he asked, going over to the stove and stirring what was bubbling.

'Can't a mate drop by and say hi?'

Foxy raised an eyebrow.

'Plus, I want to know what's up with you,' she said as she sat down in one of his big leather comfy chairs. 'You're being weird, and I want to know why.'

'I'm not being weird,' he said, turning his back on her and focusing intently on the stove.

'You are so,' Sophie taunted.

'How did it go with Sam today?' Foxy asked, opening a bottle of wine.

'No, no, no,' said Sophie. 'Stop deflecting my interrogation.'

'So this is an interrogation?'

'It is. I've ruled out waterboarding, I'm going to pound you with soft cushions instead if you don't give it up.'

Foxy chuckled. 'Sophie, nothing is wrong. I'm not being weird, OK? Now, do you want wine?'

'Yes.'

'Do you want food?'

'Yes.'

'Is this a bloody hotel?' he chided her, knowing she was always saying this to Marcus.

She laughed. 'I was worried about you,' she admitted, sipping her wine.

'Why on earth were you worried about me?' he asked in surprise.

'You weren't being you. Something was up.'

'Nothing's up. I just realised… well, I thought that I wasn't giving you much space. That I might have been crowding you. You've got some big changes coming. Sam's not going to want me in and out like we do at the moment.'

'What on earth are you on about?' Sophie said in surprise.

'What I said, Sophie. Sam's not going to like me being around. So, I need to give you some space.'

'I've never heard of anything so ridiculous,' she said incredulously. 'Where the hell did this come from?'

Frustrated, Foxy ran his hands through his hair making it stick up even more.

'It didn't come from anywhere. I just think Sam will have an issue with me, so maybe it's better if I keep my distance a little.'

Sophie narrowed her eyes. 'That, Rob Fox, is a crock of shit. I've never heard of anything so ridiculous.'

'You're really embracing this swearing.'

'Only when the situation demands it. You are talking rubbish. Where did this come from, Rob? Talk to me,' she pleaded.

Foxy felt his stomach flip when she looked at him with those big eyes and pleaded with him. He realised now that pushing her away had only made her come closer and more intent on finding out what was wrong.

'I was just putting myself where Sam would be,' he said, trying to throw her off course.

'There's something else,' she said, scrutinising him. 'I know you. All your tells.'

Foxy cursed her for being so intuitive about everything. Instead, he walked over to the stove and grabbed two bowls.

'You're imagining it. Nothing's up. Everything's fine. I was just trying to think about Sam and his feelings.'

'You let me worry about those,' she said, frowning as she watched him. 'What are we eating? Smells bloody gorgeous. I could eat a scabby horse as Sam used to say.'

'How was he today?' Foxy asked, putting her bowl down on the table and giving her a hunk of bread and some cutlery.

Sophie sat down. 'Well, we had a conversation.'

'That's progress.'

'Of sorts.' She tucked in once Foxy was seated. 'God this is so good,' she said, taking another mouthful and closing her eyes. 'Did you make this?'

'Yup.'

'Jesus, feed me like this again and I'll move in for good,' she said, closing her eyes.

'Promises, promises,' Foxy said lightly. 'So, what did Sam say?'

'He got angry about a few things. Didn't want to talk. Asked me to go. Everything I expected. He is coming on Thursday though, into the MOD camp, so he's coming home from there.'

'Will he be in a bed or wheelchair?'

'Wheelchair, I think, from what Lottie says. They're arranging it all.'

'Good. Great that he's coming. Marcus OK about it?'

'Hope so. I need to talk to him. Make sure that he doesn't expect too much.'

'Good idea. I can have a chat with him, he'll be practising plenty here before the competition on Friday. I can talk to him here. Sound him out?'

She touched Foxy's hand. 'That would be amazing.'

'What else did Sam say today?'

'He said he wasn't any use. No job, etc. Felt useless. Everything you said he'd be feeling.'

'That sounds right. Do you know what they're doing with him? Medical discharge?'

Sophie shrugged. 'I asked an old friend that today. He's quite senior in the intelligence arm. Not the same area as Sam, but he has clout nevertheless. I asked him what he thought they'd do for Sam.'

'And?'

'He said he'd find out for me.'

'Do you trust him to be honest?'

'I think so. It was a bit awkward. Asking him, but I didn't know anyone else.'

'Why was it awkward if he was a mate?'

Sophie blushed. 'To cut a long story short, Connor was our friend. Close friend. Then I heard about Sam being missing, presumed dead and Connor turned up and told me he loved me and tried to kiss me.'

'Hopefully he didn't do this on the same day you found out about Sam.'

Sophie laughed softly. 'Well, he had the good grace to wait a week or so. Anyway, we spoke today for the first time since it happened. Is there any more stew?' she said, peering over his shoulder hopefully.

'I swear you eat more than me sometimes,' he said, fetching the pan and dishing her up more. 'Do you think he'll help?'

'Right now, I've no idea, but I have to hope. He did say he thought the security services would snap Sam up. With his experience, languages and background.'

'They probably would,' agreed Foxy as he cleared their bowls away. 'Coffee?'

'Please. Let me wash up.'

'Nope. Go sit,' he said, pointing to the chair she favoured whenever she came over.

Foxy cleared away while Sophie sat in the chair and gazed out to sea. Although it was dark, there was a light moon, so a stretch of ocean was visible. She saw flashing lights out to sea.

'They're cracking on with the bases for the wind farm,' she observed quietly and then gave a huge yawn. 'I've got to do some work for them out there in a couple of weeks.'

Foxy handed her a coffee and went back to clearing up. He was taking his time so he wouldn't have to get close; to talk too much. He was terrified he was going to blurt out how he felt, he'd got so used to talking to Sophie about everything.

He needed to talk to Rudi or Mack, they'd know what to do. They were solid army buddies with sensible heads on their shoulders. Foxy was thinking about what Sophie had said about the friend who had fallen for her and told her he loved her. Was he like that? Would she feel like that about him? That it was awkward?' He was at the point that he couldn't do anything else in the kitchen. He took his coffee and walked over to the other chair, touching the photograph of his late, beloved daughter as he passed. He sat down opposite Sophie and realised she had fallen asleep.

He sat for a while, watching her. Thinking. Finally, he stood.

'Jesus, Soph, you're killing me here,' he said quietly. He picked her up gently and took her into the bedroom. Laying her down on the bed, he took her shoes off and pulled the duvet over her. He tucked her in, grabbed the warm blanket draped over the end of his bed and returned to the lounge where he sat in his chair and wondered what the bloody hell to do.

He will deliver my soul from the lowest hell, so great is His mercy towards me. These people they deserve to die. They have no place here. They are a plague of society in my view. They are the devil, their wickedness runs among them. Most of them are evil. Disguised well. But I see through it. I see it all. God knows I see it. He must know. He's told me to do this when he revealed Himself to me. I am His servant. I will be rewarded. His love for me will shine down and I will be welcomed into His heavenly kingdom. Not before I have finished my work though. That must carry on. It is my calling. Heaven can wait for now.

CHAPTER 18

Edwina Pomeroy sat at the kitchen table in the empty vicarage with a cup of tea. She had shooed the vicar and Peter out to church, waving aside their concerns that she should be at home grieving for her dead husband. Edwina was doing quite the opposite. She wasn't in the slightest bit sad about Fred's death. She had identified his body the day before, tersely, then signed the required forms and left without any emotion at all.

She had assured the vicar she needed to be busy, but she was, in fact, thoroughly enjoying the attention and all the sympathy she was getting. If she hadn't had an enormous stack of mail to steam open that morning from the previous day and a cheque to help herself to, she would have attended church to soak up the sympathy on offer from the congregation.

She flicked the kettle on and proceeded to go through the post, steaming open every letter and then carefully resealing with her trusty glue stick. Fully informed, she set the post on the vicar's desk and had a rifle through his messy paperwork in case there was anything she had missed.

Finding nothing significant, she opened the drawer and brought out the cheque book. Writing herself a cheque, she carefully forged the vicar's signature. Fairly small amounts regularly didn't raise any concerns. She had been doing it for years now and was very pleased with her vicar's signature. She increased the amount slightly; she did have a funeral to pay for after all and it was only what she deserved.

She tutted when she saw a notepad with Marion's name on it and the date of her arrival. She also saw that the vicar had written 'vegetarian' and underlined it, with *tell Mrs P* scribbled next to it. She rolled her eyes and went upstairs to make up the bed for Marion who was due in the next day or so.

As she walked up the stairs, she thought she'd use the coarsest sheets she could find for the bed, she didn't want the woman getting too comfortable at the vicarage after all. She thought about how ridiculous the vicar was being about the woman's visit and pursed her lips angrily. The man was a fool. He couldn't see the goodness that was right in front of his face most of the time. She vowed to make Marion's visit as difficult and as uncomfortable for her as possible.

* * *

Kate was still painting the cottage, with plans to move in properly over the next couple of days. She had decided the kitchen needed at least one wall of colour, so she had treated herself to a blue which instantly reminded her of sunny Greek holidays.

As she painted, she hummed happily, thinking what a good move it had been to come back to the area. No more Matthew and his petulant, lazy ways. Instead, she had met Steve quite by accident. She thought of him and how he made her feel. She had practically swooned like something from a romance novel when he had come to her rescue in the café the other day.

Her dad had whispered that he liked Steve very much and he looked like a keeper, when he had bumped into them in the town the other day. Kate had pointedly ignored her mother as she had taken one look at Steve, pursed her lips and looked down her nose at him. She then started to talk loudly about how wonderful it had been to see Matthew and what a wonderful man he was. Kate had kissed her father goodbye and walked off, leaving her mother talking to thin air.

The door knocker sounded.

'You really don't need to knock, you know,' she said as she opened the door and was faced with Matthew.

'That's good to know,' he said.

Kate eyed him suspiciously. 'Actually, you definitely need to knock. I thought you were someone else.'

'The knuckle dragger? Can I come in?' he asked, stepping forward.

Kate closed the door slightly to stop him. 'What do you want, Matthew?'

'I want to talk to you,' he said pleasantly. 'I think things got out of hand last time we spoke. I was angry.'

'You said what you said, Matthew. No taking it back. Wasn't that always what you said? Say what you mean, it's always the truth?'

'Well, I wasn't being fair. I'm sorry.'

'Apology accepted. Let's move on with our separate lives.'

Matthew stuck a foot in the door. 'We need to talk, Kate,' he said firmly. 'There are things to resolve.'

'There's nothing to resolve,' she said, trying to force the door shut. 'My solicitor will be in touch.'

'Kate,' he said patiently. 'Come on. I'm your husband. We can at least be civil.'

'Matthew,' Kate said, slightly uneasy with his demeanour. 'Can you take your foot out of the door, please? Honestly? There's nothing to say.'

'Please? Just hear me out? I need to say some things.'

Kate thought for a moment, she would say anything to get rid of him. 'I'll meet you in the café in ten minutes.'

Matthew frowned slightly. 'Right. I'll meet you there then. Look, I've removed my foot. OK? I'll see you in ten minutes.'

Kate relaxed slightly.

'See you in a minute,' she said, closing the door.

As she went to shut it, it flew back open with the force of a kick. The side of the door caught her in the face; she was dazed for a moment and staggered. Matthew kicked the door shut and turned to her, grabbing her wrist tightly. His face was contorted with anger. He looked around wildly and dragged her towards the front room. She tripped and almost fell, but he yanked her arm tightly, pulling her, the pain of his grip on her wrist excruciating. She could feel her cheek throbbing and blood on the side of her face.

Matthew spoke to her coldly as he dragged her along the hall corridor.

'I think you need to remember that I'm your husband, Kate. I won't be cast aside for some knuckle dragger who carries a badge and looks like a builder. I will not be told when things are over. I will decide that.'

'Get off me!' she yelled, trying to pull away and kick him away from her.

He spun around and gave her face a backhanded swipe, knocking her over and twisting the arm that he held tightly. Matthew yanked her towards the kitchen and forced her face down on the table, yanking her hand up behind her, making her cry out in pain. Kate's nose was pouring with blood, and it smeared the table as he pressed her face into the wooden surface and spoke through gritted teeth into her ear.

'You will not tell *me* where I can meet my own wife. You are *my* wife. I call the shots here. Who the hell do you think you are?'

Kate struggled to get free, but Matthew held her tightly. As she struggled she felt him harden against her. She had a terrible premonition of what was about to happen. Matthew had always been fond of rough sex; he had always found it a real turn on, whereas Kate had often felt like she had been the victim of a brutal attack afterwards. While he had never hit her, up until this point in their relationship, he had hit walls and doors and told her he wished it had been her face.

'Get off me,' she screamed through the blood, coughing again as it flowed from her nose down her throat. She struggled to get away and he forced her arm upwards. She cried out in pain when it felt like her shoulder was being wrenched out of the joint. He ground himself against her, panting.

'You seem to like a bit of local rough.' He tried to get the button undone on her jeans. 'So I'll give you a bit of rough. I can be a knuckle dragger too, Kate,' he said, his breath hot in her ear.

His hand was vicious on her breasts, and he was fumbling to get the zip down on her jeans. She felt her jeans give and he started to yank them down. Kate was screaming at him to get off and struggling to get free when suddenly she heard a thud and Matthew slumped over her.

Kate screamed and tried to wriggle away as the pressure on her arm released. The weight of Matthew was pinning her to the table. She moved and he slid off her and fell to the floor like a dead weight; Kate lay half sobbing on the table.

'It's OK, my darling,' Maggie said, putting down one of the off cuts of wood that Steve had left. 'He's out cold.'

Maggie gently helped Kate stand, pull her jeans back up and tuck her shirt back in.

'He didn't… did he?'

Kate shook her head, she was trembling. 'Thanks to you, Mags,' she said shakily.

Maggie walked over to Matthew and gave him a hefty kick in the ribs.

'I saw him on his way up here while I was putting the bins out. I rang Steve when I saw him force the door open.'

The front door flew open, and Steve ran in.

'Jesus Christ,' he said, taking Kate's face in his hands and pulling her towards him in a hug. 'I'm sorry I wasn't here.'

Kate breathed in the scent of him and felt safe in his arms. She exhaled deeply and burst into fresh tears again.

'It's the shock,' said Maggie, lifting dustsheets and putting the kettle on. She turned to Steve. 'When I got here, he had her bent over that table, trying to get her jeans off, forcing her…'

'What?' Steve looked at Kate. 'Did he…?'

'No,' Maggie said triumphantly. 'I walloped him pretty hard with that lump of wood there just to get him off her.'

Matthew stirred on the floor and Maggie walked over and kicked him again.

'Maggie,' Steve warned. 'Much as we'd like to. We can't.'

'What are you taking about, Inspector?' she said innocently. 'He must have fallen on something.'

Steve sat Kate down and knelt in front of her looking carefully at her face.

'I don't think anything's broken, but I think you are going to look pretty bad for a couple of days.'

'No change there then,' Kate sniffed.

'Still totally gorgeous to me,' Steve said, kissing her gently. 'Let's get you cleaned up. Do you need to go to hospital?'

Kate shook her head. 'I'm OK. Just in shock a bit, I think.'

Maggie passed her a cup of tea and pointed at Matthew still lying on the floor. 'What are we going to do with him?' she asked.

'Do you want to press charges?'

Kate looked at Matthew on the floor. 'I never want to see him again. Just get rid of him. He won't be back here if he knows I've got that over him.'

'Leave it to me,' Maggie said grimly, pulling out her phone. 'Foxy, my darling. Could you come and give me a hand putting out some rubbish, please? It's a bit too heavy for me. I'm at Kate's new place. Thanks, love.' She ended the call and looked at Steve. 'You take that girl to yours for a while and look after her properly.'

Kate was dozing on Steve's sofa. She could hear gentle music in the kitchen and sounds and smells of cooking were wafting out. The gentle buzzing of her phone woke her, and she scrabbled to answer it not recognising the number. She grimaced as she sat up, her face sore and her shoulder stiff from where Matthew had forced her arm up her back. She answered the call.

'Hello?'

'Kate?' came a familiar female voice. 'Kate… I'm sorry to call you. It's Anna.'

Kate was silent for a moment.

'Kate, are you there?'

'Yes, I'm here. What can I do for you, Anna?'

'I feel terrible calling you. After, you know, Matthew threw you out. I asked him not to by the way, but he was adamant.'

'I see,' said Kate, not surprised at the narrative that Matthew had clearly created. 'What can I help you with, Anna?'

'Oh, Kate,' she sobbed. 'We used to be so close, and now…'

'Having an affair with someone's husband will do that,' said Kate curtly. 'What do you want, Anna?'

'I've been trying to reach Matt for a few days, and I don't know where he is. We rowed and he took off and I've heard nothing from him. I just wondered…'

'Wondered what?'

'Wondered whether you have any idea of where he might have gone?'

Kate was silent.

'Do you?' Anna pushed.

Kate sat up. 'Anna, I'm not going to lie to you. There's been enough of that already. Just so you know, Matthew didn't throw me out, I made the decision to leave, come home and run Dad's practice. Matthew has been here, he turned up telling me he was ready to move here and that you two were over.'

Kate heard Anna's sharp intake of breath.

'When I said no, he was abusive and a friend of mine had to escort him out of the café we were in – he was getting really nasty.'

'I'm sure it was just a misunderstanding.'

'I can assure you it wasn't. And it wasn't a misunderstanding when he forced himself into my house earlier today, belted me and then held me down and tried to rape me.'

Silence came from Anna's end of the phone.

'I think you need to count yourself lucky it's over with him, Anna. I certainly do.'

'He wouldn't do that,' Anna said tightly. 'You're making it up. You're just jealous.'

'Well, it seems he would do it. And happily lie about you two breaking up and him being prepared to move here.'

'He wouldn't do that. He's going to be a…'

'Going to be a what, Anna?' Kate stiffened.

'Going to be a father,' Anna declared.

'And when might that be?' Kate asked quietly.

'In about two weeks' time.'

Kate was silent for a moment.

'I wish you all the best with that. Goodbye, Anna,' she said, ending the call and letting the phone drop from her hand.

She felt a gentle hand on her head as Steve appeared with a cup of tea.

'You OK?' he asked, perching on the arm of the sofa and handing her the mug. 'Is Anna a friend of yours?'

'She was,' Kate said. 'She was the one having an affair with Matt. He moved her in straight after me. She tells me Matt is going to be a father in a fortnight.'

'Wait, doesn't that mean…'

'He got her pregnant around the same time as Daniel died,' Kate finished.

'My God,' said Steve, sitting next to her on the sofa and pulling her close for a hug. 'Is there no end to how low this guy will go.'

'Seems not. I don't want to see him again. Ever.'

'You won't if I have anything to do with it.'

'Here's hoping,' she said grimly, laying her head on his shoulder.

* * *

Foxy had agreed to Maggie's request and removed Matthew from Kate's cottage. He had slapped him awake and asked him where he was staying, then slung him over his shoulder, and taken him there.

247

He had thrown him down on the floor when they entered Matthew's room and Foxy had requested politely that Matthew pack immediately. Matthew, a coward by heart, had been terrified of the six foot six tattooed frame of Foxy, with his enormous arms and had literally thrown his belongings into his suitcase. Foxy accompanied him down to reception where he watched Matthew settle his bill.

'This is intimidation,' Matthew whined as Foxy stood quietly with his large arms folded, watching him.

Foxy had merely raised an eyebrow and continued to watch.

When they had arrived at Matthew's car, Foxy came and stood close to him, backing him against it.

'Now, I don't want to see you here again, mate,' he said pleasantly. 'Are we clear on that?'

Matthew drew himself up and tried to tough it out. 'You can't stop me coming here.'

Foxy raised his eyebrow again. 'No, I can't,' he agreed. 'But things won't go so well for you next time if I see you here again.'

'I will come and go when and where I like,' Matthew spluttered, trying to step away from Foxy.

Foxy moved closer to him.

'Am I not being clear enough for you? Do I need to spell it out?' he asked quietly. 'You see, by my reckoning, you laid your hands on my mate's girlfriend. In fact, Maggie tells me you tried to force yourself on her, not to mention, got a little bit handy with her. So, by my reckoning, you deserve a little bit of your own medicine.'

'She's lying,' Matthew shouted, trying to get past Foxy. With lightning speed, Foxy jabbed Matthew in the face, so quickly that he was only aware of it afterwards when he realised his face was on fire.

'Maggie never lies,' Foxy said quietly. 'So, I'll ask again. Are we clear on you not coming here again or do I need to really spell it out?'

'I'm clear,' Matthew said, climbing into his car quickly, clutching his bleeding nose.

Foxy grabbed the door preventing him from shutting it. 'I promise you,' he said quietly and dangerously, his blue eyes boring into Matthew. 'If I so much as hear you're back again – and I will find out – you will be highly unlikely to ever walk again, let alone be able to feed yourself.' He said brightly, 'Now, you have a safe journey, won't you?' He slammed the car door, tapped the roof twice and watched Matthew drive away.

* * *

Sam sat in the wheelchair by the large glass window. He estimated he was around ten stories up. He wondered whether he would die instantly if he fell from this height, or would he linger with bad injuries and brain damage. He snorted. Knowing him, that's what would happen. He wanted something that was quick and fatal, he was past caring whether it hurt or not. He just wanted to end it permanently. Chances of that happening here were zero unless he held hostage the nurse who controlled the medicine trolley. It appeared that it was more closely guarded than the crown jewels, so that option was out too.

Lottie appeared and wheeled him into physio, where the gruelling exercises left him sweaty, grumpy, and exhausted. Lottie then took him down another floor where a very quiet and unassuming man who reminded Sam of a small mouse, explained patiently that he would be fitting Sam with some temporary prosthesis until his limbs had healed completely. For ages Sam felt him fiddling about with what was left of his legs and then finally, the agony was over, and Sam was dismissed back to his ward.

The physio had told Sam that he needed to improve his upper body strength and had suggested a variety of exercises, designed to build up his muscles and stamina.

Before Sam had been captured, he had been in peak physical condition, with incredible core strength. He had completely wasted away in captivity. An attempt earlier to get himself up a rope had left him sobbing with frustration. He couldn't even pull himself up out of the chair.

As Lottie wheeled him back to the ward, he asked her to stop at the gym again, he wanted to have another go. He set himself a test in his mind: if he could get at least 3 metres up the rope, then he wouldn't think about dying for the next day or so. If he couldn't, then he'd carry on thinking about how to end his miserable life.

Lottie guided him to below the rope and watched with concern. She had already told him he was overdoing it, and that he needed to wait for the physiotherapist to be there, but he tuned her out completely.

He sat looking up at the rope dangling above him. He grabbed it and tried to haul himself up, but he still couldn't lift himself out of his chair. He slumped back, sweaty and grumpy, and promised himself he would come up with a plan to die as soon as he could think rationally.

Lottie talked incessantly about how much she was looking forward to the forthcoming weekend. She babbled on about the fact that they were leaving on Thursday and would be back at the hospital on Tuesday morning, how they were getting there and what to expect. Sam did his usual of not listening but nodding every now and again when it looked like she was waiting for an answer. He wasn't listening. He was wondering how and when the opportunity to kill himself would arise.

CHAPTER 19

Foxy was in the climbing centre with a few of the kids who were taking part in the 'ENDURE' climbing competition, which was due to happen on Friday evening to mark the start of the carnival of the sea. The kids were practising difficult holds and timing themselves; the competition covered speed and agility.

The last of the kids were picked up by a harried parent, leaving Marcus and Jude with Foxy in the centre. Jude was still struggling with some of the holds, his hands had been badly damaged when he had rescued Marcus from a mineshaft a couple of months earlier.

'Gotta keep doing those exercises, mate,' Foxy said, ruffling his hair. 'You'll get there.'

Jude nodded and unclipped himself from his harness.

'I know,' he said ruefully. 'Marcus is gonna beat me though.' He watched Marcus who was up high and hanging upside down.

'Only this year,' Foxy said quietly. 'You'll beat him, you always used to before the accident. The two most powerful warriors are patience and time,' he said wistfully.

'What are you on about?' Jude frowned, confused.

'I'm trying to say have patience and you'll beat him next year. A man who masters patience masters everything else.'

'Why are you speaking in riddles?' asked Jude, pulling a face.

Foxy shook his head. 'Wasted on the young.' He waved at Doug who had stuck his head in the door and whistled for Jude.

'See ya,' Jude said, picking up his bag and leaving.

'See ya,' Foxy echoed, pushing the door open to get some clean air in. He clicked his fingers for Solo and motioned for him to lie across the door.

'Marcus,' he called. 'Time's up, mate.'

Marcus swung himself around and dropped down in front of Foxy.

'I reckon I've got that corner turn sorted now,' he said happily.

'Looks good. You know the route is changing, though, for Friday? Gotta make it fair for everyone.'

'Yeah, Mum said you'd change it to make it fair for the out of towners.'

'She OK?' Foxy asked as him and Marcus coiled up ropes.

'Yeah. I think she's worried about Dad coming home. She keeps moving furniture around.'

Foxy sat down on a bench and passed Marcus some more ropes to coil.

'You worried? About seeing him?' Foxy asked quietly.

Marcus was silent for a moment. 'What will he look like?' he asked in a small voice.

'I don't know, mate. He'll be a wheelchair. You'll see the bits of his legs that are left. But they'll still be healing, so they'll have bandages on. They might have fitted him with some false legs as a start, if they've got him up and about.'

'Will he look different?'

'I think he's probably thinner than you remember. I don't know.'

'How will he be?'

'I don't know, mate. He's pretty confused, I think. Not making much sense some of the time. The head takes longer to heal than the body sometimes.'

'Will he want to hug me?'

'Is that a big deal?' Foxy eyed him.

'I don't know if I remember him. It might be weird,' Marcus blinked.

Foxy could see he was getting upset and nudged him.

'Do you know what I reckon, Marcus? If you want to hug him, then do. Do whatever feels right.'

Marcus looked worried. 'What if he doesn't want to hug me? What if he doesn't remember me?'

'Of course he'll remember you. He might just be surprised at how big you are now. He might feel a bit awkward. He might be feeling as awkward as you are. Maybe make a joke about it. Easier to poke fun at a situation sometimes.'

'What d'you mean?'

'Well, you know… you see him, he sees you. Do you hug, don't you? That's one of those awkward moments, why don't you think about what you might say to make it less awkward.'

'Like what?'

'I dunno. Maybe like, "Hey, Dad, are you as confused as me about whether to hug or not? Why don't we high five instead?"'

'Bit lame,' Marcus said sarcastically. 'No one high fives anymore.'

'Oh well excuse me. Suggest something else instead then.' Foxy said dryly. 'Obviously something cool and not lame.'

'OK.'

'What do I say to him? Talk to him about?'

'Anything, mate. He's lost two years of your news. I'd say that's plenty to talk about.'

'Umm.' Marcus inspected the rope closely.

'Perhaps thrill him with your escapades with Jude up the mountain?'

'Foxy, what if he doesn't like me?' he asked quietly.

'Then he's a bloody idiot,' said Foxy, pulling Marcus in for a quick hug. 'What's not to like?'

Sophie had just been about to come into the climbing centre when she had overheard the start of the conversation. She stood quietly just inside the door listening to what Marcus was asking Foxy. At the last question, she stuffed her hand in her mouth to stop herself from sobbing out loud. Not just at Marcus's question, but at Foxy's answer. She was overwhelmed by this gentle giant and how he was with her son. She wiped her eyes quickly and pretended she had just arrived, calling out to Solo.

'Hello, gorgeous boy,' she crooned as she stopped to stroke him.

'Your mother's being nice to me again.' Foxy nudged Marcus as she walked in.

Marcus rolled his eyes. 'You know she meant the dog, right?' He handed Foxy the rope. 'Thanks, Foxy,' he said quietly.

'Anytime, buddy.'

'How did it go?' Sophie asked brightly, looking at both of them.

'Good,' they said in unison.

'Ready to go?' she asked Marcus.

'I'll get my stuff,' he said and disappeared off around the corner.

'OK?' Sophie asked Foxy.

'All good.' He avoided her gaze and stacked the ropes.

'Do you need any help getting ready for the competition?'

'I'm good, thanks. Rudi's helping out. It'll be a late one and you'll have your hands full anyway.'

'Right.'

'Are you all set at home? Need anything moved?'

'I'm all set,' she said. 'Thanks though.'

Marcus appeared with his bag and climbing shoes.

'See you, mate,' said Foxy, ruffling his hair.

'Thanks, Foxy,' he said as he stopped to stroke Solo. 'See ya.'

Sophie ushered Marcus out of the door, giving Foxy a wave, and he closed and locked it behind them. He rested his head on the door and swore softly to himself as he caught the lingering scent of Sophie's perfume. In some ways on an emotional level he felt like he'd swapped one type of hell for another.

* * *

Jimmy was shitting bricks. Not only did he have the rest of JJ in a suitcase in the back of his truck, but he also realised that Steve and Jonesey were in the car behind him. His palms were sweaty, and he was convinced his heart was about to jump out of his chest at any moment.

As well as JJ, who was nicely defrosting in the suitcase, he also had two gallons of petrol, a few empty glass bottles, some old rags, a large pair of bolt cutters and a new tube of superglue. Quite the arsonist's kit.

He kept to the speed limit and indicated at the next turning, anything to get away from them and he turned hoping they wouldn't follow him.

Relieved he couldn't see them in the rear-view mirror, he swung around and got back onto the coast road. He pulled out and trundled along the road, checking his mirror again. He pulled into the layby near a farm track and locked the truck.

Grabbing the bolt cutters and the glue he ducked through the fields arriving at the Camorra's farm building which appeared deserted. He checked all around looking carefully in windows, making absolutely sure that he was alone. He deftly cut the padlock on the front lock, carefully putting it to one side with the glue for when he left, and let himself in. Invariably, if he cut the padlock in the right place with a clean cut, he could superglue it back together and no one would ever be the wiser until it was too late. He settled in to wait for nightfall and to keep a lookout.

* * *

Jonesey opened another packet of toffees and noisily unwrapped one, stuffing it in his mouth and chewing loudly. He peered through the windscreen.

'Where's he gone?'

'Inside,' said Steve. 'I expect he's waiting for it to get dark.'

'Can't we nick him now for B&E?'

'Now where's the fun in that?' Steve said, pinching a toffee.

'When are we going to nick him?'

'I don't know if we are yet,' Steve said absently as he watched Jimmy leave the building in the dimming light.

'Why the blimmin' hell are we here then?'

'We're looking for the extra piece of the jigsaw.'

'What jigsaw?' asked Jonesey, frustrated.

'The jigsaw that's largely made up of JJ's head, and where the rest of him is and who it was that took him apart.'

'Oh. That jigsaw.'

'Call in the location of this building and get a namecheck on it.'

Jonesey obliged and Steve leant forward in his seat as he saw Jimmy's truck rolling down the dirt track with its headlights off. He produced his phone and filmed him as he drove around to the side of the building and watched as Jimmy heaved a large suitcase out of the back of his truck and into the building and return with two gallon cans.

'Registered to Abacus Holdings,' Jonesey said, unwrapping another toffee. 'Are we getting food on the way back? I'm starving.'

'Shush,' Steve murmured as he watched Jimmy essentially prepare a number of Molotov cocktails and place them carefully by the door.

He disappeared inside again and when he came out, he carefully laid something on the floor. Jimmy took a few of the cocktails and walked back inside returning without them and Steve noted an orange glow in the far corner of the lockup through one of the small windows.

'He's torching the place,' he said, still filming.

Jimmy lit the last two and hurled them through the open door, then closed the door and replaced the padlock carefully. Steve struggled to see what he was doing but he fiddled with the lock for a while and then jumped in his truck, gunned the engine and drove away.

Steve filmed the back of Jimmy's truck disappearing from sight and picked up the radio to call it in for the fire brigade.

'We're nicking him now, right? For arson?'

'Not yet. It's not like we don't know who did it. I want to see what's in that lockup that's so bad it needs to be torched.'

Jimmy was ecstatic. He had got rid of JJ for good. He considered himself to be very clever, he had put JJ in the freezer area with all the other torsos and various limbs, opened the lids of the freezers and covered them all with petrol. That had been the first place he had thrown one of his Molotov cocktails and it had gone up instantly. He'd also relocated a couple of gas bottles to that area too in the hope that it was a belt and braces approach.

He'd also checked that the cars under the tarps had petrol in them and made sure that the petrol tanks had gone up too. He drove back to his lockup and carefully changed out of his clothes, leaving them under a load of old crates in a corner. Then he drove into town, leaving his truck in one of the usual places and took himself off for a congratulatory pint. He smirked to himself, he considered it a job well done and was fairly impressed with his much-improved criminal prowess.

* * *

Doug and Jesse had arrived back from their weekend away to find the place upside down and the kids high with excitement. Claire and Felix had picked up the keys to their house and were moving Claire's things across the road. The kids had chosen which bedroom they wanted and were moving some of their things into the house too. Jesse had received a tour of Claire and Felix's new house, being dragged around by the kids until she had begged off. She walked down to her own house to pack a suitcase of clothes and a few things to keep at Doug's until she was fully recovered.

Doug stood in his bedroom which had been vacated by Claire and was pleased at the prospect of having the house back to himself. He was enjoying the quiet and wondering whether he should paint the bedroom or change it at all now Jesse would be in there with him. He heard footsteps on the stairs and assumed it was one of the kids back for another load.

'Hey, gorgeous,' Jesse said, coming in and sliding her arms around his waist.

'Well, hello yourself,' he said, turning to meet her embrace.

'What you pondering about up here on your lonesome?' she asked, smiling.

'How nice it is to have my room back, how lovely it will be to have you in it and whether I should paint it or rearrange it.'

'Quite the topics for pondering,' she agreed.

'So paint it? Not paint it?'

'Don't care,' she said. 'Just as long as you're in here with me. That's all I want. We could shift some of the furniture about.'

'I think I can arrange that,' Doug said, kissing her gently.

'Gross,' announced Jude loudly from the doorway. 'Totally gross.'

'Bugger off,' Doug said. 'You can always go and live with your mother.'

'They're just as gross,' he announced. 'This could damage me for life, you know. I'm a fragile teenager. I'm not sure I can cope with all this. It's highly stressful being in these environments.'

'Will pizza for tea help?' asked Jesse dryly.

'Bring it on,' he said. 'I'm feeling better already. I get to choose toppings though.'

* * *

Steve was reviewing the post-mortem notes on Joy Brown who died at the vicar's coffee morning. Joy had died from a combination of factors, a heart attack and a resultant brain bleed, almost certainly caused by her fall and hitting her head on the table and then the hard floor. Steve placed the report to one side and moved on to Fred's.

Fred Pomeroy's post-mortem had shown excessive bleeding from the rectum, eyes, nose and mouth, which led to some sort of circulatory failure from what Steve could gather. The report then became too much for him as he read terms such as, centrilobular hepatocellular necrosis. Sighing, he picked up the phone and rang the pathologist for an idiot's guide to what killed Fred.

'Jim Murphy.' The pathologist answered absently.

'Murph. It's Steve. How you doing?'

'Hello, hello, hello,' Murph said good-naturedly. 'What's with all the work you're chucking my way? The other half's on the warpath. I've worked all weekend to clear the backlog given to me by you and he's got the right hump about it.'

'Tell him I said sorry. There's funny goings on, maybe. Just need to pin down what, really. So I'm reading your report on Fred and my tiny police brain just couldn't cope, hence the call. So, the idiot version, please, on what killed Fred.'

'OK. Ultimately Fred drowned.'

'Right. Could we not have said that in the report?'

'Well, the interesting thing about it all is…'

'Do I need a drum roll?'

'Maybe, but we have to ask ourselves what led him to probably fall overboard in the first place.'

'Do we need to ask that?'

'We do.'

'OK, so I'm asking.'

'In very simple terms, he had an incredibly painful death leading up to him going in the water. He ingested something that led to a fairly acute and highly toxic injury to the liver, which in very simple terms led to a sort of hepatic fever symptoms.'

'God. Give me an idea of what that looks like.'

'Horrendous. Vomiting, diarrhoea, fever, abdomen swells, skin feels like it's itchy and on fire. Fred basically also bled out from pretty much every orifice there was. Not a nice way to go.'

'Jesus. What was it?'

'Hard to tell. Stomach was empty since he had probably been vomiting for hours. Tox screen showed something interesting though, so I got a mate to run a few more tests to narrow it down more and it showed the presence of the amatoxins, phallotoxins and phallolysin.'

'OK, back to the idiot's guide, please.'

'I would hazard a guess that your Fred ate something like poisonous mushrooms or a product from them at some point prior to his death.'

'*What?*'

'Great time of year for them. Go into the woods and if you know what you're doing, you'll find plenty. In some types of death cap, you only need about half a mushroom and it's lights out for good.'

'Christ alive. So he was poisoned?'

'Might have been. Might have eaten them by accident. That's your realm, not mine.'

'Right. Anything else I need to know?'

'Your Joy Brown.'

'Heart attack and head bleed? Yes?'

'That's the one. She also had some trace elements of what we call amanita toxicity in her blood work. A small amount, but enough to make her feel pretty bloody poorly and perhaps even prompt the heart attack. I understand she had a fairly weak heart from what I hear. It wasn't in great nick by the time I saw it.'

'And amanita toxicity is what?'

'Simple terms. Mushroom poisoning.'

'Bugger me,' Steve said softly.

'While that's a tempting offer, I'll pass. Call me if you need anything else.'

'Murph, do me a favour?'

'Depends.'

'Can you cross-check on your system to see if this sort of tox result shows up in other deaths in the last few months?'

'I can, but I'll need to run some extra tests. I'll get a minion to do it. It'll take some time though. Meantime, try and track back to where Fred might have eaten it, probably 12 to 18 hours before he got on the boat and also Joy too.'

'You telling me how to do my job?'

'I wouldn't dare. But it will shed some light. I'll chivvy the minion.'

'Appreciate it. If the minion hurries up, they'll be pint or two in it.'

'I'll pass it on. See you, Steve.'

'Cheers, Murph.'

* * *

Kate sat in the pub opposite Steve. She drank deeply from the large glass of red wine that he had presented her with.

'God that's good,' she said, smacking her lips.

'Thirsty?' he asked.

'I've had a right old day. I'm sick of explaining my black eye to people,' she said crossly. 'I'm sure some of the old biddies have come in today just to have a look at it and gossip rather than being ill.'

'What did you tell them?' Steve asked, amused.

'Police brutality and excessive force,' she said dryly.

263

'Excellent,' Steve said. 'So, I have news.'

'Ooh that sounds exciting,' she said, leaning forwards.

'I talked to Murph the pathologist today. He had some very interesting conclusions.'

'Such as?'

'Simple terms. Mushroom poisoning seems to be a tad prevalent.'

'What?' she said in disbelief.

'Although Fred drowned, the thing that probably caused him to drown was a type of hepatic fever.'

'Jesus. That's an awful way to go.'

'Also, Joy Brown? Although she had a heart attack and a brain bleed. She was showing the same or similar toxins.'

Kate sat back in her chair, her face a picture of disbelief.

'Are you saying…' she glanced around and then leant forwards. 'Are you saying that maybe someone is killing people with mushrooms?'

Steve shrugged. 'Don't know yet. Apparently, loads of people die each year from eating the wrong type of mushroom. We have to try and find out whether it's someone dabbling in wild mushrooms and being clueless, or whether it's intentional poisonings.'

'Christ. That's pretty hard to prove, isn't it?'

'It is.'

Kate thought for a minute. 'Wouldn't that be the difference between manslaughter and murder?'

'If the mushrooms were obtained and given with intent, then it's murder. If they were there and eaten accidentally, for example, then that might be manslaughter, but it all leads to very murky waters.'

'What's next?'

'Be good to see if you can recall any patients suffering from what looks like the early stages of food poisoning. That's how it starts I'm told, well fairly similar anyway.'

'I'll talk to Dad and the practice nurses.'

'Murph's checking tox screens for previous PMs. I also need to backtrack on people's movements including where they ate.'

'I don't pity you doing that.'

'It all helps to build up my impressive stamina if there's a lot of leg work, ready for my assessment.' Steve grinned.

'We've yet to schedule your assessment, although the early signs look quite promising,' Kate said.

'Perhaps we should schedule my assessment as a matter of urgency then,' Steve said, trying not to smile.

'Perhaps we should, Inspector.' Kate couldn't stop chuckling.

'I'm at your leisure, Doctor, want another drink?'

The evil and the selfish overwhelm me. They are the marauding hordes. I wonder if there are too many… They clutter my surroundings; they dampen his voice in my head. They are a drain on society, they serve no purpose. Would the world be better without them? As the chosen one I am doing the world a service, not just God, but the whole kingdom too. He knows. He is patient. He knows the scale of the work I have to do. My work must continue. I must carry on. He's waiting for me to finish it.

CHAPTER 20

Jimmy was on the early ferry to Ireland. To say he was unhappy about the trip was an understatement. His long-suffering partner Marie had been highly sceptical about him being away for a few nights on the premise of bringing a boat back. She had given him an exceptionally hard time, convinced that once again Jimmy was dabbling in the criminal underworld that was far too quick-witted for Jimmy to keep up with.

He bagged himself a seat in the bar, ordered a pint and settled in for the journey. The weather wasn't too bad over the next few days, so Jimmy was aiming to be back at the weekend, all things being well. He didn't trust the Camorra, but even Jimmy's tiny brain had worked out that they wouldn't go to the trouble of sending him off on a yacht just to get rid of him. If they wanted to do that, they'd probably just cut him up into small pieces and freeze him.

* * *

Steve stood in the blackened building, feeling ridiculous in the white suit and blue booties. He'd signed himself in and the head of the forensic team was picking his way across the floor on the raised footplates that protected the crime scene. He stopped and beckoned Steve over, all business and no pleasantries.

'OK. So we have a number of bodies in here. We will need to do DNA obviously as they are unrecognisable. Fire brigade just couldn't get here quick enough, the fact that an accelerant was used didn't help either. But I would estimate that we have around nine torsos and sets of arms and legs and by my last count we have around eight heads.'

'Nine? Jesus.' Steve thought for a moment. 'I can probably account for one of those heads,' he said.

'I would estimate that they were all here in some sort of freezer.'

'Frozen?'

'Yes. Quite the devil's stash. Again, some sort of accelerant used, but the core of the bodies are, or were, still frozen.'

'Right. Was petrol the accelerant?'

The team leader gestured for Steve to follow. 'Most likely. Over here we have a lot of blood on the floor and I have found a circular saw, I suspect this was used to decapitate. Also a few very sharp machetes in this cupboard over here. Early signs suggest a lovely array of prints to be had. Morris over there is very excited, the prints have stayed on the machete and the saw incredibly well.'

'I'm pleased Morris is pleased,' Steve said dryly.

The team leader gestured over to another corner. 'Two cars, lots of blood in the boots. Probably used to transport this wonderful collection. So, all in all, a veritable *buffet* of bodies,' he said, standing with his hands on his hips and snorting with laughter at his own joke.

'I need to match the blood with the body that was found hanging on the cliffs a while back too, he was tortured badly before dying. It would be good to link it to here,' he said thoughtfully. 'Can you make sure that's checked, please?'

'No problem.'

'These all being packed off to Murphy?'

'He'll get them later.'

'Great. I'd better give him a heads up.'

'Already done it. He says you're paying for his divorce.'

Steve muttered under his breath. 'Like I planned to find a cache of bodies in a farm building.'

'I'm needed over there. Call me if you need to discuss anything.'

'Thanks. Will do.'

Steve signed himself out and stripped off the forensic suit. He placed a call and waited until it was answered.

'Guv,' came the muffled voice, and snaffling associated with Jonesey.

'What are you eating now?'

'Chelsea bun.'

'It's seven in the morning.'

'It's Sandra from admin's birthday. I'm showing willing. Shall I save you one?'

'Listen, see if you can track down Jimmy. Get him up at the nick. Don't arrest him yet. Just bring him in for questioning. Yes?'

'OK. Questioning about… the fire?'

'Yup. Don't say we have it on film. Take another PC with you.'

'OK. Where are you?'

'On my way back via the vicarage.'

'Mrs Pomeroy? The coldest woman on earth. Rather you than me. So do you want a cake then?'

'Not high on my list of priorities. See you.'

Steve ended the call and climbed into his car. He needed to go to see Mrs Pomeroy to try and trace Fred's movements the night before he went fishing.

Steve found Mrs Pomeroy at home. Reluctantly and rudely she admitted him to her kitchen, but without offering him a drink or a chair to sit on. Steve didn't mind. The sooner he got away from her the better. Her interview wasn't going well.

'So just to recap. You came home late from the vicarage. Fred was here watching TV and then you went out again for dinner at the Seaview Hotel and you don't know what he had for his dinner.'

'Yes.'

'What was missing from the fridge?'

'What?'

'Well, did he eat here or get a takeaway?'

'Bacon, eggs. Bread was used. And most of the butter. Always was greedy with butter that man,' she sniped.

'Anything else?'

'Such as?'

'Mushrooms, tomatoes?' Steve pushed.

'Some mushrooms were missing. He was a pig with mushrooms too.'

'Out of interest where do you get your mushrooms?'

'Sainsbury's.'

'Anywhere else?'

'Like?'

'The woods?'

'Why would I do that?'

'Just wondering. We'll need to collect the contents of the fridge and your vegetable rack for analysis. My colleague should be here in a moment to bag the items.'

'Why do you need to do that?'

'Because Fred ingested something nasty, and we need to establish where it came from.'

The doorbell rang and Mrs Pomeroy scowled at Steve. 'If that's your colleague you let them in.'

'Your house, Mrs Pomeroy, your front door. I need to ensure the fridge and vegetables stay intact too.'

Mrs Pomeroy stomped off towards the door, opened it and returned to the kitchen without acknowledging Steve's colleague.

'So, you will need to sign the paperwork to say this has to be collected. I need to get on. We will need to chat again, Mrs Pomeroy, please don't leave the area. I'll let myself out.' Steve nodded to his colleague and let himself out of the front door.

Steve drove up to the vicarage, wanting to arrive before Mrs Pomeroy could get there. In his view, he had about twenty minutes before she'd appear. The vicar answered the door in a state of excitement.

'Ah, Steve. How are you?'

'I'm good, Vicar, you look very cheerful today.'

'I have a friend coming to stay and I must say I am quite giddy about the prospect. It's my late wife's sister. She's a scream. Such good company.'

'Do you have a few minutes now, please? Peter too, if he is around?'

They moved to the kitchen where Peter was having coffee surrounded by some paperwork.

'Please sit,' said the vicar. 'Coffee?'

Steve accepted a mug. 'I'm trying to build up a picture of the last few days of Joy Brown's life if you'd be so kind.'

The vicar jumped straight up and picked up the diary from the side of the kitchen.

'I thought you might ask. I have a couple of letters that I received from her. Although I am sure I saw another one, but I just can't find it now.'

Steve took the letters and put them in a plastic evidence bag, casting a quick eye over them.

'So she wanted to talk to you?' he asked. 'What's that, if I might ask?' he said, pointing to the diary.

'That's my diary. Mrs P keeps everything in it, who we're seeing and when. Now let me think… Yes, she did ask to see me it would appear. Mrs P decided to pay her a visit last week and took her some cakes, I think. She had tea and a chat with her.'

'That really upset her,' said Peter. 'She wanted to see the vicar and not Mrs P. Mrs Pomeroy told Joy that I would come and see her the next day. So I did. That was the day Mabel had died in the night and I was with her. I came back and slept for a few hours and then went to see Joy.'

'Did you take anything with you?'

Peter laughed. 'Most of the time, I'm given something by Mrs P to take to someone. She had taken a few cakes the day before and, if I recall, she had given me some soup for Joy too.'

The vicar laughed heartily. 'Mrs P can be a little abrasive, but she is quite wonderful at keeping the community fed with soup and cakes, you know.'

'Is she now?' Steve felt a sense of dread settling gently over him. 'That's lovely. Do most of the parishioners get cake and soup then?'

'Mostly. At some time or another. The slow cooker is always on with some concoction bubbling away,' the vicar said.

'Right,' Steve mused, thinking he needed to go and get permission for a few search warrants as quickly as possible. 'OK and how long did you stay with Joy, Peter?'

'Couple of hours maybe. I'd persuaded her to come to the coffee morning, you know where she…' Steve nodded and Peter continued. 'That day she said she wasn't feeling well, but that she didn't want to let us down. I can't help wondering if she'd have been at home…'

'Try not to think like that, Peter. She was among friends when she went,' the vicar said quietly.

Steve thought for a moment. 'May I take a few pictures of the diary, Vicar? Just for reference.'

The vicar pushed the diary towards him, and Steve snapped pictures of the last eight weeks with his phone.

'Thanks, Vicar,' he said, standing, desperate to be away. 'Peter, thanks for your time. We'll need to do this formally at some point. But I'll be in touch. I'll let myself out.' He left in a hurry, seeing Mrs Pomeroy striding purposefully at the end of the road towards the vicarage.

Later, in the quiet vicarage, Mrs Pomeroy carefully moved a few things around in Peter's room. In his bedside table she placed a book about wild mushrooms, and she also placed a small basket in a dark empty drawer of his. She carefully replaced the small markers that he had placed there to check for her activity. She snorted to herself. Nobody got the better of her.

Satisfied with her work, she had a meal to make. Something special for Marion's forthcoming visit.

* * *

'Jesse, back in the room, please. Do you feel safe, Jesse?'

'I do.' Jesse blinked and stretched.

Jonathan was sitting opposite with a pad on his legs smiling at her.

'You feel OK?' he asked.

'Fine.'

'I must say, I thought it earlier when you arrived. You look very well. Clearly sending you home with Doug was a tonic.'

'And then some.' She smiled.

'Talk to me about the session just now. How did you feel?'

'Calm, relaxed. Not in the slightest bit scared.'

'Where did you go?'

'I was stood on the high cliff.'

'Where you fell?'

'I think so.'

'What did you see?'

'Nothing. Just the beauty of nature. The birds, the sea.'

'No sense of danger?'

'Not a jot, as Doug would say.'

'Interesting.'

'How are you sleeping?'

'Like the dead.'

'OK. Keep an eye on that. So, I'm not going to see you for a few weeks now, but I have a condition attached to it.'

'OK. Not sure I like the sound of this.'

'The minute your sleep changes, the pattern, your dreams. You come and see me. Immediately. Deal?'

'Deal. Why what are you expecting?

'Your subconscious is still processing. It might be a bumpy ride. We may need to revisit a few things. We need to be prepared for that.'

274

'OK. I can do that. So that's it then, for maybe a few weeks?'

'It is. Go. Live your life, Jesse. Be happy.'

'Yes, boss. See you in December.'

'Bye, Jesse.'

Jesse arrived back at Doug's house. Suddenly feeling exhausted she went upstairs to the bedroom. She'd planned to have a lie down, but she felt restless. She surveyed the room and had a sudden urge to change it. Make a fresh start. She had often thought how lovely it would be to be able to lie in bed and look out of the big picture window and see the sea. She stood eyeing the bed and the window and decided that she would move the bed round to achieve exactly that.

Half an hour later she had moved the bed and was delighted with her efforts. She looked at the rest of the room and decided that she would move the chair nearer to the window so she could sit there too. She grabbed the armful of clothes that appeared to live on the chair and whipped the patterned blanket from it. She sat down heavily on the bed when she realised what she'd uncovered.

'Jesus Christ,' she whispered, looking at the chair. Her mind going back to when she fought the monster and the red rocking chair that appeared and kept her feeling safe. She sat staring at the chair remembering facing the monster.

Doug walked in, back from an exhausting shout on the lifeboat.

'I'll never understand why adults don't wear lifejackets when they go out on a—'

He stopped in surprise. 'Oh wow! I like it.' He nodded approvingly as he looked around. 'We can lay in bed and look at the sea, why did I never have it this way before?' He frowned at Jesse. 'What I don't like is that you've moved furniture yourself.' He noticed her pale face. 'You OK? You look like you've seen a ghost.'

275

'It's a red rocking chair,' she said faintly, staring at it.

He frowned. 'That old thing. I've had it since I got my first flat. Bought it in a car boot sale and painted it red. I've always loved it. Claire always hated it, which is why she covered it up. What's the big deal?'

'When I fought the monster. There was the red rocking chair on the porch. I sat in it, I felt safe. When I got out of the sea it was there again on a big deck. Keeping me safe. I never knew you had it.'

'Now that is beyond spooky.' Doug sat down next to her on the bed.

'I don't want to cover it up. I want to be able to sit here and watch the sea.'

'Consider it done,' he said, folding up the blanket and dragging the chair over by the window. 'Here?'

'Perfect. What's that about, Doug? Me seeing the chair and you having one? It's too weird.'

'It is,' he agreed. 'Far too spooky to work out. You should ask Jonathan. Now, come here. Let's see how much of the sea we can see from the bed with it this way around.' He grabbed her and yanked her down on the bed next to him.

'You're not looking at the view though,' she said, chuckling.

'The view is beautiful from where I am,' he said, looking serious. 'And by the way, the kids are staying at Claire's tonight and you, young lady, have got far too many clothes on.'

* * *

Kate had spent a successful hour with her father and the nurse practitioner, assessing the number of patients they had collectively seen who had been displaying food poisoning-like symptoms. They had cross referenced their list and double checked those patient's health status, crossing off those that were fully recovered. This left a list of around ten people going back over the last twelve months who had experienced similar symptoms and had later died.

Kate took the list and the details and went to her office to ring Steve.

'Hello, Inspector Miller, I have some particulars I'd like you to take down.' She giggled into the phone when he answered.

'I'm in the car with Jonesey on speaker,' he said wryly, and she could imagine him grinning.

'Oh,' she said, flustered. 'Sorry.'

'Hi, Doc,' called out Jonesey.

'Shut up, Jonesey,' Steve instructed. 'What's up? We haven't got long we're just on our way to execute a search warrant.'

'Oh OK. So, we've got together a list of patients who had the specific symptoms and those that then later died.'

'How many?'

'Ten.'

'Jesus.'

'Some of them may be genuine illness as they were all over seventy-five. But we should look at their tox screens and cause of death, see what they throw up.'

'All local?'

'Yes.'

'Have we got dates when they fell ill?'

'I have.'

'You are a superstar.'

'It's been said before. How will you ever repay me?'

'Can you email it to me?'

'No problem.'

'I'll call you later. I need to organise a date for that assessment,' he said dryly.

'Get a room,' muttered Jonesey.

'Bye.' Kate ended the call, embarrassed.

* * *

Steve thought Mrs Pomeroy was surprisingly quiet and pleasant during the execution of the search warrant. She stood serenely by, while the officers firstly searched the vicarage and then her home thoroughly. Gone was the usual rude and abrasive demeanour. Years of experience suggested to Steve that something was amiss with the woman and that she had perhaps played a hand, and this bothered him. Jonesey was more bothered that no cup of tea or biscuit had been offered.

After the search, Steve had been briefed by the search team that the primary items of interest found in Peter's room were a book on wild mushrooms, and a small empty basket with some sort of earthy residue. A small basket of mushrooms were also found in the pantry at the vicarage.

In Mrs Pomeroy's home, a jar of, what resembled, dried chopped mushrooms was confiscated, it had been found behind a packet of cereal in the kitchen cupboard. Steve had these all sent off for immediate testing being sure that the team cross-checked the toxins against the recent deaths.

While they began the interminable wait for results, Steve sent Jonesey out for enough food to tide him over before the two of them began the tedious process of cross referencing the deaths against visitor logs from relevant care homes, the vicar's diary, and other local church-based events.

Steve had a sense he would find the link between the deaths, but he wasn't liking what his gut was telling him at that moment in time. Added to which, Jimmy Ryan appeared to have vanished off the face of the planet and Steve knew this invariably meant he was up to no good again.

CHAPTER 21

Marion sat in the kitchen at the vicarage. She had arrived in a flurry of luggage and presents for the vicar, Peter and Mrs Pomeroy, who had viewed hers disdainfully despite it being a cashmere scarf. The vicar was fussing around, opening wine and Peter was silently observing Mrs Pomeroy's tight-lipped cooking activity with a modicum of amusement.

'Darling Mrs Pomeroy, please can I help?' implored Marion. 'At least sit for a moment and have a glass of wine.'

'I need to get on,' Mrs Pomeroy said shortly. 'Dinner won't cook itself.'

'Can I make you a cup of tea or something then?' Marion persisted. 'It doesn't seem fair that you're doing all the hard work and leaving us to it?'

'No thank you.'

Marion glanced at the vicar who shrugged his shoulders. Marion pulled a face and then said brightly, 'Tell me all about this carnival of the sea. It sounds wonderful. When does it all begin?'

'Oh it's quite wonderful,' the vicar said happily. 'Thursday night is a flurry of activity in the town. Everyone works late into the night getting their businesses ready.'

'Getting them ready?' Marion queried.

'Decorating them. With ocean-related themes. They are wonderful. It's a wonderful sight all down the high street and down to the harbour. There's a competition for the best decorated business, it gets in the press and everything. Last year Fishy John's seafood hut won. It was quite superb. I don't know how he did it but overnight it looked like it had been consumed by a huge shark. John was a big *Jaws* fan and I think this was his tribute!'

'Sounds terribly scary!' Marion exclaimed.

'Last year the Hope and Anchor decorated the whole front of the pub and outside canopy with huge white floating jellyfish, it must have been like parachute silk or something the way it moved. It was quite wonderful. The lovely family at Joe's Pizza Place employed the local primary school to paint a huge shoal of fish that they strung across their windows and from the ceilings inside the pizzeria. It felt like you were underwater when you were sat inside. It's quite the big deal here, you know. On the Friday there are local competitions in various forms, the sailing club have a race as do the kayakers and paddleboarders. All the local schools have an inset afternoon for the kids to take part. I think even the new climbing centre is having a competition.'

'It sounds wonderful, and on the Saturday?'

'There's a big procession through the town in the afternoon, all of the locals create floats with sea-related themes to parade through the town and the Cubs, Scouts, Brownies and Guides all dress up and join the procession. It starts about four and makes it way down to Castle beach, ending up with a huge bonfire on the beach. On the Sunday morning there's a carnival sea swim where people dress up as sea creatures and swim out to the fort and back and around a marker, which is about a mile. It really is one of the best weekends of the year. The locals really go to town.'

'It sounds marvellous!' exclaimed Marion. 'I can't wait to see the high street!'

'It really is wonderful,' the vicar agreed. 'And some of them look fantastic in the day time, but also look totally different lit up at night too. So that's always another wonderful surprise!'

'A waste of time and money if you ask me,' Mrs P said sourly, placing a dish of steaming vegetables on the table. She added another dish of mashed potatoes and then put a pie on the table, along with a jug of gravy.

'Looks wonderful, Mrs P,' said the vicar, sniffing happily.

'Meat and potato pie.' Mrs Pomeroy opened the oven and put a plate down in front of Marion. 'Mushroom and vegetable turnover for you, Marion,' she said shortly. 'Treacle tart in the oven for pudding. I'm off home now. See you tomorrow.' She took off her apron, picked up her bag and headed out of the kitchen.

As she walked down the road she pulled her coat tighter around her and anticipated an evening in front of the television, where the sofa didn't smell of fish, safe in the knowledge that Marion would most likely miss most of the carnival by the sea.

The vicar was topping up Marion's wine glass and noticed her frown.

'Everything OK, Marion?' he asked, desperate to please.

'Oh it's a little awkward and I don't want to upset Mrs P,' she said, looking a little uncomfortable. 'She's gone to so much trouble.'

'Whatever's the matter?' the vicar asked worriedly.

'Well, the fact of it is, I can't stand mushrooms.' She shuddered. 'They make me terribly ill and this vegetarian pie is full of them! I feel terrible, but I just can't eat this!'

'Now don't you worry about it at all,' he said. 'Will you be OK with potato and vegetables? I can do you an egg?'

'Veg and mash is fine,' she said with relief. 'Let's keep this between us, I really don't want to upset Mrs Pomeroy any more. I sense my presence here is enough of a challenge!'

'Quite right,' the vicar said, smiling. 'What she doesn't know won't hurt her.'

'We'd better hide the evidence though, she doesn't miss a trick!' Peter tapped the side of his nose. 'Leave it to me!'

* * *

Sam was exhausted. He felt like he had been travelling for hours. His back hurt from sitting for so long, his stumps were throbbing, and he had a banging headache. He watched through the window as the army Transport rattled along the road and into Castleby. It swept around the outskirts of the town taking the back road to his wife's home. He had never lived there permanently but had stayed for long periods at a time when he was on leave, mainly when Marcus was small, and they spent most of their summer holidays there.

Part of him itched to get on the beach, breathe in the sea air and see the town in all its oceanic glory. The other part of him just wanted to lay down in a dark room and never wake up again. The truck rumbled to a stop and the rear doors opened. Sam was lifted down gently by two men in fatigues. Lottie jumped out carrying various bags and shut the doors behind her.

'You're here!' Sophie said breathlessly as she stepped out of the front door. Sam noticed she had put a ramp there to make it easy for him to get up.

'Seems so,' said Sam shortly and felt terrible when he saw Sophie's face drop.

'Long journey,' Lottie said. 'Lots of waiting about, pretty exhausting for Sam.'

'I'm sorry to hear that.' Sophie walked towards them. 'Lads, have you got time for a cuppa before you go?'

The two men declined, thanked Sophie, saluted Sam and hopped back in the transport and rumbled off.

'Well, let get inside then, shall we?' Sophie said, picking up a few of the bags. 'Dinner's ready when you are.'

'I'm starving,' admitted Lottie.

'Sam what about you? Could you eat a scabby horse?' Sophie laughed. She glanced at Lottie who had wrinkled her nose.

'Sam always used to say that when he was starving,' she said, looking at him, hoping for a response.

'I'm not hungry,' Sam said in a flat tone. He didn't want to be reminded of all the things he used to do.

Lottie wheeled him in, and Sam immediately saw Sophie had worked hard to clear spaces for him to be able to get himself around easily.

'You're through there, Sam,' she said. 'In Dad's study. You remember.'

Lottie walked him in and dumped their bags on the bed. 'This is great,' she said, looking around. 'Sam, we need to sort a few things out for you and then we can join your adoring public.'

Lottie glanced at Sophie. 'I need to do a few things for Sam if that's OK? We'll be out in a minute.'

'O-OK,' Sophie stammered. 'I'll be in the kitchen then.'

Sophie fumbled around in the kitchen and wondered why she was close to tears. She looked at the clock just as Marcus walked in the back door.

'Hey,' he said warily.

'Hey, love. You OK?'

'Uh-huh,' he grunted. 'Is he here?'

'Yes. He's in the bedroom, just having a few medical bits done. Don't be nervous.'

'What's for dinner?' Marcus sat at the table.

'Nothing changes,' Sam announced as Lottie wheeled him in the kitchen. 'You used to ask that every single time you'd come in the kitchen after school.'

'Hi, Dad.' Marcus smiled shyly.

'My God. You've grown,' Sam said, looking emotional.

'I'm a growing boy. I'm starving. I could eat a scabby horse.'

Both Sam and Marcus laughed together. 'Got a hug for your old man or are you too big now?' Sam asked and Marcus jumped off the chair and threw himself at his dad.

'Missed you, son,' Sam said, his voice muffled in Marcus's shoulder.

'Missed you, Dad,' Marcus said, squeezing his eyes shut to hide the tears.

Sophie watched the exchange, her eyes filling with tears. She was relieved that Sam had been as normal as he could be with Marcus. She'd take that. As long as he was nice to Marcus that was all that mattered. She'd take Sam being rude to her, but she didn't want Marcus to suffer.

* * *

Despite it being well past 11 p.m. on a Thursday night, Castleby town centre was bustling with activity. The outside of Fishy John's seafood shack was covered with blacked-out Heras fencing to hide what was being done, and the Hope and Anchor had adopted the same idea.

The sounds of hammering and drills pervaded the dark streets. The restaurants and shops were also busy ushering late diners out and closing for the night to get ready for their oceanic transformation. Maggie was complaining loudly to anyone who would listen that her mermaid's flashing boobs wouldn't work so she was changing fuses and wiggling wires about hopefully.

Rudi had turned up, and he and Foxy had got to work. The two were fixing a series of ropes onto the outside of the climbing centre to drop straight down. Foxy had also strung a rope across the road at a high level from his roof to Maggie's, as well as setting up his secret weapon in a waterproof box on the roof of the café. The two had also dropped ropes down from the highest point on the massive outside climbing wall back to the centre.

Now ensconsed inside, Rudi was sitting on the floor surrounded by a dozen black frogman wetsuits. Their idea was that the scene would look like a series of frogmen attacking the building, swarming in from all angles. They were projecting underwater images with sharks, submarines and other frogmen swimming around onto the building in the dark for extra effect. It was quite close to home for both of them. They now had the tedious job of stuffing the wetsuits to pad them out into human-like shapes. As Rudi stuffed, he watched Foxy; something was up, he'd known him long enough to know something wasn't right.

'What's up, mate?' he asked. 'You're not yourself. What gives?'

Foxy debated getting into it. Once he'd said it out loud it made it all a bit too real for him.

'Nothing, mate. All good,' he said dismissively, fixing goggles and flippers to the first complete frogman and holding it up.

'Looks good,' Rudi said. 'Seriously though, you've got a right face on. From what I remember that face is usually associated with women troubles.'

'I'm fine.' Foxy avoided his gaze and started on his second frogman.

'I'll just keep going on and on,' Rudi said. 'Like an old nag.'

Foxy grunted. 'Honestly, mate, I do want to talk to you about it. But I can't do it now. I'm still trying to get my head sorted.'

'Worried that if you say it out loud then that makes it real?' he asked quietly.

'Bingo.'

'OK. Here for you, mate. Anytime. You know that. Always an ear for you.'

'Appreciate it. How's this one?' Foxy held up another one.

'Great!' Rudi said enthusiastically. 'So we've got these to do and then change the climbing routes for tomorrow?'

'Yup. Mike's giving a hand, he should be here in a sec, he had a gig tonight, but it was local. He'll do most of it. We planned it all out yesterday with Tom.'

'Better crack on then. How about this guy for the rope between us and Maggie's?'

* * *

The next morning the town was busy with many people wanting to see the decorations before their day began. Maggie's was doing a brisk trade. Doug and Jesse were up early walking Brock on the beach with a view to having an early breakfast at Maggie's and walking back through the town to admire everyone's work from the night before.

As they walked up the jetty from Castle beach, Jesse spotted the frogmen swarming all over the climbing centre, with one upside down on the rope between the climbing centre and Maggie's. They walked past Fishy John's shack which had been transformed into a yellow submarine. The pizzeria opposite had hung a series of huge clear balls all over the front with trailing ribbons to signify jellyfish. As they rounded the corner, Jesse gasped.

'How the hell did they do that?'

The Hope and Anchor had been transformed into a huge pink octopus with blue spots, the legs crept along the building and up the walls and the giant head of the octopus had the front door to the pub as its mouth. Further up the high street, businesses had gone all out, with the fish and chip shop being transformed into a huge red crab with large googley eyes and claws that moved. The George pub had covered the bottom of the wide front of the building with small red crabs up to about a metre in height and on their first-floor balcony they had created a row of cut-outs of kids who were crab fishing with lines dropped down to the crabs below.

A few of the shops opposite had teamed up and shared a huge whale that spanned the four shop fronts. Anyone who peeked closely would have seen a small snail sitting on the whale's tail.

The surf shop had created a huge wave that looked like it was about to break over people who walked past, with a surfer emerging from the tube in the middle. The Italian had covered the outside of their restaurant with starfish and seahorses in all shapes and sizes and had continued the theme inside.

'This is fantastic!' Jesse breathed, looking around in wonder. 'Some of these are so clever!'

'Favourite?'

'Ooh, I don't know. I need to see them at night. Some of them are even better at night. Tell you later.'

Doug pulled her close and kissed the top of her head. 'I need to get to work. You go home and rest for a bit. No moving furniture. Got it?'

'Yes, boss. I'll see you at Foxy's later for the competition.'

Doug winked and headed down the hill. Jesse watched his retreating back and thought yet again that the man wore a pair of jeans well.

* * *

Jimmy had picked up the boat and was making good time. He had dropped anchor for the night and grabbed a few hours' sleep, but he had been unable to get into the cabins. They were firmly padlocked, so he had spent an uncomfortable night half stretched out on the seats in the galley, constantly banging his head on the table all night. He'd awoken with a stiff neck and a high level of grumpiness.

Running the engine as much as possible, he'd calculated his route using the top-of-the-range equipment on board and had wondered momentarily whether he could easily pinch any of it for his boat without anyone noticing. He had then stopped himself thinking things like that when he remembered whose boat this actually was. He checked the weather and adjusted his course, set the autopilot and settled himself comfortably on deck. He reckoned he'd be back in Castleby by the Saturday evening. No problem. As he sat on the deck he noticed that some of the seats were storage units. Ever the petty criminal, he moved the seat covers aside and opened the cabinets; he was delighted to find a crate of champagne.

He picked up the bottle and read the label, having no real idea what he was looking at. He shrugged and peered around at the empty ocean.

'Don't mind if I do,' he said, opening the bottle and taking a swig. He settled himself in to enjoy the bottle.

Ten miles away on the same stretch of ocean between the Irish Sea and the Welsh coast, Christopher Cherry was on the old trawler. Despite the brothers' efforts to rescue him when he was found near death and floating, and their hospitality in helping him get well again, he had without any conscience whatsoever, gone out fishing with the brothers that morning and pushed them both overboard. Neither wore life savers, Chris had made sure those were lost. At their ages, they wouldn't have lasted long in the cold sea.

He was in the wheelhouse of the trawler struggling to remember how the navigation machines worked on board. This was one of the legacies of his fall onto the rocks, he just couldn't remember things. In truth he had no real idea of where he was going or what he was doing. He couldn't get the water pump to work and he had blocked the toilet too. Nothing was going his way today. He glowered at the equipment before him. Fuck. He hoped he just needed to go straight, and he would eventually end up at his destination.

He was sitting in the captain's chair keeping his route as straight as possible towards what he thought was the coast on the funny machine. He thought about what he would do to Jesse when he found her. How he would kill her and make her life a living hell. He smirked and started whistling. Wouldn't be long now. What a wonderful and rewarding reunion this would be.

CHAPTER 22

Sam awoke early. The house was silent. He manoeuvred himself to the side of the bed and clumsily managed to get himself into the wheelchair. He wheeled himself into the kitchen and managed to flick the kettle on. He made himself a coffee and opened the back doors to the garden. He breathed in the air and enjoyed the cold morning wind. He thought about how he felt about being there. This would be home now he supposed. Did he want to live here? Truth was, he didn't want to live anywhere. He didn't want to live at all.

He'd watched his son yesterday evening, and he had seen the man that the boy would become. He'd seen Sophie, her exhaustion, the tired face and dark circles under her eyes. They would both be better off without him. He couldn't add to their life at all. All he would do was make it worse. He moved away from the doors and rolled over to look at the huge bank of photos that sat above the long church pew which Sam recognised had come from their old home. He saw photographs of him and Sophie. They'd been happy, but neither of them were happy now.

He idly wondered how he could kill himself and when the opportunity might present itself. He knew he'd be doing everyone a favour, and he'd convinced himself this was the right thing to do. For Sophie. For Marcus. He wanted them to have a better life. He wondered if he could make it look like an accident. Maybe that would be easier for them to deal with.

* * *

Mrs Pomeroy had let herself into the vicarage and scowled when she heard laughter. She dumped her coat and stalked into the kitchen which she considered to be her own personal domain. Marion was standing at the stove making eggy bread and laughing with the vicar and Peter.

'Oh, darling Mrs P!' she said brightly as Edwina walked into the kitchen frowning. 'Would you like some eggy bread?'

'Had breakfast,' Mrs Pomeroy said shortly. 'I see you've made yourself at home. How are you feeling today?'

'Sorry about that,' Marion said, deftly dishing up a slice for Peter. 'After such a delicious dinner last night and all the sea air, I'm feeling wonderful this morning!'

Mrs Pomeroy grunted. 'I'll get on then,' she said, taking her apron from the hook behind the door and putting it on.

'Mrs P, any news on when we might be able to bury dear Fred?'

'They won't release the body. Still investigating, apparently,' she said shortly, stomping out of the kitchen.

Mrs Pomeroy thumped up the stairs angrily. Marion should have been in bed, sick to the stomach by now. She walked into the vicar's bedroom, made his bed and tidied up. Then she grabbed the hoover and took out her bad mood on the upstairs carpet.

Steve knocked on the vicarage door and it was opened almost immediately by Peter who had his coat on and a large bag with him.

'Going somewhere?' Steve asked.

'Oh hi,' Peter said pleasantly. 'Yes. Off out to see a few parishioners.'

'Have you got time to come to the station for a quick chat?' Steve asked pleasantly.

'You're not really asking, are you?' he said quietly. 'You're telling.'

'Friendly chat. That's all,' said Steve, gesturing towards the car.

Peter inclined his head and got in the car with Steve.

Mrs Pomeroy stood at the upstairs window and watched; a smile of satisfaction spread across her features.

* * *

Steve pressed the record button and went through the preliminaries. He had already cautioned Peter, who had declined a solicitor.

'Peter,' Steve said. 'I need you to talk me through how it works when you go and see parishioners at home or those in care homes.'

'What do you mean?' Peter said, frowning.

'Who decides who you see and when you see them?'

'Oh,' Peter said, understanding. 'Well usually it's Mrs P. She'll take calls from family or friends who have said they'd like me or the vicar to visit. Or we have heard from the congregation that someone's ill, so Mrs P will tell us that and put it in the diary.'

'Right, so you don't ever just turn up?'

'Goodness no. Don't want to be accused of trying to brainwash people!' he said. 'In this day and age we have to be so careful and

293

make sure people know we're coming. There are so many vulnerable people in the community.'

'I see. So Mrs Pomeroy organises it all.'

'I'd say 99 per cent of it.'

'OK. Peter, can you tell me about any hobbies you might have?'

Peter laughed. 'I don't have time for hobbies.' He frowned. 'Why do you ask?'

'We found a book on wild mushrooms in your room and a basket with traces of mushrooms in it. This is quite the hobby for some people.'

'Well, they're not mine,' said Peter. 'I don't have a lot, but I know I don't have anything like that.'

'Sure about that?'

'Absolutely,' he said firmly.

'Can you explain why we found them in your room?'

'I can't.' He shrugged. 'Maybe they belonged to the person who had the room before me? Or maybe someone put them there?'

'Does the vicar have access to your room?'

'Everyone does. Mrs P has a good old poke about too.'

'Right. You've seen her do that?'

'I know that she's often been through my things. I see things out of place.'

'Right. And do you think that's Mrs Pomeroy or the vicar?'

'The vicar is a good man. He respects privacy,' Peter said firmly.

'And Mrs Pomeroy doesn't?'

'I don't think so.'

'Talk to me about where you were before here.'

'Why is that relevant?'

'Humour me.'

'I'd prefer not to.'

'You've had a troubled past haven't you, Peter?' Steve said, opening a file.

'My record is behind me. I'm different now.'

'Still, I can't help feeling that it's relevant?'

'I was young. Stupid. In with the wrong crowd.'

Steve leant back in his chair. 'Peter, if you were me. What would you do? I've got at least ten unexplained deaths of people all over 75 years old in this community. You have been in these people's lives at some point prior to their death. Your record as a juvenile sees you being sent to the naughty boys' school for killing two pensioners. Now,' he said, leaning forward and looking at Peter intently. 'Killing two pensioners is a little bit worse than being young, stupid and in the wrong crowd is it not?'

Peter dropped his head into his hands. 'I didn't kill them,' he mumbled.

'Record says different.'

'I didn't kill them,' Peter shouted angrily, standing suddenly, fists clenched.

'Sit down, Peter,' Steve said quietly. 'I haven't accused you of anything. Tell me what happened.'

'You've seen the record.' Peter sat down heavily.

'I want to hear it from you.'

'I was in with the wrong crowd. Living on the streets.'

'No parents?'

'Yes, I had parents,' he said sarcastically. 'But I preferred to live on the streets, so they didn't pimp me out to their punters to fuel their drug habit.'

'How old were you when it started?'

'Eight.'

'Pretty big thing to deal with when you're that age.'

Peter shrugged. 'I left and stayed with my aunt. She was lovely. I stayed with her until she had to go into a care home, then I lived rough.'

'How old were you?'

'Fourteen. I lived on the streets. Made a living doing odd jobs for a meal or a bit of cash. Never touched drugs. Then I moved into this old hospital that was all boarded up. Great place to crash, but then this new group moved in. They were pretty hardcore. All criminals.'

Steve encouraged him to continue.

'One night, I was on my way back from doing some work for one of the local hotels and they were turning over a house around the corner from the hospital. It was one of those immaculate homes that old people have. Lawn mown, perfect garden. Really well cared for. They were in there chucking stuff about spray painting, pissing up everything. They thought the old couple had gone out, but they'd just gone to bed early. They basically threw them both down the stairs. The old lady, she hit her head on the bottom step, her neck was at a weird angle. I think it was instant. But the old man was trying to protect her. He tried to fight them, and they went to town on him. Anyway, I came in when I heard them and tried to stop them, but they legged it. By then a neighbour had called the police, but the old man was still alive. I was trying to help him, doing CPR. Police arrived, took one look at me and thought I was trying to kill him.'

'Who were the gang?'

'Only ever had nicknames. They were ghosts when the police got to the squat. They never got them.'

'So the old man died, and you went down for it.'

'Police had to convict someone.'

'I'm sure that wasn't the case.'

'Excuse me for being more sceptical than you. Ten years inside will do that.'

'I need you to put the past aside for a moment. Are you prepared to look at the vicar's diary with me for the last eight weeks so we can go through each person of interest in turn? I need you to remember when you went, what you did and whether you took anything with you.'

Peter thought for a moment and then shrugged.

'OK, I've got a pretty good memory, so I reckon we can fill in the blanks.'

Steve dropped Peter off at the care home he was planning to visit, after he'd finished interviewing him. He had confiscated everything that Mrs P had given Peter to take, but they had parted on good terms.

'Don't go doing anything silly like running off, will you?' Steve said as he pulled to a stop at Peter's destination. 'I'm trusting you to stick around.'

Peter thought for a moment. 'Thanks for believing me. Nobody ever has before except the vicar. I'll have more of a think and let you know if I can come up with anything else.'

'Take care,' Steve said and drove off back to the station.

* * *

'Sam, this is Rob. He owns this place. He's been wonderful, helping Marcus out… well, helping us both out really. Rob, meet Sam.'

Sam put the wheelchair brake on and looked up at Foxy's huge frame.

Foxy held his hand out. 'Good to meet you, Sam,' he said pleasantly. 'Call me Foxy, most people do.'

Sam shook his hand. He glanced between Foxy and Sophie and said in clipped, formal tones, 'Yes, I heard you've been helping my wife out with a variety of things. Stepping in as it were. Helping my son out too, rescuing him from mountains and such. You're quite the local hero from what I see and hear.'

'Sam… Come on,' Sophie protested.

Sam watched Marcus move away to speak to Jude.

'Tell me, do these duties also include fucking my wife?' Sam asked coldly.

Foxy gave a bark of laughter and regarded him with amusement.

'Excuse me?' he said, laughing and clapping a hand over his heart. 'Jesus, I wish, mate, heartbreakingly for me though, she only has eyes for you.'

Sophie stared at Foxy in total surprise.

'Now, I need to get things started,' Foxy said, all business. 'Sam, I've cleared a space for you guys over there, so you will pretty much be able to see everything. Hope that's OK. Marcus has been working so hard, he's quite amazing to watch.'

'No children of your own taking part today?' Sam asked him loudly. A shadow passed over Foxy's face and he frowned slightly.

'Nope. Not today.'

'Just happy watching other people's children then?' Sam pushed.

'Sam,' Sophie warned.

'I get to make a pretty good living out of it.'

'Still, doesn't beat watching your own though, does it?'

'Leave it, Sam, for God's sake,' Sophie said urgently. 'Stop being so rude.'

Foxy moved sightly closer to Sam and said quietly, 'Do you know what, Sam? I'd give my life in a heartbeat to have one more second with my daughter, let alone be lucky enough to watch her climb in a competition. So, yes. Absolutely. Nothing does beat watching your own kid if you're lucky enough to have that option. Hope you enjoy the competition.' He glanced at Sophie. 'You're over there, Soph,' he said, pointing as he stepped away and spoke to Rudi who was ticking off names of kids on a clipboard.

Marcus ran up with his phone.

'Lots of shots? Yes, Mum? For my Insta?'

Sophie nodded and waited until he had gone again before rounding on Sam.

'For God's sake!' Sophie exploded. 'What the hell was that about?' She grabbed his chair and wheeled him towards the area that Foxy had thoughtfully raised up for Sam to be able to see. She craned her neck to see where Lottie was and saw her chatting to Foxy and Rudi.

'I don't understand what the big deal is,' Sam said coldly as Sophie adjusted his chair.

'Rob's daughter died,' Sophie said quietly. 'In a climbing accident.'

'Not very good press for the climbing centre, is it?' he said with a small laugh.

'It wasn't here,' Sophie said shortly. 'Christ, you're heartless. I feel like I don't know you anymore.'

'Two years in captivity will do that,' he bit back.

'You always had a good soul. You were never cruel.'

Sam sneered. 'Wake up and smell the coffee, Sophie. This is what's left. Someone with no soul who takes pleasure out of being bitter and cruel.' He saw the look on her face. 'Yup. I wouldn't want to be around it either.'

He turned away and watched the climbers lining up in groups. He watched Foxy and felt a pang of envy. He had such a natural way with people. Sam watched him smile, encourage, greet and manage the proceedings with military precision. Part of Sam liked the man, admired him for starting again after the military; but the other part of him loathed him. For having legs. For being his wife's friend. For being such a genuinely nice, fucking good-looking bastard.

Foxy called for quiet in the centre and welcomed everyone to the competition. He explained the rules and the various heats that would be run and how the winners would be calculated. He introduced Rudi as timekeeper and Mike as first aider and then cracked a few jokes that had everyone laughing. Finally, he called for the first group to line up for a staggered start.

Sophie craned her neck to see Marcus. She spotted him standing with Jude and caught sight of Jesse and Doug, who waved and made their way over. Claire and Felix arrived behind them and stood by the doors.

'Hey, guys,' Sophie said as Doug approached. 'How are Jude's hands holding up?'

'Not great,' Doug grimaced. 'I think he's been doing too much.'

Sophie turned to Sam. 'Sam, this is Doug and Jesse. You might remember Doug from the lifeboat, when we used to come before…'

'I don't recall, but nice to meet you,' Sam said absently and then resumed watching the competition.

Sophie shook her head and mouthed an apology.

She watched Marcus. He was waiting in line, his hands were chalked, and she saw him gaze at the walls. She saw the absolute focus in his head as he prepared. Sophie looked over and saw Foxy talking to Jude quietly and loosening up his hands. Foxy caught Marcus's eye and Sophie saw him mouth something to Marcus and nod questioningly. She watched Marcus reply soundlessly and give him a huge grin. Her heart lurched for a second, seeing the closeness of their exchange.

Lottie had reappeared and introduced herself to Jesse and Doug. She whispered to Sophie, 'My God, Sophie! Foxy and Rudi. How do you ever get anything done around here? I'd be in here all the time just drooling.'

'They are lovely,' Sophie agreed.

'Either of them involved?' she asked idly.

'I think Rudi's single. Rob, sorry, Foxy has a wife, but they're separated as far as I know.'

'They are quite gorgeous, the pair of them,' said Lottie appreciatively.

'Wait till you see Mack,' Sophie said, laughing. 'Blond, blue-eyed. Gorgeous. They make quite the lovely trio. Mack's totally spoken for though.'

'Shame.'

'Marcus is up,' Jesse announced.

They watched in amazement as Marcus scaled the course route like a gecko.

'Jesus, he's fast. He'll spank Jude.'

Marcus dropped to the floor and hit the finish buzzer. Rudi shouted out the time and added it to the huge whiteboard. Rudi announced that Marcus had taken the lead. Jude was up next and climbed around the course quickly, but only made it to third place after his hand gave way on the last hold. The two boys came over while they waited for the next phase to begin.

'Well done both of you!' exclaimed Sophie as the boys came over. 'So impressive!'

Doug chipped in. 'You boys have improved so much since you started here. Your technique, your focus. Brilliant! You've worked really hard.'

The two boys fist bumped and recited Foxy's mantra together, 'Fail to prepare, prepare to fail!' and burst out laughing.

'What did you think, Dad?' Marcus asked.

'Very good. Very impressive. You have to have core strength to do that, so well done to the both of you,' he said curtly to them both. 'Someone's waving. I think you're needed over there.'

The boys headed back over to the start line and the second round started again. Jude fell halfway around as his hand gave out and was disqualified, but Marcus went on to win the next two heats and was pronounced winner.

By the end of the competition Marcus was sweaty and exhausted, but happy that he had won. The competition finished with a small prizegiving ceremony.

Jude won a pair of climbing shoes for being 'climber with the most potential', which he beamed happily about, and Foxy presented the awards for second and third place. When Marcus was called up for his trophy and name on the climbing wall of fame, Foxy presented him with his prizes and told him to say a few words. Marcus stood looking out at the faces across the crowd. He lifted the trophy, and everyone cheered again. He cleared his throat.

'Foxy said I had to say something,' he said awkwardly. 'So, I just want to say a big thanks to Mum for ferrying me about and letting me do this. And, er, thanks to Foxy. Best coach ever.' There was a huge cheer from the crowd. Jude beamed. 'I wanna share this with Jude. He should have won today. He's by far the better climber. He only lost today because he saved me and busted his hands. So, Foxy, would it be OK to have Jude's name on here too?'

Foxy nodded.

Marcus shifted foot to foot. 'I also just want to say that today is special because my dad was here to see it. He's been away a long time and he's been really ill. But he made it here today and I'm really proud of him. This is for you, Dad!'

The crowd cheered and clapped again, and Marcus went over and hugged Sophie and bent down to hug Sam.

'Well done,' Sam said gruffly, fighting back the emotion. Feeling too emotional to be in public, Sam moved backwards out of the way of all Marcus's well-wishers. He asked Lottie if he could go outside, so she pushed him through the crowd and out of the door into the evening air.

'Thanks,' he said. 'You go back in, I just need some space.'

'Sure you'll be OK?'

'I'm just going to sit here a while.'

Lottie went back inside after firmly putting the brake on for Sam. He sat there for a while, enjoying the quiet.

'Hello, soldier,' said a quiet voice.

Sam knew who it was instantly.

'Hello yourself,' he said.

Maggie handed him a coffee. 'Hot and strong. Just as you used to like it. Bit like you,' she said, tittering at her own joke.

'A bit like the old me.'

'Been a long time, soldier. We thought we'd lost you. How you coping, my love?' Mags asked, sitting down on the bench near him with a big sigh. 'No bullshit.'

'Do you really want the no bullshit answer, Mags? Really?' Sam raised an eyebrow.

'I've known you long enough to deserve the truth.'

He shrugged. 'OK.' He paused for a while. 'I feel awful. Although awful doesn't even do it justice. I'm in constant pain. Everywhere. My legs are agony, and that's just the bits that aren't even there anymore. The bits that are left are on fire all the time.' He gulped in air. 'I would happily lay down and die right here, right now

303

and that would make me a very happy man. I don't want to go on, Mags. I am no use to anyone. I'm a burden to Sophie and Marcus and I know they'd be better off without me. They've made a life here. They have a community that loves and cares for them. I'd be in the way.'

'Have you said this to Sophie?' Maggie asked quietly.

'Of course I haven't.'

'Perhaps you should.'

'What would be the point?'

'She loves you, Sam, she never gave up hope. All that time. There's not been anyone else.'

'Not even Mr Muscle in there?'

'Ah, now you stop that. Foxy's a good man. He's a good friend. He loves Sophie as a friend. He's been wonderful to Marcus.'

'I can assure you, Maggie, he loves her. But not as a friend. I've seen the way he looks at her.' He paused, looking out to sea. 'She deserves better than me. She deserves a full life, with someone who looks at her like that. Not someone who's half a man, that dreams the darkest dreams and can't even remember what joy is.'

'Oh, he dreams dark dreams I can assure you. He's not had it easy, but he got through it. Perhaps you should talk to him, see how far he's come before you go giving up.'

'I don't see it as giving up, Mags, I see it as a merciful release for Sophie and Marcus.'

'I don't know what to say to you, Sam, apart from that you're wrong to think that.'

'Here you are!' Sophie said brightly as she came out of the climbing centre. 'I wondered where you'd got to!'

'We're chatting,' Mags said, smiling. 'Doesn't seem like two minutes ago you used to be around here all the time when Marcus was small, any excuse or holiday and you were all here. So I'm thoroughly enjoying catching up with my favourite soldier.'

'I thought I was your favourite?' Rudi announced indignantly as he walked out of the building and overheard.

Maggie laughed. 'You are a wicked tease for an old lady like me. You're just after my breakfasts and steak and kidney pies, you butter me up and try to keep me sweet.'

'Well, in fairness, all of that applies,' Rudi said, putting his arm around her and kissing her on the cheek. She swatted him away.

'All you ever do is think about food…' she chided playfully. 'You soldiers are all the same.'

Rudi pretended to look affronted. 'I think we could take offence at that couldn't we, Sam?'

Sam shrugged. 'I'm not a soldier anymore. I wouldn't know.'

Rudi nudged him. 'Mate, once a soldier, always a soldier.' He rubbed his hands. 'Now where is that delicious nurse of yours, she said she might have a drink with me?'

The devil is teasing me. I know he is. He is putting obstacles in my path for me to overcome This is a test. But I will persevere and rejoice. But why is my Saviour testing me? Does He not realise the depth of my love? Of my commitment? My sacrifices for His blessings? For an eternity of being His servant? This is another test. It has to be. He loves me. He needs me. He cannot be without me. I have to carry on. He will witness the depth of my love soon and He will lay his hands on me and make me His and we shall rejoice.

CHAPTER 23

Jesse was dreaming. She was walking along the beach with Brock and in the distance, a woman with long red hair was walking slowly towards her. The wind was blowing, and the woman was barefoot wearing long white robes that were blowing in the breeze, as if in slow motion. As Jesse got nearer the woman she saw she had startling green eyes that reminded her of Emma, Chris's sister. As she drew closer, the woman held up a hand and pointed at Jesse.

'He's coming for you,' she said. 'You need to be careful. You won't survive it again. You'll die this time. He's coming for you.'

Jesse had awoken suddenly, the dream fresh in her mind; she experienced a wave of familiar dread wash over her. She lay for a moment wondering who the woman was and why she would have said that to her. She sat up, remembering the red rocking chair and wondered how this had appeared in her mind while she was fighting the monster. She grabbed her phone and called a number, waiting while an answerphone clicked in.

'Jonathan, hi, it's Jesse. Hope you're OK. Look, you said to let you know if I had a weird dream. Last night I dreamt about a woman who told me Chris was on his way and I wouldn't survive him again. I don't know what that means. Be good to hear your thoughts. Cheers then.'

She thought for a while longer, and reaching no conclusions, flicked back the covers and headed for the shower.

* * *

Jimmy had grabbed a few more hours sleep on the yacht's uncomfortable seats, waking very early on the Saturday morning. Late the night before he had stopped the engine for a while, dropped the anchor and napped for a few hours until the sound of another boat in the distance had woken him. He had risen, scrabbled about in the kitchen for some food and coffee and felt more normal. He emerged on deck and looked around, taking the opportunity to wee over the side of the boat.

Jimmy reviewed the equipment and saw he was bang on course, conditions were good, and he estimated that he had about four to five more hours and he would arrive back in Castleby in good time. Satisfied, he switched on the autopilot and settled in on the comfortable seats out on deck to enjoy the ride.

In the old brothers' fishing trawler, all was not well. Chris had realised that he was not the best sailor. The choppy night had left him feeling sick and the boat stank, not just of fish but of blocked toilets and vomit. He had rushed to the toilet to be sick before realising that it was already full and had thrown up pretty much everywhere. Annoyed, he had kicked the door, which now wouldn't close, so the putrid smell wafted freely through the boat.

Chris was gasping for a drink. He couldn't find anything apart from whiskey, which he hated and every time he drank it, he threw up. In the galley he had found a very out of date tin of pineapple, which he also hated, and had managed to half open it, cutting his hand deeply in the process. He drank the juice and ate most of the fruit and then, taking him by surprise, promptly brought it all up again, this time all over the wheelhouse floor. So not only was he dealing with the rank smell of the toilet, now the smell of his own sick in the wheelhouse was making him ill.

As he hung his head out of the side window gasping for fresh air, he saw a nice-looking yacht some distance away. He thought for a moment and decided this was his ticket out of here. They probably knew what they were doing and where they were going. He sat there for a moment and wondered how to get rescued.

He jumped up suddenly, ran into the galley and grabbed a box of matches. He opened the engine compartment and threw a couple of lit matches into the engine area. The fire took hold much quicker than expected. He dropped the lid of the engine compartment back down, but the flames licked up through it, running along the length of the boat. Smoke was pouring out. For good measure he turned on the gas in the galley slowly and lit the gas rings, dumping stuff that was flammable on the cooker so that it would catch fire. He remembered what Jesse had always said about a fire on a boat and it being as bad as it could get. Get people off the boat to safety was the rule. He ran out onto the deck and started waving his hands around and shouting at the nearby yacht.

Jimmy had opened another bottle of champagne and was lazily swigging and dozing as the boat motored beautifully through the water. He opened an eye and saw smoke in the distance; he sat up to get a proper look at it. Grabbing the binoculars he noticed a man on the prow of the boat waving his arms as the deck of the trawler was engulfed in thick black smoke.

'Shit!' Jimmy scrabbled at the wheel to change course. He flicked the boat off autopilot and adjusted his heading to bring himself near the yacht.

Jimmy's instructions from Alexy had been clear. He was to come in under the radar. No contact at all on the radio. He dithered for a second with the radio in his hand and then heard an explosion which made him throw down the radio and run back up to deck. He was nearer the boat now and could see the man coughing and fighting back the flames with a fire extinguisher.

'Jump in!' shouted Jimmy. 'Swim to me!'

* * *

Kate had risen early and had been for a long walk along the beach to clear her head. She had received a text from a friend who worked at the local hospital where Kate used to live, telling her that Matthew and Anna had the baby in the early hours of the morning. A boy weighing nearly seven pounds. Healthy. Kate had needed to walk to clear her head and unpack how she felt about it.

By the time she arrived home, she realised she actually wasn't that bothered when it came down to it. It had occurred to her halfway along the beach that she had spent very little time thinking about Matthew, and more time thinking about Steve.

She was sitting by the large window in her kitchen munching on toast and drinking coffee, looking out to sea, when the doorbell rang. She answered it to find Steve leaning against the doorjamb.

'Well hello,' she said, opening the door, taking in how good he looked out of a suit and in jeans and a T-shirt.

'For you,' he said, whipping an enormous bunch of flowers from behind him and presenting her with them.

'Wow,' she said. 'You can definitely come in bearing gifts like that.'

'That's what I hoped you'd say,' he said, stepping in and pushing her back against the door as she closed it and kissing her.

'To what do I owe this pleasure?' she said, coming up for air.

'I just wanted to see you,' he said, going in again for another kiss. 'Mmm, you taste of toast and honey.'

'Come and have a coffee before these flowers die from being ignored.' She laughed and pulled him into the kitchen where she could think straight. She made him a mug and he sat at the table.

'Isn't that view gorgeous today?' she asked as she arranged the flowers. 'I don't think I'd ever tire of that.'

'Yup. Me neither. Quite some view,' he said, smiling as he watched her.

She glanced over her shoulder. 'You're not looking at the view,' she chided.

'I'm looking at what I consider to be the best view.' He grinned. 'So, fancy spending the day with me doing sea carnivally things like tourists?' he asked, coming to stand behind her and kissing the back of her neck lightly.

'Love to,' she said. 'Although I am official helper to Barry, our very serious and committed first aider. Perhaps you could be my wingman.'

'Anytime.' Steve raised an eyebrow.

* * *

The afternoon was bright and sunny, but the November chill was settling in. Sophie had suggested that Sam had an easy morning and they have a late lunch at Maggie's before the carnival started. She had asked Maggie to save a table that would be easy for Sam.

Marcus also wanted to get to the climbing centre to see his name up on the wall of fame and take a picture for his Instagram page.

As they were settling in, Foxy and Rudi arrived and asked to join them, so Maggie pushed another table together so they could all eat together.

The table was full of banter and laughter. Sam sat watching the interplay between them all. He felt huge comfort that Sophie led a good life. She had people here who cared about her and plainly loved her. He knew, deep down, that whatever happened to him, she would be OK with people like this around her.

Suddenly he needed air. He needed solace. He was still getting used to being around people, around noise. He quietly wheeled himself out and sat on the slipway watching the sea roll in and out in its relentless quest of filling the beach.

Foxy had watched Sam; he had been keeping an eye on him and saw him wheel himself out awkwardly. Maggie had come around filling up coffee cups and Foxy got Sam's refilled and took it out to him.

'Here you go. Maggie just did refills,' he said, passing the mug to Sam and sitting on one of the benches next to him. They sat sipping their coffee in silence for a while.

Foxy said quietly, 'I remember that it was the noise, the constant noise, that just got too much for me. I craved solace and silence in equal measure. But it might be different for you.'

Sam inhaled sharply. He gripped the arm of his chair. It was exactly how he felt. He didn't know what to say. They continued to sit in silence, drinking coffee and watching the sea.

'I'm sorry for what I said yesterday about watching your kid. It was cruel. I didn't know.'

Foxy shrugged. 'No problem.'

'Must have been hard for you.'

Foxy focused straight ahead. 'Yup.'

'Sophie said you served.'

'I did.'

'She said that your unit looked for me. When we first went missing.'

'We did, among others. All over the drylands and up in the mountains on the northern border of Syria. You were known as the ghost unit.'

'Sophie said we have a lot in common.'

'Sophie's been talking too much.'

'She told me about… you being captured… Tortured.'

'Not what I consider to be my finest hour.'

'How long?' Sam's voice shook. 'How long were you…?'

'Three months,' Foxy said shortly. He looked out across the beach. 'I thought it was only a few weeks…'

'Time gets lost,' Sam said quietly. 'Quite bizarrely, there's things… elements that I miss about it.'

Foxy was silent for a moment. 'You mean the moments where it's dark and quiet, when you know they won't come for you any more that day?'

Sam swallowed hard, fighting back the tears. 'I thought it was just me losing my mind that missed part of it,' he whispered. 'How can I miss something so terrible?'

Foxy frowned. 'It was part of your life for a bad time. For a long time. The bits where it was quiet and peaceful were a gift. It's only right that you would miss that. Feeling that way. The respite from the horror.'

'Did they…' Sam gulped and tried to form a sentence. 'Were you injured? You look in good shape.'

'I was pretty rough, but I recovered. The cold nights saved me apparently. Otherwise who knows. But my problems weren't really physical. It was all up here afterwards.' He tapped his head.

Sam swallowed heavily and whispered, 'I can barely think about it and then some days it's all I think about. It's like I relive it over and over and over.'

Foxy finished his coffee. 'I know that feeling. I couldn't forget it, couldn't deal with it. But for me, it wasn't just about being captured and tortured. It was being tired of a life of killing and constantly being alert. Constantly looking for danger, even when I was at home. I began to see the faces of the collateral damage. Kids mostly. I knew no peace. I realised I needed help and I think that's the hardest thing. Admitting it out loud. I thought I was doing OK and then… then my daughter…' Foxy coughed as his voice cracked.

Sam exhaled deeply. 'I don't think,' he paused and blinked rapidly, 'I don't think I'll ever get past this. Part of me wants to try and forget it, move on from it. The other part of me wants to—'

'To be left alone to die and not be a burden?'

Sam nodded.

Foxy whistled out a big breath. 'That's some dilemma, Sam. There's enough of us that have been there wondering the same thing. The big question here is, which part of you is winning that battle?'

Foxy stretched his legs out and tilted his face towards the sun, which had broken through a cloud. They sat in silence for a while, each thinking different thoughts. Foxy tried to break the sombre mood.

'So, Marcus did well yesterday, didn't he?'

'All thanks to you, I suspect. He was always a good climber, but now. His focus, his technique is outstanding.'

'I think he'll go far if he keeps it up. I'm happy to help him do that.'

Sam watched him. 'Appreciate that.'

Foxy checked his watch and stood. 'I need to go. Sam, I mean this genuinely. If you ever need to talk. I'll always listen. I can't imagine how you must feel, but for what it's worth I remember how I felt and how I pushed my family away because I thought I was useless and a burden to them.'

'Says the man with two working legs,' said Sam lightly.

'Yes, but the man with the broken mind, Sam. I don't know which is worse. I mean it. Anytime. See you later at the procession maybe?'

'Thanks.' Sam watched him go and realised with an element of frustration that he had begun to quite like Foxy.

Sophie had been watching the two men talk through the window. Maggie had come and stood beside her.

'How's he doing?'

Sophie's eyes filled with tears. 'Well, he's being nice to Marcus.'

'Have you talked?'

Sophie shrugged. 'He doesn't really want to. He actually avoids being alone with me.'

'He wants to die. He said he'd be happy to,' Maggie said quietly.

'Foxy said he'd probably feel that way. I only hope that seeing us, being home with us here is enough for him to think differently.'

'If he's in a deep enough spiral, my love, I don't know what would get him out.'

'That's what I'm afraid of, Mags,' she said, laying her head on Maggie's comforting shoulder. 'What if he just doesn't want to be here with us?'

CHAPTER 24

Jimmy watched Chris leap off the burning trawler and swim towards him. He leant over the side of the boat.

'Anyone else on there?' Jimmy shouted as he reached down to haul him in.

'No, just me,' Chris gasped as he heaved himself over the side of the boat.

They both watched silently as the trawler quickly became engulfed in flames.

'What happened?' said Jimmy, watching the last part of the boat bubble and go under in a cloud of smoke.

'Engine blew something, I think. There was a huge bang and then there was fire everywhere,' Chris replied, eyeing up Jimmy. He wasn't what he expected to see in a boat like this.

'Big boat to be on your own,' Jimmy said, eyeing him up suspiciously. 'You'd need more crew than just you.'

'This your boat?' Chris asked, ignoring the comment and looking around.

'I wish. Just bringing it over as a favour.' Jimmy eyed up Chris. There was something about him that was vaguely familiar, but he couldn't place it.

'Are you alright?' Jimmy asked. 'Not hurt or anything? I've got a first aid kit around here somewhere.'

'I'm OK, just really thirsty. I'm Chris by the way.'

'Jimmy. Help yourself to some water,' Jimmy said, pointing to the open hatch to the galley and steering the boat back on course, flicking on the autopilot.

Chris went into the galley and helped himself to water. As he stood drinking, he noticed the padlocks on the various cabin doors. He went back up on deck and sat opposite Jimmy.

'What's with all the padlocked doors?' he asked.

'Owner wants it that way,' Jimmy said warily. 'I don't ask.'

'Aren't you interested? Padlocked doors? Smacks of something dodgy to me.'

'You sound like filth.'

Chris laughed. 'Nah. Just interested in what you're bringing in that's all. I'm nosey by nature.'

'Filth are nosey by nature too.'

Chris smirked. 'I'm not police, OK? Couldn't be further from it.'

Jimmy regarded him silently. 'Perhaps you shouldn't be so fucking nosey then. Where were you headed?'

Chris thought quickly. 'I was heading for a place called Castleby. Got a friend lives near there,' he said vaguely. 'You know it?'

'I do. Am headed there myself.'

'How far out are we?' Chris asked

317

'Few hours if we stay at this speed,' Jimmy said. 'I'd get comfy if I were you.'

'Got any dry clothes?' Chris asked.

Jimmy shook his head. 'Sorry, mate.'

The two sat in silence as the boat powered though the water with Chris shivering.

'Why don't you go below decks? Warmer down there.'

Chris stood stiffly.

'Thanks. Appreciate it. Don't suppose you've got any food?' Chris asked. 'I'm starving.'

Jimmy gestured towards the hatch. 'Some crackers and stuff in there. Help yourself.'

Jimmy watched him go and made himself comfortable, stretching on the comfortable seats.

Below decks Chris had managed to prise open one of the padlocked cabins. He didn't care that he had ruined the door in this expensive yacht, he wanted to know what was behind the door. If it was anything remotely likely to make him some money; he was interested. He had no source of income on the horizon, so he needed some cash desperately. He pushed open the door quietly and stood there staring.

'Fucking jackpot,' he said quietly.

He closed the door quickly and prised open the remaining cabins which were all empty, apart from the cabin furniture. He crept back to the first cabin and slipped inside. Stacked around the cabin and all over the bed were large grey and brown wrapped blocks, each quite uniform in size. Chris picked them up; his best guess was cocaine, and this was quite the stash. In one corner he found a roll of bin bags. He ripped a few off and started stuffing the packets in them. He laughed, if he could offload this lot, he'd be quids in.

He thought for a moment. He needed to offload that twat on deck and keep this for himself, but he knew he couldn't drive this type of boat in, let alone know where he was going. Had he seen a small RIB on the foredeck, he wondered? He could take enough of the packets of drugs to see him right for years and get away in that as soon as they were near.

He decided on a charm offensive with the bloke who had rescued him, not giving him any cause to be suspicious and he headed upstairs to see how far out they were and then he would decide when to take his chances.

He crept up on deck to see Jimmy had fallen asleep and he took the opportunity to check out the boat. It was small, but it had a tiny engine. He checked it over and reckoned he could work it. Feeling like he had a plan, he crept back along the boat and sat down opposite Jimmy, making himself comfortable.

Jimmy had been dozing and awoke to find Chris stretched out on the seats opposite him. He appeared relaxed and his eyes were closed, so Jimmy reckoned he had been there a while. Jimmy raised his head and was pleased to see land in the distance and estimated that they would hit Castleby in the next hour or so. He settled back down and then dozed off again.

Chris had been watching all of this. He sat up a little straighter and watched the direction they were headed. After a while he estimated that land was close enough. He sat up rolled his shoulders and crept over to stand in front of Jimmy.

'Hey,' he said. 'Wake up.'

Jimmy opened a sleepy eye and saw Chris towering over him.

'What's up?' he said dozily.

Jimmy had no inkling it was coming. The huge fist that smashed into his face broke his nose and sent his head snapping back so it caught the edge of the boat. Knocked unconscious, immediately he slumped on the seat, his nose pumping blood down the front of his clothes.

In a rare moment of compassion, Chris left him on deck and didn't tip him over the side. He had, after all, come to his rescue. But he did take the opportunity to punch him again in the face for good measure to make sure he wouldn't come around any time soon. He peered at the headwound and nudged Jimmy with his foot. He reckoned he might have killed him. He leant in close and couldn't hear him breathing.

Satisfied he was no threat, and probably dead anyway, he left him where he was and managed, with some difficulty to get the dinghy over the side, remembering to tie it on so that he could load in the packages. He hurried from the lower decks with the bags, heaving them over the side and into the dinghy.

When he had crammed as many in as possible, he gingerly climbed in and dropped the small outboard into the water, crossed his fingers and started it. It sprang into life and relieved, Chris motored away from the boat as fast as the engine would carry him.

He tried to remember the place from when he was there before. He didn't want to go into the harbour. He needed a fairly deserted beach where he could stash his gear safely and go and source a buyer. Easy for him to find one. He'd done a good stint in vice in his younger days, and knew exactly the type of person he needed to approach and where people like that would be.

He motored past Kirby Island and carried on, following the coastline further out of the town. He chugged along the wide stretch of beach and saw a series of large boulders at the end. Above it, was a fairly inaccessible flat area that appeared to be reachable with some difficulty. The beach was empty with the exception of a few dog walkers, and he steered the boat in and up the beach as close as he could get to the area with the boulders.

Jimmy came round with a large groan. He raised a shaking hand to his face and grunted when his hand came away covered in blood. With difficulty he sat up and was sick immediately, only just managing to get it over the side. His head throbbed and his nose felt like it was on fire.

Half draped over the edge of the boat, panting as he recovered from being sick, it suddenly occurred to him that the boat was going around in circles. In panic he reached over and flicked the engine off, the sudden quietness a welcome relief. He struggled to his feet and stood for a moment, disorientated. Through the hatch below decks he could see one of the previously padlocked doors was now open.

'No, no, no!' he shouted, stumbling down the steps. All the doors had been forced open.

Despite the fact that he had no idea what was in the cabins he had made a pretty accurate assessment fairly early on. He rushed back up to the deck and saw that the small RIB tender had been taken too and that, in simple terms, he had been completely fucked over.

He sat for a moment and thought. The first priority was to find out what had happened to the boat. He leant over the back, looking to see if the rudder had broken and was horrified to see something wound tightly around it. He closed his eyes in dread. All he fucking needed.

He grabbed a pole and tried to see what the problem was. He poked around with the pole and saw that it was some sort of rusted chain. With difficulty, his face throbbing, he grabbed the chain and heaved, hoping that the rust would mean that it might break the chain and release whatever it was. He heaved and something large bobbed to the surface.

Jimmy almost passed out from fright.

What had appeared was an old, unexploded naval mine. It was large, rusty, round and had rods sticking out of it. And it was attached to the boat. On the rudder.

He scrabbled backwards on the deck away from it. He had heard about these things suddenly blowing up. He sat for a moment looking at this thing bobbing happily in the water. He knew he needed to try and keep it away from the boat.

Jimmy realised that the rest of the day was not going to go well for him. By his reckoning the boat had been full of something illegal; probably drugs, which were now missing; the Camorra would definitely kill him for it. Plus, what seemed to be an unexploded bomb was now attached to the boat.

He didn't know whether Pearl wanted the boat because she liked boats or because she wanted the drugs. He suspected it was a combination of the two. Either way it meant almost certain death for him. He put his head in his hands and wondered how the fuck he was going to get himself out of this particular fix and not end up in pieces like JJ.

Jimmy thought for a while. He decided that he could radio for help because the drugs had gone, so that wasn't an issue. He went below decks and radioed in a Mayday, specifically requesting bomb disposal attend.

Jimmy watched the yacht slowly disappear as he sat in the inshore lifeboat heading towards Castleby.

'Jimbo, it can only happen to you, mate.' Mike laughed good-naturedly as he drove the boat towards the harbour.

'What happened to your face?' Tom asked, looking concerned, with a first aid box on his lap.

'Some fucker punched me. They're not going to blow it up, are they?' Jimmy asked worriedly, squinting at the horizon and watching the two bomb disposal guys walking over the deck of the boat. 'It's not my boat.'

'No, they'll try and get the mine off carefully, then drag it out to sea and set it off. They're going to tow the boat into the harbour when it's free. You OK with that?'

'S'pose so,' said Jimmy.

'Whose boat is it anyway?'

'Don't fucking ask.'

'I think that's broken,' Tom said, looking at his nose. 'You should get to hospital and get it set.'

Jimmy waved the comment aside.

'I need to get on. People to see,' he said dismissively. The inshore lifeboat bumped against the harbour wall. Jimmy stepped out and swayed, suddenly feeling dizzy.

'If you're not going to hospital, then come with me,' Tom said firmly, taking hold of Jimmy's arm and marching up the ramp from the harbour.

'Kate,' he called to a blonde woman who had her back to him. She turned and pulled a face when she saw Jimmy.

'Jesus,' she said, frowning. 'What happened to you?'

Jimmy was confused. This was the pathologist that would be able to link him with JJ's head. What was she doing here at the first aid stand for the carnival?

'Er,' he stammered.

Tom stepped in. 'Kate, this is Jimmy. I reckon his nose is broken but he won't go to hospital to find out.'

Kate looked at Jimmy. 'Are you happy for me to take a look at it?'

He frowned at her. 'Don't you cut up dead people?'

Kate guffawed. 'Only on a full moon.' She laughed. 'I'm a GP here. Of course I don't cut up dead people.' She snapped on some nitrile gloves. 'Now let me feel this nose.' She held his face in her hands gently. 'This is going to really hurt,' she said wryly. 'You might wanna sit down.'

Steve strolled over after spotting Jimmy being led up the harbour ramp.

'Hello, Jimmy. What have you been up to? We've been wanting to have a little chat with you.'

Jimmy took a look at Steve and scowled. 'Great. And here's me thinking my day couldn't get any fucking worse,' he snapped.

Kate had worked wonders on Jimmy's nose. He felt vaguely human again and she had been nice and gentle and also given him some painkillers. The throbbing had now reduced to a dull thud in his face. He had managed to slip away when Kate had been sidetracked, and Steve had followed her to help. He couldn't deal with speaking to Steve right now.

Jimmy wasn't sure where to start. How did he look for something when he didn't know what it actually was? He concluded he needed to talk to Alexy and come clean, before breaking it to Pearl and then no doubt dying in a horrible manner.

He called Alexy, closing his eyes and feeling his stomach roll in nervousness as the phone rang.

'Ah it is my friend Jimmy the fisherman!' Alexy said good-humoredly. 'You have parked boat?'

'Little bit trickier than that. We need to meet. Like now.'

Silence came from Alexy and Jimmy's terror ramped up a notch.

'Alexy? I said I need to meet. Right fucking now.'

There was a large sigh from Alexy. 'Where?'

'Drop from last time. I'll leave now. OK?' Jimmy was desperate.

'Alexy think this is not good news,' he said, sighing again. 'OK. I leave now.'

Jimmy breathed out heavily with relief and hurried up through the town to get his truck.

Ten minutes later he pulled into the car park and saw Alexy already parked. He pulled up next to it. The tinted window slid down and Alexy regarded Jimmy.

'Did you fall?' he asked, pointing to his nose.

Jimmy had come up with the only plan that he could think of. It involved a lot of lying and half-truths. Jimmy's special gift.

'No, I fucking didn't fall on something. Who knew I was bringing in the boat, Alexy?'

Alexy frowned. 'Why?'

'Because someone was waiting for me, and they stole all the drugs. Every single packet.'

Alexy's face was like thunder. 'What?' he snapped.

Jimmy jabbed a finger at him. 'You've got a fucking leak in your organisation, mate, and you've been proper fucked over.'

Alexy inhaled sharply. 'Say what happened,' he said, regarding Jimmy through narrowed eyes.

Jimmy took a breath. 'So I'm minding my own business. Come across an old trawler, which is on fire. Bloke screams for help. Jumps off and swims to me. Boat sinks. Mighty big fucking trawler to be manning on your own; plus, the bloke stank of sick which says to me he wasn't any kind of sailor. Anyway, he settles in for a ride back and knocks me out from behind, I didn't stand a chance, gave me a good kicking, broke my nose. Broke all the padlocks and took the stash on the small RIB.'

'Where is boat then?'

'Well, here's the other thing. I don't know how he did it either. Must have had someone else in the water doing it. They only managed to find one of those sea mines and wrap it around the rudder.'

Alexy was confused. 'What is this thing?'

'They used them a lot in the war. Probably your lot, back in the day. Round metal ball with spikes, full of explosives. They would anchor them to the bottom of the ocean and let them hang on a long chain. Boats or submarines would explode if they hit them.'

'Boat has exploded?' Alexy said, shocked.

'No. Bomb squad are taking it off and are bringing it back to the harbour for me.'

Alexy frowned. 'So. This… man you pick from water from burning boat. He took small boat with whole stash?'

Jimmy shrugged. 'Assume so, all the rooms were broken into and empty.'

Alexy narrowed his eyes and eyed Jimmy closely.

'Jimmy, we are friends… no?'

Jimmy swallowed. 'We are, Alexy. This is why I'm here.'

Alexy rubbed his dark stubble thoughtfully. 'Jimmy, you would not lie to your friend Alexy would you?'

'Fuck no,' Jimmy said nervously. 'Definitely not. Nor Pearl either. Wouldn't dare.'

Alexy thought for a moment. 'Jimmy, whole stash could not fit in tiny RIB.'

Jimmy looked confused. 'What? All the rooms were empty… I assumed—'

Alexy laughed. 'That was leftovers! In one of the cabins. In case we get bust they would see and think that was payload! Most of stuff is in special areas… yes. Special… oh, what is word?' He tutted. 'Compartments. Yes. This is very special boat for this.'

'Special boat?' Jimmy said, confused. 'That means someone knew all about this. You've been fucked over, mate. I don't know if anything else was taken.'

Jimmy's phone rang. He glanced at Alexy.

'I need to get this. They said they'd call when the boat was back.'

'OK. Put on speaker.'

Jimmy answered. 'Hello?'

'Jimmy Ryan? This is Tony from the bomb squad, we met earlier. Your boat is back in the harbour safe and sound. You had quite the lucky escape.'

'Oh, er… yes. Thanks,' stammered Jimmy. 'Everything OK?'

'Yup. My colleagues have taken it out and made it safe. I've got your keys here, where do you want them?'

'Oh, er. I'm about 10 minutes away.'

'No problem. I'll grab a coffee and hang on for you. See you in ten.' The call ended.

'Guess we should go and see whether it's all missing or just the leftovers,' Jimmy said.

Alexy raised an eyebrow. 'Leftovers worth pretty penny, my friend.'

'How many leftovers were there?'

'About 30 packets, each pack is a kilo. It add up, my friend.'

Jimmy tried to do the maths and eventually got to an answer.

'What, so that's over a million quid? For leftovers?' he asked Alexy doubtfully.

Alexy raised an eyebrow and started his engine. 'Come. We see what's left,' he said grimly.

Alexy hung back while Jimmy got the keys from bomb squad Tony, who headed off, waving cheerfully in his large Land Rover. Alexy appeared at Jimmy's elbow and together they went down into the boat. Alexy instructed Jimmy to stay on deck and keep watch while he went below to check compartments. Jimmy was still sitting on the deck when Alexy finally appeared through the hatch.

'You are lucky man,' he said as he jogged lightly up the stairs to sit next to Jimmy. 'Definitely cat with the nine tails.'

'Lives. Not tails,' Jimmy corrected absently. 'So, is it all there?'

'Yes.'

'How much… roughly?'

Alexy thought for a moment. 'Without leftovers… maybe 200 kilos?'

Jimmy swallowed. 'Two hundred kilos?' He couldn't even do the maths in his head. Wholesale, a kilo was roughly around £40,000. His brain couldn't add it up.

Alexy laughed and clapped him on the shoulder. 'It is a lot, my friend. But you have saved your legs today at least.'

'Thank God,' Jimmy agreed. 'Will it be OK in here, is it safe? Do we need to move it?'

'It goes Tuesday, around to the port. It will be fine here. I set up a little security and hey bingo… we can keep eyeball.' He beamed at Jimmy. 'Now, we need to find leftovers. We don't want Pearl being cross. No?'

'Christ no.'

'Alexy has an idea. Come, my friend.'

CHAPTER 25

Chris was hanging about in the places where he knew dealers would be. He had narrowed it down to two men he had been watching for a while. One he was starting to discount due to the clientele. He smacked of a pothead weed dealer to him. He focused on the other guy. This looked more promising. Definitely dealing a bit of blow here.

He wandered over.

'Mate,' he said casually, looking around.

The dealer stopped and eyed him suspiciously. 'Help ya?'

'If you do there's a wedge of cash for you.'

The dealer glanced around. 'Fuck off. You look and smell like filth to me,' he said.

Chris shook his head. 'No. Hear me out. I need to speak to your supplier. Or your supplier's supplier. I wanna talk to the head honcho. See, I've got a load of blow I need to shift quickly. You see me right and I'll see you right.'

'How much?' the dealer said suspiciously.

'How much have I got, or what I'll pay you?'

The dealer shrugged. 'Both.'

Chris looked at him and considered hitting him. He inhaled deeply, trying to control his temper. He was actually going to kill this little scrote just for fucking him about, so the amount was irrelevant.

'I've got enough to make them very interested,' he said. 'If you set the deal up I'll give you five grand. Cash.'

The dealer's eyes widened. 'Cash?'

'Absolutely. Give me your phone number. I'll call you later, see how you're doing.'

* * *

The sky was darkening with the onset of evening and the high street was a sea of people noisily exclaiming over the lights and creations by the local businesses. Maggie had claimed an area at the top of the harbour where the procession would pass by, and she had a bird's eye view of most things. Ever the feeder, she had set up a table filled with food and drink, and invited her favourite people along.

Rudi and Foxy had rocked up early, adding beer to Maggie's already overflowing table, and their good friend Mack had arrived hand in hand with Gen. He had finally returned from hospital in Germany, where he had been recovering from being shot while on a covert op.

Foxy enveloped him in an enormous hug. 'So pleased to see you, mate,' he said, holding Mack at arm's length and inspecting him. 'See what happens when you go on an op without me? You get shot.'

Mack rolled his eyes. 'Er, if I recall, the first time I went on an op with you I also got shot.'

'Tiny insignificant detail. Good to have you back.' Foxy laughed.

Rudi wandered over. 'And the dream team is complete again,' he said, hugging Mack. 'Missed you. You look good.'

Maggie smiled indulgently as she watched them. She had adopted these three soldiers since their arrival in the town and had fussed over them constantly ever since. Her late husband had been military, and she had always found military men to be great company. They were straight to the point, with no fussing; honest and true. She loved each of them for it.

Doug and Jesse arrived with Jude, and he and Marcus immediately left to look for their friends. Maggie embraced Jesse. 'You look wonderful, my love. A few days away with the man of your dreams is clearly the perfect tonic!'

Jesse gazed up at Doug. 'You're not wrong there, Mags.'

'Mags!' Maggie turned to see Sophie waving as she walked down the street with Sam, Marcus and Lottie. Lottie was pushing Sam, and Rudi ran over to help push him up the steep path to Maggie's small camp.

'Allow me,' he said, giving her one of his winning smiles. 'How are you doing, Sam?'

'Fine, thank you.'

In truth Sam wanted to curl up and die. The pain level in his legs was off the scale and he was bone tired. He just wanted to lay down and sleep. Or die. He'd be happy with either option.

He told himself he had a few hours of this, then he could take painkillers and sleep. Tomorrow he would think seriously about how he could die this weekend. He was too tired and in too much pain to think clearly.

Rudi manoeuvred him so he had a great view of the road below him.

'You OK there, mate? What can I get you? We've got coffee, beer…'

'Coffee, thanks,' Sam said, just wanting to be left alone.

'Soph!'

Sophie whirled at her name being shouted and saw Kate and Steve coming through the crowd. Kate and Steve made their way up, greeting people as they went. After hugging Sophie, Kate headed straight for Sam. She bent down to kiss his cheek and then stayed on her haunches in front of him.

'Ello, gorgeous,' she said in a mock cockney accent.

'Hello yourself,' Sam said. 'Heard that you got rid of that cock of a husband.'

'I'm certainly trying to.'

'Pleased to hear it. Thought we were going to have to send the boys around for a moment,' he said gruffly.

Kate had known Sam since he first had eyes for Sophie. She had loved the man, full of mischief and love, with the huge smile and dimples to match, and his infectious laugh. The man before her was broken and in immense pain. Her eyes filled with tears suddenly. She touched his face gently.

'Exactly how much pain are you in, my love?' she asked quietly.

Sam closed his eyes for a moment. A muscle pounded in his jaw. She watched as he opened eyes that were full of tears. He broke her gaze and looked away, blinking.

'It would appear I have swapped one kind of living hell for another,' he said quietly.

Kate held his hand tightly, her face full of concern. 'I can't bear to see you like this, Sam.'

Sam looked at her. 'I can't bear to be like this, Kate,' he said quietly. 'I want out.'

'No, Sam.'

'Yes, Kate,' he said, sighing and closing his eyes.

Maggie had been watching the exchange and came over with a flask of coffee.

'Hello, Kate love,' she said. 'Hello, soldier,' she said to Sam and filled up his cup.

'Everything OK? Sam, can I get you something else to eat?'

Sam shook his head. 'I'm OK thanks, Mags.'

Sam gestured to Steve who was chatting to Foxy and Rudi. 'Who's the new squeeze?'

Kate sighed happily. 'Steve. He's the local police inspector. And I don't know if squeeze is the term…'

'You look happy.'

'I am.'

'Life is short, Kate. Don't waste it.'

Sophie wandered over and placed a hand on Sam's shoulder. 'Procession starts in a minute. Sam, are you warm enough?'

Sam moved his shoulder away. 'I'm not five. Yes thank you, I'm fine.'

Sophie shrugged. 'You look cold.'

Kate said. 'I think Sam could do with some pain relief.'

'Right. I'll find Lottie.' Sophie hurried off to ask Lottie, who was totally engrossed in flirting with Rudi. Sophie came back with a couple of tablets which she dropped into Sam's hand.

'Lottie said you need to take those with something.'

Maggie handed him a hot sausage roll. 'Here you go. You always loved these.'

'Thanks,' Sam said, swallowing his tablets and then eating a few bites of the sausage roll.

Kate watched him from the corner of her eye. She was worried about him. She watched Sophie standing by Sam awkwardly and for about the hundredth time in her medical career, she wished she had a magic wand to make it all better.

The ocean procession was in full swing, and Sam's tablets had kicked in which meant he felt slightly more human. He laughed at the costumes for the Brownies, all with clear umbrellas and white tights, and singing a song about jellyfish. He laughed some more at the Cubs who were all dressed as Aquaman, complete with false six packs.

Foxy stood slightly removed from the group and watched Sophie sitting on a cool box next to Sam pointing at things and laughing.

It was universally agreed that the winners of the best group in the local parade were the local gig club, who had all dressed as seahorses with huge fins and false heads. Runners up had been the reception class at the local school, who had made themselves look like a big group of crabs with bright red umbrellas with googly eyes and cardboard claws with little red legs.

The parade came to an end and the Hope and Anchor won the award for best dressed business, with its enormous octopus; the climbing centre came second and the surf shop won third place.

People were heading off for the gathering on the beach and Maggie was fussing around her posse.

'Right,' she said. 'Off to the bonfire. If we go to the café, I can open the doors and we can all watch it from the deck. That work for everyone?'

Everyone knew the gesture was for Sam's benefit, so the group gradually made their way down towards the beach and got set up on the deck of the café.

Sophie stood on the deck leaning against the rail and watching the bonfire, it was huge; crackling and roaring. She could feel the heat from where she was standing. She enjoyed the warmth on her face. The glow cast her face in an orange light and Foxy watched her for a moment, his stomach lurching as she turned around and faced him.

'Hey, you,' she said softly.

'Hey yourself,' he said, leaning against the railing. 'How you doing?'

She looked away, unable to meet his eye. 'I'm OK,' she croaked.

Foxy took a step towards her, his face full of concern. But she held up a hand.

'Rob, please don't be nice to me. It'll make me cry and I can't cry.'

'Soph.'

Sam had been wheeling himself out onto the deck and had seen the exchange. He felt instantly guilty that Sophie was upset because he had been so abrasive to her. He wheeled himself over and tried to be pleasant.

'Congrats on coming second. You were robbed. Should have been first. What you did with the frogmen and the projection was brilliant.'

Foxy nodded. 'Thanks. I thought the surf shop was pretty damn good though.'

* * *

Chris was damp and cold and needed some food. He'd managed to secure a phone by beating up a teenage boy who'd been buying weed from the pothead dealer. It was basic but it would do. He'd texted his number to the dealer and now he just had to wait. He had heard that there was a bonfire on the beach, so he decided to see if he could warm up and ponce some food.

He walked past a launderette and peered in hopefully. He found a few dryers with clothes in just sitting there, with the empty bags on the side. He rifled through one and found nothing but old lady's clothes but on the second he struck gold. Jeans and a sweatshirt. Bingo.

He stripped off and chucked on the clothes, pleased to be rid of the underlying smell of sick that he had caught the odd waft of. The jeans were a little long, but he rolled them up slightly and they fitted fine.

Chris walked towards the beach, keeping his head down and sat on the sand by the fire, enjoying the heat. It was packed with people. He let his eyes wander around and they settled on a family finishing a picnic. He watched as one of the small children let go of the lead of their excitable dog which ran off, prompting the entire family to get up and run after it. Chris stood immediately and walked over, stopping to pick up some rolls and a bottle of drink. He grabbed a chocolate bar for good measure and wandered over the other side of the bonfire to settle down and eat his stash.

Jesse and Doug were leaning against the rail watching Jude and Marcus chat up a couple of girls. Doug was standing behind Jesse, his arms wrapped around her. She was watching Jude and laughing as the girls seemed to be playing hard to get.

'Another beer?' Doug asked.

'Lovely,' Jesse said, sighing happily from contentment.

Jesse watched him go, smiling, and turned her attention back to Jude and Marcus, but couldn't see them. She scanned the crowd and for a moment she thought her heart would stop. She gasped loudly.

'Jesse?' Steve was nearby and heard her gasp.

Jesse's head was swimming. She felt faint. Unsteady. Sick. She felt her world spinning. She fell to her knees. Unable to catch her breath.

'Jesse? Jesse, breathe slowly,' said a calm voice.

Jesse closed her eyes and breathed. She felt sick, dizzy. She realised tears were pouring down her face.

'Did you see him? Oh God… He's…' she said and fell into a dead faint.

Chris had received the call and finished his stolen picnic quickly, eager to get to his meet. The dealer had done good. He was due to meet the kingpin of it all. He didn't know where he was going, but he had seen a town map in the high street. He'd go and look at that. The phone he'd nicked from the teenager was basic: just calls and texts, so he had no chance of looking it up.

He stood, brushed himself off and walked around the bonfire towards the slipway up to the town. He passed the café quickly, briefly catching the eye of a blond man who was standing on the deck looking around, frowning. He carried on past him and found the map.

Steve was scrolling through his memory. Where the fuck had he seen that face? Jesse had fainted, and Steve watched as Kate tried to find out why. Steve recalled she had asked him if he'd seen something. Or was it someone?

His brain abruptly provided the missing piece. Chris. The man who had attacked Jesse twice. He looked around panicking. Was it him? It didn't look that much like him. Very scarred and he limped. But could it have been him? Steve couldn't be sure. He prided himself on a superb memory for faces. But this time, he just wasn't sure.

Jesse had come round and was sitting on a chair, her head dropped down to her knees. Doug was sitting next to her.

'Sweetheart, what happened?' he asked gently.

Jesse raised her head. 'I saw him. He was here. Oh God. I'm going to be sick.'

Doug stood. 'Chris?' he said loudly. 'You saw Chris?' He turned to Steve. 'Did you see him?'

Steve grimaced. 'I saw someone that might have looked like him. But I'm not sure, Jesse. I'm just not sure.'

'We'll look then.' Foxy put his beer bottle down loudly.

'I'm in,' Rudi said. 'Mack?'

'Don't need to ask.'

'He went through town? What was he wearing?' Foxy asked.

'Jeans and a grey Gap sweatshirt.'

'You coming?'

'Let's go.' Doug said grimly.

Jesse covered her face with her hands and sobbed. 'The woman in the dream. She was right.'

Foxy and the others had scoured the area and not seen him at all. After an hour of thorough searching, they had returned to the café. By that time, Sophie had taken Sam home and Doug had taken a very shaken Jesse back to his. Maggie was sitting out on the deck with Kate.

'Any luck?' Kate asked as they all piled in.

'Nothing,' said Rudi. 'Oh, has Lottie gone?' he said sadly.

'She has but she wondered if you wanted a nightcap by the fire when she's settled Sam?' Kate said.

Rudi nodded enthusiastically.

'I told her you'd meet her here at ten,' Maggie tittered. 'Like you'd say no!'

Foxy thanked Maggie for the evening and headed off home. He felt like he needed to be on his own. He was still trying to get his head around Sophie and how he felt. He genuinely felt heartbreak for Sam. He could relate. But seeing Sophie so unhappy almost broke his heart all over again. He had overheard what Sam had said about swapping one type of hell for another, and in an emotional way Foxy felt he was in the same position. He had come to Castleby wracked with guilt about the death of his daughter and struggling to cope with her loss. He had been in a self-imposed purgatory. He had learnt to live with that, but now he had the agony of seeing the woman he loved deeply being so troubled and unhappy, and he couldn't do a single thing about it.

* * *

Chris was happy. He was on his way to the deal of the century. This could set him up for years. He was mentally spending the cash already. He had worked out where he needed to be, and he was limping quickly up the road, cursing his leg. He waited in the car park of the deserted social club, huddling in the doorway. He checked his watch. He was early, they weren't late. Not yet. He waited, shivering, and stood a little straighter when he saw a truck sweeping into the car park and the rumble of a large engine. He stepped out into the glare of headlights.

I've not heard from my saviour. I wonder if He has abandoned me. I glorified him on this earth. I've accomplished the work which He has given me to do. But still He does not reveal himself. Should I stop? Has my Lord and saviour abandoned me? All I see now is the devil. I hear him in my mind. See him in my dreams. He is trying to seduce my mind. Has my Lord and saviour decided that my work is not good enough? Not quick enough? Is he angry that I have disciples helping me? Sometimes I wonder if it was the devil all along... tricking me. Seducing me to do his work. Have I lost my faith or is this a test of my faith?

This surely must be a test of my faith. I will continue to do my work and my Lord will reveal Himself and we shall prevail, and we shall rejoice.

CHAPTER 26

Sam was in the dark room again. He was laying on the hard-packed earth floor. The door opened and he scrambled to his feet. He had a moment of confusion when he realised he had his legs again. For a fleeting moment he felt pure joy. Legs! He had legs! In front of him stood a huge man, he was tall and broad-shouldered, and he had his head wrapped in a traditional Shemagh, leaving only his bright blue eyes free. Sam wondered for a moment if it was Foxy, the eyes were the same.

He beckoned to Sam and walked back through the doorway. Sam stepped out into the open air. Everywhere around him there was fire. Long lines of it. Hot, driving him back. The heat on his face unbearable. Through the flames and the smoke he saw something in the distance. The small boy that had been in his dreams before. He was screaming as the fire was getting closer. Sam stepped forward to try and rescue him but the man in the Shemagh held him firmly and shook his head. Sam struggled to get free, but the man held him fast. Sam saw the fire approaching the small boy who screamed again from the heat; Sam struggled and lashed out, finally breaking away. As he ran towards the boy hands grabbed him again, and he wildly struck out.

'SAM.'

He lashed out again and ran faster, he looked down at his legs and realised that they were plastic mannequin's legs; he saw them melting from the heat as he tried to run over the hot burning earth.

'SAM, WAKE UP.'

Sam jolted awake and lay panting in the darkness. A light flicked on and he saw Sophie kneeling on the bed next to him with blood running down her chin.

'What…?' he said confused.

'Sam, are you OK? You were having some sort of night terror,' she said, wiping his face with a cool cloth.

Sam blinked and tried to focus on what was happening. He reached out and touched her face.

'Sophie, what happened to your lip?'

'You caught me when you were in your dream. It's fine.'

'My God, I'm so sorry. It's really bleeding.'

'I said it's fine. Don't fuss. You didn't know. I'm more concerned about you.'

Sam struggled to sit up in bed. His head was pounding, his mouth was dry.

'Sophie, let me see it.'

'It's fine, Sam. Really.'

She sorted through something on his bedside table.

'Lottie said you needed to take one of these if you woke.'

She passed him a tablet and some water. 'Go on… take it.'

Sam obediently took the tablet and drank the water. Sophie wiped his face and rested a hand on his chest.

'Try and calm down a bit. Your heart is going like a freight train.' She helped him lay back down and rearranged his pillow.

'I'm OK.'

'Thing is, Sam, you're not. Stop fighting it.' She put a hand on his face. 'We have to get through this.'

Sam took her hand and held it. 'I don't think I can,' he said quietly. 'Soph, I don't think I can come back from this.'

'You can, Sam. You're the most resilient and strong person I have ever known.'

'Not anymore, Soph. They broke me. I can't live with the memory of it. I can't live knowing you are sacrificing a good life for me.'

'I'm not sacrificing anything,' she said angrily.

'You are. You're sacrificing everything for a shadow of the man I used to be.' He closed his eyes. The tablet had kicked in and was making him sleepy. 'Sophie, you need to let me go.'

'Stop talking like this.'

'I mean it, Sophie. I need you to let me go. I'm not who I used to be.'

Sam slipped into a deep sleep. Sophie sat for a while watching his face relax as he slept. She tucked in the covers around him and switched out the light.

'So… just to be clear. You and Jude are swimming around the point this morning dressed as lifeguards.'

'Uh-huh.'

'And Doug has given his blessing?'

'Uh-huh.'

'And allowed you to wear the uniform?'

'Uh-huh.'

'So if I texted him now to ask, he'd say yes to all those questions?'

'Uh-huh.'

'Sure? I'm texting him now.'

'Sure. Go for it.'

'So just to clarify for my own sanity here. Everybody else, however many hundred people there will be, are all going to be dressed as something from the sea or a sea creature. And you and Jude are going as lifeguards.'

'Yes.' Marcus rolled his eyes. 'God, Mum. There's going to be fit girls there. We're not going to go looking like a couple of idiots. We've all seen Zac Efron in *Baywatch*. This is the vibe we are going for.'

'My God,' she said, staring at him. 'Who are you and what happened to my son?'

Marcus grabbed a piece of bacon off the plate and winked at her.

'I'm the new improved Marcus, Mum. Get used to it.'

He walked out of the kitchen eating the bacon, and Sophie watched him go.

'He'll be going to university before you know it,' Sam observed from the doorway.

'How do you feel?' she asked, searching his face for clues about his mood.

'Good. Rested. God, I'm sorry about your lip. Look at it.'

'It's fine. Hungry?'

'I am,' he said. 'Let me help.'

Sophie glanced out of the kitchen window at the sound of a door slamming and saw Rudi's tree surgeon truck. Rudi was walking with Lottie, his arm slung over her shoulder. Sophie went to the back door.

'You staying for breakfast, Rudi?' Sophie called.

'Well, if you're asking,' he said happily. 'Love to.'

Lottie stepped in the back door and looked at Sophie and Sam sheepishly.

Sorry,' she said. 'Sophie, what happened to your lip?'

Sam held up his hands. 'Me. My fault. I was having a bad dream, thrashing about. I lashed out. I didn't know Sophie was there.'

Lottie frowned. 'Sophie, that needs a stich. I've got some steri-strips that will do. Come on. Sam, you come too, we need to change your dressings. Rudi take over breakfast duty.'

'Yes, ma'am.' Rudi saluted.

* * *

Jesse had spent the night in a kind of half-sleep limbo, waking every few minutes at various noises around the house. She kept reliving the moment she saw Chris. Every time she thought about it, she felt sick and dizzy. Twice she got up and checked all the doors and windows were locked.

'Shall we call Jonathan?' ventured Doug, dishing up pancakes for the kids. 'Jude… mate. Come on. One at a time. No one is going to take it away.'

'And say what? That I think I saw him? Tell him about the woman in the dream?'

'I don't know, love. All I know is that you hardly slept and you're a bundle of nerves. Christie love, Marmite on pancakes? Really?'

'I can't help it. I know it was him. I feel it. The woman in my dream. She was right.'

Doug placed a pancake in front of Jesse and came around to envelop her in a hug.

'Gross,' announced Jude, eyeing them.

'Are you coming to watch the swim? We'll be out in the big boat,' Doug said.

Jesse thought for a minute. 'I don't want to be alone; but then I don't want to be in the crowd either.'

'Come on the boat then. Just don't do anything that you can get told off for!' he said, smiling. 'You're on sick leave for another few weeks.'

'OK,' she said. 'Deal.'

'Kids eat up,' he said. 'You're going across to Mum's in a minute.'

'Do you reckon we can have breakfast there too?' asked Jude hopefully.

The lifeboat swept down the slipway and motored gently around in a large circle positioning itself carefully where they would have maximum visibility of the swimmers. The race organisers had marked a wide route for the swimmers with colourful floats, and strict instructions were being issued to the crowd to stay in the marked areas. The beach was a blaze of colour. People were dressed as fish, sharks, octopus, whales and jellyfish, and a few brave souls had pushed the limits with their costumes: there was a submarine, a battleship and a small sailboat.

Spectators were lined up all along the beach and the harbour walls. Sophie, Sam and Lottie were making room through the crowds for the wheelchair which Rudi was pushing. Rudi lived in a cottage opposite the pier, so he had suggested they pick a spot there, near to his place in case anyone needed anything. The huge stone pier had a perfect view of the bulk of the swim, so they made

346

themselves comfortable, easily picking out Marcus and Jude in their lifeguard outfits.

Sophie was fretting about Sam being too near the edge and kept telling him to keep back, but he told her to stop fussing.

Sam felt the most relaxed he had in weeks. He had a plan. Today was the day. He had asked Sophie in the early hours to let him go. She knew how he felt. She didn't agree. But the fact that he had asked was enough. He was at peace. Happy. He knew the end was near. He had woken early and written letters to both Sophie and Marcus which he had left where it would be found if anyone went through his possessions.

He jumped as the siren to start the race blasted out loudly. The sound of cheering was deafening as the colourful hordes sprang into the water.

* * *

Steve had been hoping that he could catch the start of the race. Instead, he had gone to the office in the hope he could scratch the itch he had been having about Mrs Pomeroy. He'd gone into work after the parade the previous evening, reluctant to leave Kate, but needing to break the case. Something wasn't chiming with him, and he couldn't put his finger on it. Years of experience had told him he needed to indulge these feelings; so he went to work with a view of reviewing everything again until something clicked.

He sat at the large conference table at the end of the office which was reserved for meetings and briefings with a giant coffee and one of Jonesey's penguin biscuits, and got stuck in.

He reviewed the evidence from the search warrants and wrote down what was found and where. He noted that a substance which resembled dried fungus had been found in a jar in Mrs P's cupboard and he flicked through the analysis reports. He read that these were described as dried psilocybin mushrooms. Not understanding precisely, he investigated further. What he found made him smile.

'Mrs Pomeroy. You on the old magic mushrooms?' he murmured.

He dialled a number and waited impatiently, tapping his pen noisily in the quiet room.

'Murphy.' The voice sounded annoyed.

'Murph. It's Steve. Sorry to call, mate.'

'Make it quick?'

'Psilocybin mushrooms.'

'What about them?'

'Would they have killed Fred?'

'No. Poor bastard might have had a better trip out if he had taken some.'

'So they are just used for tripping?'

'Pretty much.'

'Can they kill you?'

'Not directly… they're not poisonous. You'd feel extremely poorly if you had way too many, but nothing like poor Fred. These are like opioids. You get lots of weird effects if you use them so I assume if you have an underlying health condition, like a very poorly heart they could kill you in conjunction with that. But bottom line – people tend to use them infused as a tea, mainly to get a bit trippy.'

'Trippy like E trippy, or more like weed trippy?'

'Depends entirely on the person, the type. Somewhere in between I would say. However, I have known people have a trip on these and report all sorts of out of body experiences. Big in Ibiza apparently. Lots of people making money out of stuff like this and people desperate to trip out and find themselves. You know, usual bollocks for those people with too much money and not enough sense.'

'OK. That's helpful.'

'One thing, Steve. They can be quite addictive, not the mushrooms themselves as such, more like psychologically addicted to what they do for you.'

'Interesting… so what, need it every day or every few days?'

'Varies… but yes. Pretty often.'

'Murph, you're a superstar.'

'I know that. It's everyone else that's the problem. See ya.'

'Bye.'

Steve felt like he was at an impasse. Nothing had shown up as being of a severely poisonous nature. The broths and the cakes that he had confiscated from Peter before their chat had shown to be clear of anything suspicious, but Steve knew that something wasn't right.

He laid out all the reports across the table and walked around them slowly. His eye caught Joy Brown's name. He picked up the file and the report and felt a familiar surge of excitement. Joy Brown. A detailed analysis of the small cakes found in her house showed traces of amatoxins, phallotoxins, phallolysin, and antamanide; defined as the biologically active components of poisonous mushrooms. Steve inhaled sharply. He flicked to the next page. Analysis of stomach material and contents of a Tupperware container in the fridge containing some sort of soup: the same again.

He frowned and searched for Mabel's file. Deeper analysis of the stomach contents showed a light broth-like substance with the presence of amatoxins, phallotoxins, phallolysin, and antamanide.

He grabbed the visitor logs for the care home and saw Peter's name scribbled in the day prior to her death and reason for visiting written as: 'Prayers and Soup!'

349

Steve grabbed his notebook. He had almost a total recollection of phrases that people said to him. He remembered Peter saying that he was always given something by Mrs P to take and he had taken Joy some broth. He thought for a while longer and then wheeled himself over to the terminal that held one of the large police databases. He plugged in Mrs P's name. The results flashed up in front of him and made him sit upright in his chair and stare at the screen intently.

'Fucking bingo,' he said loudly to the empty office.

* * *

The race had finished with a clear winner; the same man who won it every year, along with all of the local Iron Man or triathlon competitions, who was dressed as a shark.

'Apt really,' Maggie said snippily. 'I don't know why he doesn't let the kids have a chance. Always has to win everything. Plus, he's always dressed in Lycra and no one wants to see that on a bloke who looks like that.' She eyed up Foxy. 'You ever worn Lycra?'

Foxy almost spat his coffee out. 'Over my dead body, no one wants to see that.'

'Oh, I don't know…' Maggie grinned lasciviously.

'Oh, stop it,' Foxy said good-naturedly. He walked to the end of the pier and whistled loudly as he saw Jude and Marcus running up the beach. He gestured to Rudi's house, and they gave him a thumbs up, grabbed their bags and changed direction running around the harbour.

'Kettle on Rudi,' Foxy said. 'The boys will be back in a minute. Doug and Jesse are still out on the boat.'

Maggie, Lottie and Sophie headed into Rudi's cottage.

'You need a hand, mate?' Foxy asked Sam.

'I just need a little peace and quiet for a minute if that's OK?' Sam asked. 'I'll stay here for a little while. Which house is Rudi's?'

'White one.'

'OK. I won't be long.'

'Sure?' Foxy said, unsure about leaving Sam on his own.

'Sure.'

Foxy reluctantly turned and started to walk away, and Sam couldn't help himself. 'Rob.'

Foxy turned, eyebrows raised. 'Yup?'

'You'll look after them, won't you? You know… if anything happens.'

Foxy narrowed his eyes. 'What do you mean if anything happens?'

'In case I don't make it past this.'

'But you're going to try, right?'

'Of course.'

'I'll take care of them.'

'Promise?'

'Don't have to promise, mate. I will. Enough said. Come on in with me.'

'I just need a minute. A little quiet. You know.'

Foxy scrutinised his face for a second. 'OK,' he said. 'See you in a minute.'

Sam watched Foxy disappear into Rudi's cottage, ducking his head as he went. Nearly time, he promised himself. It was nearly time. He untied the scarf from around his neck and tied it tightly across his lap and to each side of the chair, so he was bound tightly. He watched Jude and Marcus come back and Marcus ran towards him.

'Well done,' Sam said. 'I'm so proud of you, son.' Marcus beamed happily. Sam made a shooing gesture. 'Go inside! Get changed your lips are blue!'

He watched as the boys went into Rudi's house and heard all the exclamations and clapping. He wheeled himself closer to the edge and stared at the deep water below. *Time to go*, he thought. He turned the chair, checked around to make sure no one was near and rolled off the edge of the pier backwards into the water.

The water was cold and the shock of it forced the air from his lungs instantly. He held on to the chair as the weight of it sank quickly. He focused on not struggling against the sensation of not being able to breathe. He closed his eyes and tried to relax as the chair hit the bottom. In a moment his body would insist that he take a breath and that would be it. He looked upwards in the deep water seeing the edge of the solid stone pier. Then he closed his eyes and waited for the end.

Kate saw it happen. She'd just been leaving her house when she had seen him fall backwards over the side of the pier. She ran down the narrow path towards the pier shouting for help as she went, but people ignored her. As she ran past Rudi's house she shouted again.

Reaching the side of the pier, she kicked off her shoes, dropped her phone in them and jumped in. The shock of the cold water almost sent her back to the surface for breath, but she carried on. She searched wildly, he couldn't have gone far. She saw him below her and swam downwards, but the need for air forced her back upwards. She broke the surface, gasping, and saw Foxy skidding to a halt at the edge above her.

'Sam?' he shouted. She nodded and Foxy dived in. Straight down.

Foxy reached Sam in seconds. He was an incredibly strong swimmer. He grasped Sam by the front of his clothes and pulled but Sam and the chair didn't move.

Sam opened his eyes suddenly and clamped a hand around Foxy's arm. He looked Foxy in the eyes and shook his head. His eyes pleading to be left alone. He closed his eyes and took a deep breath of water; air bubbles being forced out of his nose and mouth.

Foxy shook him and Sam opened his eyes again. Foxy shook his head and tried to lift Sam out of the chair, but it was too heavy. Sam pushed Foxy away, shaking his head. Foxy scrabbled to see what was keeping Sam in the chair and saw that he had tied himself on. Sam fought his hands. Foxy's lungs were hurting. He forced himself upwards for air.

As he swam towards the surface, he passed Kate on her way down. Foxy surfaced, breathed in air and yelled for Rudi. Rudi appeared and dived in.

Sam fought them, and Foxy and Kate suffered the brunt of angry arms as he tried to push them away. Then suddenly he stopped. It was like the fight had left him. He sat still in the chair, his eyes open wide; unblinking. Finally, the three of them managed to pull his dead weight and the chair towards the surface. Sam's face was pale, and his head lolled to one side, his eyes remained open, unseeing.

A crowd had gathered on the quayside, watching the drama.

'We need to get him up and out,' gasped Foxy as he watched Kate trying to untie the scarf that Sam had tied himself in with. Maggie grabbed a rope from one of the boats and threw it down to Foxy.

'Can you tie this around him, and we'll haul him up from here?'

Kate finally freed Sam and the chair sank quickly to the bottom. Foxy and Rudi floated Sam on the surface of the water and tied the rope under his arms. Kate swam to one of the metal ladders and hauled herself up out of the water.

'Clear a space for when he's up,' she called as she ran to the group hauling Sam in.

Sophie was pale with shock and was standing, staring, unable to move. She had shouted at Marcus to stay in the house, but he had ignored her when he had seen Foxy dive off the edge of the pier. He was part of the group who were trying to haul Sam back up the unforgiving steep stone walls of the pier.

Finally, they hoisted Sam up to the edge and the group stepped back as they laid Sam on the ground. Kate knelt and loosened the rope around his chest. She felt for a pulse in his neck and then cleared his mouth and started to perform CPR.

'Come on, Sam,' she said breathlessly. 'Don't do this.'

Kate's arms were aching, and her back and shoulder muscles were screaming in agony as she carried on doing compression after compression. She stopped to breathe for him and sat back for a moment feeling for a pulse. Nothing.

Sam was back in the hot room. He was lying on the floor, but he was happy to be there. The warmth was nice. There were no flies, no rats. The floor didn't seem as hard. The door opened gently, and a woman walked in wearing black robes, her face completely covered with a veil. The wind blew her robes gently.

She reached out to him and said in a gentle, accented voice, 'Come. Come and rest in peace with me, my friend.'

Sam stood and took her hand, admiring the intricate henna tattoos that covered it. He felt comfortable, happy, peaceful. Holding the woman's hand, he stepped through the doorway into the bright light.

'Kate, take a break. Let me.' Lottie put a hand on her shoulder and took over.

Kate and Lottie carried on and after ten minutes of CPR the ambulance arrived. The team quickly assessed Sam and used the electronic defibrillator on him.

'I have a thready pulse here,' announced one of the crew to his colleague who was using the bag mask on Sam to help him breathe. 'I don't think it's going to last.' He flashed a light into Sam's eyes.

'Fixed and dilated pupils. Is he breathing on his own?'

The colleague shook his head. 'Nope.'

'Let's get him to hospital,' Kate said. 'I can bag him on the way. I'm a GP here.'

'Let's go.' They lifted Sam onto a stretcher and wheeled him into the back of the ambulance. Kate carried on bagging him.

Sophie stepped forwards. 'I'm his wife.'

The paramedic beckoned her in. 'You can come, but no room for anyone else,' he said, slamming one of the back doors. Sophie called to Foxy as she climbed in the back.

'Rob, can Marcus stay with you till I get back?'

'No problem. Keep me posted.'

The paramedic went to shut the other door. Foxy stepped forwards and said to the paramedic quietly.

'Mate, what are his chances?'

The paramedic pursed his lips. 'Can't really say, his pulse is weak. Not a great prognosis. But we have to hope. See you.'

A sombre crowd watched the ambulance weave its way up the high street, the sirens blaring. Foxy stood at the quayside watching it go. He remembered Sam's face; Sam shaking his head; Sam's eyes pleading for him to let him go. Foxy looked down and saw his arms were covered in small cuts, and he realised these were from Sam's nails when he was fighting him off.

He sat down suddenly on the quayside. How hard had he actually tried? he wondered. Because he loved Sophie wasn't this the perfect solution for him. Had he tried his hardest to save Sam? Foxy felt the weight of guilt settle heavily on his shoulders. If Sam died it was his fault. His fault for not seeing it was going to happen. His fault for leaving Sam on the quayside; his fault for not realising when Sam had asked him to look after Sophie and Marcus.

Sophie would never forgive him for that.

CHAPTER 27

Mrs Pomeroy was enjoying a cup of her special tea and writing in her diary. A loud knock at the door made her jump. She tutted loudly and made her way slightly unsteadily to the front door. She carefully put the chain on and opened the door a crack.

'Evening, Mrs Pomeroy,' said Steve politely. 'I wonder if you might accompany me to the station to answer some questions.'

'I'm busy,' she said, trying to shut the door.

Steve rested his foot against the door jamb, preventing it from closing. He said quietly, 'Mrs Pomeroy, you have two options. You can come now, or I can call a large and noisy police custody van with the sirens on and unceremoniously arrest you in handcuffs, but only after I'm completely sure that every single one of your neighbours are staring out of their windows. So,' he said, rubbing his hands together and smiling. 'What's it going to be?'

Steve sat down opposite Mrs Pomeroy. He pressed record and went through the formalities of introducing everyone for the tape.

'Just so you are aware, Mrs Pomeroy, we have extended the search warrant granted for your home and we are doing another sweep as we speak. I will furnish you and your solicitor with the paperwork confirming this in a moment. Now,' he said brightly, shuffling some paperwork around. 'I have a few questions I need answers to.'

Mrs Pomeroy folded her arms tightly, and pursed her lips in a thin flat line.

'How long have you worked for the vicar, Mrs Pomeroy?'

Edwina shrugged. 'Can't remember.'

'Where did you work before the vicarage?'

Edwina shrugged again. 'Here and there.'

'More specifically?'

'Don't recall.'

'Try.'

'Why is this relevant? Why am I here?'

'As I mentioned, we are investigating a number of deaths of the elderly in the community.'

'Don't see how that's relevant to me.'

'Mrs Pomeroy, talk me through your employment at the Nightingale Care Home and the Lawn Vista Care home, please.'

Edwina sniffed haughtily. 'What about it?'

'Looking at my notes you were at the Nightingale for three years and Lawn Vista for four years.'

'Sounds about right.'

'And what were your duties there, in both instances?'

Edwina snorted and shuffled in her seat. 'General dogsbody the way they treated me. No respect.'

'Did you look after patients?'

'Sometimes.'

'What else? What other duties?'

She shrugged. 'Cooking, cleaning. Running errands.'

'Am I right in thinking that you had always wanted to be a nurse?'

'Maybe.'

'Why didn't you achieve that?'

'Don't know. Hardly relevant, is it?'

Steve smiled brightly. 'No, I suppose not. So, could you tell me why you used your married name at the Nightingale care home and your maiden name at Lawn Vista?'

'Must have got confused at the time.'

'Really?' Steve said. 'Could it be maybe that you were dismissed from the Nightingale and then categorically refused a reference?'

'Rubbish,' Mrs Pomeroy said haughtily. 'Foreigners were running it. Bloody clueless they were. Staff were all bloody foreign too. Bunch of spicks, ruskies and darkies. Didn't have a clue. The whole damn lot of them.'

'I see. Mrs Pomeroy, if you could refrain from using words like that to describe ethnicity or nationality, I would be grateful.'

Edwina rolled her eyes. Steve pressed on.

'I notice at the time, during the period you worked there, there were a number of unexplained deaths of some of the older residents.'

Edwina grunted. 'Unexplained deaths in a care home? Are you some sort of idiot? There is never an unexplained death in care home. They are all old and waiting to die anyway! They *want* to die.'

'What about the money that went missing, Mrs Pomeroy? The forged cheques?'

Edwina inhaled sharply. 'I don't know what you're talking about,' she said waspishly, her eyes glittering. 'All those foreigners did it. They couldn't prove anything.'

'So you moved over to Lawn Vista, using a different name, and stayed there for quite a time.' Steve leant back in his chair and folded his arms. 'And then we see the same pattern emerge again. More money missing. More deaths. Nothing too obvious. It really is very clever.'

'Nobody could prove anything,' hissed Edwina.

'Remind me how long you have worked at the vicarage?'

'I can't recall. Vicar couldn't do without me though. I run that place.'

'Yes, I have heard that you make it your business to know... everything.'

'What do you mean by that?' Edwina's eyes narrowed.

'I won't be getting into that now. I think we'll save that for another day,' Steve said.

The duty solicitor shifted uncomfortably in his chair. 'Will you be charging my client, inspector?'

Steve raised an eyebrow. 'Who said anything about charging anyone? I just wanted to chat to Mrs Pomeroy here about her work history. She's the one who asked for a solicitor to be present for a friendly chat.'

Edwina glared at him with malevolence. 'If you recall, I am a widow. I recently lost my husband, and I'm upset and still grieving.'

Steve stood. 'Forgive me, Mrs Pomeroy, if I don't believe that for a moment. I'm done here for the day. I'll no doubt speak to you again soon.'

'I certainly hope not,' she said, standing up. 'I want to go now.'

Steve gestured to a PC in the corner to escort her out.

'Bye, Mrs Pomeroy. You take care now!' he said cheerily as she left.

Jonesey had been hopping about in excitement outside the door and rushed in as soon as Mrs Pomeroy and her solicitor left.

'Oh my God, I've been waiting ages to show you this,' he said, slamming down an evidence bag holding a leather notebook. 'Have a read of the diary of a madwoman,' he said dramatically. 'She's away with the fairies.'

Steve flicked through the pages in the evidence bag with difficulty, smoothing out the bag so he could read the neat writing. He read the most recent entry.

I hate them with their withered hands. Their foul breath, their thin hair. Their inability to go to the toilet properly. Their sense of entitlement just because they're old. Why should they live a life of being waited on when I have had to scrimp and save all my life? Why do they get to be treated like royalty when I have been put upon all of my life? People don't see me. They don't like me. They just want me to do things for them. I'm not like the others that sit around all day being waited on. Being looked after. Being cared for. Being loved. Why does nobody love me? They are too needy, too self-serving. They expect everything and give nothing. I hate them. I hate them. The time they take up. Selfishly. Expecting time from those that have other things to do. They don't deserve it. What makes them special?

Jonesey stood, nodding and watching Steve's face as he read the rantings.

'See? Told you. She's fucking batshit crazy, huh?'

'Is this definitely Edwina's?'

'I just assumed...' Jonesey stammered.

'Never just assume, Jonesey. Source a verified handwriting sample and get it confirmed. Oh, and get the vicar on the phone. I need him to check the church accounts for regular amounts of money going missing, probably cheques that he can't remember or explain.'

'Guv.'

'I want all my ducks in a row, and everything watertight so that the next time I chat to her, I can damn well charge her.'

* * *

Peter had also been at the police station that afternoon and had watched Mrs Pomeroy leave, stomping off up the hill. He had been telling Steve about the strange, overfamiliar woman called Sadie who he collected special packages from for Mrs Pomeroy. He was honest and said he didn't know what they were, but they always smelt funny and musty. He wasn't stupid. He knew exactly what they were. He also knew with some certainty that this would be a valuable piece of evidence.

Steve had suggested that Peter help them out and that it might stand him in good stead. Peter had agreed. He liked Steve; he was the first decent copper he had come across in years. Peter had his coat fitted with a small camera, so he could go and collect the package from Sadie, while being watched by Steve's officers. In his view, it was certainly more exciting than sitting next to people who were about to croak.

Peter had done well. Sadie had been half expecting him and the surveillance team in the van had cracked up when she had pressed herself up against Peter, her enormous cleavage taking up the whole of the camera lens.

Peter extricated himself and left as quickly as possible being sure to keep the package in sight the entire time before he handed it over to them. The whole operation had taken less than an hour and all Steve could do was wait until the analysis came back.

* * *

Sam had arrested twice on the way to the hospital, and they had stopped to try to resuscitate him.

Sophie was white-faced and Kate recognised all the signs of serious shock. She wrapped her in a blanket and kept an eye on her, Sam was the immediate priority.

The ambulance screamed into the A&E bay and a doctor came running out. The paramedics and Kate briefed the doctor, and they followed the stretcher as it was wheeled through the door and into a bay.

Kate took Sophie aside and sat her down. She asked the nurse for a cup of tea, and Sophie drank it gratefully while they waited for the doctors to work on Sam.

She saw the doctor come out and look for her; standing, she gave a small wave. He beckoned her over.

'You're the GP?'

'Yes. I was there. I saw it and tried to get him out of the water.'

'What's the story?'

Kate clicked into professional mode. 'Army. Back from two years in captivity. Tortured. Very bad. Legs recently amputated following severe trauma. High levels of pain and been fighting off all the usual infections. He did this deliberately. I saw it. There was no mistake. He meant to do it. He was in the water probably seven minutes? Maybe one or two more. He had tied himself to his wheelchair and he rolled off the edge of a pier. The wheelchair dragged him down and he fought us to let him be. We managed to get him loose and out of the water and then started CPR and we've been bagging him ever since.'

The doctor thought for a minute, nodding. 'We've had to intubate. He can't breathe on his own. His pupils are fixed and dilated. He's comatose. We'll take it slowly and then run the neuro tests a few times. Next of kin?'

Kate pointed to Sophie, who was sitting and staring blankly, wrapped in the red blanket.

'Wife. Very shocked.'

'Do you want me to…?'

'I'll do it. You go back to Sam. Thank you.'

Kate asked the nurse for the relatives' room and guided Sophie in and sat her down. Kate knelt down in front of her and took her hands.

'Sophie, can you hear me OK?'

Sophie frowned. 'Yes,' she said mechanically.

'Sophie, it doesn't look good. Sam's in a coma. He can't breathe on his own. The doctor isn't that hopeful that he will come out of it. They need to get him stable and then see if his brain has any activity. He was without air for a long time, Soph.'

'He asked me to let him go,' she said quietly. 'In the middle of the night. He asked me twice. How did I not see this coming?' she wailed, the tears pouring down her face. 'How could I have been so stupid and left him alone?'

* * *

Foxy had taken Marcus back to his flat. He had taken Jude to the lifeboat station and had explained to a shocked Jesse and Doug what had happened. Rudi had taken Lottie to the hospital to see if she could help.

Doug and Jesse had wanted to help and offered to have Marcus, but Marcus had said he wanted to stay with Foxy. The two of them had collected Solo and had gone for a long walk on the beach.

As they strolled along the sand Foxy primed himself for what was coming.

'He's going to die, isn't he?' Marcus said suddenly, kicking the ball for Solo.

'We don't know that,' said Foxy.

'What is it you say? Let's look at the facts? He was under the water a long time. That's not good, right? I mean it's not like he was Tom Cruise in that *Mission Impossible* film when he held his breath for like six minutes. This was Dad. War damaged Dad.'

'Truth is, I don't know, mate,' said Foxy. 'He was under a long time.'

'Why are your arms covered in cuts? Kate's were too.'

'Because your dad was pushing us away.'

'What? He wanted to die?'

Foxy decided he would embark on a white lie to try to ease Marcus's pain.

'Sometimes when people can't breathe underwater they panic and fight and flail. It's a weird hypoxic response.'

'Like a panic attack?' Marcus said doubtfully.

'Exactly like a panic attack,' Foxy agreed.

'Did he fall off the pier?' asked Marcus suddenly.

'I don't know,' Foxy said quietly. 'I guess so. He had been close to the edge. Maybe it was an accident.'

'My dad was a captain in army intelligence. He was super brave and super intelligent. He couldn't... no, wouldn't have made a mistake like that.'

'You don't know that.'

'Stop treating me like a kid!' Marcus shouted. 'He wanted to die. I heard him tell Maggie. I heard him! He couldn't look at himself. Couldn't live with himself the way he was. It wasn't an accident. He did it on purpose.'

'Marcus…' Foxy said desperately.

'So that means he didn't love me or Mum enough to stay and tough it out. Make a different life with us.'

'It doesn't mean that.'

'It DOES!' Marcus shouted. 'HE DIDN'T LOVE US ENOUGH TO STAY!'

Marcus was red from shouting. Then his face crumpled. The tears came.

'He just didn't love us enough, Foxy,' he wailed, throwing his arms around Foxy's waist and sobbing into his chest. 'He just didn't love us enough.'

Foxy's heart almost broke. He held Marcus tightly while he sobbed his world out. Solo, who found crying very confusing, came over to Marcus and pawed his leg. Marcus lifted a head from Foxy's chest and then threw his arms around the large Alsatian and sobbed into his fur. Foxy surreptitiously wiped his own tears away and laid a hand on Marcus's shoulder.

'Come on. Let's get you back to mine and feed you.'

Marcus put an arm around Foxy's waist as they walked and hugged him again.

'Can we eat in front of the telly, have ice cream and watch a film?' he said, sniffing.

'Absolutely.'

'I can't think of anything else I'd rather do at the moment,' Marcus said, resting his head against Foxy as he walked.

Foxy hugged him back, unable to say anything else because of the huge emotional lump that had lodged itself in his throat.

* * *

Sophie watched the doctor leave the relatives' room, closing the door gently behind him. She was struggling to process what the doctor had said. She couldn't think straight. Couldn't remember what he said. What did he say? She wondered what to cook Marcus for tea and whether there was any petrol in the car. Did she have any bread at home? Had she remembered to put the tumble dryer on? Had she locked the back door? What if she'd left the oven on?

'Soph, sweetie. Come on. Back in the room,' Kate said softly. She was watching Sophie with concern; she was in serious shock and not coping well.

'Hold on one second,' Kate said, stepping out quickly. The doctor was still talking to the nurses at the desk and glanced at Kate.

'Anyone got a blood pressure machine I can pinch and a pulse oximeter?' Kate asked.

'For Mrs Jones? Are you concerned?' The doctor frowned.

'Yes. She's showing signs of serious shock. She's confused, dazed, not present, talking nonsense. I think her blood pressure might be bottoming out.'

The doctor headed towards the relatives' room. 'I'll have a look,' he said, opening the door. 'I need help here,' he called out.

Sophie looked past him to see Sophie on the floor. She ran in and knelt next to her.

'Soph?' she said, rubbing her hand. 'Come on, Soph.'

The doctor examined her and took her blood pressure.

'Blood pressure is way too low. O_2 isn't great either. I'm not happy about this. Nurse, I want Mrs Jones on a bed for monitoring for the next few hours, please. I want bloods done, urine and glucose. I want her obs checked every fifteen.'

The nurse came in with a wheelchair.

'Let's get her into the chair when she comes around and then into a bed.' The doctor turned to Kate. 'Anyone to call? She might appreciate a visit from a friendly face after what she's just heard.'

'Will do. Her son and her best friend will come in,' Kate said.

'Good idea. I'll keep you posted on Mr Jones.'

Kate waited until Sophie was in a bed and popped out to call Foxy.

'Hey, Kate,' he said, answering on the second ring.

'Hi.' She exhaled heavily.

'Tell me.'

'OK. Very simply, they think Sam's suffered brain damage from being under water without oxygen for too long. Usual responses to tests aren't good, they are trying to treat him, but the next 24 hours will be the decider. There's a raft of different tests they have to perform to see if there's brain activity. We have to wait for them, but they are being pretty pessimistic.'

Foxy exhaled heavily. 'Christ, I wish we'd got him up and out sooner.'

'Hey,' Kate said softly. 'He wanted to do it. I saw it all happen. He did it on purpose. I watched him do it. If it hadn't had been then, it would have been another time and another way.'

Foxy was silent for a moment. 'I didn't realise you saw it.'

'I won't be forgetting it any time soon.'

'Are you OK, Kate? Do you need anything? How's Soph doing?'

'That's really why I'm calling. She's struggling to process this. She's in shock. She passed out.'

'Is she OK?' he said urgently.

'They are monitoring her for a few hours. Her blood pressure's low, she's confused, exhausted, not making a lot of sense. Doctor suggested maybe a friendly face pop in to see her a bit later.'

'I can do that. Marcus needs to see his mum. He's had a bit of a meltdown here. I've dealt with it, but it will be good for him to see her.'

'Bring him in. I'll text you where we are.'

'Kate, what do you need? Any clothes or anything? Food?'

'I just want to see Sophie come through this. You guys will be a tonic.'

'Have you eaten?

'No… but.'

'We'll bring food then. If you don't eat it. Marcus will. His capacity for food astounds me. See you in a bit.'

'Drive carefully.'

CHAPTER 28

Jesse couldn't shake the sense of unease she was feeling. She hadn't slept properly; she had been awoken in the early hours by a voice in her ear, it was the woman from the beach telling her he was close, and he was coming for her again. To Jesse it sounded like the woman was standing right next to her and she had awoken shaking and sweating. She had got up to sit in the red chair and watch the sunrise.

'What's up?' Doug said sleepily from the bed as he propped himself on an elbow and watched her sitting in the red chair, wrapped in a warm blanket. 'You dreaming about the woman again?'

'Not as such. I just heard her.'

'What did she say?'

Jesse rubbed her face wearily. 'She said he was close and that he was coming for me again.'

Doug flopped back in bed. 'Wow. All these semi-premonitions I can't help wondering if we should start doing the lottery.'

Jesse threw a cushion at him. 'Shut up.'

He threw the cushion back at her. 'Come here and say that.'

'Maybe I'm playing hard to get,' she said coyly.

Doug leapt up and grabbed her, yanking her back into bed. 'I think we're way past the playing hard to get stage, don't you?' He laughed and pulled the duvet over them both.

Jesse came to the station with Doug. She didn't want to be at home alone. Despite the fact she was on sick leave for another fortnight she wanted to be busy, so she promised Doug she would do light duties and stay in his office or in the shop with Nessie if the boys went on a shout. She just couldn't shake the feeling that something was about to happen.

* * *

Jimmy was convinced he was going to be killed for allowing himself to be robbed and that his death was just a matter of time.

Alexy had dropped him back at his truck and had told him to wait for his call. He was going to see what his contacts had heard. Jimmy was slightly reassured that Alexy had seemed to believe him. He tried to reason that Alexy wasn't going to admit he had lost a significant proportion of Pearl's drugs if one of his men had talked and been responsible for the robbery.

Jimmy genuinely didn't know whether to try and run, or whether to sweat it out and wait for Alexy's call. He decided to wait. When it came down to it, he didn't fancy living on the run plus, it could mean that he kept his legs or even his life.

* * *

Chris was hanging upside down in a large industrial unit. He had been there for so long he had lost all feeling in his feet. He drifted in and out of consciousness. He remembered seeing the headlights sweep into the car park. He recalled climbing into the passenger seat of the large truck and being grabbed from behind. Something chemical smelling was clamped over his mouth.

He vaguely heard the sound of footsteps approaching. Suddenly an ice-cold blast of water hit him full in the face. Coughing and spluttering he opened his eyes to see a tall, dark-haired man with a pronounced scar which ran from each side of his mouth up each cheek; he was holding a dripping bucket. Thick, crude prison style tattoos covered his large arms.

'Now that's what I call a Chelsea smile,' Chris said arrogantly, swinging gently. 'Even from this angle.'

The tall, dark-haired man produced his phone and made a call.

'I have him here,' the man said in a thick Russian accent. He listened for a moment and then said, 'My pleasure, my friend.'

He ended the call and put his phone back in his pocket. He raised a hand and clicked his fingers loudly in the cavernous space. The sound echoed. Another man appeared holding a chair, and he placed it carefully down in front of Chris.

'So.' The dark-haired man sat down, brushing a spec of something off his trousers as he crossed his legs. 'You will tell me what I wish to know, and we won't inflict any unnecessary pain on you.'

Chris turned his head so he could see him. 'Look, mate, I don't know what you think this is. I have got a lot of blow and I'm just looking to sell it on and be on my way.'

The dark-haired man laughed. 'I am interested to know what you consider to be a lot of blow my friend?'

'About 30 kilos.'

The dark-haired man raised an eyebrow. 'Where did this come from?'

'I'm not going to get into that. Are you interested or not?'

'I might be. Depends.'

'On?'

'Quality. I do not buy rubbish… plus,' he shrugged casually, 'other factors.'

'Such as?'

'Provenance. I do not want to be paying for something that might belong to someone else. This can be… a cut-throat business.'

'It's come in from out of the country, mate, so you're OK there.'

'I see. Out of the country meaning?'

Chris was becoming annoyed. He swung around with difficulty to face the dark-haired man.

'Look, mate, let's do this in a civilised manner? I don't respond well to being hung upside down and treated like a piece of fucking meat. So how abouts you take me down and we discuss this like proper businesslike grown-ups?'

The dark-haired man laughed loudly. 'What is your name, my friend?'

'Chris.'

'Chris what?'

'Chris is enough. Yours?'

'I am Nicholai.'

'Good. Nice to meet you, Nicki, now how about you untie me?'

'In moment. First things first. Tell me how you have 30 kilos.'

'You don't need to know, my friend. All you need to know is that it comes from somewhere else.'

Nicholai thought for a moment. 'OK.' He snapped his fingers and Chris fell unceremoniously to the floor. Nicholai stood over him.

'For now, we do this your way,' he said. 'Where is it?'

'Safe,' Chris said, looking up at him and hoping the feeling would return to his feet soon. Much as he would have liked to beat this bloke senseless, Nicholai's tattoos told him everything he needed to know. He needed to be careful here. He saw the eight-pointed star which meant a convicted thief of rank in a crime organisation, along with a number of skulls on each arm. Each skull usually meant an important kill; undertaken personally.

Nicholai shrugged. 'OK. You have deal if you bring here. We test. If OK, we give you cash. Everyone goes away. Yes?'

'We need to discuss price,' Chris said, narrowing his eyes.

'Price that I consider to be… reasonable,' Nicholai said.

'Which is?'

Nicholai folded his arms and considered. 'If is good quality, I pay twenty a kilo.'

'It's worth twice that and you know it.'

Nicholai inspected his fingernails. 'You want quick sale. You still walk away with six hundred K.'

'Thirty grand a slab and you've got a deal.'

Nicholai narrowed his eyes. 'Twenty-five is my final offer. Take it or leave it. Cash today.'

Chris thought for a moment. He hated being fucked over but had little choice. 'Deal. Do I have your word?'

'Not until I see the product. Then I will honour the deal.' Nicholai stood up. 'You bring here by…' He consulted the enormous diamond encrusted Rolex on his wrist. 'By six tonight and we have deal. Everybody happy.'

'If you try and fuck me over you won't live to see another day,' Chris said harshly.

Nicholai raised an eyebrow and pointed at Chris. 'Let us make deal. If your stuff is good, then I will buy and then you will go. If I see you here again. *You* will die. Understanding me? So, let us stick to doing this and then we end. Yes?'

Nicholai's colleague broke the cable ties holding his wrists and feet together and Chris struggled to his feet.

'Thing is…' Chris began.

'There is problem already?' Nicholai asked, his eyebrows raised.

'If I can borrow a truck, I can get it here for then.'

Nicholai shook his head in disbelief. 'Maxim!' he called loudly. A large man appeared in the shadows.

'Give our friend here truck to use. He will bring back by six tonight. Nothing too nice, Maxim.'

Nicholai glanced at Chris dismissively. 'I see you at six. Here.'

'I'll be here.' Chris followed Maxim out and was given the keys to an old grey Ford Ranger. He took the keys and then looked around.

'Where the fuck are we?'

Maxim spat on the floor next to him and walked away. Chris found himself in the middle of an empty car park. There were some other industrial units in the distance, but everywhere appeared deserted.

He started the truck, pulling away slowly and came out onto a main road. He saw a sign for Castleby and realised with satisfaction that he wasn't very far away. He took note of the way for his return and drove off feeling quite happy at the forthcoming deal. He was even willing to forgo the fact that they had hung him upside down all night.

Chris drove quickly to a car park at the far end of the beach. He left the car and furtively checked around before heading over to the boulders where he had left his boat and the drugs. He saw with dismay that the tide was in and there was no access to it.

'Fuck,' he shouted, annoyed for not thinking about the tide. He scrambled over some rocks and noticed a path leading up to the cliffs. He followed the path and stepped out looking down on the round clearing from above. He couldn't see a way down to it that wouldn't involve him breaking his neck. He decided to go back down the steep path and then see if he could cut across and get to it that way.

Chris emerged from the undergrowth, scratched and dirty, but closer to his stash. He crawled carefully along until he could drop down on top of it. It now occurred to him that he had a lot of stuff and no means to carry it back to his car. He peered over the edge and couldn't see the dinghy anywhere, he assumed that had been swept out. He needed some sort of large bag or sack to heft it all to the car. He peered over the edge again and saw what looked like a tangle of old fishing net caught on a protruding shrub, so he carefully scrambled down and grabbed it, almost slipping in his haste.

It took him nearly an hour to lay out the net and try to make it suitable enough to be able to carry the drugs back to the truck. His next problem was how he was going to get across the beach. He sat back on his haunches and surveyed the net with a critical eye. How much did he think he could get in that? Was it two trips? Or three?

He glanced over his shoulder and saw with surprise that the tide had gone out in the last hour, uncovering the original rocks and access path over the rocks. He felt the anger build up inside him.

'Fuck's sake,' he shouted. 'Stupid fucking tide.'

He leant out over the edge, peering at something white and then realised it was his dinghy upside down, wedged in the boulders. He clambered down clumsily and slithered the last ten feet, catching his arms on the jagged edges and painfully scraping the skin off his elbows. He slipped about on the wet rocks, banging his knees and ankles where he fell.

Finally, he reached the dinghy and tried to turn it over. He didn't have the strength. He saw a long sapling washed up on the shore and dragged it over, managing to use it as a lever to flip the boat. Eventually, he had the boat the right way up. He nodded in satisfaction. He could chuck all the stash in here and pull it up the beach and cover it with the net. He commended himself on his luck.

Six o'clock was approaching, and Chris was sweating. He was pulling the dinghy up the beach towards the car park, it was heavier work than he had anticipated. He was exhausted and starving, but the prospect of a big payday drove him on. He would book into a swanky hotel, eat a huge meal and celebrate in style.

Once he had rested and eaten, he would seek out Jesse and have the reunion he had been dreaming of. He didn't want to rush it. He wanted to be rested and full of energy before he started to make her really suffer. He just needed to get the cash together to see him through; otherwise it was all a missed opportunity, and he hated missed opportunities. He finally got the dinghy up to the car park and loaded the gear into the truck.

He sat slumped behind the wheel, catching his breath and saw the time. He started the engine and drove out of the car park, being careful to remember where he was going.

* * *

Foxy had met Marcus after school, and they left to pick up Sophie from hospital. The doctor had kept her in overnight but was happier with her progress so was allowing her home for rest. He had been most insistent that she rest for a few days and then return to discuss Sam's prognosis when she was feeling better and more able to cope.

Sophie was in Sam's room. She stroked the hair back from his forehead and watched for any signs he knew she was there.

'Sam, can you hear me?' she asked. 'Do something to show you can hear me.'

Sophie watched his face and held his hand; nothing. She heard the mechanical hiss of the respirator and watched as Sam's torso moved in sync with it. She lay her head on his chest and squeezed him, hoping to draw some comfort, but it felt cold and awkward.

The door to the room opened and Marcus shuffled in hesitantly.

'Mum?' he asked.

'Darling.' She hugged him close and kissed the top of his head. 'How was school?'

Marcus grunted. 'No change?' he asked, looking at Sam.

'Nope. No change,' she said. 'This probably sounds weird, but I don't sense he's really here anymore.'

Marcus's eyes were filled with tears. 'What, like he's dead?'

She hugged him 'No, like I don't sense "him" if you know what I mean. His body is still alive.' She touched Sam's face. 'Maybe he'll come back to us.'

Marcus looked at him. 'Come back, Dad,' he said softly and squeezed his hand. 'Please come back to us.'

Sophie kissed Sam on the cheek and held out her hand for Marcus's.

'Good to go?' she said. 'Is Rob out in the car?' she said, opening the door.

'Rob is here,' Foxy said from where he was leaning against the wall, arms folded, waiting for them.

'Hey,' she said, pleased to see him. 'Thanks for coming and for bringing this one last night. I owe you.'

'You owe me nothing,' he said lightly and ruffled Marcus's hair. 'You OK, buddy?'

Marcus grunted. 'I'm starving.'

'You are always starving,' Sophie said fondly.

'Let's stop at The Bottle on the way back and have dinner?' Foxy suggested. 'Saves us all cooking.'

'I'm in,' Marcus said instantly.

Sophie yawned. 'OK. I feel slightly bullied into it, but yes, the prospect of not having to cook is heavenly. OK, I'm in.'

Foxy pulled up outside Sophie's house.

'You want some coffee?' Sophie asked, watching Marcus jump out and head to the door.

'Sure,' Foxy said.

He sat in the kitchen, watching as Sophie made coffee.

'You hanging in there?' he asked.

Her hands shook slightly. 'Just,' she said. 'How was Marcus with you last night?'

Foxy decided honesty was the best policy. He checked over his shoulder and saw Marcus in the lounge with his headphones on.

'He had a meltdown last night.'

'About Sam?'

'Yup.'

'What specifically? That he saw him like that or...'

'It was more about Marcus thinking that he did it deliberately...'

'God.'

'He said...' Foxy stopped. He almost couldn't bring himself to say it out loud.

'What?'

'He said… that he didn't love you or him enough to stay and tough it out.'

Sophie put down the coffee cups and said quietly, 'I find myself unable to argue with that sentiment.'

They were both silent for a moment.

'Did Lottie go back?' Foxy broke the silence.

'Yes. I have to call her and let her know how he is.'

'Did you speak to Kate?' Foxy asked.

'About what?'

'The accident.'

'No. Why?' She looked at him more closely. 'What aren't you telling me?'

Foxy was torn. He had always maintained that honesty was the best policy, but this was significant.

'Rob…' she warned.

'Kate saw the whole thing. She saw him do it. She said there was no way it was an accident. He did it deliberately. He'd planned it.'

Sophie sat down suddenly. 'Christ. The night before he had asked me to let him go.' Her voice shook. 'I brushed it off… said we'd get through it.'

Foxy was silent for a moment.

'Just before he did it… we had a chat… he asked me to look after you both.'

'He said what?' Sophie stared at him for a moment, incredulous.

'He said if anything happened, would I look after you both.'

Sophie's face was angry. 'I can't believe I'm hearing this. So let me get this straight. He says something like that to you and you said what? OK, and then left him alone on the quayside? Did it occur to you that he might have been thinking about something like that?'

She paced around the kitchen. 'I mean, how much more bloody obvious is it that he might have tried something like that?' She ran her hands through her hair as she paced. 'Christ, out of all of us, you had the most insight into how he was feeling. I mean, fucking hell, Rob, what the hell did you think you were doing leaving him alone like that?'

'Sophie, don't get angry with me about this and blame me. We had a chat, he just said he needed some quiet and I respected that,' Foxy said in a warning tone.

Sophie stood in front of him and pointed a shaking finger. 'Don't get angry? Why the bloody hell not? You must have known what he was thinking… *You* could have stopped it, Rob.'

'I didn't know he was going to do that. If I'd known of course I would have stopped it.'

'You knew exactly how he was feeling! I can't believe you left him alone on the quayside after he said something like that to you.'

'I just thought he needed space. Quiet time to think.'

'No! He just needed a bloody window of time to try and kill himself!' she yelled.

Foxy stood and picked up his keys. 'Sophie, you busting my balls about this isn't getting us anywhere. Nor will it change anything.'

Sophie carried on pacing. 'Jesus. You were the last person he spoke to. How can you tell me you didn't guess what he was going to do?' Sophie shouted, her eyes glittering, her face red.

'OK then, yes,' Foxy snapped. 'I figured he might have been thinking about it, but I didn't believe for a minute that he would do it.'

'Why not? Why did you think he wouldn't?' She slammed a hand down on the worktop, breathing heavily, glaring at him.

Foxy headed for the back door. This was disintegrating into a row and Sophie was not in a reasonable mindset. He'd never seen her like this. He decided it was better to leave.

'I said, why did you think he wouldn't do it?' she shouted to his retreating back.

Foxy stood at the door. 'Because if it had been me—' He stopped himself talking and took a deep breath.

'Because if it had been you… what?' Sophie shouted, her hands on her hips. 'WHAT?'

'Because I love you both too much to leave you and I couldn't imagine a life without you both,' Foxy shouted, then yanked the door open. He turned, angrily. 'And just so you know. Me? I would rather die than be without you, but that's where me and Sam differ, I guess.' He slammed the door loudly behind him.

CHAPTER 29

Sophie had hardly slept. She felt terrible about shouting at Foxy and accusing him of letting Sam try to kill himself. She knew she had lashed out and behaved badly. She kept thinking about his face when she had said those terrible things. What he had said when she pushed him. He had told her that he loved her and Marcus. She loved Foxy very much. He was her friend, her go-to guy. She leant on him heavily. She had never thought he felt that way about her, or was he just saying that he loved her as a mate? Was she overthinking it?

She thought back to the previous evening in the pub when the waitress had referred to Foxy as Sophie's husband. Foxy had laughed and slung an arm around Sophie and said, 'Sadly, I'm not the husband, just the bestie', which had made the waitress laugh.

Sophie kissed Marcus goodbye as he trudged off to school and sat in the kitchen wondering what to do. The phone rang shrilly in the kitchen.

'Hello?' she said dully.

'Sophie? It's Lottie.'

'Hey, Lottie. Look, sorry I didn't call you back—'

'It's fine. I need to be quick. I wanted to have a chat with you. I probably shouldn't, but I wanted to say a few things and I need to know that you heard me.'

'Sounds ominous.'

'I've just sat in on a call from Sam's consultant here to the consultant treating Sam where you are, a Dr Randall.'

'Right.'

'Sophie, you need to prepare yourself. It's not looking good. The consultant talked about Sam having ABI.'

'Which is?'

'Basically, it's called anoxic brain injury and it's a common result of oxygen deprivation caused by drowning. It can cause severe neurological damage in people who survive. Simply, when the brain is deprived of oxygen, brain cells can begin to die within five minutes and then carry on.'

'Sam is brain dead?'

'I think it's looking that way. They're running the suite of tests that they need to. It's not looking good, Sophie. My guy rang for an update and to see whether we could move him back here for any specialist treatment.'

'But—'

'Sophie, I need you to hear me,' Lottie interrupted urgently. 'I think you should let him go.'

'What?'

'It's no life for you or Marcus. Sam's gone. He's just a shell now. Think about the future.'

'I can't get my head around this… They said he might improve in a day or so.'

'He can't improve if his brain is dying, Soph,' she said. 'It's no life for you or for him.'

'I can't think about…'

'Look, I've said too much. But you're my friend and I know I would want to know. I think the consultant is going to call you to come in and discuss options.'

'Is he?' Sophie said vaguely.

'Don't say I've said anything, I could get the sack. But I think you need to think about the future. It's stretching out ahead of you. Oh, I'm being paged. I've got to go. I'll call you later. If you need me for anything I'm here, OK? I'll come and see you very soon, I promise.'

'OK,' said Sophie faintly.

She ended the call, and the phone rang again making her jump.

'Mrs Jones?'

'Speaking.'

'It's Doctor Randall from the hospital. Firstly, how are you feeling today?'

'Much better, thank you.'

'Pleased to hear it. No more dizzy spells? Fainting?'

'None.'

'I wonder if you might make some time to come in for a chat, Mrs Jones?'

'Right. Yes. About Sam?' Sophie stammered. 'When were you thinking?'

'I believe that sooner is always better than later. Are you free today?'

'When?'

'Say one o'clock?'

'OK. In Sam's room?'

'Yes. I'll see you there.'

'OK. Bye.'

Sophie sat in the kitchen staring down the garden not seeing anything. Her mind was reeling. She thought about Lottie's call. She closed her eyes and thought about Sam in the house and remembered his words when he had woken in the middle of the night. He had told her he wasn't the same. That they'd broken him. That he couldn't cope, and she just hadn't heard it. She thought about the accident and what Sam had asked Foxy to do. She closed her eyes and wished for the millionth time that her dad was still lucid enough to talk to.

How she missed his sensible and pragmatic approach to everything. She imagined what he would say to her if she talked this through. He would say life was for the living and that Sam made the choice to go, because he couldn't see a life for himself. She felt he would say that she needed to preserve his memory for her and Marcus, but let him go. She glanced at the clock and realised she had been sitting there for nearly two hours. She needed to get to the hospital.

* * *

Sophie sat in her car. For once in her adult life, she had no idea what to do. She rested her head on her arms on the steering wheel and cried. The doctors had told her that they had been testing Sam for the past 48 hours and there was no change in his condition.

They had confirmed there was no brain or brainstem activity. Sam couldn't breathe for himself, he was not responsive to pain or any other stimulus, and they concluded that Sam was in a persistent vegetative state. They had sympathetically outlined Sophie's options for her and told her to consider all the options carefully. Now she had a decision to make. She wiped her eyes and started the car. This was a decision that she needed to discuss with Marcus.

Foxy was irritating himself. He had called himself every name under the sun for telling Sophie how he felt last night. He kept remembering and kicking himself. He had slept badly. He had been trying to keep busy all day, so he didn't have to think about it, but it was getting to the point where he needed to do something to get rid of the angst, so he left Mike in charge and went for a run along the coast path with Solo.

As he ran, eating up the miles, he replayed the conversation. Did she blame him for Sam's accident? He felt guilty enough. He should have seen it. Why hadn't he seen it? Would she distance herself from him now? Did he need to apologise? Should he leave her alone? He couldn't decide what was best. The punishing pace he had set himself was helping, but the run wasn't providing any answers to his questions. He only stopped when the path ran out and he found himself at the restricted area of the military base. It was only then he realised how far he'd run.

* * *

Chris pulled into the industrial unit car park in the borrowed truck, right on time. He saw the roller shutter go up and Maxim standing in the doorway beckoning the vehicle inside. As Chris manoeuvred the truck through the narrow roller shutter, he sang to himself. 'Show me the money!'

He jumped happily out of the truck and approached Maxim.

'Evening,' he said pleasantly. 'Where's Nicholai?'

Maxim gestured with his head to the corner of the unit. Chris looked past Maxim and saw a table with two chairs set up. In the far corner there was also a large workman's bench that ran along the side of the building, with various power tools and a large vice.

'Where did you say Nicholai was?' Chris heard footsteps and turned to face a huge, heavy-set man who was holding a baseball bat. The bat was coming towards him at speed. Chris's brain couldn't process the sight quickly enough to move, so his face caught the brunt of the force, rendering him unconscious instantly.

He came round after a bucket of cold water was thrown at him – again. He was sat at a table and became vaguely aware of excruciating pain in his hands. He tried to move them, and the sensation was so excruciatingly painful he whimpered. His head throbbed and he realised, looking down, that he had wet himself.

He saw with horror that his hands had been nailed to the wooden table in front of him. No doubt with the bloody claw hammer that had been left on the side. He struggled to process what had happened and then he felt the rage roll over him. He had been fucked over. He focused murderously on the two men sitting the other side of the table. He tried to calm himself. He would get out of this and take these two apart; piece by fucking piece if he had to.

Nicholai clicked his fingers again and another bucket of water was thrown over Chris. This time he harnessed the feeling of rage and sat straighter. He realised that he could yank one of his hands free of the table and grab the hammer, but he was uncertain how much damage that would do. He would have to sacrifice one hand to get away though, however he did it.

Nicholai regarded Chris coldly.

'I am pleased to see you, my friend, and I must thank you for the top-quality product you deliver. Now, business. This is my good friend and colleague Alexy.'

Alexy nodded. Nicholai continued.

'So. We need to know a few simple thing before we let you go.'

'Such as?' said Chris through gritted teeth.

'Where it came from.'

'I'm not going to give up my supplier.'

'I think, my friend, you will. It is your only choice.'

Chris debated whether to tell the truth.

'What I don't understand, fellas,' he said arrogantly, 'is what the fuck does it really matter where it came from? You have it here for a bargain price. So how about we stop fucking about and do the deal and go our separate ways?'

'It does matter to my friend Alexy here,' said Nicholai. 'You see he was doing a favour for a very important local businessman, and somebody decided to help themselves to it. So Alexy needs to find out who it was that told you where it would be and when.'

'What the fuck are you on about?' Chris said, looking confused. 'Fuck me. What does it matter? Do you want this gear or not?'

Alexy clicked his fingers and Maxim walked over. Alexy spoke into his ear and Maxim walked over to the workbench and picked up a large plank of wood about a metre long. He grabbed a handful of nails and walked back over to the table. Nicholai watched the exchange and shook his head. 'This is not good news, my friend. Alexy does not believe you are speaking the truth.'

Maxim laid the plank across Chris's legs. He pushed a nail into one of them and picked up the hammer.

'Wait!' Chris was sweating. 'I promise you. I'm telling the truth. I'd nicked a fishing boat, I couldn't drive it and needed to get off it.

I saw the yacht and set fire to the boat so they would rescue me. I wasn't looking for blow. I'm here to find someone.'

Maxim brought the hammer down on the nail. Chris screamed.

'I'm looking for my ex. She works in Castleby. Take the blow. Just let me go.'

Maxim selected another nail.

'I'M NOT LYING!' Chris screamed as Maxim brought the hammer down again.

'Wait… WAIT! If you must know, I was on a boat, it caught fire. Some fucking idiot in a yacht rescued me. I had a poke around, saw the blow. Knocked the bloke out and then nicked it and here we are. Nothing to do with your businessman friend I suspect.'

Nicholai laughed loudly. 'So, my friend, you expect us to believe that in the middle of the sea you come across a yacht full of blow?'

'Absolutely.'

Nicholai laughed. 'This is stuff of fairy tales, my friend.'

'I promise you this is what happened.'

Maxim selected another nail and brought the hammer down hard. Chris screamed. He hunched over the table sobbing. The pain in his legs and hands was excruciating.

Nicholai and Alexy moved to the corner of the unit to discuss Chris.

'Do you believe him?' Nicholai asked.

Alexy looked thoughtful. 'I know this man, but not sure from where. I need to think.' He glanced over at Chris. 'Leave him for now.'

Alexy had made a few calls and saw things much more clearly now. He had called Jimmy and told him to relax, and that he had recovered the leftovers. Jimmy had almost cried with relief. Alexy had laughed.

'It was noble thing to rescue man in distress, no?'

'In hindsight it really wasn't, Alexy,' Jimmy had said dryly.

'I am thinking you will be rethinking coming to people's rescue maybe?'

'Definitely. Is Pearl OK about this?'

'She will be fine. I will sort. She has a bonus that will please her.'

'Alexy, I owe you, mate.'

'Yes you do, my friend. *Dosvedanya.*'

'What's that?'

'Bye for now, my friend.'

'*Dosvedanya*, Alexy.'

Alexy laughed. 'I will make a Russian out of you yet, my friend.'

Chris awoke to yet another bucket of water being thrown over his face. His hands and legs throbbed with pain and he felt sick and dizzy. He focused his bleary eyes on a figure in front of him, sitting in a chair a distance away. The figure was dressed completely in red: shoes, shirt, trousers and coat.

'Tea please, Stanley,' she said, tapping an unlit cigarette on the side of a silver cigarette case.

Chris narrowed his eyes. 'Who the fuck are you?'

The lump of a man who was called Stanley came over and hit him hard in the side of the head. Chris saw stars.

'Thank you, Stanley,' said Pearl. She focused in on Chris. 'Stanley doesn't like it when people are rude to me, do you, Stanley?'

Stanley shook his head and looked at Chris menacingly, then lumbered off.

She regarded him for a while longer. 'It doesn't matter who I am,' she said pleasantly, accepting a cup and saucer from Stanley and sipping delicately. 'You already know my delightful colleagues, Alexy and Nicholai. I think the important thing is that we know exactly who you are.'

'What are you talking about?'

'I make it my business to find out exactly who the people are who clearly think I am some sort of idiot.'

'Look, lady, I'm just trying to get rid of some blow. I don't need you getting your fucking knickers in a twist about it.'

'Oh dear,' Pearl said as Stanley lumbered over and hit Chris again.

Pearl sipped carefully from her tea cup. 'Now, I suggest we try and keep this a civil exchange. For your benefit much more than mine. By the looks of it, Stanley can go on a lot longer than you. Anyway, as I was saying. We know who you are. You're quite the naughty boy, aren't you? Ex-police officer. Wanted for murder, attempted murder, assault, escaping from prison... oh my, and the list goes on. You are, in fact, on the local constabulary's list of most wanted. Imagine that. We have quite the celebrity amongst us, boys.'

'What of it?' Chris tried bravado.

'Well now. This leaves me in a little bit of a quandary, I think. Do I, one; give you back to the police, but run the risk of you shouting about my lovely new boat and the product you have tried to sell me, which incidentally was mine anyway?

'Two; do I take the product, give you some cash and let you go with a very strict telling off from Stanley...' Her eyes shifted to over Chris's shoulder to Maxim's hopeful face. 'Oh, and Maxim. Can't forget Maxim, he would hate to miss out.

'Or three; do I just cut my losses and dispose of you myself?' She laughed. 'Well, obviously not myself! Stanley and Maxim are positively desperate to be rid of you and do so thoroughly enjoy that aspect of things. So, I have to ask myself… what should I do?'

'I prefer option two,' Chris said as arrogantly as he could manage.

'I guessed as much,' Pearl observed. 'The thing is. I am less inclined to choose option two because of your rudeness to me. Plus, I see from my extensive research that you have a tendency to beat women, and that, my friend, is something I will not stand for. We simply don't tolerate this type of behaviour towards women in our organisation, do we, boys?'

Chris looked in amazement at the men standing about nodding in agreement with Pearl.

'You bunch of fucking pussies,' he shouted. 'You should put this fucking bitch in her place and teach her a fucking lesson about who the FUCK is the boss around here!' He looked at them incredulously. 'I mean, look at you all. Standing about like a bunch of fucking dickless pussies, taking orders from this stupid bitch. Who the fuck does she think she is? She's a fucking *woman*. She needs to be put in her place. Set the fucking boundaries. You don't take orders from a silly bitch like this. You *give* the orders and she fucking well listens! She knows her fucking place! So come on tell this bitch to fuck off once and for all and let's do a deal.'

Chris vaguely heard a door slam. So intent on his tirade, he didn't hear footsteps approaching until Pearl turned and beamed at a large broad-set, bald-headed man with piercing blue eyes who was striding towards her.

'Darling!' she exclaimed with delight. 'Oh, how lovely! You're back early. How was your day?'

Mickey Camorra bent and kissed his wife lovingly on the lips. As he straightened up, he produced a gun from the back of his waistband and shot Chris through the forehead.

He stroked her face tenderly. 'No one speaks to my beautiful girl like that. I don't care who he was.'

Pearl patted his hand and stood. She smiled at Alexy.

'Well, number three it was. Unpleasant man. Now, Alexy darling, could you do me two tiny favours?'

Alexy bowed slightly. 'Of course. Anything.'

'Firstly, I think we need to redistribute this gentleman in the usual fashion; however, I would like a special delivery to be made to that rather handsome police officer Jimmy talks to. I feel sure he will be interested in this gentleman. I'm sure there's a certain lady locally who will gain a modicum of relief from this special delivery too, and this will put her worries to rest.'

'No problem, Pearl. Second thing?'

'Jimmy. Thank him for me. Chuck him some cash for his trouble. Ten K should do it. I need him to keep his ear to the ground, though, about who it was that torched the warehouse. I expect an answer from him at some point in the near future.'

'No problem.'

'Thank you, darling. Now, home time. A busy but most successful day. Nicholai what's happening with the boat?'

'We are moving it, as it is, around to the port. Day after tomorrow. Easier to distribute there and we're using it to transport other items elsewhere.'

'It's safe though? Being watched in the meantime? Yes? Wonderful. Thank you. Have a lovely evening everyone.'

CHAPTER 30

Doug stood on the prow of the lifeboat as they chugged back into the harbour. It was his favourite view of the town and his preferred place to stand on the boat in calm waters. They had been called out as someone on the Kirby ferry had sworn that they had seen a leg floating in the water. The crew had launched and had recovered two legs and an arm in various locations.

Jonesey was waiting at the quayside with a large evidence bag and waved as they came in.

'Just chuck it all in,' he said cheerfully when Tom appeared with the items wrapped in a foil blanket.

'Where were they?' Jonesey asked.

Tom handed over a piece of paper. 'I've written down the co-ordinates of where they were.'

Doug jumped off the boat and stood next to Jonesey. 'This got anything to do with the head that the Davy Jones boys found?'

Jonesey shrugged. 'I am but a lowly foot soldier. You'll have to talk to his lordship about that.'

'I'm guessing he's busy if you're here collecting these delights?'

'He's chatting to the vicar, I think,' Jonesy said. 'It's all kicking off I can tell you. Whoever said life was dull in the church certainly wasn't living here. Right, I need to get off. Thanks, guys.'

'No problem,' called Doug. 'Give my regards to Steve.'

Steve was talking to the vicar. He had arranged to meet him in one of the care homes, away from Mrs Pomeroy's ears. As he waited, he watched in amusement as an older lady with a smart grey bun helped herself to a few handfuls of biscuits and popped them in her pockets. She caught Steve's eye and winked.

'Get in now,' she said, tapping the side of her nose. 'Trust me.'

Steve watched in amusement as an old man shuffled in and helped himself to a variety of biscuits, taking a bite out of each one and putting the ones back he clearly didn't like.

'Marvin,' warned one of the care workers who was topping up the teapot. 'I've told you before about doing that. No taking bites out of them and putting them back.'

The old man waved the comments aside and shuffled off. The old lady came back to top up her tea and she winked at Steve.

'Told you so,' she said, chuckling and heading off.

The vicar arrived and helped himself to a cup of tea and unknowingly selected a few of Marvin's leftover biscuits. Steve couldn't be bothered to mention it, but he did catch the eye of the old lady who had also noticed, and they shared a secret smile.

'Right,' the vicar said, frowning at one of the biscuits before he took a bite. 'You asked me to look at the accounts.'

* * *

At SOCO's instruction Jonesey had dropped off the limbs for analysis and then collected a colleague before going in search of Jimmy. As expected, he was found coming out of his favourite pub.

'Hello, Jimmy,' said Jonesey. 'Inspector Miller asked if you'd come in for a little chat.'

'About?'

'This and that.'

'When?'

'Now.'

Jimmy rolled his eyes. 'Like I have a fucking choice.' He opened the car door and got in, hunkering down in the back seat. Last thing he wanted was to be seen by anyone, especially anyone connected with Pearl or Alexy. A few minutes later, Jimmy was escorted into the station and put in an interview room.

'Cuppa?' asked Jonesey.

'How long is this going to take?'

Jonesey shrugged. 'No idea. Steve will be along in a minute. How'd you have it?'

'White with two.'

Steve returned to the station to find Jonesey leaving the interview room.

'Who's in there?' he asked.

'Jimmy. He finally appeared.'

'Right. I'll be with him in five.'

Steve balanced a coffee on top of his files and laptop and opened the door to the interview room.

'Jimmy, how's that nose?'

'OK,' he said sullenly. 'That your girlfriend then?'

'I like to think so.' Steve grinned.

'So she's not the famous pathologist you said.'

'It appears not.'

'That's lying. Thought you weren't supposed to do that.'

'Well, we all do things we're not supposed to, don't we, Jimmy?'

Jimmy slouched down in his seat. Steve sipped his coffee.

'Jimmy, I'm not going to record this. We're going to have an off-the-record chat here. No one else but you and me.'

'And whoever else is watching.' Jimmy pointed at the cameras.

'All off. I swear,' said Steve.

'This sounds dodgy.'

'You'd know all about that, Jimmy.'

Jimmy snorted.

'I want to show you something.' Steve lifted the lid on his laptop.

Jimmy raised an eyebrow and Steve pressed play. The video showed grainy footage of a man creeping around a large building and throwing what looked like petrol bombs inside and then driving off in a truck similar to Jimmy's.

'What's that then?' Jimmy asked, trying not to show he was crapping himself.

Steve pointed. 'Oh, this old thing? This is a film of you, Jimmy, torching this building.'

Jimmy leant forwards. 'Doesn't look anything like me.'

'This is your truck.'

'It was stolen for an evening the other night. I left it outside the pub, and it was gone.'

'Did you report it?'

'I did actually.'

'I'll look into that. Did it turn up?'

'In a car park on the edge of town. Next day.'

'Convenient.'

'Not really.'

'So, getting back to this warehouse.'

'What warehouse?'

'This warehouse, that you torched.'

'I didn't torch anything.'

'This looks awfully like you.'

'Lots of men with blond hair about my height.'

'True.'

'If you could make this stick, you'd be arresting me by now.'

'Thing is, Jimmy, you can deny it all you want, but I was there. It was me filming it.'

'Didn't do a very good job, did you? Bet Ridley Scott's quaking in his boots. Look, you can't make anything out clearly. It's more like that *Blair Witch* film.'

'Back to the warehouse.'

'Which warehouse?'

'Don't test me, Jimmy,' Steve warned. 'So, the warehouse that you know nothing about was full of bodies. Well, parts of bodies. We found lots of interesting things there. We found that this was the place where Huey was tortured. We also found some more of JJ. So I can't help but try to join the dots... JJ's head in a lobster pot, you setting a fire, the burnt warehouse being full of body parts that include the rest of JJ.'

'You and your fucking dot to dots,' Jimmy muttered.

'Anything to say?' Steve leant back in his chair and narrowed his eyes.

'Like what?' Jimmy scowled.

'So, here's what I think,' Steve said. 'And humour me here. I think you got roped into something that JJ was into after they killed Huey. JJ was basically as thick as shit, so he came to you for help, although Christ knows why, he must have been desperate. You fenced whatever it was to one of your nefarious contacts. That naughty JJ clearly upset someone, and you were gifted his head, partly as a warning I wonder or something else. And I bet I know who that was from too.

'Now if I were you, I would think… shit… how can I get rid of a head? I would think, I own a lobster boat with lobster pots. I'll dump him out to sea and the sea life will do the work, not banking on the Davy Jones boys clearing the seabed. So, when JJ's head was found and it went public, I think you got quite the telling off about that from the powers that be, and you had to redeem yourself. How do you redeem yourself? I'm working on that theory, so bear with me. I suspect you'll have to do them some sort of low-level favour. Anyway… I digress…' He glanced at Jimmy. 'You still with me?'

Jimmy swallowed heavily.

'I think maybe, you were gifted the rest of JJ, but you didn't know what to do with him. I mean that's bigger to get rid of, isn't it? So I reckon you go to this warehouse because JJ had told you about it, or you'd been there. Now, Jimmy, I know this because we had been looking at it anyway as it was in JJ's phone data. In fact, Jimmy, if I'm not wrong, he sent you a pin from there, didn't he? Anyway,' Steve carried on. 'You cased the joint and found it packed full of body parts and decided that was the place to leave JJ. What better way to get rid of a sticky problem than that? You essentially give it back to them and then destroy the fact that's what you'd done. Quite a good plan really.' He sat back in his chair and folded his arms. 'How did I do, Jimmy?'

Jimmy was white-faced. Could this man read his mind? See into his soul? How the fucking hell did he know all this?

'No comment,' Jimmy croaked.

'So let me tell you where I am with all this,' Steve said, smiling, thoroughly enjoying himself. 'I think you fenced a deal for JJ. I would hazard a guess that it was reluctantly too as I haven't ever put you two together for anything.'

'No comment.'

'But I reckon you didn't have anything to do with JJ's death, or Huey's come to that. You see, Jimmy, you're not a killer. Far from it. You're actually a nice bloke, it's just your judgement that sucks… oh, and the company you keep.'

'What's your point?'

'My point, Jimmy, is that I think you're in over your head. Just like last time. You got off fairly scot-free with that little escapade. But I think you have been welcomed into the fold of something that you don't want to be welcomed into. Am I right?'

'Maybe.' Jimmy narrowed his eyes. 'What of it?'

'I think we might be able to help each other out.'

'I help you out, mate, and I end up like Huey or JJ.'

'Jimmy, we're really not interested in the petty stuff. We are interested in people like Mickey Camorra and his associates.'

Jimmy shifted uneasily in his chair. 'You don't want to be fucking with them.'

'So I hear. How can I make the film go away, Jimmy, so that I don't have to charge you with arson? It's a long sentence if an accelerant was used and it was done with intent.'

Jimmy thought for a moment. 'What so… you'll leave me alone, not try and pin the fire on me… lose the film. Forever?'

'I'll leave you alone.'

Jimmy gave him a look of disbelief 'For real?'

'For real.'

Jimmy thought for a long time and then shifted in his chair. He exhaled heavily. 'I can help you out, but it has to look like an accident. I mean really fucking look like it. And then we're totally square.'

'Talk to me.' Steve leant forward.

Steve was having an excellent day. He was eager to collate the information he received from the vicar and list it all out comprehensively, double-checking it was watertight. He had a couple of facts to check with Peter and then he reckoned he could get Mrs Pomeroy in for a proper grilling and hopefully charge her.

He was at the large table at the end of the incident room, going through various pieces of paper obtained from the vicar when Jonesey came in with a large box. Jonesey had a donut stuffed in his mouth and handed a sheaf of paper to Steve as he juggled the box.

'Vicar's personal accounts,' he mumbled.

'What's in the box?' Steve asked as Jonesey chucked it on the table and sat down, removing the donut and licking his fingers.

'I dunno. It's addressed to you.'

Steve picked up a pair of scissors and scored the brown tape holding the two leaves of the box together. He lifted the flaps, took out the white packing material and inhaled sharply.

'Jesus fucking Christ,' he said, sitting down suddenly.

Jonesey stood up, stuffing the last piece of donut in and peered in the box. His eyes widened.

'Shit! Isn't that?'

'It is. Someone's done us quite the favour.'

He pulled out a piece of paper. It was a printed list from the local constabulary website which highlighted most wanted criminals. Steve noted with some amusement the red line through the name.

'Quite the sense of humour,' he said. 'Jonesey. I've got to go out. Get this to the lab. I bet it matches the arms and legs that Doug found earlier.'

'Guv.'

Steve rang the doorbell at Doug's house and waited. He heard Brock barking and Doug opened the door.

Hey, mate,' he said, surprised to see Steve on the doorstep. 'You OK?'

'I'm good. You got a minute? Jesse here?' Steve made a fuss of Brock.

'She's in the kitchen. Everything OK? She's been a bag of nerves since the bonfire.'

'Everything is very good,' he said, walking into the kitchen. 'Hey, Jesse.'

'Hi.' She eyed him suspiciously. 'Coffee?'

'Please.'

Jesse pointed to one of the chairs at the breakfast bar.

'Sit.'

'Thanks.' Steve sat, and Doug leant against the worktop. Jesse passed Steve a mug and the cafetiere.

'This is bad news, right?' she said.

'Well, I think that depends on how you look at it,' Steve said.

'God. I almost don't want to know.' Jesse buried her face in her hands.

'Chris is dead,' Steve said simply.

'What?' Doug said in disbelief. 'Are you sure?'

'I am, yes. Fairly sure. Well, almost completely sure.'

'How can you be sure?' Jesse whispered, clutching the worktop.

'Because his head was delivered to me at the station in a box about half an hour ago,' Steve said. 'Together with this print out.' He produced his phone and showed the name crossed out in red.

Jesse sat down suddenly. 'My God…' she whispered. 'It's over… It's finally over.' She grasped Steve's arm. 'Is it real? Is it really over?'

'It is.'

'I don't understand… who would do this?'

'This has all the marks of the local mafia. They like to do this. I suspect he tried something on with them and was too arrogant to realise who he was dealing with. I have to admire them though. This is them doing a public service for us. I do like the humour.'

'I need to see it,' Jesse said. 'I have to see it.'

'I knew you'd say that. Tell me. Did he have any tattoos on his arms or legs?'

'He had a small black Chinese dragon on his right bicep,' Jesse said.

Doug stood straighter. 'Wait, the arm we found this morning had a…'

'Exactly,' said Steve. 'He's gone, Jesse. You can go to the morgue tomorrow; you have my permission to see it. But he is gone. It's over. If I were you, I would say it's time to celebrate.'

'It's really over,' Jesse said tremulously. 'I almost can't believe it.'

'Looks like it really is. We should celebrate.' Doug grinned.

* * *

Jimmy was in his wetsuit. He had a small waterproof bag with him that was hooked around his waist. He rolled his shoulders and dropped quietly into the inky water. It was very late, and the harbour was silent. He swam around the wall of the harbour quietly, stopping to catch his breath in the shadow of the odd boat. He reached his destination and took a deep breath, diving under water. Three times he quietly came up for air and then satisfied, he glided off, being careful not to be noticed. He swam around to a secluded part of the beach, stripped off his wetsuit and crept quietly home, slipping in the back door, not seeing a soul.

CHAPTER 31

Sophie and Marcus stood by Sam's bed, holding hands tightly. They had talked until late the evening before and had made the decision together. Sophie had glimpsed the man Marcus would become. From his reasoning and pragmatic approach to his father, and his love for her and wanting her to have a good life. She had been completely overwhelmed with love for her son.

'This is no life for Dad,' he had said. 'There is no chance of recovery so why would we keep the machine on? That's the only thing keeping him alive. Dad looked…'

'Dad looked what?'

'He looked dead behind the eyes since he came home.'

'I know,' she whispered.

'I think you need to think about you, Mum, and your life too. He wouldn't want you to be living for a man who is being kept alive with machines. He'd want you to be happy again.'

'I want you to be sure that whatever we decide, together, you are one hundred per cent comfortable with it,' Sophie had said.

They had talked and cried and decided that they would let him go. He was an organ donor, so they felt they were doing a good thing, donating everything. Sam had always had really strong views on helping others if you could. Sophie had signed the forms and confirmed that there were no other family members. She stood looking down at Sam. There was a soft knock on the door and Lottie came in.

'Hey, Soph,' she said. 'I just wanted to say goodbye to Sam. He was with me a while, and I wanted to be here for you.' She bent and kissed his cheek. 'So long, Sam,' she said quietly. 'I hope that you sleep peacefully now.' She looked at him for a moment, then hugged Sophie and Marcus and whispered that she would be outside.

'How long does it take?' Sophie asked the nurse, who was standing quietly by.

'Not long. It's not painful.'

Sophie took Sam's hand.

'You were the absolute love of my life,' she said softly, stroking his face. 'I will always love you, your smile, your gorgeous dimples, and the fun we had and how you made me laugh all the time. I won't ever forget you. Thank you for giving me Marcus. I will cherish him forever. I will miss you forever. Sleep well and peacefully, my love. Be free.' She kissed his cheek gently and gestured to Marcus.

Marcus took Sam's hand and tears ran down his face. He sniffed and said softly, 'Dad, it's time to go. It's best for you. I'll look after Mum. I'm glad I got to say goodbye. I'm proud of you, I'll always be proud of my dad. Love you, Dad. Don't worry, but watch over us, OK?'

Sophie turned to the nurse, who wheeled Sam away into theatre for the retrieval of his organs. The door closed softly, and Sophie looked at Marcus.

'He's gone,' Sophie said.

'Uh-huh,' Marcus said in a small voice.

Sophie steered Marcus out of the door and into the corridor. Lottie wordlessly came and gave them both a hug.

'You didn't have to come, Lottie,' said Sophie. 'But thank you. It was nice that you were here at the end. Are you staying?'

'Yeah. I've got a few days off, but Rudi has said I can stay with him. Can I see you both tomorrow?'

'Sure. Lovely. Give me a call when you're around. Right, Marcus, shall we go home?'

Marcus nodded. 'Can we order pizza?'

'I think it would be rude not to,' Sophie said. 'Lottie, you're welcome to join us.'

'Thanks, but there's someone I need to see here before I leave.'

'Oh?'

'There's a vacancy for a trauma nurse here and I've been wanting to get back into it. So I'm just exploring a few options. Castleby has quite the draw.'

'It would be wonderful to have you around,' said Sophie. 'Let me know how it goes.'

They hugged goodbye and Lottie headed off. Sophie put an arm around Marcus's shoulders.

'Come on, kiddo. Let's go home.'

* * *

Foxy had been chatting to Maggie outside the café when Rudi had turned up with a huge bouquet of flowers and bulging bags of food.

'This smacks of a man on a promise,' Foxy remarked, chuckling.

'I might be,' said Rudi coyly.

'Who's the lucky lady?' asked Maggie.

'Lottie.'

'Sam's nurse? What's she doing back?' asked Foxy in surprise.

'Jesus, mate, didn't you know?' Rudi asked, looking awkward.

'Know what?' Foxy said, confused.

'They're switching Sam off today. Sophie and Marcus. Lottie came to say goodbye to him.'

Foxy was silent for a moment and Rudi shifted uncomfortably.

'Sorry, mate. I just assumed… you know… with you and Soph being close that… you knew.'

Foxy gritted his teeth and ran his hand through his hair in frustration.

'When?' he barked. 'When were they doing it?'

Maggie laid a hand on his arm. 'Sweetheart, this is something she needs to do alone. With Marcus.'

'This morning. They went in about an hour and a half ago. I passed them on the road.' Rudi's phone rang. 'Sorry, mate, catch you later, I need to get this.' He walked away and answered the phone.

'Shit,' Foxy said, scowling.

'What's the problem?' asked Maggie.

'We had a row.' Foxy looked sheepish.

'Ah.'

'We said some things.'

'Ahhh. For what it's worth, my love, Sophie doesn't hold a grudge.'

Foxy sat down and put his head in his hands. 'She accused me of allowing Sam to kill himself. That I let it happen.'

Maggie raised her eyebrows. 'Ouch. Bit harsh.'

'I told her that Sam had asked me to look after her and Marcus if anything happened to him. He asked me just before he… and she thinks I should've seen it.'

Maggie snorted. 'You just had to spend a few minutes with him to know that if it wasn't then, it would have been another time, somewhere else. That man was broken. He didn't want to break his family by sticking around. I saw it.'

'I did too, but—'

'But what?'

'I don't know, Mags,' he said. 'I couldn't have left them if it was me.'

'Christ you've got it bad haven't you, my love?' she said softly.

Foxy looked rueful. 'Seems that way.'

'What did you say to Sophie then when she accused you of letting it happen?'

'I lost it a bit.' He pulled a face. 'I said I couldn't have done it because I loved them both too much to leave them and I couldn't imagine a life without them both.'

'That's it?'

'I think my final parting shot was telling her that I would rather die than be without her. Great time to lay all that on her, eh? Go, Foxy, with your immaculate timing.'

Maggie reached out and held his hand. 'This is no surprise to me or anyone else. I think the only two people who didn't realise how you feel are you and Sophie.'

Foxy looked glum. 'Well, either way, I shouldn't have said it. She doesn't feel that way about me at all. So I should shut the fuck up about it.'

'Quite right,' Maggie said, amused.

'You don't agree?' Foxy said dryly.

'I think that poor girl needs all the help, support and love she can get at the moment. So I think she needs her mates around her. Park how you feel about her and what you said. Just be there for her and tell her that you just want to be her friend. Then there's no pressure or awkwardness, everyone knows where they stand, and no one is tip-toeing about.'

Foxy grunted. 'You're like the all-seeing eye.'

'I am. Now bugger off. Go and support that lovely girl. Take her some flowers. Make sure you tell her it's a sorry for you overstepping the mark and make sure you spell out the friends thing. You men are crap at that.'

'I got it the first time.'

'You men don't listen.'

'Anything else?'

'That'll do. No funeral-type flowers either. Happy stuff.'

'Well I wasn't going to take her a fucking wreath,' Foxy muttered sarcastically under his breath.

'I heard that.' She patted his arm and turned to go inside. 'You're a good man, Rob Fox. You've got a good heart.'

Foxy watched her go back into the café.

'Perhaps I'm fucking sick of always being the good man,' he sighed.

Foxy stood on the doorstep and rang the bell. He heard Marcus yell, 'Pizza's here!' as he flung open the door, one hand holding a games console.

'Sorry, mate, only me,' Foxy said ruefully.

Marcus walked back in the lounge saying over his shoulder, 'Mum's in the kitchen.'

Foxy walked through into the kitchen and put the flowers down on the counter.

Sophie was standing in the garden on the phone. She glanced up and when she saw him her face broke out into a huge smile. She held a hand over the receiver. 'Two minutes. Stick the kettle on.'

Foxy busied himself making her tea. She drank coffee in the morning, tea in the afternoon and she would say it was too early for wine.

'Sorry about that,' she said, coming back in and closing the door. 'Oh thanks, lovely,' she said, cupping her hands around the mug. 'Come sit. Those flowers are beautiful.'

'They're for you.'

'Why's that?'

Foxy tilted his head. 'Eh… how long have you got? To say sorry for shouting. For saying stuff I shouldn't have said. For not being with you today. For not seeing that Sam was going to…'

'No apologies needed for any of it.'

'Look, I need to…'

'Rob, really…'

Foxy held up a hand to stop her. 'Just let me say one thing, Soph, then that's it.'

'OK,' she said warily.

Foxy thought for a minute. 'My policy is to not lie. So I'm not going to lie about what I said. All I want to say is that you are my friend and that I hope I'm yours. I'm here for you and Marcus. Just like it's always been. Friends. Besides,' he said, adopting a serious tone and frowning, 'it's already out there that we're besties.'

Sophie hid a smile. 'True,' she said. 'We are besties. It *is* out there.'

'So we have to stick to it, don't we?' Foxy grinned.

'Pinky promise?' Sophie held up her little finger.

'Pinky promise.' Foxy caught her small finger in his.

He settled back in the pew. 'Now that's said, I'm sorry I wasn't there today.'

Sophie shook her head. 'We needed to do it together.'

'Are you OK?'

Sophie was quiet for a moment and sipped her tea. 'I am OK with it. It was for the best. I think he wanted to go, and I have to try and respect that.'

'Can I do anything to help?'

She laid a hand on his arm. 'Just be around. How you've always been. My rock.'

'Consider it done,' he said quietly.

'Powers that be are doing the funeral. Full honours and all that. It's out of my hands.'

'Is that what you want?'

'It's what I think he would have wanted.'

'They'll do him proud.'

'I know.'

The doorbell went again. 'Pizza's here!' yelled Marcus.

'Today's not dampened his appetite,' Foxy observed.

'Nothing could. Look, I have a favour to ask.'

'Anything.'

'Could you check in on him? He really talks to you. Always has. I just want to check he's OK.'

'You know you don't even need to ask.'

Foxy's phone rang loudly in the quiet kitchen, and he glanced at the display.

'It's Mike, sorry I need to get this,' he said, answering. He frowned as he listened. 'What? Oh for fuck's sake. Yes. Do that. I'll be there in five. I'm at Soph's. Bye.' Foxy turned to Sophie. 'Sorry, I've got to go. That little fucker Jacob has caused someone to fall.

413

Looks like they may have broken something too. I swear I'm going to tear him apart with my bare hands one of these days.'

'But you won't because he's a customer, and his parents are loaded,' said Sophie wryly. She kissed him on the cheek. 'Go. Thanks for the flowers and the chat. Take care, bestie.'

'See you, bestie,' he said, jogging out of the door.

Sophie looked at his departing back fondly. She had missed his presence in the couple of days she hadn't seen him, and she realised what a huge part of her life he was. She was pleased that they had cleared the air. It was clear to her that he loved her as a bestie and nothing else.

She headed into her dad's study to start clearing Sam's things. She sat on the bed, picked up the overnight bag and peered inside, preparing to sort out clothes. There were two envelopes in there. One addressed to her and the other to Marcus. Sam's handwriting.

She stared at it, her stomach churning. Her hand shook slightly as she opened the crisp white envelope.

> *My darling Sophie.*
>
> *So, I guess I've done it then? You're reading this because I've gone. I don't want to ramble on for ages… you know me… hate blabbing on. But I wanted to say sorry for not coming back as the man I was. For not being strong enough to get through it. The constant pain, the constant memories. The nightmares, remembering the horrors. It was my failure. Nothing more. It wasn't that I didn't love you enough to stay, it was because I loved you too much to stay. I couldn't bring all of my horror into your sweet lives.*
>
> *I'm so glad I came for the weekend; it gave me a chance to reassure myself that you have a good life. That you are completely surrounded by people who love you. You and Marcus will be OK,*

414

because you are loved and supported by a wonderful group of friends. I am so proud of you, Sophie, of how you have carried on and your parenting of our wonderful son. My biggest regret is that I won't live to see him grow into the man I have seen glimpses of this weekend. But I know you'll tell me. Every now and again, you will tell me. So, I'm off now for the big sleep. Remember me for the man I was, not the man I became. I will always love you, my beautiful Sophie. Be kind to yourself. I want you to love again, with all your heart. Freely and without guilt. I wouldn't even mind if it was Foxy. Much as I wanted to hate him for being everything I wasn't, I realised he really is quite an excellent fellow that even through my tired and jaded eyes I see that he loves you deeply. So, I reckon when you feel ready, go for it with my blessing.

Must go. I will always love you and try to watch over you both. Your Sam xx

Sophie folded the letter carefully and put it back in the envelope. She smoothed the envelope closed thoughtfully. He had planned it. She had known deep down that he had, but this light-hearted note took the horror out of that day for her. She knew Foxy felt guilty about what happened too. She should tell him about the note. Ease his guilt.

'Mum! There's only one piece left. Are you having any?' Marcus stood in the doorway holding the pizza box. 'What's that?' he said, gesturing to the letter.

'Letters from Dad. One for you. One for me.'

Marcus pulled a face. 'One for me?'

'Uh-huh.'

'I don't know if I want to read it. What did yours say?'

'It was a proper goodbye. He meant to do it.'

'How do you feel about it?' Marcus asked, his eyes wide. 'Better or worse?'

Sophie thought for a moment. 'Er… I think I feel better about the memory of the day he did it.'

Marcus took his letter from Sophie and passed her the pizza box. He licked his fingers and opened it. For ages he seemed to read. Then he laughed softly and carefully folded it up and put it in his pocket.

'You OK?' Sophie asked.

'I'm good.'

'Sure?'

'Yup.' He smiled at Sophie. For a second she saw Sam in his smile.

'Don't want to talk about it?' she pressed.

'No. I'm OK, Mum. Do you want this last bit?'

Sophie looked at the pizza box. 'You have it.'

'Reeesult,' he said, wandering out of the room.

Sophie picked up her envelope and put it in the desk drawer. She tidied away Sam's bag and joined Marcus.

* * *

Jimmy was high on the castle mount watching the harbour. He had seen Alexy arrive with two men. They seemed in good spirits. Alexy sat himself on the comfortable deck seats with a coffee while the other two men competently cast off and steered the boat out to open water. Jimmy lifted his phone out of his back pocket as he walked around the mount to track their path out to sea. He tapped out a text. Smiling, he watched them sail off and then headed back to his boat.

Steve was with Detective Chief Inspector Jerry Reed, who was head of the Organised Crime unit for the area. Jerry had been after Mickey Camorra for nearly a decade. Steve saw a text arrive on his phone.

'Boat's on its way.'

'Let's get sorted,' Jerry said.

Steve and Jerry climbed the narrow steps onto the main deck of the border force boat that they were using for the op. They nodded to colleagues from the National Crime Agency, who were ready and waiting.

'We should see them in just over half an hour if all goes to plan,' Steve said. 'Castleby lifeboat is aware and stood by to assist when they Mayday in.'

'If they Mayday,' said Steve grimly.

The large grey border force boat headed slowly out of the harbour. Steve and Jerry busied themselves as they waited while time ticked by at a glacial rate.

'I'm not even going to ask what stunt you pulled to get this done,' Jerry said, looking at Steve.

'It wasn't a stunt. It was a mutual understanding. That's all I'm saying.'

'From an anonymous informant.'

'Of sorts.'

'Wouldn't happen to be someone that has helped us out before, would it?' Jerry asked dryly.

'I couldn't possibly say,' Steve said, grinning.

Steve's phone rang, Doug's number showed.

'They've called in a Mayday,' Doug said. 'Rudder's broken. Are you going to get them, or do you need us?'

'We'll go,' said Steve, nodding to the captain.

'We're here if you need us,' Doug said.

'Thanks, mate.'

'Happy hunting!'

The powerful engines of the boat hummed as it surged through the water. In the distance through the binoculars, Steve spotted the yacht.

'Two men on deck,' he called to Jerry, who was briefing the team.

The siren on the boat rang out along with clear instructions about the border force and that they would be coming alongside for a search. Steve saw one of the men jump off the boat and swim off towards the coastline.

'One overboard!' he shouted. The border force dropped a small RIB into the water and headed towards the swimmer at high speed, catching him within seconds.

The large boat came alongside the yacht and border force officers swarmed onto it in seconds. The two men were brought up onto the deck of the large boat.

The officers tore the yacht apart. Steve and Jerry had retreated below decks to start the paperwork. The search took hours. Finally, the head of the search team came down to see Jerry and Steve.

'Right,' he said, sitting down heavily. 'We've gone through the whole boat. We've got a good stash. Probably about 70 kilos, distributed in various very clever places. Worth a few million, so it's a good call. I reckon it's come in from Ireland. I recognise the marks on the packets.'

'Anything I need?' Jerry asked. 'To link it?'

The search officer shook his head. 'Not unless we can prove either of the men work for Mickey or either of them testify. I do think, though, there's a corridor opening up from Ireland to here that Mickey's using. We can place him in Ireland recently.'

'Christ,' said Jerry angrily. 'This guy is as slippery as a fucking fish. We need a clear link between Mickey and this lot. Can you give me what you have on what he was doing in Ireland? Might shed some light or be the missing piece.'

'Happy to.'

'I will get him,' Jerry said grimly. 'But at least today I've dented his income and his cashflow. Right. Let's call it a day. Home, James!' he shouted up to the captain.

Jimmy was whistling as he steered into the harbour. Night was falling and he was pleased to be coming in under the cover of darkness. He had a number of crates stacked up on his boat. As he moored against the quayside, he heard an engine start and an old van drove over. A man Jimmy didn't recognise stood on the quay and beckoned for the crates. Jimmy handed them up. Someone was in the back of the van unloading them and the empty crates were handed back with quick and silent efficiency.

'Done,' Jimmy said as he received the last empty crate.

The door to the wheelhouse opened and Alexy stepped out.

'Jimmy,' he said quietly. 'I cannot thank you enough for the tipping off. You are a true friend. You were saving my bacon, no?'

'You've been good to me, Alexy. We're going to call it quits now,' Jimmy said.

'I will reward you, Jimmy.'

'No need to reward me. Just forget about me and make Pearl forget about me. I don't want to get involved with that lot,' Jimmy said desperately.

'OK. I have understanding.'

'You'd better go, Alexy.'

'*Dosvedanya*, Jimmy the fisherman.'

'*Dosvedanya*, Alexy. Oh and, Alexy?'

Alexy turned.

'Let's be the type of friends that don't speak to each other very often, yes?'

Alexy laughed as he climbed in the van and then turned and waved. Jimmy watched it drive safely away and up the hill. He heaved a sigh of relief, perhaps that was the end of it. His main aim had been to be free of the Camorra and by helping Alexy that was hopefully what he achieved. He locked the boat and headed home.

CHAPTER 32

Steve staggered out of the interview room and sagged against the wall, breathing deeply. Jonesey followed him out.

'You alright, Guv?' he said, frowning. 'It was well ripe in there wasn't it?'

Steve nodded, still trying to control his nausea by breathing deeply.

'What the hell was that smell?' he gasped.

Jonesey tittered. 'Well that, my friend, was Sadie the Stinker. Hints of odour de cats' piss, wacky baccy with a healthy selection of mouldy mushroom, not to mention the cliché that was patchouli oil. Quite the aroma!'

'I couldn't stand the smell any longer.'

'Good thing she was pointing the finger then!' Jonesey said. 'We gonna charge her for dealing and possession?'

'We will. I just want to check in with the drug boys to make sure they haven't got her on their radar for anything else and whether the mushrooms will stick as a narcotic; I'm fairly sure they will but I want to be certain. She can fester in her own smell for a while. Get her statement about supplying Mrs Pomeroy and their various dealings typed up and signed before we either charge or release her. OK?'

'Yup. I'm on it.'

'I'm almost there with the cold-hearted Mrs Pomeroy. Can you or Sarge call Peter and ask him to call in tomorrow quickly to dot a few Is, but if she answers, don't say it's you; just find out where he is.'

'Will do. What are you doing now?'

'Little chat with Jimmy.'

'Ahh…'

'Exactly.'

Steve left the station and decided to walk to the harbour to see if he could track down Jimmy. It was the time of day he usually returned on the boat, so Steve enjoyed the fresh air as he walked.

He jumped when a car behind him tooted loudly. He turned to see Kate behind the wheel, and she rolled to a stop next to him, her window buzzing down.

'Are you on patrol, officer?' she said, grinning at him.

He rested his hands on the edge of the door through the open window and shook his head sadly.

'Madam, no point buttering me up. You've just committed a driving offence, you may only use your horn if another road user poses a genuine danger. I may have to take down your particulars and issue some form of punishment for this serious violation.'

'Goodness, officer. Perhaps you could give some consideration to how I might be able to show my appreciation if you let this terrible infraction go,' Kate said, trying not to smile.

Steve narrowed his eyes. 'I'll give it some serious consideration. I must, however, insist that you accompany me to dinner at a public house of my choosing later.'

Kate pretended to think. 'Well, if that's my punishment, I feel I have no choice but to comply.'

Steve leant in and kissed her softly. 'Perfect. See you in the Hope at Seven?'

'Absolutely. See you later, gorgeous!' she called out of the window and tooted again, leaving Steve in the road shaking his head and chuckling.

Steve grabbed a coffee from Maggie's and strolled around to the harbour. As he walked slowly down the ramp to the lower harbour an old transit passed him; the driver was a large man with a baseball cap pulled low. Steve glanced at him, but the man was careful to look the other way. Steve mentally noted the registration plate and carried on.

Jimmy was on the deck of his boat. He had been hosing it down when he glanced up and saw one of Alexy's men stood on the quayside with his hands in his jacket pockets. Jimmy's blood ran cold, as he became immediately convinced the man was going to shoot him or do something unpleasant to him.

'Alright, mate?' he'd called up trying to be casual.

The man kicked a large black bag down towards Jimmy. It landed on the deck and Jimmy was terrified. Last time he had seen a bag like this it had contained money along with a head.

'Alexy said to say hello,' the man said in a thick accent. 'He said he need to speak to you. You will call him, yes?'

Jimmy stood nodding, not looking at the bag. The man turned suddenly and walked away. Jimmy prodded the bag with his foot. If Alexy had given him a head, whose would it be?

He dropped to his haunches and unzipped the bag carefully, peering in. The bag was full of rolled up banknotes. Jimmy stuck his hand in the bag, moved it around and was relieved to feel no head or any other body part. He heard footsteps approaching so he zipped up the bag quickly and kicked it over to the side of the deck.

'Jimmy, Jimmy, Jimmy,' Steve said, standing on the quayside looking down at Jimmy.

'I thought all our business was concluded,' Jimmy said, looking up at Steve.

'Why d'ya do it, Jimmy?' Steve asked softly.

'Do what?' Jimmy asked.

'Oh come on now... don't be coy,' Steve said, smiling. 'It was a bit of a stroke of genius if you ask me. Keeping one on side and half fucking the other one over, but not so much that they would think it was you.'

'Dunno what you mean,' said Jimmy, hosing again.

'Genius really...' said Steve. 'So what did Vladimir want?'

'Who?'

'Your mate that just left.'

'He was just saying hello.'

'He was, was he?'

'Yup.'

'So... any repercussions from your trip the other day?'

'Such as?'

'The wrath of Mickey C?'

'Why would that affect me?'

'Oh I don't know... join the dots up and Jimmy's part of the picture.'

'What is it with you and the fucking dot to dot?' Jimmy asked, exasperated. He said quietly, 'No one's come looking for me. I think they're looking a bit closer to home.'

'That was the idea, though, wasn't it, Jimmy?'

'Keep your fucking voice down,' he hissed, checking around the harbour.

'I think you've dodged the bullet this time.'

'Fucking telling me,' Jimmy mumbled.

'If it all blows up in your face, call me. Don't leave it until it's too late.'

'Yeah right. I'll ask if I can make a call once my hands and legs are nailed to the table.'

'If you get a whiff of trouble, ring me. Yes? I don't want to be pulling you off the cliff like I did Huey. Yes?'

'Yes. Bugger off.'

Steve saluted. As he walked away he called over his shoulder, 'Better stash that bag of cash, Jimmy... there's thieves and undesirables everywhere.'

'Fucking twat,' muttered Jimmy at his departing back.

'Heard that,' Steve called.

Jimmy dug his phone out from his pocket and made a call. He waited for it to be answered.

'Jimmy, my friend the fisherman.'

'Thanks for the bag.'

'No problem. I think you might be expect a head, no?' Alexy laughed loudly at his own joke.

'Very good. Your mate said I needed to call you.'

'Ahh yes... little thing Pearl asked.'

Jimmy quaked. 'Alexy,' he warned. 'You said we were square.'

'Pearl want to know who set fire at warehouse. She want you to find out. Soon, Jimmy.'

Jimmy closed his eyes in dread. Just when he thought he was free and clear.

'I'll see what I can do. No promises.'

'OK, Jimmy the fisherman. Soon, eh?'

'*Dosvedanya*, Alexy.'

'*Dosvedanya*, my friend.'

* * *

Mrs Pomeroy had answered the phone when Jonesey rang and had been instantly suspicious of whoever it was who was calling and wanted to speak to Peter, or know his whereabouts. Jonesey had put down the phone feeling like he had been under interrogation himself. He finally managed to track down Peter and had asked him to come in the next morning to tie up a few loose ends. Peter had happily agreed.

Peter turned up at the police station bright and early. Before he had left, Mrs Pomeroy had been highly suspicious of where he was going and had flung down the diary in front of him, informing him he wasn't due anywhere until 9.30, so what was so urgent that he needed to go out early?

Peter had politely suggested to Mrs Pomeroy that everyone was entitled to a private life and that private usually meant private. Peter was still chuckling over her face when he had made the comment. It had been a picture of righteous indignation. He really did enjoy winding her up, it was about the one thing that really made his day. His loathing of her was now off the scale, particularly when he compared her to Marion, who was an absolute delight to be around. The absolute polar opposite of the sour-faced Mrs Pomeroy.

Peter spent longer with Steve at the station than he had intended to, and he left the station in a hurry for his appointment at one of the care homes. He was frustrated that he was running late, which would throw his whole day out. He figured he could rush through the first couple of appointments and then he might catch up later. He had something important to do. He decided this morning, after seeing Steve, that it just couldn't wait any longer. He hurried through the day and thought about the evening ahead.

Peter packed up his rucksack and left the vicarage quietly. He walked softly down the dark road, he had a warm black hat pulled down low over his ears and his hands were in thick woollen gloves. He reached his destination and carefully climbed over the back fence. He dropped lightly to the ground and opened the back door; this wasn't the first time he had been here. He crept into the kitchen and saw a stew bubbling away on the stove. He sniffed it. Nicked from the vicarage no doubt. He dropped the rucksack on the floor and carefully picked out a small Tupperware container. He opened the lid and carefully scraped the contents into the stew, picked up the wooden spoon and gave it a good stir. Smiling to himself he picked up the container and rucksack and silently let himself out of the back door.

Mrs Pomeroy awoke the next morning feeling awful. She was confused; she'd had her flu jab. Of course she'd had her flu jab. She was vulnerable around all of these sick old people the vicar insisted on seeing. She didn't want to catch anything from them. Horrible old needy sick people.

She got up slowly and went to the bathroom, feeling dizzy for a moment, and washed her face and cleaned her teeth. She was thankful it was a Saturday, and she had a day off, so she shuffled down the stairs and made herself a cup of tea, took two paracetamol and went back to bed.

She slept for most of the day and awoke again suddenly in the afternoon. She rushed to the bathroom and was violently sick. She lay on the bathroom floor, clutching her stomach, too weak to get up and get herself some water. As she lay there, the sky darkened and evening fell. She lost track of time, the pain was so extreme. She felt like her skin was on fire. Suddenly the light in the bathroom was flicked on, momentarily blinding her.

'Well, well, well. What do we have here? Are you feeling poorly, Mrs P?' Peter said, pulling a sad face and speaking in a soppy voice as he casually leant against the doorjamb.

Mrs P opened her eyes. 'What are you doing here?' she gasped. 'How did you get in?'

He shrugged. 'Easy. A childhood of petty crime always pays off. I'm here to make sure you're feeling OK. You're certainly not looking your best, Mrs P.'

'Call an ambulance,' she managed to get out through gritted teeth and then retched again.

'What's that?' Peter pretended not to hear.

'Ambulance…' she whispered.

Peter disappeared for a moment and then returned with a chair which he placed in the doorway. He sat down and made himself comfortable. He opened his rucksack and pulled out four cans of lager and popped the tab on the first one. He sipped and savoured it.

'Delicious,' he said, smiling. 'Should have bought myself a few nibbles, thinking about it. This will be quite the show. He disappeared again, and the sound of a radio was heard playing.

'Can't have that nosey old fucking bitch next door overhearing our discussions now, can we?' he said.

'Why… are you… here?' she said, crying out and writhing on the floor as a fresh wave of pain struck.

Peter's lip curled cruelly. 'That is an excellent question, Edwina. Well firstly, I'm here to make sure that you've eaten enough of that stew to make you as ill as I had hoped you'd be,' he said. 'Tick. Secondly, I'm here to see you die a slow and painful death, which I am quite enjoying already I must say.' He pulled a face. 'Why are you looking so shocked, Edwina? I only used the filling of the turnover that you made for poor Marion and popped it in your stew. And the final reason is to tell you that I know what you did. That I know who you are. I know what an evil old bitch you are and that you deserve to die.'

Edwina writhed on the floor. 'What are you talking about? Please get me an ambulance…' she begged as she convulsed from the pain in her stomach.

Peter shook his head. 'Not a fucking chance in hell. You deserve to die in pain. Cast your mind back… The care home? The Nightingale? The one that sacked you? My aunt was in there. You killed her with your poisonous stews and broths. Deliberately. Slowly. She died screaming in agony. You took her money. You took everything from her. The only reason you got away with it then was because I was in prison. But I know it was you, Edwina.'

Edwina retched again, her face red. She was throwing up blood now. She looked at Peter murderously.

'You can't prove it,' she gasped.

Peter folded his arms. 'You really are quite the psychopath. I know you've been trying to get rid of the congregation. Your hatred of old people is staggering. But you hide it well. I've read your notebooks, your poisonous rantings about the sick, the elderly, the frail and how they are a scourge of society, it's really quite fascinating reading. You feel like they get all the love and attention that you never had. Did Mummy and Daddy not love you? Was little Edwina not loved? Was she always the last to be considered?'

He smirked and opened another can. 'I've been asking around about you, Edwina. Your parents devoted their lives to helping the elderly and the frail. That must have hurt. Your parents loving old people more than they loved you? Is that why you got pregnant so young? So desperate for love? Desperate for the escape from the family that loved helping the elderly and the frail… but didn't love Edwina?'

'You don't know anything…' Edwina said through gritted teeth as another wave of pain rolled over her.

'Oh but I do, Edwina, I know everything.' He laughed. 'I've read your diaries. I know you get a little trippy on your mushrooms and have a good old rant into your notebook. You have got some naughty thoughts about the vicar too, haven't you? Do you fancy yourself as the vicar's wife now? Edwina the widow marries the vicar. Oh, how you'd love that. You always thought Fred was beneath you, didn't you? I've watched you, Edwina. You hate anyone who takes the vicar's attention. It's like you want him all to yourself. No old people dragging on his time.' He swigged from his can and bent down to Edwina. 'Do you love the vicar, Edwina? Does your little heart beat more wildly when he is around? Is this unrequited love?'

He finished his drink and dropped the can carefully back into his rucksack.

'You don't know what you're talking about…' Edwina sneered.

Peter laughed. 'Oh, but I do, Edwina. The thing about the old people is that they remember you as a young person. I've heard quite the potted history about you from the locals. Some remember

430

you as a young girl. Unhappy. Parents never around, always helping the frail. Poor lonely, unloved Edwina. Apparently you had quite the thing for a certain young man who was quite the local Casanova by all accounts. I know who used to hang around with the vicar when they were younger, I've been very thorough with my research, I've listened to the stories. In his heyday he was quite the "love 'em and leave 'em" type, but Edwina fancied a future with him, didn't you? You tricked him into bed, got yourself knocked up, but he couldn't remember a thing about it the next day, could he? Because he was so drunk – but not so drunk he couldn't manage a quick fumble though.' He opened another can. 'But poor Edwina, she loved him. But he ignored her. He had no idea, didn't remember a thing. So what did Edwina do? She tricked poor Fred into marrying her. Did you promise poor Fred a life of misery or did it just happen that way?'

Edwina was retching almost constantly now. 'Please… an ambulance…' she gasped desperately.

'No can do,' said Peter cheerfully.

'Did Fred know?' Peter asked suddenly.

Edwina glared at him, not understanding but unable to talk.

'Did Fred know that the boy you loved, who got you pregnant was the vicar that you still worship, but has no idea of the fact?' Peter thought for a moment. 'I think we should tell the vicar!' he announced. 'He'll be stoked.'

'No!' Edwina gasped, writhing.

'Yes!' said Peter, delighted. 'Let's go and tell him now!' He walked into the bathroom and grabbed Edwina painfully under the arms and hauled her up. He half dragged her along the landing until they were at the top of the stairs.

'No, no no,' Edwina mumbled, half crippled from the pain.

431

'Second thoughts,' he said, looking at her with a cruel smile. 'Let's speed things up a little.' With that he pushed Edwina with some force off the top stair where she tumbled down and fell to the bottom, her head at an awkward angle up against the front door.

'That's that then,' Peter said softly. He zipped his rucksack up carefully and then moved the chair back to where he had found it. He crept quietly down the stairs, stepped over Edwina, and let himself out of the back door and climbed over the fence.

CHAPTER 33

Steve awoke early. He lay for a moment enjoying the warmth of the bed and the weight of Kate's arm across his chest. He thought about their dinner the night before and how they had ended up in bed together. For the first time in a long time, he realised he felt really strongly about a woman and wanted a real future with her. He turned to study her sleeping face for a moment in the dim December morning.

'Weirdo's watch people sleep,' Kate said, opening an eye. 'Don't tell me you're a weirdo.'

'Fully paid-up weirdo,' he said lightly, stroking her face. 'Good morning.'

'Good morning,' she said, snuggling closer to him under the covers. 'It's far too early to be getting up.'

'Who said anything about getting up?' Steve said, pulling the covers over their heads. 'You've got the rest of my assessment pending. We've got a lot of work to get through. We'd better crack on.'

Steve sat at the conference table in the briefing room. In front of him was the case against Mrs Pomeroy. It was quite the buffet of offences. He had listed them all out for the arrest warrant.

Jonesey wandered into the room, balancing two coffees and a bakery bag. He put down the coffee and handed Steve the bakery bag. 'Bacon sarnie,' he said, grinning. 'From what I hear, you've had a busy night. You need to keep your strength up.'

Steve looked at him. 'I'm not even going to ask how you think you know that. But thanks, I'm starving.'

'Too busy for breakfast,' Jonesey said knowledgeably.

'Not even going to comment,' Steve said, swigging his coffee, then taking a huge bite of his sandwich.

Jonesey looked at the files in front of him. 'That the arrest warrant?'

'Yup,' Steve mumbled through his sandwich.

'Can I read it?'

'Fill your boots.'

Jonesy picked up the arrest warrant and let out a low whistle. 'Jesus. She's nicked over twenty grand from the vicar?'

'Uh-huh. Maybe more.'

'Been linked to poisoning of at least ten elderly people in the local community who later died?' Jonesey read.

'Uh-huh.'

'Probably killed her husband.'

'That genuinely might have been unintentional...' Steve said through another mouthful.

'Purchased narcotics in the form of magic mushrooms.'

'Not forgetting the death caps she bought from Sadie the Stinker,' Steve clarified.

'Christ alive.'

Steve flicked the edge of the warrant. 'Of course, this doesn't include all the deaths and theft from the care homes she worked in prior to the vicarage. I'm just getting into those. But we'll add that to the list later.'

'When are we picking her up?' Jonesey rubbed his hands together.

Steve rolled up the wrapper from his sandwich and tossed it into the bin. 'No time like the present.'

* * *

Steve, Jonesey and another two PCs drove towards Mrs Pomeroy's house in the custody van. As Jonesey drove, Steve briefed the two PCs.

Jonesey pulled up a few houses down from her house.

'Right, one of you around the back. The rest in the front door. Jonesey? Got the big red door key?'

Jonesey held up the battering ram.

'Let's crack on,' Steve said, using one of Foxy and Kate's favourite terms.

Jonesey hammered on the door. 'Police open up!' he shouted.

They waited for a moment.

'Can I, Guv?' he said, brandishing the battering ram.

'Go for it.'

Jonesey smashed the door at the Yale and it opened slightly and then shut again. Jonesey kicked it and it closed again. He pushed the door open feeling resistance and carefully peered around it.

'Er… Guv?' he said, looking at Steve with a worried face.

Steve walked over and peered behind the door where he saw Mrs Pomeroy's head at a grotesque angle, her body half down the stairs. His brain snapped the picture and stored it. Where had he seen that before? He stepped back from the front door.

'If the fall didn't kill her, the door being smashed against her head twice probably did,' Jonesey said drily.

'Get forensics here pronto,' Steve said. 'Fuck!' He scowled, stomping away, running his hands through his hair in frustration. 'I was going to nail that murdering bitch to the fucking wall.'

* * *

Jesse hugged Jonathan goodbye. 'I'm beyond grateful,' she said, smiling.

Jonathan put his hands on her shoulders. 'Go and be happy. Any problems, weird dreams, etc., come see me. What's interesting is that a lot of the issues you were having were deeply rooted in fear. Fear of him coming back and doing it again. And maybe not surviving a third time.'

'I feel fine,' Jesse said. 'Honestly. I would say if I didn't. I think seeing him, like that, really meant once and for all it was over, and I can move forward.'

'It is. You are in a good place. Enjoy it. Look forward not back. There's nothing behind you that's worth thinking about. Just look ahead. Go and live, Jesse, you deserve it.'

'OK, will do if it's doctor's orders.' Jesse picked up her jacket.

'It most certainly is. Always here for you though.'

Jesse shrugged into her coat, as she was about to open the door she turned.

'Oh, I meant to tell you.'

Jonathan raised his eyebrows.

'You know I talked about the red chair in the dream where I fought the monster?'

'Yes. First thing you said when you woke.'

'Doug has a red rocking chair in his bedroom.'

'So you knew that?'

'Well, that's the thing. It was always covered with a blanket, so I had no idea. I found it the other day.'

'So there was no way you knew that?' Jonathan frowned.

'Nope.'

'Now that is a spooky coincidence.'

'Isn't it?'

'I wonder if it was some sort of subconscious transference from Doug to you…' he said and then shrugged. 'Whatever it was, it kept you safe.'

'It did.' Jesse checked her watch. 'Bugger. I'm late to see Felix. I'm officially being signed off as fit and well today. Thanks again.'

'Take care, Jesse.'

'Bye, Jonathan.'

Jesse climbed into Doug's truck, sat back and closed her eyes.

'Man, I hate the smell of hospitals.'

'Can I suggest you try and stay out of them for a while then?' He leant over and kissed her gently. 'Hello.'

She smiled. 'Hello. Thanks for picking me up. Let's go home.'

Doug turned in his seat to face her. 'About that.'

'What?'

'Home.'

'Why are you being all weird?' She glanced at him.

Doug looked at her with his wolf-like eyes and her stomach did the familiar flip. 'So, you've just had the sign off that you're OK. Does that mean you'll want to go back to your house?'

'Do you want me to go back to my house?' she chided. 'Is my excessive untidiness and random meal combos getting a bit too much?'

Doug leant over and took her face in his hands, looking serious.

'I'm not going to lie, the cooking thing needs work, and errm… the untidiness needs some training, but…'

'But what?' Jesse said indignantly.

Doug laughed at her. 'But I don't want you at *your* house. I want you at *my* house with me. All in. Till we're old and grey.'

'Aww, you say the nicest things,' she said. 'And you *are* going grey.'

'Hm, by then hopefully you'll be tidy and able to cook properly,' Doug said straight-faced, trying not to laugh.

'Seriously. Do you mean it?' Jesse batted him on the arm.

'Of course, seriously. Come home with me. For good.'

She sighed happily. 'Since you asked so nicely. I'll give notice on the house.'

'Good. That's settled then.'

'I might have some conditions though,' she said, eyeing him playfully. 'What if you're not up to them?'

'I'll do my best to accommodate. What are they?' Doug raised an eyebrow.

'I don't know yet. I'll think of something.'

'You never know, I might have a few conditions of my own,' he said, starting the engine and looking at her sideways as he pulled away.

'Such as?'

He shrugged. 'Pretty important stuff.'

'Oh God. Such as? It's the cooking, isn't it?'

He glanced at her as he drove. A hint of a smile.

'I was thinking more along the lines of naked Sundays when the kids are at Claire's for the weekend.'

She looked at him in surprise and pretended to consider it for a moment.

'Doesn't seem unreasonable,' she said after a moment. 'I'm in.'

* * *

Once again, Steve felt faintly ridiculous in his forensic suit and waited for the head of the forensic team to appear and walk him through the scene. A white clad arm with a blue glove beckoned him in around the door.

'Here we are again!' he said cheerfully. 'Careful where you walk, it's a bit messy. Now… kitchen. Some sort of stew left in the fridge, so we will test the contents of that. The fluids we've found upstairs are vaguely reminiscent of Fred's boat, which makes me wonder if she met the same fate. Right, up we go to the bathroom. Horrid mess up here. Suspect she got out of bed and ended up in the bathroom and then couldn't move from there to either hit the toilet or call for help.'

'So how did she fall down the stairs?' Steve asked.

'Ahh, well, did she fall or was she pushed? This is the question.'

'I think there may be traces of paint or wallpaper under her fingernails, which might suggest that she was dragged along to the stairs.'

'Or that she was pulling herself along to get help?'

'Perhaps. But unlikely in my experience.'

Steve looked around. 'Where's the nearest phone?'

'Bedroom.' The team leader pointed.

'So why go down the stairs?' Steve frowned.

'Exactly.'

'You think she was pushed?' Steve asked.

'Uh-huh.'

'Why?'

'The force.'

'Talk me through what you mean.' Steve leant against the wall and folded his arms.

'OK. So, if she had dragged herself along the floor, we would expect to find fibres embedded deep into her elbows and arms. She would have probably been unable to stand and walk down the stairs properly, but Murphy will be able to confirm that. So the likelihood would be that she would somehow maybe try to sort of half roll herself down the stairs or go down on her bottom or something. Yes?'

'With you so far.'

'Looking at the way she fell, I think she was shoved with some force that meant she went out and then down. Essentially, she flew down the stairs and landed at the bottom, her neck being snapped by the door.'

'So she needed to be pushed out that way to be able to fall like that.'

'I'm simplifying it, but essentially yes.'

'OK.'

'I honestly don't think she would have even been able to stand, looking at the array of bodily fluids in there. I think she could have been in incredible pain if this is what I think it is.'

'Poisoning like Fred?'

'Murphy will confirm, but it looks to be the same. I'd wait for his thoughts.'

'If the fall hadn't killed her, she might have died of whatever was in her system?'

'I'd lay money on it.'

'OK. Great. Anything else?'

'Minute traces of what looks like lager on the carpet by the bathroom door. Very odd. No lager of any sort in the house, nothing in the bin either, but we will check to be sure it is that. Don't know what that's about. Also, a couple of splatters of blood on a chair leg.'

Steve raised an eyebrow. 'Where's the chair?'

'Back bedroom. No idea if it's the same blood as the stuff in the bathroom. If it is, then that's another worry.'

'So the chair would have been in the bathroom at some point then, or in the vicinity?'

'Exactly.'

'Curiouser and curiouser.'

'Precisely.'

'Let me know if you find anything else?'

'Of course.'

* * *

Maggie's café was closed, but it was full. Maggie had laid on a big dinner for Sophie and Marcus. She wanted them to feel loved and cherished by their friends, she knew they would have had a difficult day. Doug, Jesse and the kids were there. Rudi and Lottie too, with Lottie considering whether to make the move to Castleby; she had been offered the trauma nurse job. Jesse suggested to Lottie that she take over her house she was going to give notice on.

'You can stay with me,' said Rudi, leering at Lottie.

'I don't think I'd ever make it out of the front door if I stayed with you. Besides, I don't want to rush into anything. I want to take it slowly. I'm not moving here just because you like the idea,' she said, nudging him in the ribs.

Rudi stomped off grumpily to refill his drink.

Foxy had set up Maggie's large barbeque on the deck and was outside, cooking. He was happily watching everyone through the window, enjoying the brisk night air and sipping a beer. He was trying to make peace with himself and how he felt about Sophie. He knew what she needed was strength and support, so he was aiming to provide exactly that and trying not to think about anything else. There was part of him that felt he should try and get over the way he felt about her and get the idea of her out if his head.

'Hey, bestie.' Sophie came through the door and stood next to him. She took a sip from her wine glass and closed her eyes.

'Needed that?' Foxy said, smiling.

'God, yes.'

'Tough day?'

'Yup. Memorial Service for Sam from his unit,' she said, the words catching in her throat, her eyes filling up. 'I found out from a friend today that they would have almost definitely medically discharged him.'

Foxy was silent for a moment. 'Those memorial services are a tough gig. Dare I ask when the funeral is?'

'Next Friday. After much debate they've agreed for me to have it locally and a cremation.'

'You sure?'

'Yes. They're doing some bits for it, though, to honour him which he would love.'

'Can I do anything? With that or anything else?'

Sophie looked at him. 'After today, I could really do with a hug from my bestie.'

'I can do that.' Foxy put down his drink and wrapped his arms around her.

Marcus stepped out on deck and looked confused. 'Mum?'

442

Foxy held out an arm. 'Marcus, your mum needed a hug from her bestie, come on. Bring it in. Let's make it a trio.'

Marcus stepped in, and Foxy wrapped his huge arms around them both.

'OK?' he said.

'Better,' Sophie agreed. 'Much better.'

'OK, I s'pose,' said Marcus, but hugged Foxy back fiercely.

Maggie, who was beaking out of the window, sighed fondly when she saw the three of them. Foxy caught her eye.

'Friends,' she mouthed and waggled her finger at him.

'Friends,' he mouthed back, rolling his eyes and turning his head away from her.

Lottie knocked on the window and beckoned Sophie inside. Marcus headed back in and Sophie went to follow and then stopped. She produced an envelope from her pocket.

'Thanks for that. You give the best hugs, they make everything better. Look, when you get a sec, read this. It's not for everyone's eyes. Just yours. Made me feel a whole lot better about the day he did it. It's what Sam left for me.' She handed him the letter and went inside.

Foxy took the letter and moved to stand under one of the outside lights to read it.

As he cooked, Foxy considered Sam's letter, watching everyone through the window. He saw Sophie smiling with everyone and his stomach lurched when she caught his eye and winked at him. He focused on the barbeque and thought about how he needed to stop mooning after her. She hadn't even buried her husband yet, plus they had agreed to be friends. He needed to try and get her out of his system, or he'd be behaving like a lovesick teenager and then that might start to seriously affect their friendship. He certainly didn't want that.

His phone rang, cutting through the cold night air.

'Well hello, you,' he said, seeing it was Carla. 'How are you?'

'I'm OK,' she said. 'You OK?'

'Yup.'

'What are you doing?'

'Right now?'

'Yes.'

'Cooking for about a hundred people at Maggie's on the big barbeque.'

'Party then?'

'Seems that way. What's up?'

'Can't a girl ring her ex-husband for a chat?'

'Course you can. But I know this tone of voice. I repeat, what's up?' he persisted.

'Nothing. I just wanted to hear your voice.'

'Come on…'

'Look… I had an idea… So Christmas is a few weeks away and I'm due some leave…' Carla left the sentence hanging.

'So… you wondered what exactly?' Foxy wasn't going to make it easy for her.

'I wondered whether you fancied any company over Christmas.'

'Is this you asking me for sex and a free holiday after you heartlessly friend zoned me recently?'

'I'm happy to take whatever is on offer,' she said lightly, her voice cracking slightly.

Foxy frowned as he listened. 'You don't sound good, Carls. Are you OK?'

She exhaled shakily. 'I'm OK. I just need to get away for a bit. I need to think. Stuff to work out. I could do with one of your massive hugs. They always make everything better.'

Foxy looked in through the window at Sophie and thought about getting her out of his system and back to being just friends.

'So I'm told. Carla, come whenever you like,' he said softly. 'Free holiday definitely. We'll have to see about the free sex thing.'

'You met someone?'

'It's complicated.'

'It always is with you. You sure it's OK to come?'

'Course. Stay as long as you like. Just let me know when you'll rock up.'

'OK. See you in a few weeks then. I'll look forward to it,' she said haltingly.

'Carla… Are you OK? Really? You know you can talk to me about anything?' Foxy pushed.

'I'm fine. See you in a few weeks. Lots of love.'

'Back at ya.' Foxy ended the call and thought about Carla. He knew this tone of voice. Something was wrong. Maybe she would talk to him when she saw him. Either way, she would be a distraction and as far as he was concerned it was probably for the best.

* * *

Steve sat at the conference table gloomily surveying the files on Mrs Pomeroy. Jonesey was providing emotional support with tea and a KitKat.

'So…' Jonesey said, chomping on his KitKat and waving the last finger about. 'What I don't get is that she is like "the dark Lord." Bumping everyone off with her bad ju ju mushrooms and then she meets the same fate as Fred and some of the others. It doesn't make sense to me.'

Steve sipped his tea thoughtfully. 'Exactly,' he said and rubbed his head.

'What?' said Jonesey. 'You look like you're thinking.'

'Trying to remember something.'

'What?'

'Where I've seen that picture before…' he said, shaking his head. 'Where have I seen it?'

'Picture?'

'Her at the bottom of the stairs. I've seen the same thing somewhere else. Just can't think of where – it's driving me mad.'

Jonesy rolled his eyes. 'Jesus, you being in *lurve* is pickling your brain. It was Peter's file. It's what he went down for, isn't it? The old man? The wife at the bottom of the stairs?'

Everything suddenly clicked into place in Steve's brain. 'That's it.' He grabbed Jonesey. 'You little beauty.' He gathered up some files and rushed out the door.

Jonesey watched him go and picked up the KitKat that Steve had left. 'Finders keepers.' He shrugged, unwrapping it and tucking in.

Steve went back to Mrs Pomeroy's house armed with Peter's file and the notes he had made from his chat with forensics. He spent time wandering around; looking and thinking about what forensics had said about the oddity of some elements of the scene. He looked in detail at the forensic report from the crime that Peter had gone down for. He was just about to leave the house and was standing in the doorway when he heard a voice.

'Good bloody riddance too, I say.'

Steve turned to see the elderly neighbour standing there, arms folded, looking triumphant.

'Ah. Mrs Evans, isn't it?'

'It is,' she said. 'As I said. Damn good riddance to that one. No more than she deserved.'

'I see.'

'You'll be wanting me to come in then?' She folded her arms.

'Come in to where?'

'The police station,' she said impatiently. 'Are you not the full ticket or something?'

'I can assure you I am the full ticket,' Steve said with amusement. 'Do you have something to report?'

'Of course! You'll be wanting me to make a statement about what I saw last night, won't you?'

'Mrs Evans. What did you see last night?' Steve said, confused.

She tutted, rolling her eyes. 'I'll get my coat. You can drive me in your fancy car. I'll be expecting a cup of tea at the station as well, mind you. And a biscuit.'

* * *

Peter let himself into the vicarage and listened for a moment. All quiet. The vicar and Marion were obviously out. He checked the rooms downstairs and ran upstairs to his bedroom, quickly dragging out the rucksack from under his bed which contained the empty cans of lager that he had drunk at Mrs Pomeroy's house. In the semi-darkness, he dumped the rucksack on the bed and scrabbled about for the Tupperware that he had kept the poisonous mushrooms in before he had dumped them in Mrs Pomeroy's stew. He opened his bedside table and couldn't see it anywhere. He had put it there! Where was it?

'Hello, Peter,' Steve said in the darkness from the armchair.

447

Peter jumped. 'What the hell are you doing here?' he asked, flicking the light on.

'Why did you do it, Peter?' Steve stood up.

Peter made a run for the door, only to be blocked by a very tall PC. He spun around and glared at Steve.

'Why, Peter?' Steve repeated.

Peter stood shaking, his eyes wild.

'She deserved to fucking die. Miserable, interfering old bitch. I wanted her to suffer. To be afraid, to die being scared and in agony. She killed my aunt. She worked in my aunt's care home. She killed her and took all her money. She was an evil bitch and deserved to die.'

'I had more than enough to charge her, you knew that,' Steve said, frustrated.

'What? And let her enjoy prison for the rest of her days? No way. I wanted her to feel real pain. To feel real agony. To be terrified. I'm happy knowing she died feeling all of those things.'

'You sat and watched her die,' Steve stated. 'You had a beer and watched.'

'Yes I did. And she didn't fucking die quickly enough!'

'So you helped her along.'

Peter gave Steve a sullen expression.

Steve began. 'The old woman you pushed down the stairs, the one you went down for—'

'I didn't push her—' Peter began, but Steve waved his words away.

'You see, Peter, I think you did. I think you got a taste for it. After you got out of prison you didn't fall into finding God for a few months, did you? In the interim, we find a woman dead at the bottom of the stairs, local plod just thinks she's fallen down the stairs and died. Ruled as an accident. But no, the dead woman was a nurse at the same care home as your aunt was. I think you threatened and tortured her and found out about Edwina Pomeroy and then came looking.'

'You can't prove it.' Peter raised his chin defiantly and gave a cruel smile.

Steve gave a long-suffering sigh. 'Oh I think I can. Peter Ford, I'm arresting you for the murder of Edwina Pomeroy and for the murder of Rose Smith.'

Steve beckoned to the tall officer who handcuffed Peter as Steve finished reading him his rights. Together they escorted Peter out and into the waiting squad car.

* * *

The vicar sat solemnly by the side of another patient who was at the end of his life. His mind was racing. He couldn't believe that Mrs P had been killed and that the police were about to arrest Peter. Steve had briefed him and requested he and Marion stay clear of the vicarage for a few hours.

The vicar had put on a good show and had been convincingly both horrified and distraught to hear the news. This suited his plan wonderfully. He sent up a small prayer of thanks to his saviour for silencing Edwina before she could implicate him. He knew Steve had been close to charging her. She had been quite the willing and ruthless accomplice. She would always be his servant she had said. He knew she would have done anything for him. He had played on her unhappy marriage, her overwhelming and blind hatred of old people and her need to feel wanted and loved, and he had played her well.

He remembered her as a young, attractive girl. He remembered exactly what he had done. What had happened between them; he hadn't forgotten. He just never wanted to admit to it. It made it easier to forgive himself that way.

He studied the patient. It wouldn't be long now. The care home was quiet, with only the occasional sound of night staff moving about. The vicar liked the care homes at this time of night. He felt like he was in the waiting room with God. He felt close to his saviour. Felt his presence. He would wander the corridors and see the patients in their beds. Old, asleep, waiting to die. He felt invincible here, he felt like he could do anything. Some days he imagined he was God himself, randomly choosing who needed to be sent to the heavenly place.

One of the care home nurses interrupted his thinking, and put her head around the door.

'Any change?' she asked quietly.

The vicar shook his head. 'It won't be long now, I'd say.'

'Call me if you need me,' she said, closing the door gently.

The vicar watched her go down the corridor and said one last prayer. He stood and watched the man who was around the same age as him but was withered with Parkinson's and dementia and said softly, 'Time to go now. If nothing else, to stop you blabbing to anyone who would listen about my past.'

The vicar picked up a pillow and placed it gently over the old man's face. There was no struggle, there was no clawing at the pillow. There was acceptance. The vicar kept the pillow there for a few more minutes and then removed it gently and closed the old man's eyes. He sat and took his hand and said one last prayer.

The vicar was pleased with himself. One less of the annoying congregation to take up his time which was even more precious now he planned to make Marion his wife. Plus, the last real link to his past was gone. He figured he could get away with using this method for a while now; everyone would be looking for poison and no one would suspect him. He needed to work harder at getting rid of them, but do it carefully, discreetly. No one could ever know.

If only they knew how much he knew! How utterly complicit he was! It was such a wonderful secret.

He said a quick prayer for his sins, but he was safe in the knowledge that his Lord knew what he was doing and accepted it.

He sat for a while longer and produced a small notebook from his pocket. He wrote quickly.

Once more I have helped another poor and helpless soul pass into the next life. I have the gift of helping people cross into another dimension. My saviour knows and blesses what I am doing. Together we are growing His kingdom of heaven. I choose the best flowers for his garden. He chose me because I choose them. I am the chosen one. I am the new Messiah. They will come to me to pass into the next life. I will serve the Lord for as long as I can. I will gather them together, to deliver us from these heathens, so we can rejoice in our work, and we can glory in his praise.

The vicar closed the notebook and then placed the pillow carefully back in the wardrobe. He needed to go. He had planned to propose to Marion this evening, but perhaps with Mrs P dying and Peter being arrested it was inappropriate. Maybe another day then, he thought. Besides, he was here in this rich environment; there was absolutely nothing wrong with scoping out who the next sacrifice would be. Humming quietly to himself he walked out of the room, closing the door gently behind him.

The End.

ACKNOWLEDGEMENTS

As always, it's time to leave the dark pit of writing to say a heartfelt thank you to the people that are intrinsic to the journey of getting this book out to lovely readers.

Love and thanks as always go to my 'first readers' posse, Sal, Jane, Mette, Tracy, Linda and Julie. You see the first attempts and your feedback and comments are invaluable to me. Thank you for your interest, your time and your commitment to the books and the characters.

Enormous respect and thanks have to go to my 'dream team'. My editor, Heather Fitt, for her guidance and for putting up with (and trying to change) my bad habits. Abbie Rutherford for her superb proofreading and amusing comments, all with help from the lovely Thorin. Last but certainly not least, the gorgeous gals at Literally PR who are so wonderfully efficient and hugely supportive.

Massive gratitude goes to Dr Mark Ashton, Consultant Cellular Pathologist (on this book and the forthcoming Scottish series too), who answers my tediously bizarre questions, and I'm sure rolls his eyes when I promptly apply literary licence to his wonderfully detailed responses.

Love and endless thanks as ever goes to my wonderful friends. For buying my books and being interested and supportive, along with wonderful comments such as "I genuinely thought it was going to be a bit shit, but it's absolutely brilliant". (Gotta love the honesty.) You're all fabulous and *yes, yes*, beers are on me (*again*).

As always, I couldn't do any of this without the love and support from 'my crew'. Thank you for letting me escape into my fictional world for hours and days on end, and for the support and encouragement you give me, along with the love you have for the characters and the stories. I feel truly blessed (well, some of the time anyway). Oh and I'm sorry for nearly always ruining a nice moment with a comment like 'that's a great place for a body to wash up.' I'll try and do better.

I really want to thank my readers. Wholeheartedly. Self-publishing is an incredibly tough journey, wracked with crushing and endless self-doubt and a good review can mean the absolute world. The response and support I have had from readers of the first two books makes the struggle worthwhile. Some comments have made me smile in the darkest of moments, has warmed my heart, and has been the thing to bolster me to continue writing when I've wondered whether to give it all up or not.

Finally, huge love and thanks go to the lovely reviewers on the online book tours – some of you have been with me on this journey from the first book, and your love for the books and the characters genuinely inspires me to carry on and write more. Your unabated excitement for the next instalment is incredible and deeply touching. You are a special part of the Castleby family, and its continuing journey and I hope you'll come with me on the other journeys too. Thank you so much for your support, it means the absolute world to me.